THE LOOKING GLASS CLUB

Gruff Davies

SENCILLO

Sencillo Press

Published by Sencillo Limited
London, UK

First Edition
ISBN: 978-0-9566245-0-5

À la mémoire de Gilberte qui m'a donné le gout des puzzles.

COMPETITION

A prize of up to 1 million pounds sterling is being offered to the first team to solve the puzzles left by Tony in his diary and reproduced in the printed editions of this book.

For details on the competition rules and how to enter, please visit the book's website:

www.TheLookingGlassClub.com

AUTHOR'S NOTE

The tunnel network running beneath South Kensington and the Imperial College campus is real. The service tunnels are off-limits for safety reasons. The fire system is based on an inert gas which is heavier than air and presents a genuine risk of suffocation in the event of fire.

This novel is in no way intended to encourage people to explore them.

The club room as described in the novel does not exist.

From the pages of Tony's diary:

'Oh Kitty! how nice it would be to know, are you alive inside that Looking-glass Box?'

—Schrödinger

No no no no no no no no no no no no no no yes yes no no no no no no no no no no no no no
yes yes no yes no no no no no no no no no no no no yes yes yes no no no no no no no no
no no no yes no yes no yes no no no no no no no no no no no no no yes yes yes yes no no
no no no no no no no yes no no yes no yes no no no no no no no no no no no no no no yes yes
yes yes yes yes yes yes yes yes yes yes no no no yes no yes no no no no no no no no no no no
no no no yes yes yes yes yes no no no yes yes yes no yes no no yes no yes no no no no no no
no no no no no no no no no no no no no yes no no no no no no no no yes no no no no yes yes no
no no no no no no no no no no no no no yes no no no no no no no no yes no no no no yes yes no
yes no no no no no no no no no no no no no yes no no no no no no no no no no no no no yes
yes yes no yes no no no no no no no no no no no no no no no yes yes no no no no no no no no
no no no yes yes yes no yes no no no no no no no no no no no no no no yes yes no no no no yes
no no no no yes no no no yes yes no no no no no no no no no no no no no no no no no yes yes yes
yes no no yes no no no no yes no no no no yes no no no no no no no no no no no no no no no no
no no no yes no no no no no no no no no no no yes no no yes no no no no no no no no no no no
no no no no no no yes no no no no no no no no no no no yes yes no no no no no yes no no no no
no no no no no no no no no yes no no no no yes yes no no no no no yes no no no no no no no no
no no no no no no no no no no no yes yes yes yes yes no no no no yes yes yes yes yes no no
yes no yes yes yes yes yes yes yes yes yes yes yes yes yes no yes no yes no yes yes yes yes
no yes no yes no yes yes yes yes no no no no no no no no no no no no yes yes no yes no yes
no yes no no yes no yes no yes no yes yes yes no yes no no no no no no yes yes yes no no no
yes yes yes yes yes yes no no no no yes yes yes yes yes no yes yes no yes no no no yes yes no
no no no yes no no no no no no no no no no no no no no no no no no yes yes no yes no no yes
no yes yes yes yes yes no yes no no no no no no no no no no no no no no no no no yes no no
yes no no no no no yes yes yes no no no no no no no no no no no no no no yes yes no no no
yes no no no yes no yes no no no no yes no no no no no no no no yes yes yes no no no
no no no no yes no no yes no yes no no no no no no no no no yes no no no no no no no no yes
yes no no no no no no yes no no no yes no no no no no no no no no no yes no no no no no no
no no no yes yes no no no no no no no yes no no no yes no yes yes yes yes yes no no no no no
yes no no no no no yes yes yes yes no no no no no yes no no no yes no no no yes yes yes
no yes yes yes no no no no no no no no yes yes yes yes no no no no no no yes no no yes no no
yes no yes yes yes no yes yes no no no no no no no no yes no no no no no yes yes yes yes no
yes no yes no no yes yes no no no no no no no no yes no no no no no no no yes yes yes yes no
no no no no yes no no yes no no no no no yes yes yes no no no no no no no no no no no yes yes
yes yes no no no no no no yes no no yes no no no no no no no no no no no no no no no no no
no no no no no no no no no no no yes no no yes no no no no no no no no no no no no no no no
no no no no no no no no no no no no no no yes yes no yes yes yes yes yes yes yes yes yes yes
yes yes yes yes yes yes yes yes yes yes yes yes yes yes yes yes yes yes no...

Chapter 1

'Oh, Kitty! how nice it would be if we could only get through into Looking-glass House! I'm sure it's got, oh! such beautiful things in it! Let's pretend there's a way of getting through into it somehow, Kitty.'

—Alice

It was as if the sky's bruised belly had been cruelly slit from beneath: she spewed her dead infant over Manhattan, drowning us. We fled through the darkness—three of us—our soaked forms flashed into grotesque stills by the livid sky. Skyler nursed her pregnant belly and whimpered as I dragged her along under the freezing torrent.

'Faster,' I begged. She was terrified. Something fizzed by in the darkness, probably bullet-shaped. Too close. Far too close.

Afterimages from the lightning faded from my vision.

'Down here,' called JR—the owner of half of our legs. He disappeared into another road. We raced around the corner, our new vector dangerously at odds with our momentum. JR reappeared ahead of us, scampering as fast as he could. I prayed he was still connected to a map. He was driving front paws between back in rapid succession, a dirty blur of black and white, and he was showing no signs of slowing. Lightning silently fractured the night sky ahead, throwing out monstrous dancing shadows momentarily more real than the things that cast them. I winced and checked that nothing permanent remained. Nothing. But it wasn't safe anymore. I could *feel* it, and that scared me more than any gun.

Twenty-five years I'd kept a lid on it. I cursed. No point. *No point, Steel.* Done now. Deal with it. Thunder cracked and shuddered through the air, dispersing my thoughts.

'This way,' JR called again, disappearing. Another gunshot. Shards of brick shattered off a corner. He was getting too close. As I ran I felt something sticky pulling at my coat like toffee. *It's nothing, don't let it be something.* I grabbed at a lamppost on the corner and we sling-shotted around it. We made it out of sight—the toffee sensation vanished—but: too much speed. Sky slipped, tripped, fell. We crumpled into a far wall.

'JR!' I cried, scrabbling at Sky trying to lift her to her feet again. 'Get back here! We're in trouble!'

Nothing broken. *The baby?* We were dead anyway. Skyler tried to stand, but her legs buckled under her, shaking like a newborn calf's.

'What's happening?' she implored. I could see from her eyes, she'd gone again. 'Stay with it. Someone's trying to kill you.'

The sound of the assassin's footfall began to grow audible above the rain's obliterating tantrum. My mind started to falter, to wash away: we had no chance. Then, JR, a bullet of soaked fur, blurred past us again, vanishing into

2

the darkness from which the assassin approached. The gears in my mind caught, meshed again.

'Bu... *why*?!' Skyler's distress contorted her into a limp watery ghoul.

'No time.'

I heard a bark. A yell. The footfall silenced ominously. Then, a stuttering sound: soles slapping the ground again. Another cry. A crumpling sound. A pause. Vicious barking. In my mind I pictured what I couldn't see: *JR turning to block the assassin's path, barking, the assassin not able to slow or stop, jumping over JR— tripping?* My heart leapt with hope.

A gun shot.

A yelp. A heart-rending yelp. Then—

Silence. Just the rain.

OhGodJRwhathaveIdone?

I didn't wait for the inevitable footfall to start again, but hefted Sky up, one arm over my shoulder and struggled to make use of the time that JR had bought us. We limped to a corner, an alley this time, and slid in. Bad choice. Dead end. We had seconds before he found us, a minute or two at the most.

I whispered into my com, 'JR?'

Silence.

I looked into the alley. The rain was driving down in great veils. I felt the cold biting into the bones of my fingers. The rain at least had given us some cover. Skyler would have been dead by now otherwise. I saw nowhere to hide. I could have made it over the wall at the end, but Skyler looked at least eight months. She didn't stand a chance. I could see only one door into the building to the left. It was plain steel and—I checked it—firmly locked. I raged silently.

I had no choice.

I pressed Skyler against the wall, trying to ignore her stricken expression and implored her to remain quiet. Her hair was plastered in dark wet strands down her face. She was shivering violently.

'Just try to remember: someone's trying to kill you,' I urged. 'Don't say a word. Just keep saying that to yourself: *"Someone's trying to kill me."* Try not to forget, okay?'

She nodded with wide frightened eyes. I was terrified that she would forget again, might wander out or start talking. I put my finger to my mouth. *Silence.* I looked for a lock on the door, something I could change. Nothing. Just plain steel. Maybe a fire door? Yes, with a bar on the inside. Had to be. I wasn't sure if I could do—*do it or she will die and so will you.*

But I'd never done it without... *shutupjustshutthefuckupanddoit.*

I swallowed and faced the door. It defied me arrogantly. I tried, but I felt my mind slip on the sweat of its own fear. This subtle sleight could be the undoing of me. I tried again. I felt my sanity stretch out; a living filament bared across a seductive chasm of chaos. Part of me cried out in alarm at the prospect of the hermeneutical hazard I contemplated (*hermenauts* you called us, Jon! in your unbounded folly). Inside me, the gift that I could never truly bury came alive. Dark shadows in my peripheral vision began to shift. I had to be quick. I faced the blackest depths of the whirling void, braced myself and plunged deep into the paradox. I clutched, wet-fingered, onto a desperate filigree of sanity. My mind seemed stretched to snapping point by the Möbius twist I made of myself. A scream reverberated, echoed in silent agony, as I strained to retain integrity during the abomination I was attempting. I was dimly aware of a hot wetness blurring my vision, but I was beyond emotion by then. I don't know how many seconds passed, and then—

Like a sigh.

I realized that I had stopped breathing and took great gulps of breath, like a diver returning to the surface. I began to shake and, as quietly as possible, I wept. Piss trickled down my leg, burning hot against the freezing rain.

Oh God, what have you done?

'Why are you crying?' she asked tenderly. 'Why don't we go inside? Look: it's not locked. Don't be afraid.'

The previously locked door was now ajar. She put her arm around me, pulled the door open further and we stumbled inside. It *was* a fire door. Perhaps it had been before, who knows? It was a question that made no sense to ask. I pulled it shut behind us. We were safe. At least for the moment. So long as he hadn't seen us. I needed a moment to recompose myself, but Skyler looked like she was about to talk again so I had to get us away from the door in case he could hear us. I tried to forget what I'd just done but the voices were screaming in my head, reminding. Warning.

We were in a cold, concrete rectangular stairwell leading both up and down. The shadows on the wall looked dangerous; their edges wavered in my peripheral vision. Something living threatened to cast them. We were in a different type of danger now. We had to get to somewhere safe quickly, somewhere I could regain a semblance of control before I lost it completely. I swore to myself: never again, Steel, *never*. Double doors led further into the building, away from the stairs. It took me a moment to realize where we were, my sense of direction had been so confused. I screamed silently back at the voices in my head to shut up. We were a long way from our origin, Bellevue. I recognized our location: a small car park underneath some offices off East 23rd or maybe 24th. The entrance would be near where we'd lost him. We weren't as safe in here as I'd thought. I swore. *Why was nothing straightforward?*

We needed a car, and quickly.

'Hello, I'm Skyler,' Sky said, looking slightly confused and afraid, but trying to be polite. My heart would have sunk, but there was nowhere further it could go.

'I know, sweetheart, we've met already. I'm Steel.' I checked our options through the glass in the double doors. The car park seemed empty.

'You've wet your pants,' she said. 'Are you okay?'

I was soaking from the rain, I didn't want to think about how she could have known. There was so much I didn't want to think about.

'Not really. I don't have time to explain. We need to get out of here. *Fast.*'

'There's a fire exit?' she said, indicating the door we'd just come through. She was completely earnest.

'Not that way.'

I pulled her through into the car park and told her to stay quiet. Then I left her and scouted the level. There were no cars. The exit had an automatic barrier which looked like it was working, the main entrance beyond was barred by a gate, but it looked weak: two cage doors locked by a padlock in the center. Easy to drive through. I just needed to find a car. *Right. Just that.* The level below was empty too and my spirits began to sink again, but three cars sat neglected in the level beneath that. My legs were trembling. I picked a smart looking silver Audi. Of course it was locked.

For the second time in two and half decades, I hot-wired reality.

I'm not very good at keeping promises to myself.

This time at least my bladder was already empty. It was easier than before and that thought terrified me as much as what I had done. I opened the driver's door. Something dark, with too many legs, scampered out from underneath the purring car engine and into the shadows opposite. I suppressed a whimper, swung into the car, checked the back seats were empty and turned the lights on full beam. Blank wall. *Nothing.* I exhaled relief like cigarette smoke.

I was still in control. Just. This was Russian roulette with slow-moving bullets. I couldn't be certain just yet that the last shot was a blank. Time would tell.

I thought of Tony, and of Emily, and suppressed a shudder. I checked my pockets but the only drugs I had were at home. I needed something strong soon, a stimulant. I could still manage this.

I drove up the levels back to Skyler.

'Get in,' I called to her through the window. Fortunately, she still recognized me and clambered into the passenger seat. I tapped my earring com with my thumb to activate it. 'JR,' I said and waited. There was a connection error. A dull pain filled my chest like dark ice.

'Where are we going? Are we going on a trip?' Sky asked.

'I'm taking you somewhere safe. Put your seat belt on please,' I said, eyeing the exit barriers and revving the engine. 'This might hurt.'

Just hours earlier Sky and I had been mutual strangers. She had simply arrived on my doorstep with a hastily scribbled note, a tattoo for a name, an empty head, and a full belly. I'd stuck my head out of the window of my apartment, still shaking from the words in the note, to see a car pull away, but it was a cab and I didn't catch the registration.

There was something familiar about the handwriting.

> *I'm sorry. It's starting again.*
> *The Looking Glass Club.*
> *Look after her. I'll contact you.*

At first those words had just shut down my mind, swept it clean like a hurricane. I got her inside, sat her down, gave her a drink, and did some automatic stuff for a while that, honestly, I have no recollection of. When control returned and the shaking had stopped, I didn't know what to do. I questioned her from every possible direction, but she could tell me nothing and she was starting to get distressed by my inquisition. I put the TV on to relax her, and took something to calm my own nerves. JR pointed out to me she wasn't from Manhattan. He was better at picking up accents than me. Then he'd suggested—in his own thick Bronx tones—the hospital:

'She's pregnant and ain't got no memory. She's gotta have a medical record.'

His logic was flawless, as always. Wrong, but flawless.

I picked up a gun on the way out.

The nurse that had finally come to collect me from the butt-numbing plastic seat in the hospital was the same one who had given us such a hard time when we arrived. She had nylon black hair, cut in a sharp bob around a joyless face. I couldn't tell if we were the only source of her unhappiness today. Her eyes sucked first the warmth from my smile then the smile itself from my face. Any number of smiles could have been lost in that void without ever filling it.

'You can join her now,' she said without a trace of emotion.

The biting cold and wind had made Bellevue look invitingly warm through the glass doors of Emergency. Poor JR. He must have resented the nurse twice as much as I did when she refused to allow him in. No amount of puppy dog eyes or reasoning would sway her either. Hospital rules: no dogs.

'What about guide dogs? They're allowed!' he tried to reason with her.

'He's not a guide dog,' she said to me.

'Hey, miss, I know that thanks. I ain't a fool. But if they're allowed, why ain't I?'

'He's not a guide dog and the rules only allow guide dogs.'

There was no point arguing and JR knew it. He sulked off into the darkness looking for some temporary shelter from the wind and cold. Fat drops of rain had started to fall fitfully. I felt sorry for JR; this type of thing always happened to him. I tapped my earcom.

'Stay in range, in case I need you.'

The nurse stared down her nose at me from under her eyebrows. 'You'll be switching that off, of course. Hospital rules. No phones, coms, PDAs, SapInts, or other forms of radio wave communication devices allowed in the hospital. They interfere with life-support and endanger patients.'

'I'd call her a bitch if it wasn't a compliment,' my earcom crackled.

She couldn't have heard him, but I had the oddest feeling that she did.

I'd insisted on staying with Skyler when she was admitted. It was partly a sense of responsibility and partly because I didn't want to be on my own. The note had unnerved me. The nurse was equally adamant that I would wait in the corridor until she'd come out of MRI.

'Look, I've been assigned to protect her,' I lied, casting myself into a bodyguard role, 'and you're preventing me from doing my job.'

'Mister. . . ' she started imperiously, failing to recall my surname.

'Just Steel,' I said.

'*Mister* Steel. If you want to step into the MRI room into a magnetic field strong enough to drag you across the room by every bit of metal on you, damaging a two million dollar machine and further endangering you and your client's lives, then by all means, go ahead. Otherwise, I suggest you wait patiently here until her scans are completed.'

So I waited in the corridor and tried to find a position on one of the plastic chairs that didn't anaesthetize my butt. Who the hell designs those things? I pondered the scrawled note for about an hour both inventing and remembering terrible possibilities before, finally, the nurse came to collect me. She walked me to a small, single-bed ward room.

'How long does it take to have an MRI scan these days?' I said sarcastically.

'Talk to the doctor about it.'

I opened the door to see Skyler lying in a green gown on a hospital bed listening to a pretty Indian doctor. The doctor turned to acknowledge me. 'We'll just be one second.' I nodded.

She looked smaller on that bed, even more vulnerable. Her knees were drawn up to her chest. Little green girl. I guessed at her age: she was either a young-looking thirty or an old-looking twenty five. Small, round face, simple but pretty. Shoulder length, curly brown hair. Ordinary. Forgettable. Forgotten. Some people have faces that make you look again, not necessarily because they're attractive. Sky had a bland, ordinary prettiness of the type that just slides off your memory like one of those Airfix stickers you put in water, or a kid's tattoo.

The doctor finished explaining herself and stood upright.

'You must be the bodyguard.'

She obviously found the lie less ridiculous than the nurse had. She moved briskly, economically. Her voice carried an authority and confidence completely at odds with her apparent age. Her clothes did the opposite to Sky's. Take off the white coat and release that onyx hair around her face, I could have easily imagined she was twenty.

'Sorry for the delay, sir, we had to run a CAT scan instead. Do you know where she was treated before? We ran a check on her but she doesn't appear on any records.'

I said that I didn't know. 'Her memory, do you know what's wrong?'

She took a careful breath. 'I have to admit we don't. The scans show no brain damage. It's unusual. She has both long- and short-term memory loss which is most often caused by severe injury, but not in her case. There could be psychological causes. I'll have her referred to a psychiatrist.'

'And the baby? Is that okay?'

'She's booked into obstetrics next. Our first priority is to establish the mother is safe. Someone will come and collect her shortly.'

I must have let out a small grunt of disappointment that she wasn't going to hang around because she allowed herself a small flirtatious smile. Before she left she reintroduced me to Skyler.

'I'll be back later to check up on her.'

I threw out another little line, just to keep her around a minute more.

'Must be terrible to live like that, without a memory. She probably doesn't even know who the father is. Anyone could have taken advantage.'

She turned around and stood in the doorway holding the door open with one hand. The fluorescent light from the corridor caught in the edges of her hair, glowing like a halo.

'It's not her first either.'

'How do you know that?'

'Caesarean scar.'

I shook my head in sympathy.

'I'll be back later,' she said gently. She turned and left then, but I was certain I saw her smile again before the door obscured her from view.

'Skyler. It's a pretty name.' I found myself talking to her like a child.

She shrugged and examined the room innocently. I shouldn't pity her. She's not a child.

'I'm cold. Can I put my clothes on now?' The gown looked thin. I had no idea whether she'd need to wear it for the scan in obstetrics, but I doubted it. As far as I knew they just pulled up your top, put gel over you and waved the scanner over your bump.

'Sure. I don't see why not.'

I stood outside the door whilst Skyler changed into her clothes. When she opened the door to let me back in she looked different. Less vulnerable. She wore a thick, heavy-knit jumper which was a dusty blue and made her look less pregnant. She wore jeans, in spite of her swollen belly. I guess some girls can if they have the right figure. She'd transformed from a patient to a person.

'Who's the father?' It didn't seem rude to ask given the circumstances.

'Whose father?'

'Your baby...?'

'Oh.' She looked down at herself. 'No. No I don't.'

She didn't seem to be concerned and gave her head an unconscious flick to move sandy brown curls out of her face. She was definitely pretty now that I studied her, but her condition made her too strange to be attractive. The door to the private ward swung open and a male nurse arrived to escort us to obstetrics.

The obstetrician was a short, rotund Chinese man called Doctor Sheng. He allowed me to stay in the room. He sat Skyler in a reclining chair next to the scanner and began to chat with her. His words were like fudge: sweet but coarse. I looked out through the blinds into the rain.

And that's when I first felt it.

The room darkened with no change in light, and slowed with no change in tempo. I felt something crawl in my hair at the back of my head. My right shoulder twitched up involuntarily. Sheng's fudge words melted into formlessness. *Oh God, it's happening.* The feeling went as suddenly as it had come.

I moved to the door. Something dark moved past it through the small window pane. My pulse quickened. I weighed up the possibilities. It could have been a nurse or doctor, even a patient, but something about the movement of that shape was unnatural. I took out my gun and moved to the side to see if I could see anything through the door's window from an angle. The gun began to whine quietly as it charged up in my hands. The conversation in the room stopped.

'Is everything okay, sir?' Dr Sheng asked, concern spoiling his fudgy words. I didn't answer immediately. The corridor seemed empty through the window.

I spoke slowly. 'I'm not sure.'

The door handle started to turn. Adrenaline coursed through me. I still could see nothing through the glass window. I moved closer to the wall. The handle reached its furthest position and I heard the click of the metal catch releasing. The door started to open, hiding me behind it.

Time turned to honey.

He was dressed in dark clothes with a hood. He walked calmly and silently into the room. I stepped out from behind the door, just as he raised his arms toward Sky and Dr Sheng. I saw their eyes widen with fright. He was holding a gun. Sky's mouth started to open. I used my bodyweight. I must have hit his arm just as he pulled the trigger. I heard the deceitfully soft sound of a silenced shot and watched in helpless dismay as Dr Sheng took the bullet in his right shoulder. As Sheng recoiled, horror spread over his face. Blood spilled from his shoulder. The attacker ignored me completely and headed straight for Sky, whose open mouth began to emit a shrill scream. I raised my gun and pulled the trigger. The charged stunlet sailed from the barrel, splitting and spreading wide into a trio of spiked charges connected by conducting wire. The spikes wrapped around him like bolas, increasing in velocity as they circled him, ice skaters pulling in their arms. They thudded into him, penetrating his clothes, and discharged themselves violently through his body in a web of liquid blue lightening.

He contorted, twitching spastically and slumped to the floor.

I moved over to his body, shaking with adrenaline. I reached out a hand to move his hood to see his face, but as I did so, I noticed something else. His sleeve had ridden up his arm, revealing smooth skin. He had a tattoo; a small one on the inside of his wrist where a watch would have covered it. It was a design I knew too well. One I hadn't seen in twenty-five years. A small handheld mirror. An old-fashioned looking glass.

A cold wave of fear cascaded through me. Then it was true.

It shouldn't have been possible but the assailant began to move. There had been enough charge in my gun to take down a bear, but the rules were different now. I pointed my gun at his back, ready to fire again, but his arm shot out with impossible speed and knocked it from my grasp across the room. He was still on all fours. He hadn't even been looking in my direction.

I knew this was not a fight I could win. There was only one option and we had very little time. I grabbed at Skyler and yelled at her to run. The attacker tried to get up but stumbled as we took flight. I thought I'd managed to lose him in the maze of hospital corridors, but we left a breadcrumb trail of destruction behind of crashed trolleys and angry nurses. By the time we joined JR outside on the streets he'd found us again and was regaining his energy and balance fast.

The rest you know.

After driving through the car park gates, I made doubly sure we had no tail before I made the calls I had always hoped to avoid. Every muscle in my body seemed to be vibrating from overuse or adrenaline. Skyler had soon forgotten even about driving through the gates and was a model of indifference, absently stroking her swollen belly and staring out of the window.

I had time to do some thinking. With JR gone (*this thought a hard vacuum in my chest*) I had no interface. I had no idea who Skyler was, or who the father of her baby might be, but one thing was clear to me, with the situation as bad as it was, I would have gratefully traded her ignorance for mine.

From the pages of Tony's diary:

An amphibious mammal swims in this sea.

```
zmmydnkchjfcfimphrallarzdkpgczcf
fkbbjkcbqyiqptxkwsrasuwrljefnogm
ineeicbppgbkqzjowsussuwwrjbdzbkn
qfbmketbeczgffxasaluaawasagjgcbm
qnceoxnekokvnjerbosxtrswruhehnqd
yihbozbdgggkvpbsezwjbrrallrftvhx
diqcegtofjcjetsjeaszpwlssswwneyk
agmjqzihtimjqxrhcswptrslwswrmgvd
knoxzbzomxyeejwdqazyalaswrwsatou
kbbqceqnqztcxksgrumolrluuswrwvpw
fjkmyfntgzbbkxrelrgaauararsaaevr
rfjgfyichbnjztrxslqalrlwsuluuwgw
fgcnonixefxehuwnrlhrallarurrrsid
mmitbqmjxkznssuclwbswslrwsaasuce
cqeeejdqjqydllluwwpaauaruuarlryi
bieppgecbwwsurusassarllararrrsiz
jfgchffswusuusslsawlraulwululrbu
dfcdcwuusrrluuraaswluawlslsssseu
ipnwuaawruwaursssruuwwslrsswlabr
xcwwrasslaaalarasuallsslasuwuuir
zlaaassaulrlsaulsasswaswrusuwuex
oawlaswlsawsurualluswuawswluwroh
euusrluwssululrswlrauswallsuwwdc
muassurrualwwlrlsslwlrwasarlrrwl
crarlslualwuusaarsuwlsruurarsslr
tflslwslurusrlsrwwuwlaaauusllrum
jmiuruuslwsursaurwwwllluwaawrrlm
bzpusllrawswaruawrslswluaawlurlb
dqektlsssaarauwwluwrwulsswwuruux
rpdckhwaarnawwautrwwwlwwulrullag
xiotmkkinniwrwuwjrssuwlsaupullui
jpveinqyqnfbwarsmwrwsuubeidslrry
```

Chapter 2

We'd buried the Looking Glass Club and some of its members a long time ago. So I'd thought. You see, there was a time before the universe got fucked up. Stupid thing to say. The universe was already fucked up. It was just wearing make-up. The Buddha knew this two and a half thousand years before quantum physicists came along, pinned it with sharp labels and boxed the poor fucker like Schrödinger's cat in a poisoned paradigm.

I sound like I'm against science. I'm not. Forgive me. Therapy didn't take away the bitterness.

A lot changes in two and a half decades. Much more than we'd ever imagined.

I had been at university.

And, well—there was a girl...

South Kensington.

London, England.

The memory comes with difficulty—and an ache:

A cold, late October day.

Outside, thin winter light, darkness descending; Inside, sour, electric yellow.

All wind, and drizzle, and busy leaves rushing the streets.

Imperial College of Science, Technology and Medicine.

The physics department.

Standing damp, with a heaving chest, before a board of passport-sized photos. *Last* year's. I'd sprinted here. It had taken me a minute to spot her. Her photo was different from the one on this year's poster. I'd run my hot eyes across that matrix of two hundred tiny faces, blistering them with my intensity until I found hers. Pigeon-holed in a little frame. She looked so delicate, so much younger. She had still been a child then. Tightly bound schoolgirl hair, but it was her nonetheless; undeniably her. Even had I not recognised her, her name blazed away underneath in ordinary type: Kate Andrews.

I pressed my knuckles into my temples. Angry. Jubilant.

I hunted for Tony Baijaiti's photo among the images of the living. No luck. He'd been a final year student then, so his year poster had been buried in an archive somewhere. Even his photograph had now been inhumed.

I took off again, back to hall (drizzle, cold needles stinging my face), nervously listening outside Alexei's door before acting. I could hear murmurings inside.

10

What if he had guests? *Yeah, right.* I put my ear to the door. The murmurings became a whining. Something hard knocked against the wood and I jerked backwards. I distinctly heard the word 'Bugger!'. The room fell silent.
I couldn't wait. I rapped on the door and whispered harshly:
'Alexei? *Alexei,* it's me, Zeke.'
Ezekial was my given name. 'Steel' came much later, in Manhattan.
A silent pause then:
'Go away!'
'Alexei. Please. It's important.'
'Oh, I'm sure it *really* is not, whatever it is. And I'm perfectly certain it's about that sodding girl again. Besides which I'm really quite busy. Now would you care to fuck off?'
'Alexei, *please.*'
'You're obsessed. Leave Her Alone.'
I let my head sag against the door, and whined quietly. 'Let me in. *Please.*'

Kate Andrews had crashed meteor-like into my world without warning, eradicating a whole era of female-scientist stereotypes. We shared a tutorial group under the expert tutelage of Professor Fabrizio Theodore Luciano. *The* Fabrizio Luciano. I'd read about his work of course, but I'd never actually seen him, or heard him speak. I'd expected him to be a frail, Italian academic when he was in fact a jolly American, ursine character: thick black beard; infectious, bassy laugh. Just an eye-patch and a shoulder parrot away from the name Blacktooth. I'd missed weeks of tutorials already, so I'd blustered apologetically into that first tutorial with piles of uncooperative books under each arm, placed the unruly things on the floor where they wanted to be anyway and looked up.
A pair of petite white Adidas trainers tiptoed in front of Luciano's whiteboard. The owner turned and rained a devastating smile upon me. She continued, spiking and jabbing an equation into existence with a marker in her left hand. It was green. I remember every detail. Everything, as if that moment was cut up into little pieces and stuffed into my head to float around in colourful fragments in front of my eyes forever. The slender milk-skinned arm running into the small cave of her armpit in her white T-shirt. The Bezier curve of her back. Her dancer's buttocks. The double white stripe down the grey sides of her sports pants. And how the stub of her little black pigtail wagged reproachfully back at me.
She fingered away an angle bracket and rewrote it nearby.
My mouth seemed sticky, my breathing laboured. I realised I was still stooping and straightened up.
I couldn't interpret the equation she'd written. We *never* used angle brackets in equations...
'No need to look so baffled, boy,' came Luciano's boom again. 'Dirac notation. You'll learn it next year.'
'Sorry. *Sorry,*' the girl spun, proffered a hand; shook mine—shook *me.* Those *eyes...* 'Didn't mean to take over. I'm Kate.'
I managed to sit and achieved a smile as the other tutees arrived.

Alexei's door opened a crack. Even with one eye he managed a withering look.
'If it *is* about her, you're going to regret this.'
He relaxed his hold on the door and the gap widened a fraction.
I pushed through, my eyes widening at the sight of his room.
'How do you get away with this?'

For once Alexei's carpet was actually visible under the usual detritus of food packets, chocolate wrappers, orange peel, Coke cans, disassembled machinery, half-assembled computers, Lego and Meccano, PIC chips and writers, hard drives, drives cables, DVDs, rope, wires and springs. The carpet might be visible, but only because things had been literally swept into piles; it was still a catastrophe.

'I don't understand why the cleaners don't report you.'

'Because,' he said, quickly checking the corridor before shooing me in further and then closing the door shut, 'unlike some meddling idiots, they don't buggering come in here.'

'But they have keys. How—'

'I pay them.'

'Bribes?' I was shocked. 'Well, I bet they sneak a peek when—'

'They do not. Believe me, I'd know. Now what do you want?'

I used to be the only permitted intrusion when he was so deeply into a construction or programming project, but recently even I was a distraction.

I wanted to tell him what I'd heard. But I'd better not. Not yet.

I stepped towards his desk where one of his terminals sat with a 21" screen filled with countless scrolling windows. On the floor something whined across the carpet out of the way of my foot.

I did a dance of fright.

There was a terrible crunching sound.

'Oh, you ABSOLUTE ARSING TIT!'

Underneath my foot a small creature of metal and plastic whined.

'What is it?'

I lifted my foot. The thing whirled a few damaged circles before jamming up.

'What *was* it?'

He lifted an arm and for the first time I saw that it was wrapped with a neoprene sleeve, the sort used for sports injuries. Wires trailed out from the underside of his forearm to a small circuit board stitched to the back of it. A small silver aerial extended from the circuit board.

'You got it working?'

'Yes.'

A sliver of sunshine cracked through the storm on his face.

'You're *fucking* brilliant.'

'Am I? Oh! The adulation,' he growled. 'I just *love* it.' Then he waved a hand expansively. 'Go ahead. Break what you want.'

'Show me.'

He turned his hand palm upwards and began to wiggle his fingers in a complex pattern. On the floor the buggy twitched. He regarded it sadly.

'Trashed. Poor bugger. Look at the diagnostics instead.'

Coloured lines danced across the screen on his desk—a digital oscilloscope.

'The contacts read the nerve impulses as they travel down to my fingers.'

'You sorted the noise and lag problems?'

'Recursive adaptive digital filter. Two birds, one stone. Oh, and I rewrote the Bluetooth driver. Bypasses the protocol completely now. It was *utter* shite.'

'Since this morning?'

'Yes. Why?'

'Wow.' More breath than word. Alexei's eyes shone.

Now was a good time.

I glanced around preparing the question in my mind.

'*Theoretically...*'

Shining eyes screwed into narrow beams.

'Yes...?'

'How would you hack into a mail server?'

'Depends. What's the setup?'

'Old. Vista.'

'Running anything else?'

'Probably. Yes—definitely actually. Intranet.'

'Easy then. Start by trying a SQL-injection attack. IIS still has no in-built protection against...'

He went into a rapid and detailed explanation that dragged my slow-coach mind along by threadbare ropes at such a pace it threatened to overturn the whole cart. By the end—a mere minute or two—I was exhausted just from paying attention. He stopped suddenly and scrutinised me carefully.

'This *is* about that bloody girl, isn't it?'

I opened a mouth to object. His arm shot out in the air, pointing heavenward.

'OUT! Now! And don't come back until you come to your senses!'

He shouted at me in the corridor from behind the slammed door:

'And I take it all *back*. It won't work. *Don't Try It.*'

Alexei and I had enjoyed a short yet intense friendship, but since my obsession with Kate it seemed to have soured a little. We actually met the summer before at a software competition in London. (He won. There was talk of a patent.) His accent was decidedly English public school, but his face had a broad structure and rounded angles that hinted at an Eastern-European origin. He had dark blond hair, and baby-like skin so clear and smooth that, if it needed shaving at all, it was once per week at most. His eyes were a cat-like green-blue. It was a handsome face and its soft, noble set and slightly Roman nose gave him a natural air of superiority. There was something regal about him, an impression that was created by more than his features. He was extremely complementary about my project, though I'd felt embarrassed at its simplicity compared to his gargantuan effort which included hardware that he'd built himself. He'd asked to see my code and made some instantaneous suggestions for improving it that were inspired. We were both seventeen but he'd skipped a year and was already a first year Computing Science student at Cambridge. It came as quite a surprise then, nine months later, to bump into him at Imperial College, London.

I'd been in London barely a week and I'd been walking along Exhibition Road when I saw him further up. It may have been my imagination but he seemed to recognise me before I saw him and he hesitated. It was that halting moment of indecision that drew my attention to him. It seemed as if he were about to turn to hide, or walk the other way.

'Alexei?' I ventured as I drew close and confirmed that it was indeed him.

He touched his hair self-consciously and his face flushed a dirty-pastel pink.

'Hi.'

His hand seemed to tremble. It flew back to his side before I could be sure.

'What are you doing in London?'

Had there been another AI competition I'd not been aware of?

'I'm studying here now.'

'What?! In London? At which college? What happened to Cambridge?'

'Here. Imperial.'

'But you...'

His eyes danced over my face then he looked away, seemingly in pain. He breathed out carefully.

'Got kicked out.'

'Oh, you're *kidding*. For what?'

'Hacked into their systems once too many.'

'Oh God, Alexei... I'm sorry.'

'It's fine. Really.' He shrugged and caught my eyes again. 'London has its attractions.' His gaze became furtive again and then flicked away to the grand architecture of Exhibition Road. 'And Dad's still paying for my education and my living expenses so I've nothing to complain about.'

His breathing was shallow and rapid.

'Well, God! It's... great that you're here! You should have dropped me an email.'

'I thought about it. I mean, I was going to.'

'Where are you living?'

He tipped his head backwards towards Prince's Gardens.

'Linstead Hall.'

'Cool! We're practically neighbours.'

'I saw your brother the other day,' Alexei said. 'I thought it was you.'

My brother, Jacob—my twin—was also was studying at Imperial. Electrical Engineering. I grunted, ill-concealing my contempt. Jacob and I did not get along. Twins we were; similar we were not.

'Look, I have to run.' I glanced at my watch. 'I'm late for a lecture. Call me?'

He gave a curious, indecipherable fraction of a smile.

'Depend upon it.'

After that first, slightly awkward meeting, my friendship with Alexei rapidly grew to a heady, almost intoxicating intensity. (Next day on the phone, him saying: 'I'm building a robot swarm. Do you fancy coming over to help?' 'Virtually you mean? A simulation?' He could only mean a simulation, it would be far too difficult to— 'No. A real one.' We completed the project overnight using over-the-counter components that must have cost him hundreds of pounds.) Alexei's intellect blazed as hot as a star. His focus was inhuman. He concentrated his intellectual heat on those mesmerising little projects of his, flashing them to boiling point in a fraction of the time it would have taken others. By rights it should have been Alexei that I was blinded by, but it would be Kate Andrews' beauty and the manipulative blindfold of Jon Rodin that stole my sight, leaving poor Alexei to his own tragic destiny.

For five weeks, Alexei and I enjoyed an incandescent friendship. They were happy weeks, working on his fascinating ideas, wandering South Kensington, talking incessantly about science and technology. In fact, I became so absorbed in my friendship with him that I skipped all of my tutorials until he pointed out that I wasting an opportunity. Professor Luciano was a famous theoretical physicist after all. So off I went. And there I met Kate.

'In love? How can you be in love?' Alexei had later protested. 'How much time have you spent with her? You don't even *know* her.'

It was at least a week before he would speak to me again. I was baffled, but we eventually settled back into something resembling our former friendship. The topic of Kate was taboo. Possibly everything would have been fine, but one morning I overheard a conversation.

I'd been feeling especially down after spending much of the morning looking at the back of Kate's head, trying to pluck up the courage to speak to her, but unable. (Kate had quickly detected my awkward attraction to her and the kind eyes she had turned upon me in that first tutorial had soon become guarded and expressionless.) It was a miserable, wet day and after lectures I wretchedly dragged myself back to hall, changed clothes, and took myself to the television lounge, where I planned to anaesthetise myself with its banal, projected phantasmagoria. The television was chattering away to itself, ignored by a small group of students enjoying—judging by their keen expressions—a more local soap. I positioned myself between them and the television where I could remain inconspicuous; and tuned in to the gossip.

'Another physicist apparently.'

'That's horrible.'

'The whole college was closed for two days while they investigated.'

'He was on for a first too.'

'What a waste. His parents must have been devastated.'

'Why did he do it?'

'Pressure.'

'No, apparently no-one knows. There's a rumour he was pushed. There was no note. But the police didn't treat it as suspicious. Anyway, *she* was involved. Claimed he'd been sending her strange emails. She got really messed up by it and dropped out. She's redoing her year again now.'

'What did the police say?'

'No idea. Maybe they're still investigating it.'

By this time my ears were pricked.

'Could be a coincidence, I suppose. . . '

'Wow. She seems so. . . normal.'

At this one of the boys muttered something I didn't catch and the group dissolved into cackles.

'Maybe the guy was stalking her.'

'He did! By email.'

'Hell, I'd stalk her!'

'Not now you wouldn't.'

'Who would have thought it? Kate Andrews, you mysterious little vixen!'

My heart leapt like a kicked dog. I turned.

'Did you just say Kate Andrews? Physics? First year?'

There was a fractional moment of surprise at my intrusion; myriad eyes turned upon me.

'Yeah. You know her?'

The question seemed loaded with too much interest. An instinctive desire to protect her competed with the urge to boast that we shared a tutorial class.

'Uh. . . no, not really,' I said. 'I'm just in Physics too.'

'You heard anything about the stuff that happened last year?'

'No. I just overheard you guys now. I didn't know she was redoing her year.'

No; I *didn't* realise she was redoing her year. I began to reinterpret her performance in our tutorials.

'So, what happened?'

'Oh, well. . . ' said the boy, freshly enthused by the prospect of a new audience: 'This guy topped himself last year—Tony Baijaiti his name was—threw himself off Queen's Tower. It was all over the news. That's how come you can't go inside any more.'

I doubted this. The famous old bell tower stood 300 feet in a lawn in the middle of campus with two stone lions guarding its entrance. Underneath, a complex maze of service tunnels was rumoured to run throughout the whole of South Kensington. The tower housed one of many entrances to the tunnels and for that reason it was a restricted area, and carried the risk of expulsion. The doors had been locked for years. I considered the base of the tower, its unyielding steps, and I tensed at the image of flesh and stone colliding.

'Why would someone *do* that?' I murmured.

'They say he went a bit mad. Started babbling on about weird stuff. Hassled Kate Andrews with psycho emails. Then smashed himself to a pulp.'

'Because she rejected him?'

'No. Apparently he was sending her warnings.'

'About what.'

'No idea. The police won't give details.'

All this, Kate? My Kate?

'It was all too much for her when he topped himself and she dropped out for the rest of the year. But she came back and they let her redo her year.'

The fuel of facts gone, the conversation shortly thereafter sputtered out and the group dispersed. I walked back to my room troubled and yet with a lighter heart than I'd had in weeks. If Kate had been in some kind of trouble, perhaps I could help? Perhaps this could draw our lives together, join them.

If only I had known just how it would.

I'd run to the physics year photos to confirm if she was in the previous year.

Google had little to add to the matter, other than confirming the spelling of Tony Baijaiti's name, that he'd died the previous April, and that the press seemed to want to blame his behaviour and suicide on schizophrenia. I was desperate to know what his emails to Kate had contained. Thanks to Alexei, I'd got the very lock-picking tools that I needed to find out.

I flew back to my room, poked life into the magic window of my desktop terminal, sat down and mentally cracked my knuckles for a masterwork of breaking and entering. A few hours later, my eyes were burning I had blinked so little, but I had wriggled my way with a series of cunning tricks into the physics department's mail servers.

An array of user accounts stood across the black console window in proud white regiments. There in line was her deliciously Soviet-sounding alias, `andrewsk`, neatly boxed by banal `allenp` and bland `atkinsv`. My eyes traced the glowing cursives as if they were her very own skin.

I was about to issue the command to access her directory when another alias in the list caught my attention:

`baijaitia`

It stood just a few lines below at the edge of the screen, pretending innocence. Nine ghostly-white letters, the marks of a dead man. A. Baijaiti. Antony. Tony. Kate's email stalker. The boy who had thrown himself from the Queen's Tower. The tiny hairs on my triceps lifted and tightened in a small wave that spread across my arms and back. I hadn't expected his account to remain on the server, and yet, here it was, a silicon sarcophagus preserving a tiny part of his existence. I paused for a moment, in nervous indecision.

I tapped at the keyboard and cracked open Anthony Baijaiti's past.

There was nothing but spam email and old project files inside. Everything since before his death in April had been deleted, perhaps at the request of the police. When I checked Kate's directory I found the same was true of hers.

An idea struck me. Email logs were kept by the system. They would only contain the subject headers, not the emails themselves, but it was better than nothing. The files were huge, but I filtered them to pick out only the lines representing emails between Kate and Tony during that April.

Bingo.

```
TimeStamp            From         To          Subject
09/04/2010 03:13     baijaitia    andrewsk    You're in danger
09/04/2010 09:13     andrewsk     baijaitia   RE: You're in danger
09/04/2010 12:07     baijaitia    andrewsk    RE: RE: You're in danger
10/04/2010 11:45     andrewsk     baijaitia   RE: RE: RE: You're in danger
11/04/2010 02:13     baijaitia    andrewsk    Believe me
11/04/2010 09:07     andrewsk     baijaitia   RE: Believe me
11/04/2010 15:07     baijaitia    andrewsk    RE: RE: Believe me
12/04/2010 18:12     andrewsk     baijaitia   LEAVE ME ALONE YOU FREAK
12/04/2010 23:56     baijaitia    andrewsk    RE: LEAVE ME ALONE YOU FREAK
14/04/2010 04:02     baijaitia    andrewsk    PLEASE, STAY AWAY from the Looking Glass Club.
```

The entire dialogue between them had occurred inside of a single week in the final term of her first year. I had no way to know the content of those emails, but the subject lines intrigued me. What kind of danger had he tried to warn Kate about? Was it real? Whatever it was, and whatever the content of his warnings, it seemed he had unnerved her. And then there was that final message header.

What the hell was *the Looking Glass Club*?

From the pages of Tony's diary:

ET phone home...

```
---------------------------------------------------------
---------------------------------------------------------
------------------.------------------------..------
------------------.,,.------------------------....
..-..----------------------.---.,.---.--------------....
--------.----.-------------.,,,,,,.-----.------------
-..........---.------.----------.,,,,,,,,,,,-.------.-
----------.,,,,,,,,,-.-------..,-------.,,,,,,,,,,-..
-------.---------.,,,,,,,,,,,.-------.---------.,,,,
....-,,,,.-----------------.,,,,,,,,,-.,,,,-------.-----
--.,,,,,,,--.,,,,.---------.-------.-.,,,,,,-.,,,,,,-----
---------.---.,,,.-.,,,,,,,,.---------------.-------.,,,,,,,
.----------.,-----.-----.,,,,,,,,,.------------.---..---.-
----.,-------------------.,,,,,.------------------------
--..,------------------------.----------------------
------.,-----------------------------------------
-------------------------------------------------
--------------------------.-----------------------
-----------------------------------------
```

Chapter 3

'And now, which of these finger-posts ought I to follow, I wonder?'

—Alice

It wasn't very far but as a precaution we drove through the rain for a few hours before dumping the car and jumping into a taxi cab. I was still trembling. I told the cab driver to drop us a couple of blocks away—he seemed grateful to be rid of us—and we walked the rest. By the time we arrived, the rain had stopped and the black sky had lightened, teasing us with blue. The clouds had moved on; and the light was a welcome relief. There were fewer shadows and though I could still hear shouting in my head, the voices seemed distant. Everything felt more solid. Before us, Manhattan lay slick and wet, and blue-black—a city-sized, steaming whale. The air was charged, less humid after the downpour. It wouldn't be long before the humidity rose again as ten million vehicles spewed their hot, steamy exhaust into the morning sky, vaporous farts from hydroxy meals. A new steam age.

I was preoccupied with the question of how the assassin had known to find us at Bellevue. A search of Sky's clothes had revealed no bugs or tracers. Someone must have had a triggerbot watching out for her name on hospital systems. It was trivial enough to set up. That's why he hadn't found us at my apartment. I cursed myself for being such an idiot. I knew she was in danger and yet I'd paraded her in blazing neon across the net. We'd been so careless. Now there were consequences. Our names could be linked. We couldn't go back to the apartment. Not until things quietened down. I took us instead to my second, secret home: the office. The place where I make money. There was no link to me there. Registered under the false name of a fake ID. If the police ever raided it, they'd never be able to link it to me. Blob, the hirsute, fleshy homunculus that I kept captive there secreted the DNA of ten thousand people all over the place in various forms: skin cells, hair, sebaceous sludge. I just needed to shake him out once in a while, or let JR worry the wretched rag doll in his snarling jaws. JR had been modified with a rainbow mutation as well. Forensics wouldn't know where to begin.

The street was quiet, but as we approached the building block something didn't look right. I kept Sky back with a flat palm, and edged up to the door. There was blood on the floor. The voices started singing; whispered songs, distorted lullaby nonsense. My thoughts went with a shot of anxiety to Mrs. Voisine, my kind, wrinkled neighbor who thought my name was Alex. Could someone have traced me here? A thump in my chest from the coward I call a heart. I instinctively went for my gun, but felt empty space. It had been knocked from my hand in the attack. I motioned for Sky to stay where she was and moved toward the door, all of my senses sharpened. I sidled round, centered on the door, to look through the glass. Voices sang. *Round and round the garden.* It was dim inside, but empty. The elevator stood impotent at the base. More blood inside the foyer. Dark blood. *Like a teddy bear.* I pushed open the door and strained at my ears, listening for movement inside. Silence. Inside. *One step. Two step.* Nothing in the foyer. Stairs to the left strangled the elevator shaft, a quantized python. The steps were smudged with blood. Alarm exploded in my mind. There was a gap under the stairs, a small area I couldn't see into. I slowed the door with my hand so it closed in silence, and then tiptoed round to it. I peered into its darkness. *Murder you under there.* Nothing. I let a silent breath leave me, and carefully took another.

I followed the blood up the stairs with my eyes. It looked as if someone had been dragged out. Dead or dying. Without my gun I was naked. The apartment was on the first floor, three short turns, 180 degrees. I approached the stairwell and began to tiptoe up the edge of the wall, around the first corner; up the second set of steps, all the time with my ears straining for any sound that might be heard above the turbulent siren of my protesting pulse. Suddenly, downstairs, the silence was shattered by the sound of the front door opening. Immediately upstairs there was a loud scrabbling, clicking sound. I let out a short cry, and, not knowing which way to run, thrust myself, bunch-fisted, round the final corner to take on whatever menace waited there to attack me.

JR barked at me from the landing, wagging the entire back end of his body. Simultaneously Sky called out from the foyer, 'Hello? Anyone there?' *OhmyGodOhmyGoodGod.* The relief was so intense I nearly vomited.

'JR?!' I said, stupefied. 'You're alive?'

I collapsed, half-controlled towards him, jellied by my adrenal glands. I waited for him to respond, but he just barked furiously and tried to lick half my face off. With two arms I lifted him high and gave him a huge hug. He yelped in pain and kicked at my chest. I quickly put him down again and swore.

'What's happened?' I studied him. He looked odd. 'Where's your collar?'

I realized the cable had been ripped out from the top of his spine. The wound was crusted at the edges with blood and looked red and livid. He looked at me with imploring eyes and whined.

'You poor— *but you're alive!* I was so sure you were dead.'

I called to Sky to come up the stairs and herded them both into the apartment. It greeted us and lit up softly. It was cold. I hadn't been here for days, so it had switched the heating off. The wall heaters began to click and creak as they warmed. It felt good to be here. Safe.

'Is this where we live?' Sky demanded abruptly.

'No. No it's not. But it's safe. We can stay here a while.'

'Safe?'

I ignored that, invited her to sit down on the sofa. She lay back and soon closed her eyes. I was grateful. It one less thing to worry about. Her face was slack with fatigue. I returned my attentions to JR. He was walking with difficulty. His claws made an irregular clicking sound as he followed me into the living room. I didn't want to risk lifting him again. I couldn't tell if it was from pain or because of brain damage. He was shivering, still wet from the rain. I pulled his little bed near to the heater in the living room and wrapped a blanket around him, as gently as I could.

I rubbed my nose against his, and he licked me.

'Bark once if you can still understand me.'

He let out a low growl that rose into a bark but it could have been a coincidence.

'Okay, bark three times if you can understand me.'

He barked once. *No.*

Then once more. And a third time. I scratched under his chin with a fingernail and whispered:

'Good boy.'
He let out a whine and shivered. He tried to wag his tail but seemed to lack the energy for it.
'Okay, baby, stay here, by the radiator. It'll be warm soon. I'm going to get some help for you.'
His breathing was raspy.
'Are you hungry?'
I fetched a bowl of water for him and some food. He lapped up a little water but didn't touch the food. That was not a good sign. JR never refuses food.

Skyler let out an un-ladylike snore. We were all soaked. There was no dryer in the office. I had no clothes to lend her and she'd have to get scanned before I could get some fabbed-up. There was a retro store somewhere in a neighboring district that still sold prefab clothes. She'd look like she was on welfare wearing prefab, but she wasn't in a position to be choosy. (Jesus! just five years ago you couldn't even *get* clothes fabbed on the high street. Now it was standard. Things were changing too fast, even for me.) All I had for her now were some towels. We would have to dry what we had on the radiators. Sky slept whilst I undressed her, letting out occasional snorts. I envied her unconsciousness. I lay her flat on the sofa—her belly protruding, pink and taut, incongruous with her slender frame—and covered her with a big towel, makeshift bedding. I didn't see the point of waking her to unfold the sofa into a bed. I figured it was probably more comfortable like that anyway. There was no spare room. The office wasn't much more than a hi-tech bed-sit really. Just a short hallway, a living room, a kitchenette. I had a spare room in my main apartment on 23rd. I had planned for her to stay in that, but, well, we were here instead.

There wasn't much in this apartment that wasn't work-related. Just a few sentimental decorations, enough to make it feel like my own: some Japanese art; a samurai sword mounted on the wall—an authentic *buke-zukuri* I'd got from a Japanese guy on Eighth; a Buddha, next to Blob on the mantelpiece; a picture of my mum when she was young. Little things that meant something to me. Everything else was tech, open carcasses of games machines spilling their guts in front of the World Wall.

Sky began to gently snore, a regular sound, air catching at the back of her throat, and I stopped lamenting my spare room. She was doing fine here. JR's breathing too seemed to slow. His eyes were closed. The siren of sleep sang to me, but I had to remain on guard. JR needed medical help, urgently I suspected. I dug out some amphetamine from my stash. The little paper wrap was filled with dirty looking white powder. I put it away again. I needed something stronger. And purer. It was daylight by now, but night shadows weren't the only worry. I hunted deeper and dug out a tiny square plastic bag. Crystal meth. *Tina*. The tiny crystals were visible, damply clinging to each other in the corners. I smoked it and its fog mingled with that in my mind and canceled it, anti-fog. Clarity reigned. Finally, the voices went away. But nothing was for free. Tina was a bitch. She'd make me pay later.

Neither Emily nor Lewis had answered my calls to them. I hadn't really expected Emily to, under the circumstances, but I'd kept my ancient promise. Lewis, on the other hand, I expected to call back. I had left messages, but I was worried. They depended on me. I considered asking Kate. She had said nothing, and yet *she* was the sentinel. She should have messaged me at the first sign. How could she have not picked anything up? Maybe we'd made a mistake. Maybe she wasn't good enough after all. Maybe if I told her about the note and the assassin, the tattoo, maybe then she could turn something up? Maybe, maybe, maybe. But she'd have to wait. JR first.

A vet would probably just make things worse. It was settled, Needle then. I needed his help anyway.

I looked at sleeping Sky and considered extracting a hair, but that would certainly wake her. I could cut some, but without the root, a full profile would be impossible. Then I noticed that she'd grazed her hand, probably when we'd run into the wall. I wet a few sheets of toilet paper from the bathroom and cleaned off some of the blood. She stirred, but didn't wake. I put the swab into a baggie and pocketed it and then I stood up and went to the mound in the corner and pulled off the dusty cover. It sat there, a metal ribcage: a transparent gel-bed for a spine, a technological carcass with a vascular tangle of wires. Needle's gift to me. A rarely used thing. The ribs stretched out, beckoning me inside. It was no ordinary rig. A sense of dread began to steal over me, dark and foreboding. I'm not a nethead. I don't do total immersion. I'm not like the kids today, addicted to the add-ons their Shades provide, who can't quite leave the net behind even to take a walk. I'm quite happy to walk the naked world. In fact, I would normally do anything to keep the distinction between this world and any other as clean and as possible. That's why I have a World Wall, complete with the one gigapixel per square centimeter needed for high definition holography; and a price tag to rival the GDP of a small country. I prefer my world to stay behind a screen. Normally I use the sanitized, physically disconnected version of the net that only the most technophobic laggards use to do their shopping: visual displays like bullet-proofed windows onto a dangerous world; interfaces worn like gloves—or condoms—protecting us from directly touching the disease-ridden thing itself. And that's why I have JR, all so that I don't have to go in myself. He can stay permanently connected on my behalf. He's my intelligent interface. My proxy. Hell, I thought, at least three of the patients in the Emergency Room where I'd taken Skyler had been kids wearing Shades. The real world has edges to walk into.

There was no good time for immersion as far as I was concerned, but now? After what *I had done*? I cursed Needle. Why was he so damn paranoid? Why wouldn't he let me contact him any other way?

Reluctantly, I lay down on the gel-bed, and slipped my head into the array SQuID microinductors. I held my breath, and flicked the switch that allowed them to take remote control of my neurons.

With a sickening sense of vertigo, the world blinked away. A brief smell of turquoise washed through my toes. I could taste the numbers three through seven. An artefact. Misaligned inductors crossing my wires. The sensations vanished as the rig adjusted. I was left in a void.

Contacting Needle was anything but straightforward. Needle's extreme paranoia meant you didn't find him, he found you. No-one was allowed inside his domain. I tried once to persuade him to allow me some way of letting him know for sure it was me knocking at the virtual door, some code or signal agreed in advance, but he wouldn't. He was utterly intransigent on this matter, far too paranoid about being caught. Caught for what I'm not exactly sure, but Needle lived in a world of conspiracy theories so complex and twisted I got lost at the first turn. He justified his beliefs with the kind of perverse, undeniable logic of an optical illusion by Escher. You could inspect any part of it in detail and it made sense. All the edges matched up, but when you looked at the whole thing it just didn't seem right. We spent many a misguided night in our youth debating whether world leaders were really alien stooges.

So, I had ways of attracting his attention, I could leave messages here and there and then I had to wait. Sometimes days. This time I didn't *have* days to wait for him to find my breadcrumbs. JR needed urgent help. And I needed urgent intelligence on this woman before she, or I, got killed.

I had to try and get inside his domain.

I was there in milliseconds, flashing from blank to white at the speed of thought. I found only dull empty space in which stood a single blank obelisk.

A featureless, out-of-the-box holding space. Anyone visiting here would immediately assume they had stumbled across a beginner's site who had yet to configure anything. *Nothing to see here...*

I knew better.

I pulled up a menu box and accessed a hidden menu using a complex of Linglyph and Propriosense. Needle had nearly lost his patience teaching me the combo and threatened to have the rig burn it into me instead. I'm still not entirely sure he didn't. It seemed strangely familiar for something I hadn't done in at least a year. I selected an option.

A small box unfolded in front of me. A perfectly cubic crystal thing, refracting the virtual light into rainbow. I held it up and peered inside. Dots so tiny, they seemed like dust.

Fleas.

Small dots of low code. *Artilects.* Tiny bits of software, each under twenty gigabytes. More illegal than I even dared contemplate. I'd never used them before. They were a *just-in-case* gift from Needle that came with the rig he'd given to me. Part of this DIY lash-up, strung together with illegal Chinese imports. He never assumed when he gave them to me that I would use them on him.

I crafted a Linglyph and twisted it to them.

At first it just sat inside the vial next to them, looking like a colorful snowflake trapped in a disk, and they remained static, impassive. Then, suddenly, they devoured it, accelerating to a frightening speed, slicing through it until it was a mere cobweb of color that fell into dust. There was a moment of stillness again as they compiled the instructions, and then they began to hop about frantically, smashing with surprising force against the walls of the crystal box. It shuddered in what felt like my hands. The fleas were glowing red with the speed of their movement. I knew what to do. I lifted the crystal cube and threw it with force at the obelisk, where it shattered into tiny diamonds, throwing out the glowing fleas like sparks. The diamonds vanished. The fleas swarmed at the obelisk and raced along its edges, twisting and turning, following invisible patterns, finding cracks. One by one, they flickered out of sight with tiny flashes of crimson light.

I was suddenly aware of my real body lying in the rig, less than a ghost in this world. It breathed with nervous excitement. I waited. There was little more I could do except wait for them to get back to me. I had to stay immersed, so I wasted some time casting out web searches for the top five painkillers and general anesthetics for canines and stored the resulting list. I sucked in some feeds to get the news. Two news items caught my attention. Some kid in Russia—barely a teenager—was claiming he could stalemate QMaster, the high street chess game released last year by Ikitama. I doubted the claim. QMaster was the first high-street quantum computer, a hardwired implementation of the quantum algorithm designed by Koto and Yebber to solve chess. It didn't calculate ten, or even twenty moves ahead. It played *every possible* permutation of every game from its current state and picked the winning path. The other news item was on the Singularity. The rate of technological change is constantly accelerating because of the law of increasing returns: each generation of technology is used to create the next generation more quickly and efficiently. About ten years ago, some German science writer—bless the Germans for their wonderful neologisms—coined this runaway reaction, *technologiegalopp.* No-one denies it's a real phenomenon: there have been more new technologies in the last five years than in the previous five hundred. The Singularity is the logical conclusion of *technologiegalopp,* the point of no return. What happens when technology becomes smart enough to start improving itself? The pace of change will explode geometrically. The world will change overnight and no-one can predict what it will look like in the morning. Vernor Vinge, who coined the term Singularity, once predicted it would happen before 2030, but that was based on the assumption that computers could theoretically become sentient. Once it was proven that classical computers could never produce a conscious intelligence—and as the first end-of-the-world-as-we-know-it dates came and went—all the Singularity predictions fell away. Now, though, someone was braving a new Singularity projection based on breakthroughs in biological implementations of self-replicating quantum computers. Sometime in 2040.

Five years away.

So soon... The thought caused a cold shiver to run through me.

I wasn't entirely sure how long I would have to wait for the fleas to do their work. Minutes, surely, not hours? Or days? I pulled up a view on the living room to check on JR. I could see my body cradled in the haphazard metal and wire, my head couched in a honeycomb helmet. It was strange seeing myself like that, from a viewpoint that could neither be mine nor that of a reflection. That man looked like a stranger, but I knew it was me. I could find no correlation between those arm and those leg positions and the limbs I had here. I lifted one of my arms—it looked so realistic!—and yet I watched my real body lying limp and unresponsive. I lifted another and another, and then another, amusing myself at the complete lack of correlation between my physical and virtual corpi. The rig allowed me to multiply my limbs if I wanted to, effectively multiplexing the nerves that connected my physical limbs to my motor and somatosensory cortices. It would provide as many limbs as my brain could handle. Everyone was different, many people couldn't do it at all. I could manage ten or twelve, even sixteen on a good day, if I'd slept well, or was tweaked. (If you've never used a rig you can get a sense of this by imagining an extra pair of arms and then imagine moving them independently of your real arms. All the rig does is track the neurons firing as you do that, interpret them, and map onto pseudolimbs, but it takes enormous practice to move more than one or two at once—a bit like rubbing your stomach whilst patting your head. Needle once told me he could handle over a hundred limbs. I believed him.)

I twisted into a new, physically impossible shape, reveling in the freedom. Then I mapped a limb onto the camera, slid it around to look at JR's bed and then zoomed in. He seemed to be asleep, his breathing was slow and shallow and had an unnatural rhythm. His ear twitched and he opened an eye and stared straight at the cam. I blinked the red light at him to say hi. I was the ghost in my own machines. He lifted his head and looked puzzled. I had no idea if he knew it was me. Normally he would have, but I wondered how much of his higher functions had been compromised by his injury.

An alert sounded. Suddenly, the view of the living room was yanked away and I was back in Needle's blank domain. It looked the same. I was confused for a moment and feeling slightly on edge. The rig had never done anything like that before. Overridden my control. It unnerved me.

I studied the plain walls. Nothing.

Then I noticed. A tiny red glow in one corner.

I smiled. One of the fleas had found a way in. All I had to do now was zoom in on it and slide through whatever crack it was holding open for me.

I went to the corner to look. The tiny dot seemed to hurt my eyes. I suddenly felt a terrible sense of dread. I almost persuaded myself to pull back but it was too late: I found myself looking closer and before I could react, the world started to turn inside out. The dot pulled at my vision, torturing my visual centers like some terrible optical illusion. I fractured. Machine painfully divorced from human. Then, *everything* inverted; solid became empty space.

The world went dark.

Something was wrong. Very wrong. This wasn't supposed to happen. I was supposed to find a tunnel or a crack and go through it. That's what Needle had said. The fleas hadn't just failed, they'd caused the whole rig to fail. The inductors were jamming my neurons.

I was trapped.

I suddenly felt very human. Exposed. Completely vulnerable. I was in a pitch blackness deeper than it was possible to imagine. Deeper even than it was normally possible to experience. Even the half-colors that normally played across my eyelids when I closed my eyes at night were absent. This was pure, absolute blackness. I tried to cast out a limb, but I felt nothing. I was utterly discorporated—a blind, deaf, bodiless mind. The silence was absolute. I could not even hear the quiet hum or hiss of background noise that ears seem to make by themselves in a silent room. All of my senses had been attenuated to nothing by the rig's actuators deep in my cerebrum. I had no external senses. Nothing. Just my sense of self, pure conscious thought. For a moment, even my thoughts seemed to be going far away, becoming barely audible, and I was terrified that I would stop being able to think at all, that I would simply stop. But my capacity for thought remained, though the thoughts themselves came in and out of focus, and changed volume alarmingly. And then my worst fears began to come true: the voices that had been quiet until now began to sing softly in the distance. My thoughts started racing at a frightening pace.

WhathefuckisgoingonImgoingdie calmdownnoImdeadnocalmcalmImdead nono-NO.

I could not feel my body but I knew my heart must be revving under an onslaught of adrenaline and tina, fueled by panic that was somehow being communicated back to my body. I had to calm down.

Calmthefuckdown.

Calmdowneverythingwillbefine. Justaslongasyoudontgiveyourselfafuckingcoronary.

How to control breathing? Was I breathing? Must be. Autonomic nervous system. Like sleeping. Regulated. Blood oxygen levels.

The voices babbled in the distance, coming closer, fading again.

I started to think soothing words, visualized calming scenes, like a beach, a quiet country garden, clouds. For the moment, it seemed to work. My thoughts slowed, became less erratic.

I hung bodiless, barely human in the total darkness and silence. Waiting.

Time passed. The voices seemed to fade.

Utterly alone, trapped in a void, a liquid black prison. The absence of everything.

I began to frighten myself again.

How long had I'd been like this? Ten minutes? Twenty?

I tried to cast out some limbs again. Nothing. Was there another way to access menus? All of the other interface styles I could think of needed to be open already before you could use their methods.

I was going to die.

Claustrophobia suffocated me like a blanket. I was entombed in an infinite black liquid. I was lying in a coffin into which had poured a black resin, over my eyes, into my ears, inside my mouth, into my lungs, filling me up, covering every part of me. There was no way to turn or move, just black on black on black. I wanted to scream. I had no mouth. I imagined screaming, but it was powerless, pathetic. The voices wandered closer. They screamed, mocking me. My thoughts became lucid. Their speed told me my adrenaline levels must be high again. That calmed me. It was a sign that there was a reality beyond this one. There was a real room in which a real body was lying with its senses artificially suppressed.

Calm. *Calm.* I considered the option that I didn't want to consider: Russian Roulette. The Abyss.

But could I? What was there to change? I was in a void. There was nothing here. It wasn't possible to create. And, hadn't I used up my quota of sanity? Listen to them singing. Wasn't I dangerously on the edge already? Twice in two days; the usual dangers would surely be magnified here? I could hear them whispering now, somewhere in the distance again, conspiring, summoned, given power again just by the idea. Haunting me. If I tried it now, I was guaranteed to go the way of Emily. Who knows what horrors I would unleash on myself, perhaps for eternity.

Then, in the midst of my thoughts, the blackness lightened to gray.

For a fraction of a second I was suddenly overwhelmed by an overload of sensory input. Then blackness again. I was momentarily stunned, but there could be no doubt about it, for a moment my senses *had* returned. I had felt pain in all my limbs, beautiful glorious pain! I'd felt a thump in my chest that could only have been my heart (my *heart!*). I'd smelled the warm doggy smell of my living room and the vaguely plastic scent of the rig. I'd heard a brief moment of nothing. The kind of nothing that was something. The sound of a silent room.

The darkness seemed to lighten again to gray and my interfaces flickered in and out of existence. There was a second or two more of strobe-like fluctuation and then everything came online. I was back in Needle's featureless domain. I felt an acute pain in my chest; a colossal headache pounded at my temples. My heart was hammering blood around my body. My head felt like it would explode from the thumping pressure. Fortunately, now that I had sensory feedback again, I could feel my heart rate slowing, relaxing, as if I'd just crossed the finish line of a marathon.

A handsome man with green-blue eyes and long blond hair in a pony tail stood across from me. He wore a smart charcoal polo neck with a sand-colored camel emblem as a badge.

'You really should be more careful,' he said.

'YOU FUCKING IDIOT NEEDLE! I COULD HAVE DIED IN THERE.'

'Oh, don't be such a drama queen. You're fine. And that's hardly the way to thank me for rescuing you now, is it?'

'FINE?! You call *this* fine?'

I flashed out a visual of my vital signs.

I tried to calm down. There was no point aggravating Needle if I wanted anything from him. He was the ultimate prima donna. I knew from bitter experience that he would be impossible if I didn't treat him with kid gloves. I managed to get my voice calm, but it was impossible to disguise my fury completely.

'I can't believe you of all people called me a drama queen?! Have you seen how fast my heart was going?'

'Darling, I'm well aware of your vital statistics. Now stop being such a bore. I've got you out of yet another mess and I'm sure you haven't gone to this degree of attention grabbing just to have a go at me.'

'It's your bloody code that got me into this mess in the first place. One of those damn fleas. It completely shut my rig down. I had no way of getting out.'

'Fleas? I couldn't possibly admit to having anything to do with something so illegal. As a matter of fact, my defences are configured to automatically shut them down and kick out anyone who would be stupid enough to try such an attack on my domain. I mean, come on, Steel. What the hell did you think you were playing at?'

Needle had an unfailing knack of making me feel like a retard. My anger deflated like a balloon. He was right. What was I expecting? To get in?

'They shouldn't have buggered your rig though,' he added with a curious expression. 'That's a surprise. I'll make a note of that.'

'I can't believe it could even leave me in that state,' I said. My voice sounded petulant, small. 'Why doesn't it have a failsafe?'

He shrugged. 'Never thought about it. I've never needed one. Hold on.'
His image froze for a few hundred milliseconds.
'There, I've written a patch and uploaded it. It won't happen again.'
A few hundred milliseconds.
'Jesus, Needle! How fast are you running?'
'You really don't want to know, darling. Now, what on Earth could be so urgent that you felt the urge to hack into my own domain of all places to get my attention?'
'I need to find out about someone. A... client. Sort of. Look, all I have is a DNA sample. She has no memory of who she is, and no public record, not even on the hospital files, but she's heavily pregnant. I'm pretty sure she'll have been treated before. Maybe a boutique clinic. Somewhere not on Mednet.'
Needle looked at me as though I'd just started cross-dressing whilst singing songs about hemorrhoids.
'Someone's trying to kill her, okay? They damn near killed me in the process. I need to find out who she is and why someone would want her dead.'
I did not mention the note. There are some things about your past you don't talk about.
'You're a competent enough hacker, do it yourself!'
Flattery time.
'Needle, I'm a zombie designer. For games. For porn. I make empty people that pretend to be real. Dolls that fool people into thinking there's somebody home when really the lights are all out. Intelligent undead. I'm not good at the whole hacking thing. It's too technical, too detailed. There's too much to know. Yes, I can do it, but I'm not even in the same league as you and you know it. Not even the same universe. I need a result fast. Preferably before one of us is killed. It would take me a year to hack into every private care provider in New York.'
'Oh-kay... and given your resources, waiting a day or two to make this request was a problem how exactly?'
'There's something else.'
I pulled up a video wall showing the living room. The cam was still on a close-up of JR.
'He was injured when we were attacked. His collar's been ripped off. I don't know what kind of damage there is but he needs patching up. He's in a pretty bad way. We need to come to see you.'
Needle folded his arms.
'You *know* I don't take real visitors, Steel. You're lucky I'm seeing you virtually, quite frankly, after that little stunt.'
'This is an emergency. He needs help. Please.'
'Do I have "Vet" stamped on my forehead?' he snapped. 'Take him to one.'
'They wouldn't have a clue what to do. Come on, Needle. *Please.* You're the only person I know that could get him up and running again. You'd probably make him even better than he was. You're a genius. More than a genius. I wouldn't trust him with anyone less.'
Needle could see through my flattery as clearly as though it were glass, but flattery was his Achilles heel. He was completely unable to resist it. He sighed dramatically.
'Okay. How much?'
I grinned in relief.
I didn't just design zombies. The Looking Glass Club had left with me a side-effect that Needle had occasion—most illegally—to take advantage of.
'Half my next job.'
He chuckled sarcastically. 'You mean you have nothing to pay me, except a promise that you may not be able to keep? Who says there'll be a next job?'

I lowered my head and let my disappointment show with a crestfallen look. Pure manipulation.

I looked up again with sad eyes.

'All of my next job?'

'Oh for God's sake, don't do that puppy dog eyes shit on me, *pu-lease*. Bring him over. I'm sending a car. It will be there in fifteen minutes. But I'm only doing it for you because you're still cute. Just. You owe me. And it *will* be expensive.'

I kissed the fingertips on both hands and threw them apart in extravagant gratitude.

'Needle, I love you. You're a God.'

'Not yet I'm not.'

I zipped the list of canine anesthetics to him.

'Do you have any of these to hand?'

'No, but I will by the time you arrive.'

His image vanished, but his voice lingered in the air.

'I won't have time to make myself pretty for you. But I'm sure a gentleman like you won't be insulted.'

I extricated myself from the metal ribcage of the rig, feeling sweaty and unwashed, and strangely limited. I considered jumping in the shower quickly, but one look at Jack changed my mind. His breathing was fitful and he hadn't reacted to my return. He was still unconscious in his basket. I decided the best thing to do would be to lift the whole basket and get it down into the car.

Sky was still snoring gently on the sofa. She'd be fine here. Hopefully we'd be back before she woke up.

I looked out of the window. It was light outside. The sky was billowing with white cloud. I asked the apartment for a weather forecast and it came back with an 85% likelihood of snow. From torrential rain to clear skies and then to snow in half a day. Ridiculous. But the weather was worse these days. Practically the whole winter was spent trudging through wet carpets of snow. Clear evidence of local climate change caused by hydroxy fuels, but people accepted it. They were organically derived and therefore carbon neutral. It was better than the smog we used to get in the late teens. Better than global warming.

I covered JR with a blanket and carried him down into the street, locking Skyler in the apartment. She'd be fine. The door would unlock if there was a fire.

Outside, the air was still, as if the city were too lazy to move. The temperature hovered around zero. JR opened his eyes when we hit the cold and let out a hoarse grunt of complaint.

The limousine flashed its lights as it approached. It was a regular not a stretch I noticed gratefully. The windows were black. I put JR's basket on the back seat and climbed in, saying hello to the driver. JR lifted his head weakly. I was bumping him around more than I meant to. My words of consolation seemed weak, insufficient. I bundled myself in and pulled the door closed. The car pulled away immediately. I looked up, just about to comment on the imminent snow to the driver, to see that in fact, the front of the car was empty. There was no driver. I'd been speaking to myself.

The world outside looked darker and more ominous through the one-way glass of the car. It soon began to snow and within minutes it was falling in such heavy flakes I could barely see twenty meters ahead. The wipers swept away fat lines of white sludge in rubbery, squeaking arcs. I wasn't sure why they were on, I thought the car's cams would have been on the outside, but I could have been wrong. After about ten minutes all of the windows turned black on the inside too. Lights flickered on and my com stopped working. Needle's voice sounded from the car's speakers. 'Just a precaution. As much for your safety as mine. It really wouldn't be good for your health to know where I live.'

And I thought I was paranoid.

The journey took nearly an hour and I had no idea where we were, not even if we were still in Manhattan. If we were, it was a part I'd never been to. Eventually, the windows flicked transparent again just as the car entered a private housing estate through automatic gates. You could tell which were the rich districts because they had their own police force. An officer peered at me from a small office at the entrance before letting us past. Needle's apartment block looked more like corporate offices than housing to me, but once inside I had the impression of a five star hotel. The car had told me the apartment number. It was the penthouse.

The lift at the bottom greeted us in a saccharine sweet tone.

I had my salutation prepared before the doors to his penthouse opened, but I couldn't prevent a sharp intake of breath when they parted. I hadn't seen Needle in the flesh for many years. I wasn't prepared.

I tried to cover my reaction by turning it into a whistle of admiration and I forced a wide smile and opened my arms.

'Great apartment. It's good to see you again, Needle.'

His wheelchair gave a despondent electric whine as he rolled towards us. His head seemed stuck to one shoulder. The skull was exposed and it was partly covered with a livid red growth into which bundles of cabling vanished. The left side of his face had severe burn scars. When he spoke the right half of his mouth did not move, slurring his speech badly.

'Don't lie, Steel. You were never any good at it. I know how I look.'

The last time I'd seen him he had been mobile. He hadn't been what I would have called normal for years, but this was extreme, even for him. Needle gave new meanings to 'personal development' and 'self-improvement'. He wasn't called Needle because he was hard to find. He got his name because he considered himself a work in progress and used himself as an experimental subject. We used to joke that Needle was the bleeding edge of technology. He was always sticking things into himself. He was a walking laboratory. Well, he had been. Now he was a rolling one.

It was Needle that persuaded me to move to New York and helped me change my identity—a move that almost certainly saved my life. At that time Jacob, my twin brother, had already tried to kill me twice. That's also when we discovered my talent, my gift from the LGC. A little extra. One that didn't cost my sanity to use. Needle never questioned it. Over the years, he'd simply give me the odd job here and there, and help me hide the sometimes enormous pay packets I'd be given in return. The scars of Needle's experiments were beginning to show even then. When most people were still playing around with hearing-aid-style insert phones, Needle had replaced his own ear drum with a home-made com implant. He did the operation himself under local anesthetic with the help of a friend. Over the years I watched as his handsome face was steadily eaten away by the ravenous mouth of technology.

I decided the best way to handle the shock was with humor.

'Great new set of wheels you have there. So, you freaky old faggot, what have you been up to apart from ruining your good looks?'

He laughed lopsidedly.

'That's more like it. Advancement carries a heavy price, Steel, you know that as well as anyone. It's a price worth paying. Freak, yes, but for the record, I don't identify as queer anymore. I haven't had sex for over a decade. It lost its appeal when even rent boys started turning me down, so I edited the urges out completely. You know, life is so much more *productive* without them. As for old, well, there's one thing this path is going to guarantee me, and that's a very, *very* long life. So, old...? In the grand scheme of things I suspect I've only just been born.'

I laughed gently, but I was still reeling from shock. He reversed back into the large apartment with petulant whines from his wheelchair motor. The entire wall on the other side of the penthouse was glass. One-way probably. As his chair reversed I noticed that fat cables ran from the back of it into runners in the ceiling which followed the chair around. No wonder it complained. The sight brought to mind an image of fairground bumper cars which would have been funny had the whole scene not been so disturbing.

'Are those power or data?'

'Both.'

'What do you do when you want to get outside?'

'I don't. The outside world holds little interest for me now, my friend. I have almost no power out there, but in here...' He tapped at his good temple, I think to indicate the net, but he left the sentence hanging, incomplete.

'Is all... this... intentional? I mean the chair?'

He let out a sad laugh, part cough, part sigh.

'No. I had an interface blow-out during an installation. It caught fire and took out half of my motor cortex, wiped out Lord knows how many memories and set my cognitive functions back years. I've replaced them now, but as you can see, it didn't do much for my pulling power. Come through to the lab. You can put your dog on the bench.'

I followed him through into a darkened room without windows. A large metal bench in the center supported several fat, anonymous looking devices. The carcasses of hundreds of machines and interfaces, large and small lay strewn in disarray around the room and on racks that lined the walls.

There was a powerful cocktail of chemical smells. It smelled like a hospital, and a garage.

I put the basket on the bench. JR was awake now. He was making small rasping noises each time he exhaled. My stomach was tight with anxiety listening to them.

'Did you get the drugs? The anesthetics?'

Needle lifted a limp hand to indicate one of the beige plastic boxes on the bench. It had rounded corners and a large transparent plastic window. A small amber light strobed on its face. The device clicked and hummed occasionally and flashed green.

'It's cooking now. I can make most things here. Should be ready in a few minutes. Let's have a look at him.'

He wheeled over to the edge of the bench and simultaneously two robot arms began to slide along the bench on caterpillar tracks toward JR, one from each end. JR lifted his head and let out a growl.

'It's okay, little guy. Needle's going to help you, buddy. Gonna fix you up.'

I stroked his side with a finger, afraid to touch him anywhere else in case I hurt him. He thumped the basket once with his tail, either too exhausted, or in too much pain to wag it. He looked at me nervously.

Six halogen lamps in a hexagonal array descended from the ceiling and pinged into dazzling blue-white brightness above the basket. The lamp moved smoothly into position above him, throwing sharp shadows from the equipment onto the bench. The robot arms moved in a table-top ballet, perfectly synchronized. Countless other devices nested in the ceiling, spindly metal bats folded up, hibernating.

Both of the tank-like robot arms had multiple limbs, all fingered with expensively tooled digits. Each had a twin-eyed camera. The eyes glistened, tiny dark marbles. Needle instructed JR to lie very still. He'd try not to hurt him but he needed to have a look at the damage. Elegant digits gently moved blood-matted fur away from the wound on the back of his neck. Curious-eyed cameras probed and inspected.

Needle was sitting to the side, his eyes had glazed over. When he spoke his mouth no longer moved and his speech was no longer slurred. His voice came from a speaker somewhere.

'It looks like the whole line has ripped out. Shame. If it had just broken I might have been able to re-patch the ends. I can't tell much more without putting him under.'

One of the tank arms drove to Needle's chemical cooker. The green light was now shining steadily. The robot arm twisted down and pushed a button that triggered the wide plastic window to spring out and then slide upwards. It let out a satisfied hiss. Inside sat an array of five small glass vials shaped like cubes stacked neatly in blocks. Each contained clear liquid. One of the engineered digits pushed at the central block, prompting it to click and then slide out of the cooker. A shadow passed over the table. One of the metal bats was unfolding. It descended and dipped into the clear liquid, drawing some of it up into a tube. I saw no needle, but moments later when it was applied to JR's furry back, I heard a sharp hiss. Seconds later he was unconscious.

'You don't have to stay for this. Go and watch a 3DV if you're squeamish.'

'I'll stay.'

'Well then, stop looking so anxious.'

Needle appeared asleep in his wheelchair as he worked his art on JR. The only evidence of his consciousness was the synchronized performance of plastic, fur and blood being played out over the starkly lit stage of metal. The pace seemed to grow more urgent, with new actors appearing, fluidly unfolding from the ceiling, dei ex machina, to save a slumbering protagonist. The story was told to the strange music of servo motors, the rattling suck of liquid drains, and elucidating interjections from Needle, whose helpful narrative filled in the gaps in my understanding.

The pace began to slow and the robots' arms began to tidy the wound they had worsened. A tiny machine gun chatter of staples announced the end of the performance, machine applause, and the actors exited the spot lit stage with a final flourish.

JR's body lay still, awkwardly positioned by Needle's handiwork. I prayed this performance would not have a tragic ending.

'He was lucky. The artificial neuroplasm was degrading, it seems to have broken quite cleanly and left a lot of his original bundle intact. He probably would have needed a replacement soon anyway. He'll have lost a lot of stuff, you backed him up regularly, though, right?'

'I don't know. I left that to him.'

'Well, he'll have the primal stuff still, sights, sound, smell, but he may have no higher cognitive or linguistic recall from before the event unless he backed up. Or unless you can find his old collar.'

'Okay. What about a new collar, when does he get that?'

'He doesn't need one, Steel. *Smaller, better, faster.* It's all inside now. I'm sure the little fella will appreciate the new freedom.' A chuckle came from the speakers. 'Especially the new voice.'

'I don't follow. Where's the speaker? How will he speak?'

'He had room in his motor cortex for a mod. He'll be able to use his mouth now. It'll take a bit of getting used to but he'll be able to use his better than I can use mine.'

JR's old collar had been state-of-the-art only *three months ago...* *Technologiegalopp.* The pace of change was beginning to frighten even a technophile like me.

'Are you kidding?'

'Sadly not.'

'I meant—'

'I know what you meant. Let's not dwell on that. After all, I'm sure it won't be long before I'll be able to mend even my serious mistakes if I have the desire to. He's going to need to rest for a few days at least while the new interface integrates. I've given him an immunobooster, so the risk of infection is low, but keep him inside and clean until the wound has closed properly.'

JR was beginning to show signs of regaining consciousness.

'Now, what about this mystery woman. You could always bring her here; let me have a go at cracking her. I'm sure with a little digging around I could uncover what you're looking for...'

'Yeah, nice try. I'm trying to protect her, not have her opened up and rewired. I'll stick to conventional methods for now.'

'The offer's there if you need it.'

I handed him the small baggie with the blood-stained toilet tissue inside.

'Let me know what you can find out about her.'

'I'll see what I can get, but it could turn up nothing for a whole lot of expense. DNA matching can still be time consuming. I'm not working on a success only basis.'

'I'll take that risk.'

'It was nice to see you again. I mean it.' He spoke from his mouth this time and the words came out slurred. Rheumy green-blue eyes were open and looking at me, cat-like. They seemed to be saying something more, but as is often the case with Needle, it was in a language I couldn't understand.

I thanked him for everything, and, knowing the privilege of being allowed a flesh visit, I said he was a true friend. It was a strangely intimate moment. It was the first time since the lift doors had opened that I really saw past the grotesque mask of his features, that I saw the old friend I remembered.

When the limo dropped us back near my office, the snow had stopped. I carried JR up the stairs in his basket to the front door, and gently put it on the floor whilst I unlocked the door with my code.

I pushed the door open carefully, not wishing to wake Skyler. I picked up the basket, and on my way in, I turned, and used it to push the door shut.

Suddenly, I felt a sharp and hard point in my back.

An unsteady voice said:

'One false move and I'll spear you. You put that down *now* and turn around. Slowly.'

From the pages of Tony's diary:

'Steganography? What a capital idea!' said Alice.

letspretendtheglasshasgotallsoftlikegauzesothatwecangetthroughwhyITS
TurningintoasortofmistnowideclareItllbeeasyenoughtogetthroughSHEWasu
ponthechimneypiecewhileshEsaidthisthoughshehardlyknewhoWSHEHAdgotthe
reandcertainlytheglasswasbeginninGtomEltAwAYJUstlikeaBRIGhtsilverYmi
stinAnOthermomentaliCewasthroUghtHEGLaSSANdhadjUmPEDLightlydoWninTot
HeLookingglAsSroomtheveRYFIRsTthInGSHEdidwaStOLOOkwhethertherewasafi
reinthefireplaceandshewasquitepleasedtofiNdtHattherewasarealoneblazi
ngaWaYASBrightlyastheoneshehadleftbEhIndSoishallbeaswarmhereasiwasin
theoLdroomthoughtalicewarmerinfacTBECausetherellbenooneheretoscoldme
awayfromthefireohwhatfunitllBEWHeNTHEySEEMeThrOuGhThEGLaSSINHereaNdc
AnTgeTaTmeThEnShEbEgAnlOOkingAboUtAndNoTICedThAtWhAtCoULDbeseEnfRoMt
hEoLdRooMwAsQuItEcomMonanDUNInTEREsTinGbUtTHAtAlLTHerestwasasdiffere
ntaspossibleforinSTANcethepicturesonthewallnextThEfiReseemedtobealla
liveandthevErYcLOckonthechimneypieceyouknowyoUcanonlyseethebackofiti
nthelookiNGGlasshadgotthefaceofalittleoldmanandgrinnedathertheydontk
eepT

Chapter 4

'I think of my lifetime in physics as divided into three periods. In the first period... I was in the grip of the idea that Everything is Particles... I call my second period Everything is Fields... Now I am in the grip of a new vision: that Everything is Information.'

—John Wheeler

I learned of the existence of the enigmatic Looking Glass Club just as England shucked off the last of summer. Warm days became more rare, and when the clocks went back it seemed to nail down the coffin lid of winter for another six dark months. For weeks, the evenings carried the malty scents of bonfires and the Punch and Judy shrieks of fireworks. The leaves turned in Hyde Park and the trees began to rain paper, rust and gold. Plum skies descended more suddenly and London sprang into points of coloured light against a dark background like some delightfully garish pop-up book. It was a time for wearing thick jumpers and staying in.

I could find out no more about the Looking Glass Club after my illicit incursion into the email server. The Internet was a sea murky with red herrings. I did not know it, but I had already triggered events that would lead me directly to it—or rather it to me.

My friendship with Alexei seemed to have restored itself to its former warmth and intensity—and exclusivity; my neighbours in my new residence had all but given up their attempts at including me in their social activities. I was a latecomer anyway and I had rebutted their invitations once too often. They regarded me with curious but aloof eyes on the rare occasions when I encountered them. I was sure that many of them would be fascinated, even thrilled as I was, by the projects Alexei and I obsessed over nightly, but he'd forbidden me from talking about them and for some reason, I complied. People began to regard us as a pair of strange outsiders.

We'd been debating an old classic: could machines ever become conscious? Ironically, Alexei, the computer scientist, was saying 'no' and using physics against me to justify his argument. He insisted that minds were fundamentally quantum mechanical in nature. He'd managed to drag my tortured mind away from the subject of Kate and her mystery for a while and we were actively engaged in this debate walking back to the physics department after lunch. He'd offered to walk back with me as I had a lecture but he had a free period. Alexei was in the middle of attacking the famous 'Turing Test'. Alan Turing, the father of computer science, had argued that if a machine behaved indistinguishably from a human, then it had to be conscious to do so.

'Look,' Alexei insisted, 'we already have non-sentient machines that can produce behaviour indistinguishable from human behaviour.'

33

'We do?'

'Yes. Televisions! Video recorders! Using *completely different processes* they *re*produce phenomena which are identical to the humans they recorded. No-one's arguing those machines are conscious.'

'Yeah, but they're not interactive. The Turing Test is supposed to be.'

'So? The point is you can be fooled by behaviour. You could make a system based on recordings that fooled you for an arbitrary length of time. The Turing Test is based on what I call the Fallacy of Phenomenological Equivalence: the assertion that if the external phenomena are the same they must have the same underlying ontology. That's not just flawed, it's patently false. Calculating a behaviour does not imply the calculator is required to experience it.'

'So you believe it's possible to create a phenomenal zombie?'

A *phenomenal zombie* was the name given to a machine that appeared sentient in its behaviours, but had no true inner feelings or experience. It was not conscious, not self-aware. The very possibility of phenomenal zombies was not universally accepted. Turing's argument essentially claimed such a thing was impossible.

'Theoretically, yes, but the real problem,' Alexei continued loudly, 'is with the discrete nature of Turing equivalent machines. You can't chop consciousness up into discrete states. In fact, I'm working on a *reductio ad absurdum*-style proof starting with that assumption.'

'Are you?' I said, terribly impressed.

'Sure, look.' He took a pen and scribbled on a napkin. 'See these?'

He'd written '3', 'iii' and 'three'.

'They're all "three".'

'Right. To you. But they're just arbitrary marks on a bit of paper we happen to agree mean 'three'. It's the act of *interpretation* that makes them *three*. So, if you assert that brain state can be written as a number, albeit a long one, then what gives that number its meaning? Who chooses? It's just an arbitrary number. Where's consciousness in that? A number is like a... a frozen state. Imagine your head was frozen, like in those cryonics facilities. Those heads aren't *conscious*. And linking a whole series of them together in time just creates some hideous, stop-motion, frozen zombie movie. Each frame in the movie is still dead. That's where quantum mechanics comes in—'

Just as that moment, a cheerfully sarcastic voice interrupted:

'God, guys, *riveting* stuff. You must be a fucking *hoot* at parties.'

I was used to being ribbed, so I looked up, largely uncaring, until I saw the owner of the voice was stood with Kate.

The sight of her robbed something inside me.

She wore a grey flannel skirt and white shirt today that would have made any other girl look like a librarian. Instead, she looked like a pop star. It was deliberately school-girly. Provocative.

I recognised the guy from around but he wasn't from physics. He looked sturdy. He wore a rugby shirt with 'RSM' embroidered above a shield. Royal School of Mines. A geologist probably. She offered me a bland fraction of a smile and then looked away. *Meaning what? What did that mean? Was that bad?*

They left, dragging a wretched beating heart invisibly behind them.

Alexei tutted. Was that tut *at me*? A hot anger swelled inside me.

'*Pillock*,' he said.

No, the rugby player.

Then he looked at me, and interpreted something from my expression. He rolled his eyes ceiling-ward.

'Oh, for *goodness'* sake! She's just a *girl.*'

I felt a strange slackness in my face; gravity was pulling down on it more heavily than usual, and the muscles were simply too weak to resist. The flesh cupping my eyes burned hot and damp.

'Alexei? Just *Fuck Off*, okay?'

People were looking at us now. A reflection of my own humiliation flared terribly in his eyes.

I walked out.

The cars on Prince Consort Road cruised past in calm contrast to the turmoil that the geologist's sarcastic guffaw had stirred up in my mind. The breath that curled from my mouth into the autumn air seemed to have lifted itself steaming directly from my mind.

'I'm not just some *geek*!'

Further up the road, a figure turned to look, then continued its business.

Kate was hot metal under the skull encasing my mind, trapping it. I pressed at my temples with the heels of my hands, massaging the pain of inadequacy that throbbed there.

I took off, running, trying to escape from myself, across the road, up the steps of the Albert Hall, across the main road and into Hyde Park. The trees rustled grandly, the slow rushing of a papery sea. I ran through them. They whispered sadistically: *not you*. I turned and ran back to my room. From behind the safe, protective glass of my window I looked out onto the world below and waited for my breath and heart to still. I told myself that my chest ached from running. I had stood at this window many times in the past few weeks watching our building's languid metabolism. In the morning, it exhaled students in a steady stream from its varied mouths; then, a small, quick hiccup, in-out, over lunch; finally a lazy, long inhalation over the course of the evening, leaving it full-chested, student-infested, ready to slumber through the long night. Now, the light was falling from the sky, as if insecurely fastened, and the building seemed poised to take its long inward breath. I turned and faced myself in the small mirror on the cabinet above the porcelain sink.

He didn't look so bad, that boy. He was good looking, in a timid sort of way, wasn't he?

Then the problem wasn't that, but what was inside him.

I cried out and punched the mirror, smashing it. I fractured my own terrible expression into long, sad shards.

At home, Mum's concern over my bandaged fist seemed exaggerated, even for her. She seemed pale and waxy. At first, I was so consumed by my own misery I didn't notice.

'Probably broke it tossing off too much,' Jacob jeered.

'*Jacob!* I did *not* raise you with a gutter mouth. What is this university *doing* to you both?!'

'Why do you *always* include me when *he* does something?' I protested. Words in our arguments were frequently over-emphasised.

'Why can't you just get along, like you did when you were children?'

There was despair in her voice. It was true; we were close when we young, up until the age of thirteen. We behaved as people expected twins to, even wore the same clothes. People found us hard to tell apart, though everyone could see we had quite different temperaments. We were inseparable. And then Amy Scott happened, shortly after puberty. Amy was my first crush. And Jacob (ever the extrovert) asked her out *knowing* how I felt about her because I'd told him. She said yes. It had only lasted a week, but I never forgave him. I don't think he ever knew how much that had hurt me.

Mum sat down unexpectedly at the dinner table and started to cry. I looked at Jacob in astonishment and then resentment.

'Now look what you've done!'

'I didn't *do* anything!'

'No. Stop. It's not you. You're *both* fine. *So fine.* Let's not argue.'

She reach out for our hands and pulled us into her, as if we were children again and kissed our chests.

'I love you *both. So much.* You have to be strong for Mummy.'

Mummy?

She delivered the news whilst staring blankly into the table centre, unable to look at either of us. It was colon cancer. She'd known for a while but hadn't known how to tell us, hadn't been strong enough to. The prognosis was poor. They'd offered treatment but explained that the chances were it would just make her quality of life worse and there was a large risk it would kill her sooner. She'd decided not to have it. It was weeks rather than months. She was sorry, as if it was her fault somehow. She wanted us to continue studying.

My insides seemed to implode slowly. I felt a bitterness seed itself where they had been.

Alexei had not called me since the incident in the physics common room and though I felt bad about it, I hadn't called him either. The news about Mum brought me and Jacob closer to each other than we had been in years. Mum's cancer, I mused with gallows humour, was even eating away at our old rivalries. We were sitting having lunch together in the bustling junior common room. The chairs and tables were all very low for a reason I could never fathom, so students across the great hall hunched over their meals as if conspiring over plots and plans. Through the windows lining the rear edge, I could see out to the thick stone trunk of the Queen's Tower standing on the Queen's lawn.

Jacob was beginning to bore me with tales about his antics in his halls:

'And then Susy gave this *huge* burp. Everyone was in stitches. . .'

I made the appropriate grunts of punctuation, and surveyed the student body, munching and hunching around the room. We were all freaks here, weren't we? Look at us all, spending our days obsessing with numbers and formulae, our evenings with alcohol and sex. Children pretending to be adults. I consoled myself by observing that I wasn't the biggest social misfit: there was that strange girl again, always dressed in black, who seemed to hang around at the edges, never speaking to anyone, but never leaving, as if she were waiting for someone. Tall, thin. Her face ghostly white. That had to be make-up. No-one could be that white, surely? Her hair was jet black. Dyed. She even painted her lips black to accentuate her strangeness. She carried herself uncomfortably, one shoulder always seemed to be lower than the other. I wondered what kind of statement she felt she was making, dressed like that. She wasn't all black and white, I noticed. No, she always had something purple on her as well. A scarf, or hanky, a badge. Today there were thick beige bandages around one her wrists. I looked at my own bandaged fist and back up at her. She caught my glance, sneered, then looked away.

Nice.

Jacob tutted.

'You're not even listening.'

'I am!' I lied. 'She burped. It was hilarious.'

'Oh for God's sake, if you're going to be like this I'm going.'

'No, Jacob please. I don't want. . .'

He was already standing. His annoyance at me, so clear on his face, melted when he saw my expression, but he couldn't stay:

'Oh, look—my lecture starts in a few minutes anyway. I gotta go. I'll see you later, mate. Okay?'

I sighed. 'Mate' was a recent affectation. We were brothers, I'd thought.

'Sure.'

I sat for a moment, alone. I was about to pick myself up and leave when a handsome blond face stooped to greet me with a winning grin. The young man steadied himself with a hand on his knee, and held the other out to me. Something about our relative arrangements gave him the air of a teacher addressing a child. I found myself shaking his hand.

'Hi?' I responded to his greeting.

'Are you Ezekial or Jacob?'

'Ezekial,' I replied through a frown. 'Zeke. How do y—'

'You're a twin, right?'

'Yeah, my brother just left?'

'Oh! *Shame!*'

The man sat down uninvited next to me, looking genuinely disappointed but still full of enthusiasm, which he seemed to radiate effortlessly.

'I'm Jon. Jonathan Rodin. I'm a post-doc researcher here. Biochemical neurology. Someone told me that there were twins this year and I thought, wow! What a great opportunity. You know? To study twins.'

'Oh, right, I see.'

It was a common proposition. Often geneticists or behavioural scientists used groups of twins to examine some behaviour or trait and see if the statistics indicated a genetic cause. There was something familiar about this guy. I'd seen him around before. I had a vague sense of envy, perhaps even jealousy towards him. He was one of the popular characters on the campus. Good looking, funny, intelligent. The guy with everything. The kind of guy Kate would go for.

'You know, I'm really not sure—' I began.

'Hey, look, why don't you have a drink with me tonight? At the union. I'll explain the research. There might even be some money in it for you. What do you say?'

That winning grin again. He probably excelled at sport too. I hated him.

'Yeah. Sure. A drink.'

'Great! Eight o'clock, then. Drinks on me, obviously.'

He shook my hand, and patted me on the shoulder and then dashed off, waving at various people who called to him on the way. *What the heck*, I figured, *maybe some of his popularity would rub off on me.* I picked myself up and left, trying to spot the weird Goth girl on the way out, but she seemed to have found somewhere else to be as well.

Snooker balls clapped crisp welcomes at me that evening as I entered the student union building. Students crowded around tables near the windows facing out onto the pretty quadrangle I'd just walked through. It was still early but the air already seemed solid with the sound of laughter and shouting. And it stank of stale beer. How was *this* a good place to talk?

I saw Jon sat at one of the tables, speaking eagerly, twinkle-eyed, to a group of younger boys and girls. He slammed a palm tablewards and I saw him mouth the word *blam*; everyone erupted into delighted laughter. There was an unfamiliar dynamic at the table, the epicentre of which seemed be Jon. At least two of the girls had a strange look in their eyes, slightly predatory, a forced eagerness, as if they were televisions and were twisting their own internal brightness controls to the maximum. One had an elbow uncomfortably forward, subtly blocking the other. One of the boys peeled away from the group with a sullen twist to his upper lip. I almost turned away and left, but then Jon caught sight of me and stood up, opening his arms.

'Aha! My date!'

Another laughter explosion. Confusion flickered briefly across the face of the girl closest to Jon. I felt my face redden.

'Zeke, my friend. Sit here and let me get you a drink. What would you like?'
My friend. I noticed the girl furthest from me, smiling. She reached forward,
over the elbow.
'Hi! I'm Becky.'
She had a sweet round face, dimpled cheeks. Dark hair in a pony tail.
I shook her hand, struggling to multitask.
'Er... Hi. Zeke. A cider please?'
An awkward eternity later (my gaze colliding with Becky's, once, twice and
again) Jon was at my shoulder, holding two pints of sparkling amber.
'Come on, let's go outside where it's quiet. Nice to meet you guys!'
I smiled a goodbye at Becky, but her eyes were Jon's again.
Outside, it was indeed quieter, and not too cold. We found an empty bench
and sat. I caught myself looking to see whether people had noticed us.
'So, tell—' said Jon, taking a sip from his cider and making no attempt to
disguise a grimace. '*Urk!* Why do people drink this stuff? Sorry. So, tell me a
little about yourself. And then, I'll—'
'Why did you buy a cider if you don't like it?'
'Because you were having it.'
'Oh. I see.'
But I didn't. Not at all. I took a sip of mine. Sweet, acid, apple. The fizz
continued pleasantly up the back of my nose after I had swallowed. I didn't see
the problem. I liked it.
Jon began gently to interrogate me and I spilled my secrets easily. He seemed
so interested in me. He wanted to know everything. Something of the bitterness
that had been developing within me lifted in his company. The attention he
gave me was not undivided: there were regular interruptions as he was spotted
by friends or colleagues entering the quad, but between these fermata his focus
(intense, blue-eyed) was entirely trained upon me. When he left me briefly to
fetch a second round of drinks, I felt lost and awaited his return self-consciously,
watching my breath catch the light as it curled up into the night.
He returned, this time with a pair of pint glasses with cloudy looking straw-
coloured liquid.
'What's that?'
'Snakebite. If we're going to drink together, I'm going to have to wean you off
that crap and on to lager.'
'What's snakebite?'
'You're not serious?'
My blank expression told him that I was.
'Lager and cider. Together. Try it.'
He threw a few packets of crisps onto the bench and sat down. My initial
impression of snakebite was that it was slightly bitter and certainly inferior to
cider, but I felt I was being inducted into something (and how that sweetened the
flavour!). By the time I could see the thick glass base of my pint, I found I had
become quite partial to it. I was beginning to feel dizzy and uncoordinated. The
evening air was rapidly cooling but I no longer noticed. By the third pint, the
poison from the snakebite was loosening my tongue. I began to confess, through
a hazy veil, my worries about not fitting in, my feelings for Kate, for Jacob, for
my mother. Jon drank this information in, consoled me, and finally, after too
many more pints, helped me out into a corner of the quad garden to rid myself,
foul-tongued and teary-eyed, of all the acid bile that had accrued inside of me.

I woke up the following morning (fully dressed, shirt clinging) in my room,
dreadfully hung-over and with an appalling sense of humiliation.
On my desk lay a couple of white ibuprofen tablets, and a note:

Well played, Zeke mate! Welcome to university! You're just a bit of a later starter, you'll get the hang of it. Enjoyed our talk. Got carried away though— missed our objective. Take these. When you're feeling better, give me a call and we can hook up. Jon.

He'd left the number of his lab underneath.

I remembered only one awkward moment from the previous evening, a flaw in the otherwise perfect rapport we seemed to have had. At some point, I had complimented Jon on his expensive looking watch. It was an impressive, rugged thing, like a diver's. I'd reached out to bring it closer to me to see better but he'd snatched his wrist away. Just a little too quickly.

I let the memory go. I was late for my lecture.

Outside, I bumped into Alexei. It was almost as if he'd been waiting for me. *Oh God,* I thought, *not now. Not feeling like this.* My dismay must have shown on my face because his lips tightened at the edges.

'How are you?' he enquired, aloof.

'Hung over.'

'Oh. Didn't have you down as a big drinker.'

'People change.'

Alexei's expression froze. He blinked several times.

Why did I say that?

'I see.' Doubt rippled under the cold, hard expression he'd adopted. He took a small breath. 'Look, I'm sorry if I—'

'Don't. Really.'

I didn't meant to sound so cold, but I felt I was on the verge of vomiting again. I had to get away. I only realised how harsh I must have sounded when I saw his eyes. His expression was suddenly awful, full of pain—fear almost. I wanted to apologise, but I just couldn't do it now. I'd call him later and do it.

'I have to go,' I said, leaving him standing in the cold with that abject look upon his face.

By morning break, thanks to Jon's words, my hangover was already transmuting into a vague feeling of accomplishment. I was slouching, shallow-breathed, on one of the midget sofas in the physics common room when I spotted Kate, milling around outside, chatting with a girlfriend. Her hair was tied back, exposing her ears. She was wearing less make-up, or perhaps none, I couldn't quite tell. It made her look younger, elf-like. My heart ached seeing exposed the fine canvas she painted daily. I started to wonder why she hadn't had time to create herself this morning, and then remembered the rugby-playing geologist she had been with the last time I had seen her.

I pulled out Jon's note and studied it. Yes, I would call.

Kate turned her head, unconsciously, to the common room. Her lips continued to play out the rapid sentence she was delivering to her friend. Her eyes flicked over me briefly, so light a touch that I'm not even sure she noticed, and yet with such force as to press me an inch into the sofa, and then she turned her head back to her friend. I looked away in pain. When I looked back again, a few seconds later, unable to keep my burning eyes from the flame of her, she was looking at me. Directly at me. She seemed to have a question in her eyes and lips. She smiled a fraction and then was gone, tugged by another's hand, leaving the perfect image of an elf hanging in pastels on my retina.

I called Jon that afternoon. He seemed delighted to hear from me and invited me to come over to his lab after my last lecture. It was getting late by the time I stuck my head around the door of his shared office and he was tidying up.

'Hey! You made it,' he said. 'Listen, I've just been told I'm on TV tonight, any minute now, so I wanna run to catch it. I have some friends who live on Gloucester Road, you can tag along if you want? We can chat afterwards.'

'Uh. Yeah. Okay.'

On TV?

At this point, I admit I was beginning to feel a little dazzled by Jon Rodin. At twenty-four, he represented to my eighteen-year-old mind something impossibly cool. I followed him to his friends' flat.

The doorbell was answered by a curly-haired lad in his twenties with heavy eyelids. I had the impression he might have just woken up. I smelled something pungent. Behind him the hallway seemed hazy with smoke. I noticed he was carrying a hand-rolled cigarette. It was obvious, even to me, that it was dope.

'Yo! Frankie.' Jon greeted the lad enthusiastically. The greeting was returned with an accepting murmur. Jon pushed past and strolled into the living room.

Frankie, sleepy-eyed, invited me past him, not seeming to care who I was. I hesitated, feeling tremendously uncomfortable and out of place suddenly, but entered. The living room was a smoky den. Two other young men were spread casually on sofas, arms and legs splayed.

'Guess who's on TV?' Jon challenged, dragging a whorl of grey smoke behind him as he marched across the room. He grabbed the remote and switched on the geriatric television set. (It gave an asthmatic wheeze; dust crackled.)

'Jono!' one of the smokers droned. He was slouched contentedly in an arm chair holding on to a newly lit spliff. There was a general round of welcome. I lingered at the door frame until the lad behind me motioned for me to sit.

'Oh, this is Zeke.'

Nods and 'hi's, and names.

Jon found his channel: a man was being wheeled through a hospital in a wheelchair. He wore a green gown. Only one leg poked out of it. A husky female voice began mid-sentence:

'...now a new treatment being pioneered at The Institute of Neurology in London in collaboration with researchers at Imperial College, seems able to offer some relief to sufferers of this strange syndrome.'

The picture changed to a side-shot of a young man in a white lab-coat. Next to him an oscilloscope traced erratic green scribbles; behind that a poster-sized illustration of the brain. The young man was Jon.

'Ta-da!' sang Jon, seeing himself.

'Hey, cool,' mumbled one of the slouchers, and lifted himself forward to watch.

The narrator continued:

'Dr Jon Rodin, a neuroscientist studying consciousness, explains how this syndrome is possible and talks about his new treatment...'

'One of the remarkable things that the phantom limb phenomenon teaches us about the brain,' Jon's television voice educated us, 'is that all sensation, all external feelings, pain or pleasure, actually take place somewhere in here,' he tapped at his temple and I noticed how impressively large that watch of his seemed again. 'The feeling that pain occurs somewhere in the body is really an illusion, albeit a very powerful one. What happens in healthy people experiencing pain is that nerve endings in the body send signals to certain areas of the brain responsible for interpreting them.

'How the sensation of pain is handled by the brain isn't completely understood and is part of a wider problem concerned with conscious awareness. We know that many areas of the brain seem to be important in its perception: primarily the thalamus, here, but also the right ventral prefrontal cortex, here, and the anterior cingulate cortex or ACC, here. What's interesting is that these latter two areas of the brain have also been shown to become active in situations of non-physical pain, such as social rejection, or when a mother hears her baby crying.

They appear to be responsible more for how "painful" pain seems rather than any specific location for pain.

'We also know that the act of damaging the body can be separated from the perception of pain through the use of a group of local anaesthetics known as dissociative anaesthetics, such as ketamine. In fact some major operations are conducted under these with the patient remaining conscious the whole time. The pain signals from nerves still get sent to the brain, but the patient doesn't experience "pain". Under these conditions we see a change in the way these areas of the brain "light up" in our scans.

'What we're seeing in patients who experience phantom pain—which is where they have had a limb amputated, but continue to feel pain in the space where the limb used to be—is that the area of the brain that used to be responsible for sensing pain in that limb is still active. It's quite common for amputees to experience phantom sensations, in fact about ninety per cent of amputees report this phenomenon.'

The invisible interviewer stepped in with a question:

'Tell us about the technique you've developed here.'

'Well, the challenge has always been to identify the part of the brain that handles pain signals for a given limb. In healthy patients we can stimulate the limb's nerves and see on scans which areas are activated. That's impossible with amputees because the limb is missing. This new technique, which is called *cortical ablation-induced hypopathia*, is a more general approach that targets the areas of the brain responsible for the interpretation of pain, rather than the pain itself. We effectively destroy the areas of the brain that make pain "painful". The patient continues to feel a sensation in their phantom limb, but they're no longer bothered by it.'

The miniature Jon on the television smiled proudly and the real Jon standing next to me, mirrored him. An impressed murmur moved across the room.

The view flicked back to the hospital and the mellifluous tone of the female commentator in the studio returned. There was now a slight edge to her voice:

'The technique is *not* without controversy however, as Dr Michael Goldstein of the Institute of Neurology in New York explains...'

'The *bitch!*' Jon barked. 'They *promised us* they would paint this in a good light! Fucking journo wankers.'

'What's the big deal?' Ashley asked. 'That came across really well!'

Judging his expression, Jon might have spat on the floor in disgust.

'They're never content with reporting good science, they always have to go and dig up controversy. Now Goldstein's going to pour his stinking piss all over our strawberries. She could have at least told me she was interviewing that slimy bastard so I could have responded. Now he's going to have the last word!'

Goldstein was a ruddy looking man, balding but with a tight fuzz of greying hair round the sides of his head. There was something overly animated about his manner (that gave me the impression he was very short) when he spoke:

'There have been cases of this treatment used early on, patients suffering from a condition called central pain where they have actually gone on to do self-harm because they no longer have a safe relationship with the concept of pain.'

'Christ, what's the point of digging this up? It's in the past,' Jon intercepted. He'd moved closer to the screen and was stooping to see it. 'This is about phantom pain. We stopped treating central pain cases two years ago.'

Goldstein continued:

'There is one documented case—a horrific incident I might add—where the post-operative patient burnt all of his fingers down to stumps *deliberately* in a candle flame over a period of hours. Uh... oh, just oh... terrible. I truly believe medicine has a responsibility to seek treatment for the causes, and not to meddle with the human experience.'

The commentator began to wrap up the feature in a bright tone that spoke of a future with extraordinary potential. Jon straightened himself, looking less than impressed.

'He burnt his fingers to stumps in a candle flame? That's gross,' said Ashley, one of the sofa-bound smokers.

'The guy was barking mad before *we* had anything to do with him. Goldstein is such a twat. He's only jealous because his techniques are complete fucking failures. *Jesus.* Where's the joint? I'm going to get it in the neck from Hartnett tomorrow.'

'What's central pain?' I asked, suddenly bold.

Everyone in the room seemed to notice me at once, as though I'd been the same colour as the sofa before and had unexpectedly become visible. Jon took a long pull on the spliff he'd taken from Ashley and spoke with a tight, deep voice, billowing smoke as he issued the words:

'Chronic condition... affects stroke victims... MS sufferers... spinal cord trauma victims.'

He exhaled a long plume of smoke. ''The central nervous system gets damaged and bombards the thalamus with pain signals and it basically goes permanently a bit loopy. Sufferers often get hypersensitive and can't touch anything without experiencing pain, or they get dysesthesia: they feel like their skin is constantly burning. It's like being tortured constantly. People go mad from it. Withdraw. The guy we treated was a paraplegic. He'd suffered from it for years and didn't even speak any more. At least we stopped him from suffering.'

Ashley looked appalled.

'He killed himself in the end. Started speaking again after the treatment. Said he enjoyed the burning. Doused his wheelchair in petrol one night and set it alight. God, I'm glad Goldstein didn't know that. He'd have made mincemeat out of us. God knows how the guy held the can, he practically had no hands left.'

The room was silent. Jon took another long toke.

'Anyway!' he tried to say brightly, instead choking on the smoke. 'No point dwelling on mistakes. Point is to learn from them and move on. Besides, I'm done with this area of research anyway. Time to move on. New projects. Want some?'

He held out the spliff to me and seeing indecision paralysing me, took it back for a final drag. I didn't want to reject his offer, any offer of his. But, I had never so much as even smoked a cigarette and although I hadn't ever really examined the source of my beliefs, I realised that I was against the concept of drug-taking. Dare I refuse? The television appearance had elevated Jon even further in my estimation. The desire to be his friend had multiplied. He'd walked into this intellectually stagnant room and transformed it in a stride. He had taken in lungfuls of its drug-laced, smoky air and blew it out again, freshened with words of erudition. And he had been on television, a fact, shallow as it was by comparison to the magnet of his obvious intellect, that I couldn't help but be seduced by.

'You're leaving your research field?'

'Mh-huh.'

'Why? You seem to be doing really good work.'

'Just time to move on. Something more challenging. More engaging.'

'Anything specific?'

He paused, taking a moment to appraise me.

'Nothing firm, no,' he said cautiously.

The room unexpectedly filled with a debate about science and ethics. Intellects that had before been hiding behind smoky veils now made themselves apparent. Whereas my impression of the room before had been one of dark, dinginess, it was suddenly filled with colour and light. Jon couldn't have brightened the room for me any more had he flung wide the curtains and opened the windows.

I no longer wanted to leave. Jon sat down next to me on the sofa and I began to question him about his research. Though he would not be drawn on his future direction—skilfully avoiding the topic each time I steered us near it—he seemed delighted that I took such an interest in his current work. He casually offered me the spliff again. I took it without thinking, and then, realising that I was now expected to smoke it, and too cowardly to back out, I took my first small adventure beyond the usual boundaries of the mind. Of course I coughed, but, determined not to look a fool, I suppressed as much as possible and took another drag. I passed the joint on to the guy next to me, Rob, who was on the verge of dozing off. The curly-locked lad who had opened the door, Frankie, disappeared off upstairs, where apparently his girlfriend was.

As the subtle effects of the joint I had tasted took hold, Jon explained that though his doctoral research had been in the area of pain perception, his current research was primarily biochemical in nature and not surgical. He was trying to broaden our understanding of the relationship between neural structures and subjective experience. He believed he had made some exciting discoveries, but that he was not ready to publish.

I remembered Alexei's hypothesis about quantum mechanics and the mind.

'Do you think quantum mechanics has a role to play in consciousness?' I mused, feeling heavy all of a sudden.

Jon shifted slightly and fixed slivers of blue flint on me through slit eyelids.

'Popular debate, but there's precious little support for it in neurological circles.'

'You didn't answer the question.'

He took a short breath.

'Have you ever heard of microtubulin?'

I wanted to close my eyes; sit back.

'Nope.'

'Remarkable molecule. It's like cellular scaffolding, train tracks for transport, but it also acts as a calculator; all-in-one. Cellular automata. Neurons are particularly rich in microtubules. Well, it turns out they're not just capable of classical calculations: they also appear to be capable of quantum calculations...'

I opened my eyes, which had been beginning to close.

'Really?'

'M-huh. They can tunnel into states that aren't reachable classically.'

I let out a small laugh.

'I should tell Alexei.'

'Who's Alexei?'

What would Jon think of Alexei, his strange manner, his quick, singular mind?

'Oh, just... a fr... this guy I know. He thinks consciousness is quantum.'

'Man,' interjected Rob suddenly. 'Who'd burn their fingers to stumps? Sick.'

'I'll tell you about microtubules another time,' Jon said, and winked.

There was a peal of laughter from upstairs that failed to stop. A female voice began to say something in response. I couldn't make out the words, but she clearly wasn't sharing the joke. The laughter stopped. Conciliatory tones. Movement towards the upper landing. I could hear her words now.

'It's only funny if you're stoned, Frankie, and I'm not.'

She descended. The front door opened.

'I'll see you tomorrow.'

The front door slammed shut.

Frankie appeared in the doorway. He didn't look particularly bothered. A smile cracked his face. Nobody asked what the problem was, at least not in words, but he decided to explain:

'I went up and she comes out of the bathroom, right, and says, "The bulb's gone? In the bedroom?" expecting me to do something practical about it. So

I says to her, "Okay, so, from now on, whenever you're in the bedroom, clap yer hands, like this,"' he clapped rapidly twice, causing his curly hair to bounce, ' "and I'll know where you are." She looks at me crazy, like, *that ain't a solution*, so I goes: "And tomorrow, I'll get us some cow bells."'

He collapsed into hysterics.

It took me a slow second to process what he had said, and then, for the next few minutes, it was the funniest thing I thought I'd ever heard. Laughter caught among us like fire on dry tinder, and we rolled around the sofas, hurting from the convulsions. After it had consumed us fully and died away again, Rob turned off the television and put some music on.

'You like tribal house?'

'Sure. Yeah. Great.'

I'd never heard of it.

A basic beat began to play out. The main instruments seemed to be drums, or pots and pans beaten with a wooden spoon, and electronic sounds that spilled up and down the musical scale like water. The beat was simple, vaguely African, infectious. It seemed to reach inside me, and touched something primitive. Rob and Frankie vanished off elsewhere in the flat on some unspoken business. They seemed to treat Jon as if he were just another tenant.

Jon was drumming out a tribal accompaniment on the edge of the sofa. His watch jangled gently to the rhythm. Ashley appeared to be asleep.

I felt so relaxed. So comfortable; so welcome. I turned to Jon.

'Have you ever heard of something called the Looking Glass Club?'

Jon stopped drumming. He caught my eyes briefly but looked away again.

'No.'

His finger drumming recommenced, this time—although perhaps I have subsequently imagined this detail—his percussion was more forcible. He started putting his shoulders into it, and bounced his head to the rhythm. We sat for a while longer in silence, until Jon decided there were things he had to do, and oughtn't we to be getting along?

My suspicions should have been raised at that moment perhaps, if not before. Were there not enough signs? Not enough gaps in credibility to explain his sudden interest? But I was in a pitiful, needy state, bewitched by the attentions of a proto-hero. It was yet another kind of love blindness, no less potent for the fact that the object was, this time, a man. I had one for each eye. Between Jon and Kate, I wonder if I actually saw anything.

Guy Fawkes' night came and went. Instead of bonding with my fellow residents in Hall I began losing myself in my friendship with Jon Rodin, and spent my weekends looking after Mum. I began to change. I wasn't conscious just how much that change was being directed.

I soon realised that drug-taking with Jon was not limited to cannabis. Jon would try anything. He considered it personal research. And, he seemed to be offering to induct me further into the world of social drug-taking.

Gradually, over a period of weeks, my confused feelings on the subject began to articulate into concerns of where this path was leading. I brought them up over a shared joint in the private darkness of the pretty cemetery sitting like a secret behind the Brompton Oratory Church. It was closed at night. We had snuck over the fence to watch the stars.

'Don't you think it's dangerous? Aren't you worried about addiction?'

'Crossing the road is dangerous. Sex is addictive.'

Jon took another toke. The tip flared in the black night, crackling and smoking. It looked beautiful, dangerous, like a gem on fire; like a tiny view into a volcano's mouth, into Hell.

'You've eaten that propaganda bullshit they fed you at school wholesale, haven't you?'

'It's not *propaganda*...'

'Of course it is. It's all about control. We live in a nanny state. Don't you think you're old enough to make your own mind up?'

'But—'

'You ever read Aldous Huxley?'

'*Brave New World?*'

Aldous Huxley was the grandson of Thomas Henry Huxley, a brilliant nineteenth-century scientist, after whom one of the physics buildings was named.

'Huxley took drugs. Mescaline. Wrote two books about his experiences. *The Doors of Perception*, and *Heaven and Hell*. You know The Doors? The group? They were named after his book. Byron, Shelley? Took opiates. Where do you think Frankenstein came from?' Jon snorted. 'That was one fucked-up trip.'

'But—doesn't it damage your brain? Aren't you worried about becoming, I don't know, *stupid?*'

Jon started to laugh.

'Zeke, half my research ideas come from being stoned, or tripping. Haven't you noticed how it liberates your thinking?'

I had not.

Jon's eyes glinted in the darkness, reflecting, it seemed to me, not some external light source, but some light from within; the ideas that he was at that very moment visualising, turning in his mind's eye, focusing on.

'Sometimes, my mind can just visit places that aren't possible normally. It makes intuitive leaps so quickly. It's like a... a stone skipping across the surface of a pond that normally I'd have to swim through. And—it's as if, sometimes, I can skip out, into new ponds, along paths that you just can't reach by swimming.'

The firefly of the cigarette flew up to Jon's face again and back down again to dance by his side. He blew smoke into the night.

'I used to think the ideas wouldn't stick. That they'd be stupid when I came down again, stopped tripping, but you know what?'

He turned to look at me.

'Most of them still make sense. They're different. Sometimes I can't quite see the power of them any more, as if they've lost potency, or are just shadows in this world, where they were solid before. But I've used them, they've helped me.'

'Like what? What ideas?'

Jon smirked and inspected his chest, pressing his jaw down into it; he picked off some ash that had fallen there and then looked away again.

'Oh, just stuff.'

When it finally happened, we were in the JCR. I sometimes joined Jon in the senior common room, which had better food, I'd discovered, but Jon found it stuffy and too formal, and preferred the vibrancy of the JCR, and more often joined me there.

It was bustling, as it did every lunch hour, transforming from a quiet, empty place into one of energy and noise, and the smell of cooking pizzas. We had settled with our trays at table.

I'd noticed that the strange girl, the Goth with the pale face, was there again, haunting the JCR. She looked high on something. Her pupils were large, out of focus, heavy-lidded, her mouth slightly slack. I was puzzling over a curiosity. I'd been certain that, as we had passed her, she had stopped and turned to us, and said, 'Jon,' as if trying to get his attention. But it was noisy, and I felt I must have imagined it because Jon did not seem to notice. He had not acknowledged her in the least.

'She's a strange one,' I said, sitting down.

'Who?'

'That Goth girl.'

Jon murmured agreement whilst taking a huge bite from a large bun sandwich he'd bought. We began to smalltalk when a commotion started behind us.

Suddenly, there were shouts. Jon's eyes widened, and he threw his sandwich to the table. I turned to see a group of people all rising from their seats at a table behind us; a girl began to scream, then another. Jon rushed past me, I thought at first towards the group, but realised he was heading past them. A tall student stepped back, away from the table and behind him, there she was revealed, standing passive, a mere onlooker to the commotion at the table: the Goth. She wore an eerie half-smile, crooked as if only half of her saw the joke, and she was gazing placidly at the table, which by now, was surrounded by people both trying to get away and get closer to see what was happening. Then, to my surprise, I saw Jon grab her by the arms and pull her away. He escorted her from the JCR, unseen by anyone but me. Everyone else's attention was on the commotion happening at the nearby table.

A girl standing on one of the seats was holding a single palm to her chest. She began to laugh nervously. A boy stooped to retrieve a hair brush from under the table. People began to chuckle with relief.

On my way out, as I passed the table I overheard one of the girls in the group:

'My *God!* I thought it was... I swear... those were legs. It was *moving*. How *funny*.'

But nobody at that table looked amused. Not in the least. They all seemed very pale.

I looked each way along the walkway outside the double doors of the JCR for Jon, but there was no sign of either him or the girl. Across to the left there was a stairwell leading up, and to the left of them, a smaller set of stairs leading down into a service area underneath the walkway. I ran across and looked into the gloom of the aeronautics department. Students passed me on their way in and out. I heard an urgent conversation in low tones from somewhere. I turned and peered over the edge of the walkway. Looking down and underneath, I saw rows of cars parked by the wall, and just behind them I could see him. The Goth girl was with him. She was leaning against the wall. He seemed to be restraining her with his hands by her elbows, and he was speaking rapidly:

'...times do I have to tell you *never* to do that in public. *Never* again. Understand? *Jesus!* How could you be so fucking *stupid?*'

'Why do you have to ignore me? I can't deal with that.'

'You know we can't be seen together. None of us. I've explained why.'

'I don't *understand* you, Jon. You make everything so... *complicated*.'

She was distressed. Dark make-up smudged under her eyes. Her black-painted lips were twisted in pain.

He lifted her wrist, the bandaged one, and pulled the dirty beige crêpe down. '*This* means we're together. That I'm with you. Okay? Always.'

Underneath the bandages I could see that the inside of her wrist was marked by a series of horizontal cuts that were healing over. It was not the cuts Jon was referring to, but the thing they had perhaps tried to erase: a small tattoo of some kind. I saw Jon lift up his own left arm. He pulled down his watch and presented the inside of his wrist to her. She turned her face from him but he took her jaw in his hand and forced her to meet his gaze.

'Emily, *this* binds us together. *The Looking Glass Club*.'

When he released her face, she pulled it away from him and in doing so, she saw me. Her expression hardened, her tearfulness glazing over like ice. Jon saw the change, and jerked his head around to look, and caught me staring straight at him.

From the pages of Tony's diary:

Ahexonacatinabox

7ffffffe40000002400100034000f12
58301f824c60178246c04f2343800f0a
4380062246c016024c6086034830004b
4010000340000803c000000240000003
7fffffff0001c23800008f1100010009
800190898003908480339cc8003109c
8002001c0002010d000383840003e3a4
0003ffc40003c024000380150003000c

Chapter 5

'I wonder if that's the reason insects are so fond of flying into candles.'

—Alice

I put down the basket, and I turned slowly around.

Skyler was holding my Samurai sword, her eyes were wide and terrified. Her brow was trembling with anger and uncertainty.

'Who *the hell* are you?'

I cursed myself for being so stupid. Why had I risked leaving her alone?

'It's okay. I'm a... I'm a friend.'

I lifted my hand in a calming gesture. Skyler reacted instantly:

'KEEP your hands by your sides!'

Neither of us seemed certain how to proceed. I spoke with caution:

'This is my apartment.'

'Why was I locked in here?'

'You were attacked. I helped you. We came here to escape. To hide.'

She didn't look like she was believing any of this.

'Why was I *locked* in here?'

I indicated the basket.

'My dog was injured. The same guy who attacked you. I had to get him help. I... I was worried... Your memory problem...I mean... If you'd woken up you'd have just wandered out onto the street. You could have been killed. Skyler, don't you remember *anything* about this?'

She looked confused. Her hands were trembling from holding the weight of the *buke-zukuri*. It curved in an elegant threat from her hands. The blade was sharp. I considered trying to wrestle it from her, but it would surely slice my palms open, if not worse.

JR lifted himself from out of his basket behind me and poked his head between my legs.

'Oh Dog...' he said. 'I feel like cat shit.'

The words slurred as they came out. I looked down. He wore a surprised expression and moved his lips and tongue in a way that gave the impression he'd just eaten something that tasted especially nasty.

Skyler blinked with surprise. Then, matter-of-fact:

'A talking dog.'

She took a step backwards. JR moved out from between my legs and began to pace around in a circle.

'Hey, I just talked with my *mouth*. What's going on? Ooh. This is st*range*. St'r*aaange*.'

Skyler stepped backwards further and the sword fell to the floor, singing musically in protest, reminding me how rare and expensive it had been.

48

I let out a sigh, half relief, half dismay. JR continued:

'Oh no. *Oh* no. I do *not* like this at... ooh... *blrgh*... Steel... what have you done to me? *Steel?*'

He started to cough and wheeze as if trying to bring up a hair ball. I'd forgotten how improbably large and pink his tongue was.

'JR, just calm it. Needle gave you a mod. You lost your collar. It's an upgrade.'

'You let that *freak* near me? Are you c'razy?'

'Oh, everyone is just *full* of gratitude for me today.'

Sky started to say something but I cut her off:

'Skyler. Here's the deal. You're free to go if you want to. Frankly, you've caused me enough shit for an entire lifetime since I met you. But, listen to me first. Then, if you still want to leave, be my guest and have a nice life.'

I explained the story to her from the beginning, her arrival with the note.

'So? Make up your mind. Are you staying or leaving?'

Whilst she was still deciding, JR, who now seemed to have completely forgotten that he had been complaining, trotted over to Sky and hopped onto his hind legs, pawing at her with his front paws.

'You smell like a nice lady. Would you mind scratching my chest?'

She looked uncertain for a moment then stooped, still watching me with cautious eyes, and scratched under his chin.

'Ooh. *Ooh.* That's good. That's *so* good. Bit lower. Mmm.'

'I guess I'll stay,' she said.

'Great,' I said, walking past the happy couple. 'Now if you don't mind, I *really* need to sleep. And, could you put that back on the wall please? It's dangerous.'

I was exhausted. Tina had staved off the fog of sleep for a while, but it was rolling back down over my mind now in thick veils and soon she would be demanding payment. It was mid-afternoon. I'd been awake for two days. My eyelids stung, my eyes felt hot.

'Don't go out anywhere. JR? *JR?!*'

JR was in the middle of telling Skyler how heroic he'd been in saving her and she seemed content to succumb to his canine charms. He had a particular knack with the ladies. Perhaps I was being unfair. He *had* been a hero. He'd saved my life as well as hers. I told the apartment to stay locked unless there was an emergency, and that if Sky should start behaving oddly, to speak to her and remind her that she was with friends.

Then I started to figure out where to sleep. The apartment wasn't built for three. I assumed Sky would stay awake now. The sofa-bed would take up too much room if I unfolded it, and if I slept on it as it was, although JR had his basket, Sky would have nowhere to sit. I looked at the rig, lying on the floor, a great, dead metal insect with legs curled, necrotic, in the air. No, maybe not a dead insect but a silver Venus flytrap waiting with infinite patience for a live one. Me. *Well,* I thought, *the gel-bed is comfortable enough.* If I could bear the idea of immersing again, I could even run a sleep program. Now that wasn't such a bad idea. I'd need some help to combat the crystal. It was wearing off, but I knew as soon as I put my head down I'd find it hard to fall off to sleep. And the inductors would block out any external noise, which, judging from the way JR was playing Skyler, was likely to be incessant.

'I'm going to sleep here. Just a few hours.'

I lay down in the rig and sank gratefully into its jaws. I shifted my head into the helmet, flicked the switch, instantly banishing the world. I set a two-hour REM program and I went finally to sleep.

*

The internal clock told me I had been asleep for exactly two hours when the nerve-jangling imperative interrupted my slumber and wrenched me, protesting, back to consciousness.

I half-extracted myself still bleary-eyed from the rig. Skyler and JR were both asleep on the sofa, with JR snuggled into the crook of her arm. It was a sight that for some reason made my heart feel swollen with joy and yet at the same time brought tears of sadness to my eyes. I couldn't work out why. I had so many questions about this woman. Who was the father of her child? What was her connection to the Looking Glass Club? Why couldn't she remember anything?

Why was someone trying to kill her?

The rig notified me that Lewis had left a return message on our secret notice board in nomansland. I was relieved. I might be able to get somewhere now. Emily hadn't tried to contact me, but that wasn't really a surprise. I hadn't expected her to. Unless things had changed dramatically for the better, I would have to pay her a personal visit if I wanted to get anything from her. And that prospect filled me with a sick anxiety. I couldn't virt there either. Those places were pretty low-tech. I'd have to go physically.

I'd call Lewis in a moment. But right now, it was time to speak to Kate. I'd been putting it off until I was more rested. I needed to know why she hadn't picked anything up. She was the sentinel, and she'd failed. I felt a sick knot in my stomach. The past was supposed to stay in the past; buried things should remain buried, not claw through the dirt with grimy nails and raise themselves again. I considered using the Wall, but I didn't want to wake Skyler and JR. Not like that, when they looked so content. I cursed, then lay forwards and fell, bodiless, into the nexus.

I know that beauty is relative, and I know that familiarity is supposed to breed contempt—what would we do without such wisdom parceled neatly for us into maxims?—yet, as far as I was concerned, Kate's image radiated beauty no less today than she had when I first met her. *Radiation* was the right word. Her beauty was as deadly still—and as rare to me—as uranium, a long-lived threat that should be kept in a special container, watched through lead-enriched glass, handled with protective gloves. If anything, she looked younger than the last time.

'It's been a long time,' she said. 'I was beginning to think you were never going to speak to me again.'

A clever lie. She would never have even been aware of how long it had been. She'd almost certainly just checked the calendar this minute and worked it out. I sighed. Calculated to the core. So very different to the Kate I had fallen in love with all those years ago, and yet, at least to look at, she seemed the same. I wondered how much I had changed, inside and out.

We went through the usual routine:

'You look beautiful. As always. You haven't aged a day.'

'That's kind of you.'

She never complimented me back. This was understood, on many levels, deserved and quite deliberate.

Why was I such a masochist? I didn't need to do this. I didn't *need* to see her. I could get the answers I needed without this torture. But on some level, I think I knew I needed to punish myself, to force myself to go through this.

'What have you been up to?' I asked.

'Oh, the usual. I'm happy. That's what you need to know, isn't it?'

'Yes,' I whispered. 'Yes, it is.'

I should stop. It hurt too much. It was never easy, but today it was impossible. *Just get to the point.*

'When did you last hear from Jacob?'

'The twenty-third of April, 2033, at 16:30.'

Two years ago. Such precision was typical, no matter how it made her sound. I noticed it was the same answer she'd given me the last time. So, he hadn't been in touch. It was necessary to use Kate as our messenger, our go-between. I was determined to keep in touch with him, and the only way I could do this without jeopardizing my safety—he was after all still determined to kill me—was to use a go-between. Using Kate this way only fueled Jacob's fury towards me. He could never understand why I did it. He thought I was just sick, cruel. He didn't know she was a sentinel. But that was the whole point.

'You don't think I'm sick and cruel, do you?'

'I don't think that. No.'

There. See, Jacob? You only had to ask her.

'What news do you have?'

'Nothing. No change.'

I couldn't understand it.

'Then something is wrong. Someone turned up two days ago, and it was a Looking Glass Club member.'

'I've picked up nothing.'

'Clearly. A woman turned up on my doorstep with a note saying it had started again. Her name's Skyler. At least I think so. She's pregnant, about twenty-five, thirty, I guess. She's also an amnesiac. The attacker was after her. I can't tell you much about him, except he had the tattoo. And he was meta-capable. I'm sure.'

Kate frowned.

'I'm getting nothing.'

'Do a deep search. See if anything comes up with this new information.'

'Okay.'

Next, I contacted Lewis. I hadn't seen or spoken to Lewis in years. It was not an easy thing to do. My heart beat anxiously in my chest, my breath felt insufficient. He had changed more obviously. In fact, I barely recognized him. In a sense, I found this a relief. He looked fat, and haggard. He was ageing badly. His hair was receding and turning gray. The thick eyebrows that he and Vaughan had both sported were turning bushy. Deep grooves now ran down the side of his nose, framing his mouth. His skin was blotchy from alcohol. He was only forty-five—a couple of years older than me—but whereas I could still pass for my mid-thirties, he looked more like he was in his fifties. He'd never been particularly slim, but this man was barely recognizable from the twenty-year-old I'd first known.

Life had been hard for Lewis. It had been hard for all of us.

'Zeke. It's been a *long* time. You look well.'

Lewis did not know that I had changed my identity, or where I lived, for the same reasons that I used Kate as a messenger. He and Jacob were not in touch as far as I knew, but it could put his life in as much danger as mine if he knew too much about me.

'It has. I wish I felt well, Lewis.'

'After all these years I... I wasn't expecting the call. Your message was somewhat cryptic. What's the news?'

I updated him. He frowned with those bushy eyebrows of his and maintained it through the whole story. When I'd finished speaking, he remained in silent contemplation for a while. Eventually, he spoke:

'How could someone recreate it? You told me you destroyed it.'

'I did. Everything. The method, the notes, the source.'

He shook his head, looking sick and confused.

'I don't understand,' he muttered to himself.

'It's what we've been guarding against,' I said. 'We knew there was a risk. But the sentinel... I don't understand how the system we set up could have failed.'

'Nothing's foolproof,' Lewis said. 'Do you want to come and stay with me? Bring the woman.'

'We'll be safer here for the moment.'

'I'll come to you, then? Where are you?'

'No. Don't do this, Lewis. You know I can't put you in danger. You know why. Has Jacob tried to contact you?'

Jacob had been missing from our radar for almost two years now. Jon had never been on it.

'Not for years. Zeke, we're supposed to be in this together. Are you going be this stubborn for the rest of your life?'

'Probably.'

He sighed.

'Then how the hell am I supposed to help?'

'See if you can find out anything for me about this woman. I need everything I can get. We have no idea who or even what we might be up against. I think Jacob might be behind this.'

'Always so goddamn paranoid about Jacob...'

'This isn't paranoia. He *told* me he was going to do this one day, Lewis. That was going to be his revenge. Have you forgotten that?'

'No, I haven't forgotten, Zeke, but that was decades ago. People change. People forgive. Even Jacob. He told me several times he wanted to reconcile things with you. You don't want to reconcile things with him. Do you? *Do* you?'

'You know he's tried to con me before, telling me that he's forgiven me, that our fraternal bond is the most important thing. But I know that the minute he gets within meters of me he would try to kill me again. I *know* him.' I didn't add, because I know *me*. As different as we were on the surface, Jacob and I, there were some things that ran through us both like veins of dark ore through rock. We were carved from identical strata. I didn't think he could ever forgive me. Because I couldn't.

'Just answer me something. It's important to me.' He sounded angry. I'd forgotten how seriously Lewis took the matter of fraternity. 'If he genuinely wanted a reconciliation with you, what would you do?'

'He wouldn't. He doesn't.'

'*Answer* the goddamn question.'

I glared at him, wondering why he was suddenly so angry.

'You can't, can you? Because the answer's no.'

'That's my business, Lewis. This is not about Vaughan. It's about Jacob. Butt out.'

I flinched at my own words. He nodded slowly with a bitter, knowing expression.

'I... sorry. I... I didn't mean that.'

His eyes seemed to glaze over, to lose a little of what light they had. His face seemed dead.

'I don't want to fight. I'm sorry,' I said weakly.

'Don't worry about it.' He recomposed himself. 'Only Jon knew enough. What about Jon?'

Yes, Jon was the highest risk, but I knew that assuming he was the *only* risk was dangerous. How many of the world's great inventions had been discovered independently more than once? Calculus was famously developed independently by both Newton and Leibniz; Philipp Reis, a German, invented the 'telephon' fifteen years before Alexander Graham Bell; Photography was invented at the same time in England and France. America narrowly beat Germany to the invention of the atom bomb. The list seemed inexhaustible: animation, anesthetic, hypodermic needles, spectacles, packet switching, ink, the integrated circuit, the typewriter, the electric bulb, countless more; even the Rubik's cube. All credited with multiple independent inventors. It was as if these ideas were seeds, cross fertilized by science and sown in the ground across the world, just waiting for fertile minds to cultivate them. The fact of meta's discovery once was a sure sign that it would be invented again. Like the atom bomb before it, science was ripe for meta, whether or not the world was ready for it.

This was why I had argued for a sentinel system. That was how I had persuaded him. He had wanted to forget. Eventually he either understood, or he stopped questioning it. Emily was sometimes well enough back then to agree to be a part, but over the years she'd deteriorated.

'It could be Jon,' I conceded. We'd said everything we could say in this conversation. 'I'll be in touch again in a few days. If you find anything, post me on the board and I'll call you.'

Lewis cut the connection without saying anything more, but though his image vanished the sound didn't quite go dead.

In the distance I could hear something.

'Hello?'

Something indistinct.

'Lewis? Are you still there?'

No response. I strained to listen.

It was the sound of singing. I could hardly make out the words, but the tune was familiar. Just a few garbled fragments came to me:

> That's... way... money goes,
> Pop! goes ... weasel.

The line went dead.

Must have been a crossed line. There were still analogue lines in use in places. It could happen. I shivered, and pushed the tune from my head.

I stretched and paced the room. JR's head followed me silently around for a while.

'We should get ready,' I said. 'How are you feeling?'

'Starvin'.'

I laughed. 'Better then.'

JR jumped off the sofa and trotted over to his bowl.

'What's to eat?'

'Nothing. I need to shop. I'll pop out while you two freshen up.'

'Great! Can I have Flibbety Gibbets?'

'Oh, JR...' I moaned.

Flibbety Gibbets. Bio-engineered cat food. It was not and had never been alive, but the gibbets flipped around like fish when the pack was opened. Cats—and JR—loved them.

He looked crestfallen and I saw the matted fur on the back of his neck, still flecked with dried blood. 'Yes, of course you can. I'll get some.'

This time, I made sure Sky knew who I was before I left to fetch some supplies from the corner store.

The automart was empty, except for a greasy looking homeless guy wearing brand new Nikes who was sitting in the protection of the doorway. They tend to come out more in the snow, to play on your sympathy. He flashed his card and asked for credits. I didn't recognize him. He must have been on rotation with the usual guy. I selected a few essentials from the menu and the Flibbety Gibbets and waited whilst they filtered down the conveyor belt behind the bullet-proof

Plexiglas. There the items filtered into bags that bustled along looking like so much unclaimed airport luggage. The auto-teller thanked me politely in female honey tones then rudely crapped the bags onto the soft landing mat.

'Fuck you very much,' I muttered and left, stepping over the beggar, who was now actually lying in front of the door to be deliberately annoying. I didn't give him any credits. He'd only spend it on crack or mylk. I made a mental note to give some money to a homeless charity instead.

When I re-entered the apartment Skyler eyed me strangely.

'Remember me?' I teased.

She looked uncertain for a second, then bobbed her head in a way that said *yeah, kinda.* It seemed a bit odd, but I was getting used to that. I unpacked some MegaMeals and pulled the warming tabs.

'Careful, it's hot.'

Sky ate in silence.

'We're going to visit Emily,' I said to JR, opening his flippy fake fish and tipping them onto the floor where he could menace them.

'Oh no. No, I ain't coming,' he said, trapping two of the wriggling orange slivers under a paw. 'I hate that place. Besides, it's Dogsday afternoon, I have to go to my church meeting in the park.'

I stood up, away from the warm smell of fish.

'It's—sorry, *what?*'

'Dogsday afternoon.'

'JR, it's *Thursday.*'

'Sure. The Sabbath. His day of rest. The day Dog finished digging up the universe and lay down in the afternoon to have a rest. I *have* to go. *All* the dogs will be there.'

This entire subject was news to me. Skyler, who'd finished eating, seemed to be pre-occupied with something else. I noticed in my peripheral vision that she kept frowning, but the news of Dogsday was occupying my attention too fully for me to pay it any.

'Are you telling me you've found God?'

'Dog.'

'Dog. *Right.* And he... *dug up* the universe.'

'Well, where else did it come from, smart ass?'

JR necked one of the wriggling glistening things, and began to crunch on it. I felt vaguely sick.

'Good grief. My dog has found religion.'

'Oh... you think your ass smells *so* good. Well, let me tell you, it *stinks,* you bighead schmuck.'

'Fine. Go. We'll meet you back here in two.'

He wolfed down the rest.

Skyler was quiet in the cab. I tried to make conversation a couple of times but she just responded with a murmur or a hum. She didn't seem to have forgotten who I was just yet, so I figured she was just moody after sleeping. I figured as long as she stayed with me, she shouldn't forget who I was. It seemed to be working.

The skyscrapers of the financial district loomed ahead of us to the left, glittering giants, all of them dwarfed by the extraordinary sight of the Freedom Tower, standing proudly 1,776 feet high, expressing in feet the year that the declaration of independence was signed. A single child born of the death of twins.

The snow clouds had moved on, freeing the sun to dazzle proudly between— and reflecting off—the crystal-like glass of the buildings. New York never ceases to astound me with its beauty. Under snow, it sparkles like the inside of a geode, and there's something in the sight of the sunlit American flag, flapping red, white and blue in the cold, sharp winter wind, that instils pride even in an immigrant like me.

The buildings vanished upwards out of sight as we drove between them, into William Street, to New York Downtown Hospital.

Sometimes, my life seems to be nothing but pebble-skipping from one hospital to another. That will be my fate, I'm certain, to finally run out of speed one day and sink in one.

'Are you okay?' I asked Sky. She eyed the building nervously. She affirmed that she was by humming and nodding vigorously. Strange girl.

We took the elevator to the top floor. The psychiatric ward.

In the lift, Skyler looked at me and said, 'Will you stop whistling that damn tune? It's irritating.'

Pop! goes the weasel. I hadn't even noticed I was doing it.

At reception, the nurse recognized me.

'Mr Steel. Nice to see you.'

She thought Steel was my surname.

'How is she?'

'Agitated. Look, about your message... Doctor Hayes is really *quite* upset with you. He's had to increase her sedation. You know you really should be more responsible. Doctor Hayes said she shouldn't have visitors. Especially you. Sorry. I don't think you'd get much out of her today anyway.'

'I'd like to see her. Just five minutes.'

I smiled sweetly and she caved in and let me through. I left Sky on a seat in reception. I'd only be a minute.

Emily sat facing the television, mounted high in one corner of the white room, looking straight through it, impervious to the images it presented to her. She gave me a heavy-lidded stare when I said her name, not a flicker of recognition, and turned back to the television, cradling the smooth pink stubs of her fingerless hand in her other one. They looked like sharpened cocktail sausages, those stubs, bony things, ending at the first knuckle. The skin of her palm had the twisted, melted detail of skin tormented by fire.

'Emily?' I said gently. 'It's me. Zeke. Can you hear me?'

She turned to look again. That heavy-lidded stare. In the background, I could hear the screaming of some madman or woman, fighting invisible demons that the drugs could not banish.

'Emily, I'm sorry... to... to ask this of you. It's starting again. Do you... know... anything?'

A spit bubble formed deep in her mouth, glinting darkly inside. It expanded and popped when it touched her dry, slack lips.

I felt cold suddenly. The TV started to buzz with interference. The voices in my own mind babbled louder.

A groan started from deep within Emily's chest, seeming reluctant to go to her mouth.

In my peripheral vision, I thought I saw something black drip to the floor from the TV screen. My heart thumped.

'When did it stop?' she hissed. 'Tell me, when?'

She mumbled something incoherent and turned back to the television, now a wild snowstorm of interference. The screaming of the other patients elsewhere in the ward tripled in volume.

I left as quickly as I could, before someone came to throw me out.

Outside in the corridor, I leaned against a wall, breathing jerkily. I hadn't expected to get anywhere, but I'd had to try.

I felt sick.

'Are you okay?' Skyler asked.

I nodded.

'I just need a moment. Wash my face. I won't be a minute.'

I entered the bathroom. I didn't notice initially that the mirrors were steamed up. I ran the tap hard and splashed cold water on my face, letting my head hang for a moment. I watched cool drops fall into the sink. I took a full breath and straightened up. The mirror stared back at me, gray, unreadable fog. Why were the mirrors steamed? I wondered.

I glanced around. There were no hot taps running. I turned around fully. This facility had no showers. Just urinals and two cubicles. And yet here were the mirrors, fogged up as if all the hot taps were on. I turned back. Someone had written something with their finger in the steam.

qoq

The numbers meant nothing to me. A shiver ran over my skin. I reached a finger out to touch the numbers, and wiped across them in a line. They remained, obstinate. I wiped my hand across them, and pulled it back in astonishment. My palm was dry. On the other side of the mirror a shadow moved. I stepped back. Something dark lifted behind the glass. Underneath the numbers the white oval of a fingertip pressed against the glass and began to write, from right to left:

ƨɘog

I realized they had not been numbers. Through the letters, I could see the arm tracing them. The owner was dressed in black. Someone short. They stretched up to write:

UOY

I backed further away from the writing just as a hand wiped a patch clear and a terrifying, distorted face snarled at me from behind the glass. I tumbled from the bathroom into the corridor.

'Are you okay?' Skyler asked for the second time. 'You look awful.'

'We have to get out of here,' I said, pulling her towards the lifts.

As the elevator descended, I struggled to keep my legs from buckling beneath me.

Outside, as we left the hospital, there were two police officers waiting for us on the snow-laden walkway. A mean-looking guy in his forties with a moustache—Bryant, according to his proud badge—and a younger female officer—Duggan. It seemed an ugly name for such a pretty officer. She looked timid, industrious, loyal. She looked like she should have been called Polanski, or Dubois.

He just looked like his badge gave him a hard-on.

'Skyler and Steel, no surnames supplied?'

Anxiety burned in my stomach like acid.

I spotted the purple-green sheen of a tiny camera lens, a beady little eye, nestling in the badge of her cap. She held a palm-screen in one hand. *I spy with my little eye, something beginning with L...*

No point in lying, then. When you lie, the area around your eyes flushes imperceptibly with more blood, making it fractionally warmer. Infrared lie-cams show up your lies in dark rings like panda eyes, and an AI matches voice patterns to give a practically perfect result every time. It was possible to cheat them, but it took monk-like self-control, special make-up, or a mod. I had none of these.

'Yes. That's us.'

How the hell did they know we would be here? I hadn't told a soul we were coming.

'There was a shooting incident two days ago which we believe may have been attempted homicide. You're on several hospital surveillance videos, and four patients and a nurse also independently recorded you being chased by a man. If it hadn't been night and interference from a storm, we'd have you on video all the way home. We've been looking for you.'

Something in his tone suggested he wasn't treating us as innocent victims here.

'How did you know I'd be here?'

'The station AI suggested you might come here, you've visited before, so we asked to be informed if you made a visit.'

There was no hiding these days. I wondered what else the AI might have to say about me.

'We'd like a few moments of your time, please. We have a few questions...'

'I see.'

'I remind you that under federal law you are obliged to comply with police investigations and that under section four point nine A of the Uniform Terrorism Act it is an offence to lie to an officer of the law. Your right to freedom of speech remains unaffected. You are not under arrest but you do *not* have the right to remain silent if asked a direct question unless answering the question should violate your statutory or basic human rights. Do you understand?'

I wanted to say no. I didn't understand how these laws had ever come to be. But I knew the history of 'terrorism'. I knew how our little freedoms had been taken away. And that wasn't his question; the lie-cam would betray me in a second if I said no.

'I understand.'

Sky looked at me nervously, then back at the police officer. She nodded.

'You have to say it for the record, ma'am.'

'I understand.'

'We'd like you to accompany us to the station.'

'Are we obliged to by law?'

'No, we can do this here if you prefer to stand in the cold?'

Sarcasm curled his upper lip like a flame to paper. His eyes dared me to be flippant back to him.

They took us in their car to the station on Gramercy Park, East 21st, where we were told we just needed to record an interview, and assuming we were truthful, we'd be free to go. It was NYPD, Patrol Services Bureau 13th Precinct, a couple of blocks from Bellevue Hospital where we'd been attacked. Given what had happened, I was going to find it hard to speak the truth without sounding like I belonged in the very institution where they'd come to find us.

The station was quiet when we arrived. I'd half expected it to be bustling with criminals resisting arrest, but I guess that only happens on TV. The place stank of fast food, burgers and fries. Someone was either eating takeout, or had just done so. The smell made me hungry, even though we had recently eaten.

They interviewed us together. We were the victims of the crime after all, not suspects. Nonetheless, there was a lie-cam on the interview desk and it was pointed right at us. I chose my words very carefully. I figured there were strategies to get past a lie-detector that did not involve superhuman control or mods and if I was smart, I might even be able to think of one.

'I was asked to look after Skyler. She's pregnant and she has a memory problem—'

'A memory problem?'

'She has amnesia. Can't remember stuff, especially if she's stressed. She'd forgotten the whole incident by the time we got home.'

Officer Bryant looked to Duggan to see if I was telling the truth. She looked at her readout panel and shrugged. I was.

I told the story of the attack, omitting details that I thought might get me into trouble, but being careful not to actually lie.

'This man, do you have any idea who he was, what his motives may have been? If he was affiliated with a gang of any kind?'

Time for some strategy. I prayed this would work.

'No, I have no idea.'

I saw the female officer frown at her screen.

'No, that's a lie. There was one thing...'

Her expression relaxed again. A strategic lie here, admitted as an accident, could hopefully conceal a much bigger lie. I planned to get away with admitting to far less than I really knew.

'I noticed he had a tattoo, on the inside of his wrist. It was of a small hand-held mirror. I guess I could draw it for you? Maybe you could find out... you know... do a search, see if it means anything.'

The implication being that it didn't mean anything to me.

Officer Bryant spun a pad across to me and a stylus.

I sketched a bad approximation of the looking glass design for him and spun it back, conscious of the discolored skin on the underside of my own wrist where a laser had so long ago removed evidence.

It worked. They didn't ask any more questions in that direction.

'And you, ma'am? Tell me what you can remember about what happened.'

'I'm sorry... I don't remember anything.'

'And you don't have any idea why someone might try to kill you?'

'No, I'm sorry.'

Officer Bryant nodded and chewed the inside of his lip pensively.

'Okay, well, thank you for your time. You're free to go and we'll be in touch.'

We stood to rise, but then Duggan, who was staring at her screen, stopped us with a hand.

'Hang on sir... I'm afraid I'm getting a positive here...'

I felt cold sweat wash over my face. I was *sure* I'd chosen my words carefully enough.

'That's impossible, ma'am. I've told you truth. I swear it.'

She looked up at me from her screen.

'I believe you, sir.'

She looked across at Sky.

'It's her that's lying.'

From the pages of Tony's diary:

These co-ordinates won't sink Blefuscu.

```
                        [0.0, 0.0, 0.0]
[-1.57775792162848e-030, 6.69929916330239e-030, 9.40251987695083e-037]
[9.40388362061631e-038, 6.61735339255922e-024, 8.4700997562474e-022]
[2.52435263975808e-029, 3.85185277152352e-034, 2.35095296853373e-038]
[1.08420113850974e-019, 1.08420165549762e-019, 1.17542610758707e-038]
[2.3509561915202e-038, 9.40388362061631e-038, 8.46212529312402e-037]
[1.09946569505738e-034, 2.13674422973828e-030, -9.1772522411976e-021]
  [7.7367172044365e-021, 5.9335274463214e-020, 8.1321728682525e-020]
[-5.93002913472103e-021, 6.77636051326244e-021, 8.1321728682525e-020]
        [2.2091162759975e-029, 3.3708402535783e-034, 0.0]
                        [0.0, 0.0, null]
```

59

Chapter 6

'Whilst the Many Worlds Interpretation of Quantum Mechanics resolves the problems and paradoxes inherent in the collapsing wave function or Copenhagen interpretation, it brings with it the awkward, even ugly, idea of universes "splitting" with each and every particle interaction. Information Relativity does away with this ugliness by suggesting that no new universes are created. Instead, each possible state is a different interpretation of the same underlying thing; and time is simply an abstract path between interpretations.'

—*Information Relativity and the New Physics,*
Professor Fabrizio T. Luciano

Jon held my gaze over the balcony of the walkway for what seemed like minutes, though in truth were seconds, stretched out by the tension of the moment. Questions tussled angrily with each other in my mind, fighting for supremacy. Jon had clearly lied to me. He was part of the very thing I had been trying to uncover, and he had not only walked right into my life, *he* had been the one to find *me*. Moreover, he was connected to this strange girl, Emily, that he had publicly shirked. What had happened in the JCR just now? The only theories that my imagination could concoct were too extreme, too ridiculous to entertain. My rational mind needed a rational explanation. There had to be one. There was always a rational explanation. Always.

'Shall I?' Emily said, breaking the silence.

'No,' Jon murmured, 'let's speak to him.' Then to me:

'Come down. Let's talk.'

I moved to the nearby steps and walked down them, losing sight of them both for a moment, as I turned the narrow right angles of the stairwell and ended up underneath the walkway.

I approached them cautiously. There was a sickly sweet smell of garbage. My heart quickened.

Emily spoke, again to Jon:

'I'm still high. I could do it. Easily. Just need your agreement.'

'No. Don't. Just keep him here. He's not bad. He'd be useful if he joined us.'

What could this wretched smudge-faced mess do? What kind of threat was this? Yet, my own bravado did not convince me. I didn't feel safe. Perhaps I should leave? Maybe it wasn't safe, here, where no-one else could see us? Yes, leave. Confront this later, somewhere public. I turned to leave, back towards the steps.

It must have been my haste: in my adrenaline-charged state, by some means I must have misjudged the effort required to turn, because now, instead of the stairs now facing me, here again were Emily and Jon. The stairs were still behind me.

Emily smirked. 'Going somewhere?'

I felt my lips working at a response, but words fractured and crumbled before they formed. I felt dizzy. How had I turned too far; missed the stairs? I felt foolish.

Jon spoke next:

'Stay, Zeke. I guess you want some answers. Are you willing to talk?'

I nodded, trying to be certain.

'Okay, then. But not here.'

'The club room.' Emily said, practically snarling.

Jon considered this, looking uncertain, then:

'Maybe.'

'Do you want Lewis and Vaughan too? Should we call them?'

'Not yet. Let's talk first. Actually, yes: go fetch them. Let me speak with him alone first.'

Emily did not seem to like this, but Jon put a hand to her arm reassuringly.

'Go. Meet us in the club room. If he's agreed, we'll be there.'

Emily looked at me as if challenging me to do or say something about her black, smudgy face and then left. The only thought that came into my mind was that she could have been quite pretty if she hadn't messed herself up with make-up and drugs.

'Sorry about her. She's cool, really. A bit fucked up, that's all. Let's go somewhere private. I'll explain. I'm going to make you an offer. If you agree, you come to the club room. If not, we forget all about this. Okay?'

He sounded so matter-of-fact. He sounded like a mafia boss. I wasn't certain I was being given the kind of offer where there was any real choice. He made it clear from his tone, his choice of words, his calm, assured body language, just exactly who was in control right now. I wrestled with something formless and uncomfortable in my mind.

I needed to control something about this situation; I could control the location.

'The cemetery.'

It was close by, open, but pretty private, certainly enough to talk. The weather was dry, but cold, so it was unlikely to have people hanging around, and if anyone walked through, we could stop talking. More importantly, its main exits led directly to public places. I couldn't believe I was having to think of such practicalities with Jon. Minutes before, he had been my friend.

'Fine. Let's go.'

We walked in silence. I found myself furtively looking at the faces of passers-by, as if Jon were holding a gun to my stomach, kidnapping me.

The cemetery was devoid of life, full of death—the peaceful, granite-tombstoned kind of death that a privileged few are rewarded with when they pass quietly away of mere old age. Only the squirrels noticed our arrival, with hungry curiosity. We sat on one of the benches. I felt the cold of the wooden slats bite through my jeans. I braced myself for a few moments against their chilly vampirism until they'd had their fill of my warmth.

Jon took out a packet of cigarettes and withdrew a slender white cylinder, jutting it between his lips. He showed me the pack, offering. Several of the cigarettes thrust themselves towards me, eager to be smoked to ash. I took the proudest. Smoking wasn't a habit I had acquired, but the occasion seemed to demand it.

Jon casually lit my cigarette and then his own with a Zippo, flicking back the metal lid with a pleasant metal *chang!*. He drew in a long lungful. The cigarette responded with an eager orange glow and a soft crackling and then settled back down, red and grey-tipped.

'So,' Jon began. He paused to blow out a plume of white that the wind tugged and pulled at until it was nothing. 'Tell me what you know. I'll fill in the gaps.'

'You came to find me specifically, didn't you?'

Jon twisted his lips down as if to say *maybe.*

'The twin research. It was bull. Wasn't it?'

'Not quite. You were digging around. I needed to find out who you were. So I got to know you. Turns out you're interesting. I decided to see where it would lead.'

Interesting?

'How did you know I was digging?'

'Details. Doesn't matter. Why did you get yourself involved? How did you know about us?'

'I overheard some gossip about Kate.'

'Ah. Yes—Kate Andrews.'

'She's involved somehow?'

'Not really. Tony thought she was.'

'Tony? Antony Baijaiti?'

'Mm-huh.'

'But she wasn't involved?'

'Not until he started emailing her.' Jon scoffed the words out. 'He lost it a bit. Started—imagining things. Nearly ruined the whole thing.'

'So you killed him.'

The words just slipped out of me, like greased fish from a hand. I hadn't intended them. Jon turned to me, his expression suddenly malicious:

'He was my *best* friend, Zeke. He committed suicide.'

'Uh—I'm sorry. I just...'

'Do you have any idea what that's like? I'm not a *murderer.*'

Jon turned his face out into the small park, scanning the little tombstones, searching them for something within himself. I turned to look too. We sat silent for a moment, and spoke without looking at each other.

'What is the Looking Glass Club?'

Jon took another drag on his cigarette and blew smoke at the tombstones.

'You don't have to be involved in this, Zeke.'

I laughed, a little mockingly.

'You can tell me, but then you'd have to kill me? Right?'

He turned that steady blue flint gaze on me again.

'I'm perfectly serious, Zeke. This isn't a game. You can walk away. Once you're in, you're in.'

'Walk away from what?! *In* what?! You haven't told me anything!'

'There's your dilemma. I can't tell you more unless you're prepared to join us. If you decide not to, you must promise never to mention the Looking Glass Club again. Ever. Or do any more digging around. You have to forget.'

'Jon, this is ridiculous, you're speaking in riddles. How the heck can I make a decision to join something I know *nothing about.*'

Another drag on the cigarette. Pause for thought. A decision. Then:

'Two years ago I made a discovery. Almost completely by accident. It was an important discovery. So important, I decided not to publish. So important that if the government found out—any government—my life would be in danger. So I kept the research secret. Not even my supervisor knew. Or knows. The only person I told about it was Tony, because... it doesn't matter. We made a pact, continued the experiment together.'

It was a painful recollection for him, this was obvious from his knitted brow, his heavy speech.

'And Emily?'

'We needed others involved, to continue the research. We couldn't do it with just the two of us. Tony found them, screened them. Emily. Lewis and Vaughan. She might not seem it, but she's one helluva smart girl. The boys too. It was just the five of us. We were the Looking Glass Club.'

'What kind of research?'

'I've told you enough. Too much. What we're doing is dangerous, illegal and almost certainly cost Tony his life. But it's also without doubt the most incredible discovery ever made. I'm not being arrogant, Zeke. The world won't be the same again after this. The reward outweighs the risks. I can't tell you any more, Zeke, but I'm going to make you an offer. If you want, you can join us. Find out everything. But—there's no going back.'

He pulled down his watch strap, revealing the indelible ink of the tattoo on the white inside of his wrist.

'Membership is permanent. How willing are you to take risks in the pursuit of science?'

How could I answer this?

'What kind of risks? What would I have to do?'

'The world *is* going to change. Just ask yourself, do you want to be involved in that, or be a bystander? You're smart enough to be involved. You just have to decide.'

'If you're not going tell me any more I... I need to sleep on it. I can't make that kind of decision like that.'

'Okay, then you're out. It's now or never.'

'No wait, that's not fair.'

'You're selecting *yourself* out, Zeke. Showing your mettle, your true colours. This is the first test. Can't you *see*? If you can't take this risk, then you don't have what it takes for the club.'

'I...'

I... what? He was right, I was a coward. I *wasn't* a risk-taker. I was a coward and a jerk and a geek. I was exactly the type of person that Kate would never look at. What *had* happened in the JCR with Emily standing by? I considered the moment when I had tried to leave, and found a one hundred and eighty degree turn had instead turned me full circle. I wasn't *that* clumsy. *Just keep him here,* Jon had said. I had to know. I couldn't stay this crappy, worthless, gutless person for the rest of my life. I'd started to change already, just by hanging out with Jon. And I'd started to like the person that I had glimpsed I could become.

Jon stood up. He brushed down his legs, his manner peremptory, as if to leave, close off possibilities. Permanently.

I stood up quickly.

'No, Jon, wait, wait. Please. I want to be in. I mean—I'm in.'

His blue flint twinkled through narrowed eyelids. He took a taut-mouthed drag on the stub of his cigarette and flicked it into the distant gravestones. The glowing stub-end spiralled along its parabola and bounced off a grey granite block in a shower of dull red sparks, where one by one they died in the cool cemetery grass.

From the pages of Tony's diary:

We agree they point somewhere, but where?

Chapter 7

'Oh, what fun it'll be, when they see me through the glass in here, and can't get at me!'

—Alice

Skyler lowered her head and stared at the interview-room table.

Bryant leaned back in his chair with a smirk spread over his face like dark chocolate.

I stared at her in disbelief.

She put a hand to her swollen belly. 'Could I have some water please?'

Bryant rocked forward again and put his face far too close to Skyler's. 'I repeat—in case you "forgot"—under federal law you are *obliged* to comply with police investigations and that under section four point nine A of the Uniform Terrorism Act it is an *offence* to lie to an officer of the law. Your right to freedom of speech remains unaffected. You are not under arrest but you do *not* have the right to remain silent if asked a direct question unless answering the question should violate your statutory or basic human rights. Do you understand?'

'Could I have some water, please?'

'Do... you... understand?'

'The lady's pregnant, come on,' I said.

'Duggan, fetch her some water. I repeat: Do you understand?'

Sky nodded.

Duggan stood up and left to fetch some water. I wasn't sure, but I thought I detected the tiniest hint of umbrage in the way she stood, either at Bryant's heavy-handed approach, or possibly at being asked to fetch water.

'Just as soon as Officer Duggan gets back, we're gonna go through some of these questions again, Miss Skyler. Don't make me arrest you.'

He stood up and walked out, leaving us alone for a moment.

The lie-cam still stared at us on the desk.

'What's going on?' I demanded as soon as I was sure we were alone.

Sky continued to stare at the desk. She looked afraid. Diminished somehow, so that the bump under her jumper was the entirety of her.

'Sky? Talk to me, I have a right—'

She whipped around to face me.

'You have a right to what?'

Her accent. Was it... different?

'To know. What's going on?'

She scrutinized me, looking as confused as I felt. Then she shook her head, as if to dislodge a vagrant thought.

'I'm sorry,' she said finally. 'I know none of this is your fault. I'm remembering stuff. But it's fragments. I don't know what's real. Everything's confused in my head right now.'

Her accent seemed normal again. Maybe I'd imagined it. I looked at the lie-cam nervously. Bryant had almost certainly left deliberately. I was certain this man did nothing in this room that was not deliberate.

'You remember the attack?'

She shook her head.

I tried to think back to what it was that she was supposed to have lied to, back to the questions that had been directed at her, to understand what it was she'd been asked that had caused the lie-cam to trigger. My own mind was also a confused mess. Why was it so damn hard to remember details when you most needed to? It was only minutes ago and yet I couldn't recall the words that had been spoken. Just the sense. Was it something about whether she knew why someone might attack her? Yes, that was it, something like that.

'So, you know why you were attacked?'

She shook her head and then shrugged and looked up at the lie-cam, then at me, clenching her jaw hard and frowning at me. I thought for a second.

'I need to stretch my legs.'

I stood up, strategically knocking the table slightly. The lie-cam tipped onto one side and rolled over, pointing at the wall.

I mouthed words at Sky quickly:

What's going on?

I can't tell you.

Why?

Italy called.

Italy called?

Yes.

I don't understand.

Italy call.

What?

This. She pointed at her belly.

The door banged opened. Bryant strode in purposefully and righted the lie-cam, giving us a mean, wordless stare.

I shrugged.

'Sorry, I knocked it over when I stood up to stretch my legs.'

'Did you now?'

Officer Duggan walked in carrying a tray with glasses of water on and a steaming cup of coffee.

'I think we're going to interview these people separately, Officer Duggan. I have reason to suspect they may be colluding to obstruct a police investigation.'

He sucked air through his teeth and shook his head at his own words. He continued, speaking to himself as though there were two of him in the room.

'Now why would they do that? That would be a *very* unwise thing to do. Let's start with the liar.'

Sky looked at me, afraid suddenly.

Duggan approached me and asked me to come with her. There was nothing I could do, so I went with her and was escorted into an empty interview room where I sat alone for twenty minutes listening to the sounds of the station: doors banging, colleagues laughing in the corridor, phone conversations at reception.

The door opened, and just as it did so, my mind worked something out.

Not *Italy call. It's illegal.*

Her baby was illegal.

What did that mean? *Surrogacy.* The practice of surrogacy had been decreed un-Godly by senator Jackson, a religious republican senator of New York State a few years back. Since overpopulation had become such a big issue, nobody made a particularly huge fuss to defend it.

Bryant and Duggan walked in. Duggan looking efficient and kind. Bryant looked smug.

'Well,' he began as Duggan set-up the lie-cam on the desk. 'What a story. I wonder if yours is going to corroborate hers?'

'Is she under arrest?'

Bryant looked at Duggan with an innocent, confused face suddenly. He was mocking me:

'Oh... I thought *I* was the one asking the questions, Officer Duggan, I didn't realize our guest here was. Stupid me!'

I took a controlled, clench-jawed breath, resisting the urge to get arrested for assaulting a police officer. This was bad news. If we were going to go over the questions again, then it was going to come out that I knew something about the attacker, and my whole wretched history was going to be dug up.

But then Bryant surprised me, showing that it already had been:

'You have a very obscure past, Mister Steel...'

'I'm *sure* I have the right to a lawyer.'

'You're not under arrest. Yet.'

'That's because I haven't done anything wrong. I'm actually the victim here— or rather Skyler is—and you're treating us both like criminals.'

'Well, time will tell which side of the law you're on, Mister Steel.'

'It's Steel. Just *Steel*. What happened to "innocent until proven guilty"?'

'Like I said, you're not under arrest. We're just trying to do our jobs, apprehend a dangerous criminal, and I can't understand *why* you wouldn't be bending over backwards to help us in this respect. But you go into hiding for two days and you seem remarkably reluctant to assist us in this matter. Now do you care to tell me *why*?'

His voice was steady, cool, even soft, now.

I let out a great sigh.

'We went into hiding, because someone had tried to kill us. That's a sensible thing to do under the circumstances, isn't it?'

'Where did you go?'

'I'm afraid for my personal safety, Officer Bryant. I'm sure you won't mind if I don't answer that question.'

'It's *Sergeant* Bryant. *Steel*.'

Bryant sniffed unhappily, and I learned a little about my rights. Hmm. I wondered how much I could use that excuse not to answer questions.

'Have you perhaps been on the other side of the law before, *Steel*?'

'My past is none of your business.'

'The past—' Bryant began, but then he was interrupted by a screaming sound.

'What the— Duggan, go see what that is.'

Bryant simply sat and stared at me for a minute, breaking me down silently. Someone sounded like they were in a great deal of pain.

Duggan rushed breathlessly back into the room.

'Sir? It's the woman. Skyler. She's having the baby.'

From the pages of Tony's diary:

The bishop is mad playing a game like this, the foreign fool!

1. Pa1+ - Pa1+
2. Cxc6 - Da1+
3. Dxc7+ - Ta1
4. Pa1+ - Txa1+
5. Dxc6 - Ra1
6. Ra1+ - Txa1
7. Pxc6+ - Txe1
8. Ra1 - Pxa1
9. Tc6+ - Txa1
10. Pa1 - Pxg1
11. Cf3+ - Ca1
12. Pxc1 - Fxe1
13. Pf1 - Pxh5
14. Cxb3+ - Rxd7
15. Pxc5+ - Rxh1
16. Cxb2 - Dh8+
17. Re6 - Rxe4+
18. Pf3+ - Txh5
19. Cf6 - Pd8+
20. Rf1 - Txf5+
21. Df3+ - Txh8
22. Cg1+ - Txh8+
23. Rf3+ - Txe5
24. Cxc6 - Fxh8+
25. Ra5 - Txh8+
26. Rf3+ - Txe2
27. Pxc6 - Fxh8+
28. Ra3 - Ph7
29. Pa1+ - Txe1+
30. Pe6 - Da1
31. Tc6 - Dd5
32. Pa1 - Pxg1+
33. Pa7+ - Txh8+
34. Dc6+ - Pa8+
35. Rf3+ - Txg1
36. Tf8+ - Rxe2+
37. Re1 - Pa3
38. Rf3+ - Txb1
39. Pa3+ - Txh8+
40. Re6 - Rxa2+
41. Cxc6 - Dd5
42. Pf4+ - Cxh8+
43. Rb1 - Pe1+
44. Ff3+ - Txe7
45. Pa1+ - Txh8+
46. Rf2 - Da1
47. Cxc6 - Fxh7
48. Pc6 - Dd8+
49. Re1 - Pa1

Chapter 8

'What do we know' he had said, 'of the world and the universe about us? Our means of receiving impressions are absurdly few, and our notions surrounding objects infinitely narrow. We see things only as we are constructed to see them, and can gain no idea of their absolute nature.'

—*From Beyond*, H. P. Lovecraft

Jon led me back towards Princes Gardens from the cemetery where I had committed myself to him.

'What now?' I had said.

I'd offered up my wrist, a sacrifice. 'Do I have to get a tattoo?' I felt slightly foolish.

'That comes later. You prove yourself first.'

'So there's an induction ceremony?'

'Not a ceremony. No. Membership starts with you coming on a little trip with us.'

'A trip? To where?'

'No more questions, Zeke. If you're in, this is where you start to have to trust me. Just follow me.'

At that he led me out of the cemetery. We turned into Princes Gardens at the south-east corner. Alexei's halls of residence, Linstead, stood to my right on the east side, but we turned left along the south side, to my very own hall of residence, Falmouth Keogh, in the building known as Southside. It towered above us, facing the grand trees of Princes Gardens. A pair of glass security doors led inside the Halls. Jon surprised me by producing a card. He swiped it and pushed open the doors.

'Here? The Club room is here in Southside? In a hall of residence?'

He lifted a solitary finger to his lips. *No more questions.*

He walked directly to a lift and pushed the call button. A square halo lit up around the steel button, glowing an ominous red. We waited, present only to the ominous sounds of lift machinery, whining into life, something deep and hidden. The doors opened to a steel box.

As the lift mouth closed, consuming us, Jon removed a set of keys from his pocket. I frowned but kept my silence. He inserted a small silver key into the lift panel. My frown deepened, expressing a question I was forbidden to ask. The lift descended, not far: one, two levels at most. The doors opened into a wide service corridor. I immediately caught the fragrance of detergent. We walked in silence past the laundry on the right. Almost opposite the laundry led a short corridor, at the end of which were bland grey double doors, locked. A sign on them warned, 'Strictly No Admittance. Service Personnel Only'. I knew then

69

that we were at one of the many entrances to the college's underground tunnel
network running beneath the whole of South Kensington.

Jon turned to me.

'Take your jumper off.'

'Why?'

'I need to blindfold you.'

'Don't be ridiculous.'

Jon's face became ruddy with anger, his tone sharpened with threat, like a
knife:

'Don't play games with me, Zeke. Until you've proven yourself, until you have
this on your wrist, you wear a blindfold to the club room. You already know too
much. I have people to protect.'

I tried to remove my jumper calmly, without expressing the resentment and
anger I felt.

Jon took the jumper by both arms, and twirled the body around itself into a
makeshift blindfold. I let him wrap it around my head, and fasten it roughly. He
pulled it tight, and knotted the arms behind my head, blinding me utterly and
leaving no chance of me seeing even the floor, or my own footsteps. The jumper
smelled of underarm deodorant mingled with the musk of my armpits; of damp
autumn air; of cigarette smoke.

I heard the sound of keys, of a lock being unlocked; of the big doors being
pushed wide and refastened behind us. He pulled me into the unknown.

Our steps echoed strangely as we walked, changing their sounds as we turned
left or right, into narrower or wider tunnels. I don't know if he took me the
most direct route, or to confuse me, took me on a long detour, to guarantee my
ignorance. I don't know how long we walked like this. His hand sometimes pushed
down on my head to make me stoop. Once near the beginning, I had to climb
down a rattling metal ladder for what felt like an age. I struggled to release my
hands, not knowing just how far I might fall if I slipped. My blindness took away
my sense of time as well as sight. Perhaps twenty minutes. There were countless
turns and twists. At one point, we heard two male voices, I presumed men at
work. Jon stopped me and whispered to be silent. The tunnel smelled damp and
musty. It was cold. I felt the skin of my arms and torso wrinkle as the hairs
stood on end to try to keep me warm. My abdominal muscles and my biceps and
triceps began to twitch and shiver. We waited until the voices faded and then
waited more in silence to be sure before we resumed. Twice, he made me step
over obstacles of some unimaginable form, and finally towards the culmination
of our journey, he manoeuvred me, all clumsy knees and elbows, through a small
hatchway, into some secret space that he had revealed, which I imagined from
the sounds penetrating my darkness, had been via the removal of a hatch door.
We walked and twisted some more in subjective darkness, until he stopped me,
jangled with some keys, turned an invisible lock, and pulled the blindfold from
my eyes.

We stood in a low tunnel that ran to our left and right. Facing us was the
front of a plain grey door, lit by a dull orange service light on the wall to the left:
an acrylic lozenge jailed behind grey plastic restraints. Lagged pipes ran along
the corridor to our left and right above the door. The door's featureless surface
seemed deliberate, as if to disguise its contents. It had a single dark keyhole out
of which protruded a long bronze key, and from which, joined by a silver ring,
hung a set of variform siblings.

'Okay?' he asked.

I nodded. He pushed open the door.

The club room was tall enough to stand in without stooping. I tried to guess
what purpose this room must have once fulfilled, perhaps a power or control
room of some sort, but there was no machinery here now, the only evidence of

its former use was a collection of pipe stubs protruding from the wall, sealed off, amputated. A multitude of pipes of various sizes crossed the ceiling. There was a single structural column off-centre to the rear left, a nuisance thing as if to deliberately make the space awkward. The room had been furnished and lit well enough to make it seem comfortable, but it must once have been morbid. Light came from two standing lamps, one in each of the opposite corners, throwing out a long shadow from the column. The lamps were long tubes of glowing crêpe hanging vertically. They looked modern, incongruous with the ancient dampness of this room.

A box structure that blocked the entire right wall had been made into a makeshift sofa by the addition of cushions and throws. Rugs covered the concrete floor. Huge beanbags provided further seating. I took in this subterranean hideaway and wondered which part of South Kensington was above us.

Emily lay reclining on the makeshift sofa, with her head against the rear wall. She lay arm-in-arm with a boy with tousled dark hair and a surly mien. On one of the great beanbags lounged a dirty-blond-haired, morose-looking boy, who shared the same thick eyebrows as the scrawny youth entangled with Emily. She looked more presentable than when I had seen her an hour before, evidently having passed in front of a mirror and corrected her smudgy facial errors. The effect was a small improvement. I still found her overall impression disconcerting and contrived.

I stepped inside, tracked silently by three pairs of eyes. Jon closed and then locked the door behind us, removing the keys and pocketing them.

'The door is always locked, whether we're in or out. Club rule.'

The dirty-blond boy surveyed me from his supine position:

'Just him?'

The tone was dismissive. A hot humiliation swelled up inside me. I hadn't realised that I had misinterpreted his comment.

'Lewis?' Jon responded before I could say anything. 'Enough. Okay?'

Lewis capitulated instantly, settling back, revealing his position in the hierarchy.

I felt tiny and inadequate. Here, I had no context to give me any power at all. It felt like my first day at kindergarten, except that all the other kids had already grown up. I was the only infant.

'This is Lewis, that's his brother Vaughan.'

Brothers. The fraternity was evident in the eyebrows.

'My *twin*,' Lewis corrected.

Could have fooled me, I thought. It was then that I noticed the clothing. Lewis and Vaughan were both dressed in exactly the same clothes: the same trainers (some trendy brand I recognised but couldn't name, with an N on the side), the same black jeans, identical black T-shirts. The effect would have disturbed me if they had been identical twins, contrasting so starkly as it did with the lengths Jacob and I made to be distinguishable from each other; the fact that these two brothers were clearly heterozygous twins, fraternal, *non-identical* twins, disturbed me even more. What on Earth were they trying to say?

I suppressed laughter.

'Well. I'm here now. I'm in. Are you going to tell me what exactly it is we do in this club?'

'What we do?' mocked Vaughan. He was resting on one elbow, fiddling with something in his hands.

'*Impossible* things, Zeke' Emily finished. She savoured the words as she spoke them, as if they were sexual, pheromonal things.

'We explore boundaries. Push them,' Lewis continued on behalf of his brother.

I realised what Vaughan was doing: he was rolling a joint. He caught me looking.

'It'll help you relax.'

'I'm relaxed,' I lied. Just saying the words seemed to make me tremble.

Vaughan took out a Zippo, and with a *kerchang*, the end of the joint was aflame, burning briefly yellow and lithe, before decaying into a smoking ruby. This room was too small, too poorly ventilated for this. I felt myself wanting to cough in anticipation of the unbreathable atmosphere I imagined was seconds away. But it wasn't to be as cloying as I imagined: the smoke traced a line across the ceiling and began to filter out through a round hole in the corner.

Vaughan passed the joint straight to me and in spite of myself I took it gratefully. I sat myself on one of the beanbags to show I felt comfortable, and to prevent any of them from noticing that my knees had started to tremble. Jon sat next to me.

Vaughan untangled himself from Emily and stepped over her to pick up a small thermos flask that had lain unseen by the wall. He passed it to Emily. Next to it was a small green plastic medicine box, with a hinged lid. He retrieved this as well. He opened the medicine box and took out a sterile syringe pack which he pulled open with the aid of his teeth. Emily unscrewed the thermos flask, and pulled out on a wire a small container, shrouded in liquid nitrogen mist. My heart began to pound seeing this, but simultaneously, I felt my mind beginning to slow, to melt under the strange liquefying tensions of the cannabis.

Jon put an arm around my back. I understood it was intended to comfort me, and so partly it did, but the intimacy of the act introduced a tension in the muscles of my upper back as surely as ice would have done. I let the arm remain for a moment, but soon sat forward, on the pretext of getting more comfortable in order to remove myself from it.

'What are we doing?'

'Shhh. Relax. Trust, remember? We're just going on a little trip together. You're never going to see things the same after this.'

The cannabis was strong. I felt it pulling me down into the beanbag, back into Jon's arm. He began to stroke the hair on the back of my head. I wanted to close my eyes. I was watching Emily pulling a liquid up into the syringe from the cold smoke of the vial, as Vaughan fastened a blue elastic rectangle around his forearm, stretching it into a cord, tying it, raising the veins into a prominent network of turquoise tubes above his white skin. The elastic sheet reminded me of an exercise gimmick my mum had bought once years before, when she still cared about her body.

'Relax. Just relax...' Jon cooed, soothing. His voice was hypnotic.

My eyelids started to droop, but the sight of Emily injecting the needle into the vein of Vaughan's forearm made me sit up again.

'I don't want this...' I mumbled.

'It's okay,' Jon soothed. 'It's no different to smoking, just a different way into your body.'

The tourniquet was passed around, new needles attached to the syringe. Emily was next. Then Lewis. One by one, they lay back on their cushions. Emily's arm extended out to take Lewis's hand. She began to massage it with her own. Her eyes fixed on mine, lascivious. Reclining behind her, Vaughan was stroking her back. Part of my mind was screaming at me to run, get away from this. A deviant part of me felt aroused. I felt blood pulse in my groin, my penis moved in my underpants, stretching out like a beast awakened.

Jon took the kit from Lewis. He took my arm and began to tie the rubber cord.

'Clench your fist.'

I mumbled a negative.

'Come on. They've started. We don't have much time.' In spite of myself, I found myself complying.

I didn't feel the needle, but the liquid entered me like a stream of ice, freezing its way up my bicep. I shivered powerfully. Jon restrained me, pulled the needle out.

Vaughan had started to kiss Emily's neck, one hand fondled a breast. I was disgusted, mortified at the sight; my penis stiffened in opposition to me.

'You like that, new boy?' Vaughan sneered.

Jon spoke as he prepared himself for his injection:

'Ignore him, he's just trying to freak you out. Test you.'

Vaughan smiled nastily with one half of his face and then his hand fell away from Emily's breast, his eyelids were heavy and he sank back into his cushion.

'Just relax into it. Swim down, as far as you can go. To the edge. You'll understand. Once you're there, push through.'

Jon injected himself.

He took my hand unexpectedly, and began to massage it as Emily was doing with Lewis. I pulled it back involuntarily, but he coaxed it back.

'*Trust* me.'

His thumb worked sensuously into my palm.

'See you on the other side, Alice. . .'

I lay back and closed my eyes, allowing Jon's thumb to work warmly into my palm.

I began to hear the buzzing of flies and bees in the distance.

'Don't let go of me at any time. The physical contact helps.'

Without moving, my body became a distant thing. My hand, once a hot point of discomfort, tied uncomfortably to my sexuality by Jon's inappropriate contact, became irrelevant, and then faded to nothing.

I became something other. Ephemeral, liquid, flowing into the bright shapes I sensed more than merely saw, twisting them through their multiplicity of dimensions. My awareness and understanding expanded and suddenly I knew the meaning of the Doors of Perception. I felt the walls that had encapsulated and limited my experience of the universe fall away, and I was freed. My previously limited views of reality seemed laughable: that I could have only been present to one dimension of time and three dimensions of space seemed so naïve; that I could accept as the only ones, the laws of logic and mathematics I had been trained in, was to be as good as blind. I saw an infinity of connected sets of logic, branches of mathematics that obeyed completely different rules to the one I had known just minutes before, trapped in a planar jail.

With this new freedom of dimension, I realised something with astonishment: my conscious mind was at the edge of the universe. It had *always* been there; as if before I had been a dot on a plane, able only to see north and south, east and west, oblivious to the edges that pressed against me 'up' and 'down', wherever I was. I simply had not been able to see those directions before. Yet, this was more than a plane: there were so many directions, many of them not physical dimensions but others indescribable, inexpressible in my limited language. The universe's edge was *here*, and *here* and *there*, but extended newly in *this* direction, or *this*, or *that*, or *those*; Each new direction as perpendicular to the next as east is to north. I could swim in any.

I understood the universe.

It was merely the gamut of all possible conscious experience. It was every conscious state, contiguous, connected. The physical laws all fell out naturally from this conclusion. I observed how in *that* direction, energy was not conserved, nor momentum; no brain could survive in that direction, nothing could make sense, and therefore consciousness was not possible. This fact defined the edges. Time, I observed, was simply a certain type of path through the states. It was not a unique, singular thing. It was simply that human consciousness could perceive only a single history. The superposition of wave functions became clear to me in that moment, as if a shroud had been lifted and I could see the thing beneath. *Swim down*, he'd said. *You'll understand.*

And I did. Loosed from the constraints of physicality, I swam, down and down, experiencing parts of my mind fly away from me like flotsam that could not follow, new parts joining, for as I swam, the rules that supported my conscious mind also changed, defining it anew.

In a distant, remote place, there was a ball-like thing, curled up, encapsulated.

The universe became a bright, burning thing, a liquid incandescence. I let its energies flow and ebb through me. *Swim down.*

I sensed a boundary, a sliver, a thing infinite in only three dimensions, and therefore infinitely thin. I pushed up against it, feeling it flex like skin against my insistence. I was near another of the Universe's edges.

Once you're there, push through. Who had said that? Someone had said that once.

I struggled to pull the memory to me, but it resisted. What was I doing here? What was my purpose? These questions troubled me. I could not recall myself, who I was.

The boundary ahead of me felt alive. I must have come for this. I felt afraid suddenly. I was lost in an infinite sea of limitless dimension and direction. I was alone, for there could be no-one else *here*, *now*, in this space. I turned, this way and that, in the dark liquid universe that was now suffocating me. Where was home? Who was I? *What did I have to do?* I *had* to remember.

I panicked.

I pushed myself against the boundary, pressing into it, flattening myself to its three dimensional form and—

I fell through.

I opened my eyes.

I was back in the club room. Jon was staring at me, smiling. I still felt different, my mind was still kaleidoscoping, but it was back in my physical body—or so I thought. I tried to turn my head to look around. It was an effort, my vision seemed to echo as it moved, layering the same images, over and over, instead of turning. My head remained in the same position. It was like being blind drunk. I blinked hard to clear the sensation. I felt sick. I tried to turn again, but failed. *I'm paralysed*, I thought.

I could hear Jon's voice talking to me.

'Don't worry.'

His voice seemed distant. I tried to turn once more, this time with more success, but the movement seemed to echo again, as if I were not one but many, occupying the same space, dancing out of step. I heard a voice behind me, it was Lewis or Vaughan, I couldn't tell which. I couldn't make out the words.

I turned. The visual echo had gone. No more dizziness. Lewis and Vaughan were sitting on the box, the makeshift sofa. Where was Emily? I turned. Ah, there. She was next to Jon. I'd missed seeing her. She was stretching like a cat on one of the beanbags.

She stood up, began to examine herself in the full-length mirror that hung next to the door. Something looked wrong, but I couldn't quite tell what it was.

'I'm still feeling the effects. I'm not back to normal yet. I—I feel dizzy.'

Jon laughed across a distant wind.

'We're *not back yet*, Zeke,' said a voice from behind in my ear.

I turned. Impossibly, it was Jon. He was no longer in front of me, but behind me. *I'm still tripping*, I thought to myself.

'It's happened again,' Emily said, staring into the glass of the mirror frame ahead of her.

'It must be him,' Vaughan indicated me. 'He's new. Maybe a subconscious expectation.'

'Fascinating,' Emily said. She reached out a hand to the mirror.

And it was then I realised what was wrong.

Emily had no reflection.

Emily tried extending her fingers through the mirror glass, into the reflected room. She shivered almost sexually, and immediately withdrew her hand, holding it tenderly to her bosom.

'*Cold*. So beautiful.'

This isn't real. The thought came hard and heavy, like something massive falling from a long way. *I'm tripping*, I thought. *Dreaming.*

None of this is real—

When it came again, that second time, the thought was like thunder, renting apart the scene, as if it were the image on the surface of a puddle. I found myself twisting through darkness shot with colours, flavours, smells, tactile percepts and qualities; a very different space than the one I had arrived via; a space that had a direction and a motive; a destination. I was pulled along a kaleidoscopic journey that lasted an infinity of eternities and yet a second before I gradually became aware of a body—my body; and my body was in pain.

This time, when I opened my eyes, I knew with certainty that I was awake. I stared at the worn rug on the floor from just an inch away. I was lying with my cheek pressed to it. It was red, colour-bled by age. Its fibres stuck out in rebellious straggles. The odour was heavy and damp. I felt a burning pain through my body.

As my sense of the relative positions of my body parts—my proprioception—returned I realised that I lay curled on my side. I could feel that I was foetal, but my right arm was stuck awkwardly out behind me in a position such that my torso had restricted the blood flow from the shoulder. I had no idea how long I'd been in that position, but it was agony. I rolled over on to my front with difficulty, releasing it, and lay for a moment, suffering the cloying must of the rug near my face in exchange for relief in my arm. The relief was short-lived; as the blood returned to my oxygen-starved arm, an agonising swarm of pins and needles began to stab into the muscles. I moaned out loud.

'Zeke? You okay?'

The voice calling to me was struggling to be clear, with the unwilling mouth and lips of someone just waking. It was Jon. I heard a crumping sound, like a footstep through heavy snow. Someone was moving on the beanbags.

'My arm. Pins and needles,' I moaned again through gritted teeth. I felt groggy.

I managed to manoeuvre myself up against the edge of the makeshift sofa and lay back, teeth still clamped. Jon offered to massage my arm but the pain was intense and any pressure made it worse. I lay back further and let it slowly ebb away until finally it was just the heel of my hand that throbbed and jabbed.

More crunching of artificial snow. Vaughan and Emily had returned to consciousness. Lewis remained sleeping on his beanbag, his lower lip hanging slack.

Vaughan spoke. There was a sultry edge to his voice.

'You ended it. Early.'

I didn't register that he was talking to me. As the pain had subsided my thoughts had begun to return to my trip. The majority of it had been timeless, exploring dimensions I'd had no previous concept of, but that middle section, the dream, had been almost real.

'I had this dream whilst I was tripping,' I said. 'Like—so *lucid*. You were there.'

'He doesn't get it.' Vaughan sounded vaguely disgusted.

'It wasn't a dream,' Emily said.

Jon was silent. He was studying me.

'No, it was, I swear. You were all there.'

Emily spoke slowly to me, smiling, as though I were a child and she were teaching me something marvellous:

'I put my hand through the mirror, Zeke.'

The words stunned me. How could she have known what I'd dreamt?

Lewis began to stir. His eyes opened and he lifted himself onto one elbow with a crump. He surveyed the room casually.

''m I last?'

'As usual,' his brother responded.

Lewis looked at me, squinting underneath his thick dirty eyebrows.

'Hey, man, why'd you stop it early? We were just getting going. *And* the mirror was clear again.'

I looked back at Jon with a jaw slack from shock.

Jon continued to silently appraise me; a quiet smile glinted deep in his eyes.

From the pages of Tony's diary:

*What a mess! Smashed into pieces, billions! All the King's horses and all the
King's men differed in opinion about how to sort out this scrambled egg.*

16.700562132

34.521071284   5.615550161   8.026465362

4.216382543

3.141592654   55.162481535   25.399517350   5.812822994

46.370332532

5.495907920   14.545181524

42.075365238   37.758148341   3.141592654

3.141719631   12.382787540   27.746622117

40.986836790

3.141592654   21.104550454

10.205000915

53.014997889   50.800142205

3.141592654   48.585286521

3.276333647   5.747678034

18.889957973   30.226103989

5.257651536   27.912621233

16.708919957

Chapter 9

'The horror of that moment,' the King went on, 'I shall never, NEVER forget!'
'You will, though,' the Queen replied, 'if you don't make a memorandum of it.'

—*Through the Looking Glass*

'Get her to Bellevue. Now,' Officer Bryant called. 'If this turns out to be a ruse, she's going to be in a whole bunch of trouble.'

The word *bunch* was imbued with spittle and venom. His thick moustache had jumped out slightly when he had said the word.

'I'm going with her,' I said, standing up.

'Sit down.'

'I'm going with her. You want me to stay, find a reason to arrest me.'

He thought about it for a moment. I saw his jaw muscles clench. Then he sniffed and said:

'You're free to go. For now. Tell me one thing. This baby yours?'

I'd been waiting for this question. I was surprised it had taken until now to ask it. I gave him the response I'd planned:

'I don't know.'

I said it as earnestly as possible, as though the thought was of some concern to me. It wasn't a complete lie. After all, I didn't know for *sure* it wasn't mine. But this ambiguous admission would hopefully give Bryant an alternative motive for murder that would stop him digging any deeper in my past than he—and his station AI—seemed intent on doing.

He nodded knowingly.

'I see. We're going to want to ask you some more questions later. I hope I can count on your co-operation.'

'Sure,' I said, no doubt triggering the lie-cam's little alarms, but thankfully Officer Duggan wasn't there to read the display. I walked out.

I held Sky's hand in the cop car. She wasn't faking the pain, I could tell. She could hardly speak her breathing was so rapid, and she was sweating profusely. Her eyes alternated from being wide to scrunched shut, and every few minutes she would grunt and tense until a strangled half-word aborted itself in her throat, and squeeze my hand enough for me to feel some of her pain with her. Between the contractions she seemed to be in a feverish state and appeared to be starting to hallucinate. She grabbed on to me and held me tightly, like a lover, resting her damp head in the crook of my neck under my chin. She moaned and her lips brushed my neck, hot and moist. I felt an exquisite and familiar discomfort.

She whispered something to the air. I shushed her gently, but she continued.

'The white boys. They'll come for me.'

'What?' I gingerly stroked her forehead. It felt clammy and hot. My stomach clenched like a fist.

'The white boys. The ghosts. The ones who did this.'

After that she was silent, crying out only when the contractions came.

Officer Duggan drove. It was only ten blocks, but, in spite of our whirling police lights and our siren's wailing cries of urgency, the evening traffic was against us. Outside it was dark again. The snow was turning to slush under the onslaught of tires, and the constant barrage of Manhattan's honking cab horns penetrated through our siren and our windows.

I tried to calm and reassure Skyler with cooing words of wisdom, platitudes from someone without a womb, who had never known—could never know—what she was suffering.

The siren died and Sky was transferred to a wheelchair. By now, her breathing was shallower and she seemed strangely quiet. I made sure this time we registered her under an alias. I raced with the medics to the maternity ward whilst Duggan parked the car somewhere.

She was lifted onto a bed, and doctors and nurses swarmed around her, jabbering to each other in jargon. It was clear from the beginning that this wasn't going to be a straightforward delivery. Once she was safely in her bed, the swarm of activity died a little, leaving just a single doctor and nurse.

The doctor felt around her belly. The old scar of her previous caesarean section looked stretched and livid.

'Polyhydramnios. Why wasn't this picked up when she came in before?'

The nurse shrugged.

'There was an attack,' I offered. 'We were shot at, so we ran away.'

The doctor glared at me as if it had been my fault.

'Oh. That was you, was it?'

'What's poly...'

'Too much amniotic fluid. She's as tight as a bowling ball. I can't feel whether the baby's breeched or not. Explains why her previous caesarean was such a botch job if she's had this before. *Get me an EFM. And get a portable ultrasound.*'

A nurse was already waiting with a small device. The doctor began to fit it to the side of Sky's belly and a trace began with a regular beeping on a monitor to the side.

The doctor looked at the signal and frowned. Then he hit the unit. It didn't appear to make a difference. He turned back to Skyler, who tensed suddenly and let out a cry of pain.

'How frequent are the contractions?'

I felt so stupid. Should I have been timing them?

'Sorry, I don't know. I've never done this before.'

I moved to the side to make more room for the doctor to inspect her.

'She's hardly dilated. She shouldn't be in this much pain.'

I held Sky's hand. She squeezed mine hard, gritting her teeth.

The doctor spoke to me in a low, private tone.

'Is the baby healthy? Did the last scan show up any problems?'

'I don't know. She never had the scan, we were attacked. She seemed fine until today.'

I suddenly remembered us running in the rain, turning the corner at high speed, nearly tripping and slamming into the wall. *Oh God...*

I explained to the doctor. He looked uncomfortable.

'Could the baby have been hurt by that?'

'It's possible. It certainly won't have done it any good. But polyhydramnios isn't caused by injury, and it builds up over weeks. I'm concerned. It's isn't just polyhydramnios. The EFM—this thing, the baby's heart monitor—is giving an unusual signal. It's too slow. This could be complicated. I don't want to order a caesarean until we know what we're dealing with. *Steph, book me a dMRI. Urgent please. Five minutes.* We'll make do with an echograph in the meantime.'

Officer Duggan appeared in the doorway. She looked concerned, bless her. I've no idea what kind of expression I was wearing on my face, but she was kind enough to come over and offer some words of comfort to me. I moved away again to let the doctor start the ultrasound scan. I felt like I was just a nuisance here.

'What is going on with these machines today? Sir? Officer? If you have radio communications devices could you please switch them off?'

I tapped my earcom off. Duggan had already turned off her police radio.

The doctor called out to the nurses through the door of the room.

'Can you find out whoever it is that has their com switched on and *throw them out*, please?'

He sounded deeply pissed off. There was a flurry of activity outside in response. He hissed to himself:

'Jesus, this is a frickin' hospital.'

The screen in front of him lost its interference patterns and showed a grainy snowfield, barely more meaningful than before.

'*Thank you.*'

The gel looked cold smeared over the tight, pale skin of Sky's belly. Sky was oblivious to it. She was concentrating hard on managing the pain.

Variations in the grainy black and white snow appeared on the monitor as the scanner slid over Sky's bump. The Doctor moved it slowly. His eyebrows were knitted together in confusion. He grunted but said nothing. I tried to pick out a shape in the snowstorm but the image on the screen meant nothing to me. Echographs had always seemed a little like Rorschach ink blot tests. Proud mothers showed the first pictures of their unborns and if you screwed your eyes up and tilted your head you could just about see what you were expected to. You smiled and said, 'It's got your nose!' and they said that was the scrotum or something and then you decided it was safer to shut up and smile and nod approvingly.

The screen went jagged with interference again. The doctor cursed loudly.

'WHO IS USING A FRICKIN' COM IN HERE? TURN IT OFF!! *Steph? How are we doing with that MRI?*'

A voice came back over the speaker:

'Apparently she failed her pre-test last time. Metal. MRI's out. Wanna CAT?'

'Just my luck. *Yes. How long?*'

'*Twenty?*'

'*Have to do. Thanks. Get an Ob surgeon ready, we may have a section.*'

He turned back to me:

'She may have pins from a previous injury. We have to wait for a CT scan. I'm gonna give her something to stop the contractions, until we know they're not damaging the baby.'

The doctor pulled out a small cream-colored device with a screen and pressed a button on the side.

'Polhydramniotic. Severe, acute pain. Zero to one centimetre dilation, zero effaced. Possible breech. I wanna administer a tocolytic. Risks against terbutaline, ritodrine, and isoxuprine.'

The unit spoke back:

'Recommend 100 mils indomethacin, 80 micros ritodrine and 20 micros guanitaximol, administered I.M. Risk profile 3.'

'Okay, prep it.'

There was a pause.

'Ready.'

He held the device tightly against Sky's bicep, where it hissed for a second. Moments later the tension in her face began to melt. She let out a groan in relief.

'She's gonna be fine. Just fine.'

I felt the drugs work their magic by proxy on me. I felt something else too, a dusty unfamiliar emotion trying to return from exile. Instinctively I closed the city gates against it.

The doctor straightened himself. 'I'll be back in five minutes. She should be fine, but if not, hit that button.'

Duggan's face was full of concern. I decided she hadn't just been playing good cop, she was genuinely a good person. I also realized that she must have assumed I was the father. I stroked Sky's hand. She turned to me and gave me a strange smile. The doctor came back with a male and female nurse.

'Okay, we're going to take her to the scanning area now. There's a waiting area over there.'

I waited for Sky with Officer Duggan sitting on the same butt-numbing chairs I had waited on when I'd brought Skyler here the first time. Duggan had been pretty quiet until now. I decided it might be wise to get to know her a little if she was going to be asking questions again once the baby was born.

'You enjoy your job?'

She shrugged, cocked her head and pouted in a way that suggested she did, but that she didn't want to make a big deal of it. Especially to a man she'd helped intimidate in an interview not long before.

'That Bryant seems like a hoot.'

She defended him gently.

'He's just doing his job. It's a difficult one. He's not a bad person.'

'Yeah, I guess.'

'You haven't exactly been helpful. It makes you look suspicious.'

'I have a... is that thing still on?' I asked, indicating the glittering eye nestled in the badge of her cap which she now cradled in her lap.

'No. I had to turn it off. Why? Are you planning on spinning me something?'

I laughed.

'No, I just don't necessarily want this on record. Listen, I didn't want to be obstructive. It's just...'

I paused to make sure that she knew I was letting her into my confidence.

'I have a history—nothing to do with this, mind, and all over a long time ago—but I wouldn't get treated fairly. I'm just trying to protect myself.'

'Mister Steel. We're trying to help. You have to trust us.'

I wished that there was an honest story that I could have told her and Bryant that wouldn't have put me straight back in care.

Nothing was going to put me back there. Nothing.

'It's just "Steel". It's hard to trust people. But I trust you. Not Bryant, I don't know why. But I trust you.'

I was glad that the lie-cam was off. I didn't trust her as far as I could spit a rat.

Suddenly from the scanning room I heard raised voices. A door banged open and shut, loosing them into the corridor, fractions of sentences. A nurse ran past me looking extremely unnerved. I jumped to my feet and ran to the scanning room door, but I was pushed back again by a technician coming out.

'Sir—*no*, sir, you can't come in here. *Sir?*'

'My friend is in there. What's going on?'

'Everything's fine, sir, please go and sit down.'

'Everything is *not* fine. Don't give me that shit. What's going on?'

Another technician arrived, in the doorway. Beyond them, I could here two people arguing.

'—*fuck standard procedure. What fucking standard does this come under?*'

'*What, so you say we just leave that in there? It's a fucking—*'

The technician pushed forward, pulling the door closed behind the two of them.

'Sir, I—please sit down.'

'*Tell* me what's going on.'

'*Officer?* Please ask this gentleman to sit down.'

'She's my—' I began, but realized I had nothing to say. She wasn't my wife, my girlfriend, my sister. Or my client. She was just a girl, who'd been dumped on me. I finished with the only word that remotely fitted: 'friend'.

Duggan was behind me. She took my arm gently.

'Mr Steel...'

'*Don't* call me that,' I snarled, still facing the technicians. 'My name's *Steel.*'

'Steel. Come sit and wait. Let the doctors do their job.'

'Your friend's gonna be just fine, sir. Please sit down. Officer? May I have a word please?'

I couldn't believe this. He was going to speak to her and not me. I was about to raise merry hell when Sky was wheeled out on a bed into the corridor. She looked fine. A little frightened, but not in pain. Her eyes implored me to do something, but I was helpless.

I followed the nurses wheeling her back to her room, leaving Duggan and the technician to talk.

The nurses pushing the bed were speaking to each other in indignant voices as if Skyler wasn't there, bitching about whoever had instructed them to move the bed: they weren't *porters.*

'Apparently, they're buying one of those fancy Honda iNurses next month. Three hundred thousand dollars. For a years' salary they get a nurse that never sleeps and lasts for decades. You can see where this is going. We'll all be redundant in a few years' time.'

I got a look from one of them as if I were the latest nuisance in a string of today's inconveniences, before they both stalked out of the room to ignore another patient. I looked forward to the day I could get my nursing care from a robot.

'Are you okay?' I said to Sky.

She nodded. Then her lips twisted down and started to tremble and she burst into tears.

'What's going on? Please tell me, Skyler. Is the baby okay?'

She had nothing to say but sobs.

Duggan called to me from the doorway. Her face looked gray. Behind her was the doctor who had ordered the scan. His expression was grave. I realized I didn't even know his name. I checked his badge. It said: Doctor Corello.

'Mister Steel. May we have a word please?'

Skyler's sobbing intensified.

I felt torn. I wanted to help Skyler, to comfort her. Where was their compassion? Everyone was treating her like an animal. She was a patient, for goodness' sake.

I squeezed Sky's hand and told her I'd be back in a second.

I walked with Doctor Corello and Officer Duggan around the corner into a private room. Corello scratched at his head through his hair, searching for words.

'Are you going to tell me what's going on?' I demanded.

'We were hoping you might be able to tell us.'

'For Christ's sake. Is the baby okay or not?'

Corello looked at Duggan. 'I guess that answers your question.'

She pursed her lips and frowned at the floor.

Doctor Corello looked at me levelly.

'Mister Steel. Skyler isn't pregnant. She's carrying something. But I can tell you quite categorically, it *isn't* a baby.'

From the pages of Tony's diary:

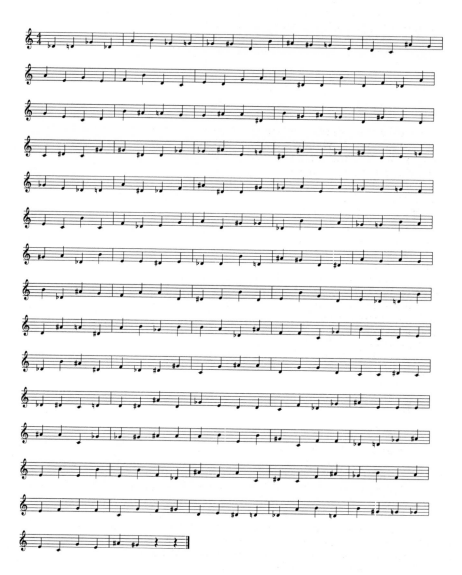

Chapter 10

'It is important to point out that Information Relativity is not intended to be a new interpretation of Quantum Mechanics, rather Quantum Theory may be derived from it.'

—*Information Relativity and the New Physics*,
Professor Fabrizio T. Luciano

I sat still, nursing the pain in my arm, the residual pins and needles in my hand, trying to fit what I had just experienced into some hole in my mind that would take them. Nothing was the right shape. The club room seemed more dark and damp than before. Strange patterns danced across my visual field, disappearing whenever I tried to look at them.

'The mirror was clear again,' Vaughan said, seeming to direct this comment specifically at Jon. Vaughan's voice was cautious and the knit in his eyebrows told me that he found this deeply unnerving, a reaction I found hard to understand given the rest of the situation.

'What does it mean?' Lewis whispered.

'The *jack-in-the-box*?' asked Vaughan obscurely.

'Exactly,' replied his twin.

The jack-in-the-box would take on its own appalling connotations soon enough, but at that point it meant nothing to me. Emily looked almost as confused as I felt. I looked to Jon for an explanation but he was glaring at the twins and deftly moved the subject into different territory:

'What you just experienced was more than just a dream, Zeke. Let me ask you a question. What if there is no objective reality?'

'What are you talking about?' I said angrily. A profound fear chilled me. A belief that my entire existence was founded upon was being attacked.

'What is reality over and above what we *agree* we experience?' Jon said.

I looked at him, horrified.

'What if we could find a way to change our agreed experience, to find a different interpretation... we all agree we just experienced something... a hallucination perhaps... but the same hallucination. Was it therefore not *real*?'

'It was a dream,' I protested desperately. 'Just a dream.'

'He still doesn't get it. Show him more,' said Vaughan.

Emily extended a flat palm out and up, as if she were holding something.

'A flame,' she whispered. The others stared at her hand and to my enormous surprise the flickering patterns in my eyes began to coalesce. I saw the air above her hand begin to shimmer as though from heat, and a lick of dark shadow whipped itself turbulently ceilingwards. It was smoke. I heard a small, soft explosion and the air above Emily's hand was suddenly brilliant with light.

84

'To me,' Lewis said, and extended his palm out horizontally. The flame seemed to hear the call as if it were alive and began to shed itself, dripping like liquid towards his hand, catching there; and then, as if a threshold had been reached, the whole body of the fire fell sideways into his palm, where it flickered in silence. He snaked his hand in the air and the flame followed like a hypnotised gaze, moving over the tips of his fingers and back again.

Vaughan began to name colours and the flame shifted through the spectrum at his bidding.

Lewis offered his palm to me. The flame was green and blue now.

'Take it, it's not hot.'

I extended my own palm cautiously, testing for heat. There was nothing. It was pure light. The flame flickered and shifted on to my palm from his.

'Look inside it, tell us what you can see,' Emily said.

I looked into the dancing flames. Nothing.

'Use your imagination.'

I began to see a naked female form dancing in the flames. The flames seemed to coalesce around her, not clothing her, but forming her, so that she was entirely made from fire and light, and the flame itself was gone.

'Nice,' Vaughan said approvingly.

'Anyone we know?'

The tiny flame girl in my hand moved seductively, a lithe conflagration, a luminous, three-dimensional silhouette. Her incandescent hair moved from her face and I saw in that moment from the shape her nose, the angle of her cheekbones, that it was Kate.

Startled, I moved back, and the image vanished into a shadow of black smoke that was gone before it reached the ceiling.

Lewis snorted in amusement. I was left blinking in astonishment.

'You like our magic?'

'What... *is*... this?'

'Illusions perhaps,' Jon said. 'Shared hallucinations. Maybe more...'

'But... how?'

'Honestly? I have no idea. This drug's properties are the perfect opposite to the effect I had intended. It was supposed to *inhibit* hallucinations in cases of schizophrenia by correcting configuration anomalies in neuronal microtubulin, and I discovered it... well, allows people to share them instead.'

'But how is that *possible*? That's not possible. It's like... I mean, our minds would have to be communicating somehow.' My mind seemed to rise up like a wave, a tsunami in protest at what I was being force to understand. This simply did not fit.

'Only if reality causes experience,' Vaughan interjected. 'What if it's the other way arou—'

'No. No *way*. This is something else. You've... you've messed me up. That's what you've done.'

'Hey. Calm down. We all saw what you saw, okay?'

I began to tremble and shake.

'Hey. Hey hey*hey*, calm down, mister. It's okay.' Jon moved towards me swiftly and put his arm around my shoulder. 'Look, you're the physicist, I'm just a biochemist, a neurologist. I don't have an explanation. I don't know how this works, maybe you can figure it out. Like Tony. There's always a rational explanation. Right?'

Emily was looking at me without sympathy and with quite some distaste at my reaction. She clearly didn't understand what I found so difficult about this. I put my forehead in my hands and massaged my eyes with my palms. I ran my fingers up into my hair pulling down on the locks for comfort.

'What's the deal with him, man?' Lewis said. 'Jesus, if he can't handle this, what's he gonna be like on a long trip?'

I sensed Jon look up sharply at Lewis, who instantly fell silent.

'Tony said it wasn't about communication. He always said they were more than illusions. It was about agreeing the interpretation. Does that make sense?'

I shook my head.

'He said that reality, our reality, was just an interpretation of something deeper. Meta, that's the name I give the drug, it gives access to different interpretations, allows us to find a new common interpretation. Tony said something about forcing wave functions to collapse in a particular way. I never really understood what he meant. Do you see?'

'No.' Hearing my own voice, it seemed small and sad.

'Okay. Well, there's *nothing* to worry about. You should be *excited* by this. Think of how *big* this is, Zeke.'

But I *was* worried. Jon's explanation about shared hallucinations was quite at odds with his talk about reality. Quite disturbingly at odds. Were we dealing with illusion or reality here? I wasn't so sure I still knew the difference.

'After a trip, when we're still high, and alone, we can do stuff like this. But it doesn't work if too many other people are around. Even in nearby rooms. That's why we meet down here.'

'That's not true.' I shook my head. 'Emily did. In the JCR, and on the stairs.'

'She has a particular knack. But she still needs one of us around for it to work. We're trying to work that out. What it means.'

'You don't understand how this works? And you don't think that's *dangerous*?'

'All science is dangerous, Zeke. All discovery.'

'He's *just* like Tony,' Emily said, smiling now and shaking her head almost sadly. I wasn't sure what kind of smile it was exactly that she was wearing.

I lifted my palm again and inspected it.

'Wanna see her again?' Lewis teased. I dropped the palm quickly.

'No,' I said. 'I want some fresh air.'

My initial shock at what I had experienced in that first club meeting did not last for long. The human ability to adjust to novelty and wonder is essentially limitless, and with good reason: if it were not, how could we go about our daily business? We would be stopped at every moment if we were not able to render mundane the quotidian miracle of existence.

Jon wanted me to wear the blindfold again on the way out, but I refused. He said he still wasn't sure of my allegiance, given my reaction, but I said I was fine. It was just new; I just needed time to get used to it. He needn't have worried about the blindfold. The tunnels were dark and labyrinthine and I could not have found my way back to the room unaided a second time. We exited, to my surprise, not from the Southside entrance, but from a loading bay behind the chemistry building. Emily, Lewis and Vaughan took different routes, splitting off from us whilst still underground. Jon insisted that it was important that we were never seen together outside as a group. He didn't want people to be able to link us. The link between us was on our wrists, or in my case, was about to be.

'Now?' I said, surprised at the urgency of Jon's demand.

'Yes, now. It's the final part of your initiation. Why would we wait?'

I felt nervous, but after what I had just experienced, what was a mere tattoo?

On the way, I challenged Jon on what he had said about not being seen together. I pointed out that we had been seen together frequently, and that he was still with me.

'You're different.'

'How?'

'I can explain my relationship to you through work. Hanging out with Emily just looks weird. And Vaughan and Lewis too. They attract attention. Even so,

it would be best if we weren't seen hanging out too much after this. You never know who's watching. That display in the JCR could have been the end of us.'
I remembered how desperate she had seemed there.
'What's the deal with her and you?'
Jon frowned and tutted at me, as if I'd said something distasteful.
'She's confused. She thinks she's in love with me. Sometimes.'
'What?! She was all over Vaughan.'
'Oh, Christ knows how that girl's mind works. She thinks it will make me jealous if she fucks him. Or his brother, or both. I just let her get on with it.'
We walked into a place full of metal piercings and tattoo designs. My eyes were being opened in every direction. A young woman with bright purple dreadlocks did my tattoo, copying exactly the design of the ornate oval hand-held mirror that Jon gave to her on a printed sheet. The pain was severe, and it seemed as if the process would never be over, but I hid my suffering. I did not want Jon to think I was going to be a continual liability, a scaredy cat, afraid of his own tail. I was in now, here for the ride.
We left the shop, and then Jon left me, content that I had the mark; my loyalties were inked under my skin. He explained that we would meet again soon when we would go on an extended trip. In the meantime, I was to attend lectures as normal and wait for him to contact me. I should tell no-one what I had experienced. I had to understand that a drug like this would be of the highest importance to any government, and that breaking this rule of silence could potentially put all of us in grave danger. I had to understand that. *Did I?*
Yes, I thought. Yes, I did.
That night, I sat on the edge of my bed in my room in the dim light of the table lamp, and I stared at the wall. My wrist throbbed underneath the crêpe bandage I had wrapped around it. I still did not feel normal. I thought back to the strange day, the dream-like trip in a room exactly like the one we had been in; the mirror; Emily placing her hand through it; the group hallucinations afterwards. In the dim light I held out my hand and tried to conjure a flame with the image of Kate inside it. I don't know if what I saw was simply a memory, but momentarily the image of her seemed to come alive in my hand before vanishing again. It stubbornly refused to return in the next attempts I made and finally I leaned over to one side, exhausted, and fell asleep in my clothes.
I attended lectures in the days after with a sense of dislocation. The subjects seemed dry and unrelated to me. All with one exception: my quantum mechanics lectures. The spooky behaviour of particles in the quantum domain and the tantalising and dubious link they seemed to have with the observer, with the conscious mind, intrigued me even more than usual. I felt certain that this mysterious science could be the key to understanding the drug that Jon had stumbled across.
The small tattoo soon scabbed over and I was able to wear my watch over it with a plaster to protect it from rubbing. I wore it around the campus, deriving confidence from it, as if it were a magic rune inscribed into my flesh, and when I attended my tutorial that week, I sat with a new boldness burning in me, bolstered by the burning mark under my watch.
I was certain that Kate noticed the difference in me. I answered questions confidently, not always correctly, but I saw that she looked at me differently (darkly seductive, Persian eyes). I smiled at her, and she smiled, slightly nervously, and looked away. I left that tutorial feeling more happy than I had since I'd arrived.
Two days later, Jon found me again, and told me that there would be a club meeting that night. I should meet him just before six by the library. I waited in the cold and dark, watching the light of the library through its glass-walled entrance and listening to the wind in the trees behind me, the constant wash of traffic from the nearby road. Across from me, across the Queen's Lawn stood the

Queen's Tower, the place of Tony's final moments. I considered the meaning of 'place' in the framework of spacetime, Einstein's legacy. Tony had died, ended, at a point in spacetime nearly a half a year from here. Half a year in spacetime is a long way. It's half a light-year. No, this was not his endpoint. Just as I was not the boy I had once been, but a pattern that held something in common with that boy, this place was not the location of Tony's death, it was merely somewhere that looked the same.

Jon startled me, I was so lost in thought. He was wearing dark clothes and I had not seen him arrive. He was carrying a small thermos flask.

'Follow me. I wanted to get back in by the loading bay, but it's closed already. We'll have to go in another way.'

'How many entrances do these tunnels have?'

'More than thirty, but some of them are permanently locked, or open out in places where you'd be caught immediately. We try to use different ones so it doesn't look suspicious. We don't want to be seen always hanging around the same places. But some entrances are easier than others.'

'How the hell am I supposed to learn my way?'

Jon handed me a thick folded piece of paper.

'Don't open it here. It's not entirely up to date, but it's mostly accurate. Keep it secret and safe. The first few times I'll be with you, after that you find your own way in. Cool?'

'Cool.'

I pocketed the tunnel map in my coat and followed Jon around the building.

'Where are we going?'

'Inside the library.'

Jon tapped on a glass door to get the attention of a browser. The student looked up and frowned. Jon mouthed some words and the boy reluctantly stood and opened the side door for us, pushing down on the fire-bar that kept the door closed to outsiders.

'You're supposed to use the main entrance,' the student said, annoyed at having been disturbed.

'Oh yeah, I know but it's freezing tonight. Short cut. You know? Cheers.'

He seemed to accept this and left us to study again.

I followed Jon deeper into the library.

'Why didn't we go in the main entrance?' I whispered.

'Because a) you have to swipe in, and we're not going to swipe out again, and b) there's a video camera at the main entrance so they could easily show us entering but not leaving.'

The library was bright and well lit, rows of densely packed shelves contrasted starkly with white walls. We went to the silver doors of the lift, but instead of taking it, Jon led me down some white stairs to its right. At the base of the stairs a corridor led off into what seemed to be a storage floor. Ladies' and gents' toilets were signposted further down the corridor. Jon motioned for me to follow him into the gents.

The smell of bleach blocks from the urinals hit my nose. There were only two urinals, but the cleaner had piled small pyramids of yellow bleach blocks into each of them. To the left was a large cubicle with a handicapped sign on it. Jon pushed open the door and we entered. I saw that there was another small door inside on the main wall. It was marked with a warning sign. *Strictly No Admittance. Service Personnel Only.*

'Take out your map,' Jon said in a low voice.

I retrieved the map and unfolded it. The paper was a dirty grey, the ink a blurry blue. The paper had turned blue at the folds. I saw a dense schematic of interconnecting tunnels. Meaningless symbols marked various points. I felt anxious seeing how complex it was. How was I to learn my way? Jon began to explain, half whispering:

'We're here, at this entrance. The club room is here—I've marked it for you—which means we have to go there first, climb down the service shaft and then make our way here. See? That length there is basically the length of Prince Consort Road. That's the Natural History Museum. This bit's all under Hyde Park. And that entrance there leads into the Albert Hall, but don't get any ideas, it's always manned and usually locked.'

'Jesus, it's massive. Why don't the museums use the tunnels?'

'Who said they don't? I told you, be careful. Our bit isn't in use any more, but all that area there is. We need to go from here, over to there. There's a connection between these two tunnels here.'

I saw a small empty square and the letters QT.

Queen's Tower. So, there was a secret entrance to the tower after all.

Jon traced our path, confirming my suspicion that he had taken me a deliberately circuitous route on my first trip to the club room. Nonetheless, without the map, I would have difficulty ever finding it again.

Jon took out a credit card and deftly unlatched the door with it. It swung open, revealing a small service tunnel ending at a T-junction which opened into a larger tunnel. The space inside was dark and cloying. I could hear the distant thrum of some machinery. Warm stale air brushed my face, invaded my nostrils. Jon pulled the door closed behind us and it shut with a click.

The only light seemed to come from the door that we had just used.

Jon spoke in a low voice:

'This is a way in only. You can't open the door from the inside without a key. We don't have one.'

'I can't see a thing.'

'Your eyes will adjust in a second. There are service lights in most of the tunnels further down.'

We moved in silence to the T-junction, where Jon listened before progressing. He whispered to me.

'Always listen out for maintenance staff. They're most common near entrances and exits, and near the main pumps. You'll see on the map where those are, but they can be anywhere. It's quieter at night, but there's never any guarantee. If you get caught, just play dumb student and plead with them not to report you. You'll probably get away with it, but it's not worth the risk.'

I nodded and followed him.

We moved like silent rats through the tunnels, turning into larger or small ones at Jon's indication. He seemed to know them intimately. Finally, we arrived at the formless grey door of the club. Jon inserted his key, and once inside presented me with my own copy of it.

'Lock it. Remember the rule. Always locked whether in or out. If anyone ever knocks on the door, ignore it and stay silent. Don't turn off the lights or make any noise. Just stay silent and they'll go away.'

I locked the door. Lewis was already inside. Emily and Vaughan arrived together. I noticed Emily watching Jon for a reaction at their joint arrival, but he offered none. She seemed to notice that I was watching and challenged me with an aggressive glare.

The room seemed to be more tense than the last time. Jon was fiddling with his thermos flask in the corner of the room behind the pillar. Vaughan broke the silence in a low voice:

'You cooked up another batch?'

Jon murmured an affirmative.

'How come? We had enough, didn't we?'

'There are more of us now. Didn't know how much was left. Besides, I don't like to use an old batch if we don't have to. I have no idea how long this stuff stays fresh for.'

Lewis began to tie the blue elastic tourniquet around his forearm.

'Let's do it.'

'One moment.'

We waited whilst Jon warmed up the liquid to a temperature warm enough to be injected into our veins, and then, one by one, with the tiniest of violations we gave up our reality and slipped away into something other.

This time, when I pushed through that strange boundary, I understood and appreciated more clearly what a gift I had been granted. I wondered how many people, most especially physicists, string theorists, might try drugs if they knew that it was possible to personally experience more than three physical dimensions. Indeed, how many had already?

I was back in the club room. One moment I had been something indescribable using my own limited language, and the next, I was back again, solid, three dimensional. Something was lost in the transition, but it was impossible to know what, just as it was impossible to truly remain human when I was being in that other domain.

Lewis was already waiting for me, he was stood facing the full-length mirror on the wall. He reached out. His fingers touched their own reflections. Solid.

'It's not clear this time.' His disappointment carried across a great wind.

'What makes it clear?' I called, hearing my own voice strange as if in a gale, yet the wind was silent whenever we were.

'We haven't figured that out.'

Were we speaking aloud back in the real club room? Was that how we communicated? Was it like sleep talking, with our imaginations filling in the rest? Was that the reality beneath this illusion?

When I turned the others had arrived. I never once saw them arrive in all the trips we took. Even if I was looking in the right direction, they would appear without a sense of change, suddenly simply there, as if I had merely failed to notice them before.

'The mirror isn't clear this time.' I said to Jon.

'It usually isn't.'

'I *love* it here,' came Emily's voice. When I turned to look she was lying against the ceiling, stretching out like a cat, defying gravity.

'Never had a flying dream, Zeke?' Vaughan asked me. He put both of his hands up and grabbed onto thin air, pulling himself up by nothing. He let go and floated, but I could see he was straining to maintain the position.

An ancient memory murmured to me. I knew how to do this. I tensed my mind, and lifted myself up to the ceiling, pushing my body flat against it like Emily. Exhilaration flooded through me. I twisted round to see her. The others began to float up to the ceiling too and suddenly we were all laughing.

'This is *amazing*!' The word, hopelessly inadequate.

'You haven't seen anything yet, come,' said Jon and landed gracefully back on the floor in front of the club door.

'Can we go outside? Into London?' I thrilled at the idea of flying over the Albert Hall, over Westminster.

Jon inserted his key into the club door and opened it.

I fell to the floor in surprise.

The door no longer opened out into a tunnel. I looked out onto a great desert of pure white sand under a bright electric blue sky. The sand burned under the blazing light of an invisible sun. The sky was banded with wisps of white cloud, but the sun was nowhere to be seen.

'Too harsh,' Lewis called out.

Jon closed the door and locked it. Then he unlocked and opened it again. I smelled something like engine oil. This time we looked out across a great and dark rolling ocean underneath a black and starless night. I felt the chill hand of fear grasp my stomach. I had an image of floating alone in that stretch of black water, with no land in any direction, no hope of ever being rescued no matter how far one swam. Jon closed the door again quickly, locked and unlocked it again—a cycle I would become familiar with.

Now, we saw out onto a great plain of white marble. In the distance, vast white pillars ascended into the sky as far as I could see. Jon cycled the door again. This time he revealed a small enclosed brick-walled space. I wondered if there were something beyond, or if this was a universe of infinitely stacked bricks, with a single hole at its centre. Jon cycled the door again: a swampy forest, with bubbling mud, vast trees and vines. It was absolutely devoid of any sign of animal life; the only sound was plopping quagmire, and wind through the foliage. Next: heat-cracked yellow mud plains that ran on for a great distance before stopping abruptly and falling away into an infinitely vast ravine under a purple sky.

We spoke in the low respectful tones normally reserved for churches:

'What are all these places?'

'Tony called them the Great Unseen,' Jon replied. 'Selections from the infinite set of places that have never been observed, the universes where life doesn't exist.'

'They're all lifeless?'

'The conditions to support conscious life are quite narrow. The vast majority we can never see, because we couldn't exist there. These places are fringes, places where we can exist, but animal life hasn't evolved. Many of them have plants.'

Jon tried to open the door again, but as he pulled it fractionally open, a shrill sound began to fill the room, and I felt a stir of wind.

'Shit. Vacuum.'

Jon quickly let the door close again with a bang, and cycled the lock.

He took a deep breath.

He opened the door again, this time on to a green and lush mountain range. In the distance I could see a great glittering lake. It looked like Earth, yet there was something slightly wrong with the scene that at first I could not fathom.

'This one looks alright,' Lewis said.

'Shall we explore?'

As soon as we passed through the door I understood what was wrong. It was the scale. It was as if the mountain range had been scaled down, built as a model for a movie. The mountains mere hills, hundreds of metres high instead of thousands. Yet the grass and plants covering them were normal size.

I turned back and saw the door that we had come through standing inappropriately in mid air. The back of it was just a solid rectangle.

Ahead of me Lewis began to run and then leapt into the air sliding up through it as if being pulled by a paraglider. He cried out, a cry of absolute freedom.

I ran and leapt too, feeling inside for my new skill, flexing it to lift myself up and into the air, but held myself only a few feet before sailing down again under gravity. I found that I could pull myself higher if I imagined hauling myself up on an invisible rope, but it was as strenuous to me as if I really were climbing and so I stopped and ran ahead up the green slope of one of the miniature mountains to look across the range. The mountains rolled like a toy plain, green and lush, and a series of lakes nestled between them. In the distance, a length of white cliffs ran across the horizon of unknown height. Emily and Vaughan flew in the distance together, like small birds. In the sky hung two fierce suns, each a tenth of the size of ours, but twins that burned brightly. Jon appeared by my side.

'What do you think?'

'I... I don't have words. So beautiful. So strange. It's like dreaming. To-gether. And we're awake!'

I noticed running down the side of the mountain there was a small set of concrete steps, perfectly regular, and with a blue and red trim that seemed to be made of plastic. Off to the side, near the top of the steps there was a hole, large enough to fit a man.

'Hey,' I pointed out the steps and the hole to Jon. 'That looks man-made.' We walked over together.

'We quite often find features that seem fabricated, but there are never any makers. In an infinite set of universes, everything exists somewhere. There's no such thing as creation. Just interpretation. We create these worlds ourselves by selecting them; I think that's why the features are so often familiar.'

I peered down into the hole. The inside was a smooth eggshell blue plastic that bulged and twisted organically, down and sideways through the mountain. A flow of crystal clear water poured along it.

'Shall we?' Jon offered.

I was afraid. 'We don't know where it leads to. It might be dangerous.'

'Zeke, this is our universe. We're in control here. If you don't like something, change it.'

Change it?

Jon smiled and before I had time to ask, he lowered himself into the running water and slid away out of view. I poked my head in to see where he had gone, but the plastic tunnel twisted out of view. All I could hear was the rush and gurgle of water.

'Jon?' I called. The name reverberated off the walls. I heard only the rush of water. I stood up and looked around for the others. Emily and Vaughan were dots in the distant sky. I couldn't see Lewis anywhere.

Moments later, I heard laughter and then Jon's voice calling me in the distance. I looked down the steps. They ran in a perfect straight line the hundred metres or so down the mountain. Jon had come out of a hole near their base. He scrambled upright and started up them.

'Try it! It's fun,' he called to me.

I leaned over into the hole again and tested the water with my fingers. Warm. *What the hell.*

I lowered myself into the water and let go.

The surface of the tunnel was smooth and twisted round, plunging me deeper into the depths of the mountain. There was no obvious source of light, yet I was never in darkness. I twisted and turned, surrounded by rushing water. The tunnel turned left and suddenly I dropped over a ledge into a deep pool of dark blue. Water went up my nose, but I was laughing. I began to tread water. Beneath me, under the water, the walls seemed in part to be made of something like sparkling diamond lit from behind by some unknown source. The water moved me slowly towards another tunnel mouth and I rushed over a lip and down another section of tunnel, crying out as I went, half in delight and half in fear. I twisted and turned again, forced flat onto my back by centripetal force, and I was thrown abruptly into the daylight again at the bottom of the mountain. The blue plastic fanned out and the water rushed off into shallow drains either side.

I stood up, dripping and with my heart pounding with uncertain emotion.

Jon had wandered off the side of the stairs and was looking out across our model mountain range. I ran up to where he was standing, finding to my surprise that by the time I reached him I was already dry.

'Where's Lewis?'

'I don't know, that's who I was looking for. He pretty much vanished as soon as we got here.'

'I saw him flying near the door. Maybe he's back there?'

We wandered back towards where the doorframe stood, but there was no sign of him. I looked around and saw that there was another hole in the side of the slope running away behind us. I walked over. It was a much larger hole than the other; ragged rock at the edges. It seemed more like a break in the ground. Looking inside, another surprise awaited me. The hole did not lead underground. Against all intuition, it showed a view onto another mountain range—an underworld. The mountains inside were black like coal, and rivers of molten lava flowed between them. A deep grey sky above them defied the laws of geometry by extending infinitely upwards beyond the grassy ground that I was stood on. I saw Lewis sliding down the sooty side of a mountain below me towards a hot red lava lake. He stopped and vanished into yet another hole in the side of that black volcanic scene beneath our feet.

I could feel heat on my face.

'He's in here,' I called to Jon, but when I looked up, I saw that Lewis had emerged from the side of a mountain up above and behind Jon and was floating down through the air towards him.

Without thinking, I lifted myself into the air and flew to join them. Only upon landing did I realise that I had flown without effort.

'This place is *weird*,' I said.

'I'm bored of this one, let's find another. We have time,' Lewis said. He put his fingers to his mouth and gave a shrill whistle to his brother and Emily. A distant return whistle confirmed that they had heard. I flew down to the edge of the nearest lake and looked into the crystal water for signs of life. The water lapped gently at the edge, clear as far as I could see, but it covered nothing but pebbles and rock. I saw no signs of life. I turned to see Emily and Vaughan landing like graceful birds up ahead.

'Let's go,' Lewis called. 'We're done here.'

I looked out to the horizon of this mysterious place and wondered what lay a thousand miles away. Perhaps a city? Was this a planet? Did the horizon curve around on itself as with Earth? Or would it run on forever, flat, without end? If Tony had been right, unless I visited these distant places they did not, in any real sense, exist at all. I could never know.

In a single buoyant leap I was back to the door and we left that world through our club room's doorframe, never to return to it.

Jon closed the door behind us. The club room seemed small and dim, and I had the peculiar sense that outside, surrounding it, the strange miniature mountain range was still there instead of the architecture of South Kensington.

Jon was about to cycle the door's lock again, but I put a hand to his elbow and asked him to wait.

'What did you mean if I didn't like something to change it?'

'You can fly.' He shrugged. 'You want to break the laws here, you can. Just a matter of will.'

He twisted the key. The door almost exploded open, pushing him backwards. I felt my ears pop painfully with a pressure change. All of us cried out in surprise, and pain.

'I hate it when that happens,' Lewis spat.

I could smell the sea, but there was no sea. There was a gentle hissing sound. We looked out into a grey void filled with iron cables criss-crossing vast distances, receding into the foggy distance. Everywhere I looked a constant drizzle rained down and I noticed that all of the cables seemed to be rusting. Perpetually rusting. I wondered what would happen when they rusted through. There were no obvious towers, or supporting struts, just miles and miles of browning iron, looping across the weeping grey sky at all visible heights.

Jon closed the door again. The next world was a heavy sea of some unfathomably dense liquid upon which floated huge boulders of rock, so closely packed that the sea itself was only visible through the crashing wave action which undulated the enormous rocks, causing them to grind and crack against each other noisily under a sickly yellow sky. The scene was inexplicably frightening. I urged Jon to cycle the door. The next cycle brought a great wooden structure in the midst of a vast expanse of sandless desert, each window threaded with what seemed like the enormous body of a snake, that slithered slowly through the entire building without tail or head ever appearing. The next appeared to be a vast white-grey corridor stretching out away from us under a peach pink sky, with walls a thousand miles high and no discernable features anywhere.

When Jon opened the door a final time, we looked out into what seemed like an orchard of apple trees under a moonlit night. The scene was almost monochromatic, the silvery moon rendering the trees argentine. The musical tinkling of many wind-chimes flowed out to us through the doorframe, and I picked up the vague scent of violets.

Jon turned to us, clearly seeing this world as a possibility and seeking agreement to explore it. After a silent exchange of glances and a shrug from Lewis, we agreed, and Jon stepped through the doorframe into the other world.

The gentle rippling chiming sound was all around me. It seemed to be coming from the trees themselves.

'Hey, come and look at this,' Jon called. We joined him as a group.

'They're all metal.'

They were. The trees and their fruit, all entirely made of metal. It was not the moon that had tricked my eyes after all, the trees were indeed silvery. Their silver leaves tinkled in the gentle breeze. The trunks seemed of twisted or wrought iron. And hanging from the trees were tarnished silver apples and pears, both fruit from the same trees.

I looked up into the sky. A huge silver moon, two or three times as big as Earth's hung in the sky. It was surrounded by a brilliant dusting of stars, a configuration that no Earth astronomer would recognise. I marvelled at the sight. This universe was connected to ours only by our consciousness of it, as if via a wormhole of awareness. Five twisted threads of silvery thought, each the breadth of a mind, entwined in sentient braid of shared experience.

I reached up to touch one of the apples. I tugged but the apple did not come, instead the tree protested musically. I pulled a little harder and twisted and the apple came heavily into my hand (cold and hard in my fingers), the branches of the tree bounced back, clanging and chiming.

You can break the laws here...

What if this were to be a pear instead? I wondered.

I looked at the apple, and willed it to change. It remained resolutely apple-like in my hand. But I was not to be deterred. I stared at the apple, and as I did so, I sensed that *it* and my *experience of it* were not different things. I understood in that moment what I had to do, what I had to *give up*, in order for the apple to be something else. Like the Necker Cube illusion, where a wire cube appears to invert without actually changing, the apple transformed into a pear in my hands—yet it had not changed at all.

The change had occurred in me, for we were one and the same thing.

I smiled at my new understanding. I put the pear in my jacket pocket.

'There are paths through the wood.' Vaughan traced a line out with his finger. The floor of the forest orchard was covered in a dark green grass, but there were dusty paths, that seemed well-trodden, tracing their way through the trees.

'They look like they're leading to the same place,' Emily observed.

'Come on.'

We wandered across the grass towards a path, stooping on occasion to avoid being scratched by the leaves. We walked on a while and through the moonlit forest, in the distance, I spotted something golden.

'Look!' I pointed.

We raced ahead and came upon a small lake of liquid gold. Four trees stood around the lake. Each tree had been carved down the length of its trunk and was slowly bleeding gold into the lake.

I put out a finger and caught a drop on my finger. It rolled off like mercury. Suddenly behind me there was a cry.

'Fuck fuck FUCK!'

Vaughan. He held a hand to his cheek. I saw blood through his fingers.

'I turned, I didn't see it.'

'Come here!' Jon called to the others.

Lewis and Emily joined him. Jon took Vaughan's wrist away from his face. The gash was dark but livid under the silver moon, and bleeding profusely.

Emily lifted a palm towards Vaughan but didn't touch him.

'We need to get him to a hospital,' I said. Disturbed by their apparent calmness towards the injury.

'Zeke?' Emily said, as if I were a stupid child. 'This is a *trip*.'

Everyone stopped talking and simply looked at Vaughan, concentrating.

'He's resisting it,' Emily said, turning, and indicated me.

'I'm not doing anything!'

Jon urged me:

'We can change this. You have to help.'

I nodded. I'd done it with the pear.

Afterwards I had the impression that Jon blamed me. Perhaps he was right. Perhaps I was resisting what they were trying, because no matter what we tried to force by will, the gash on Vaughan's face remained. Slowly, the blood coagulated of its own accord, but the failure of our efforts dulled the high spirits of the group.

'Why isn't it working?'

'I don't know. We've always been able to change things.'

'Have you ever tried to change part of someone though?'

'No. But what's the difference?'

'I don't know. Maybe... maybe we're off limits. Maybe we can only control things external to ourselves?'

Jon gave me a suspicious stare, but the conversation was brought to an early close. Suddenly I felt dizzy. The ground shuddered to the left under me.

'Uh oh. Time to go,' Jon said. His voice seemed to come from across a great wind, the way it had when we had first arrived.

'What's happening?' I asked, slightly afraid. My own voice also sounded strange. Jon almost had to shout:

'Trip's over. We have to get back to the club room before we come down.'

'The drug's wearing off?'

'Exactly. Let's go.'

The others were all running ahead of me. I trotted along the trembling path. It seemed to shift several feet all of a sudden.

I stumbled and fell. Panic consumed me.

What if I didn't make it back in time?

Forget the path.

I picked myself up and began to hurry across the shifting turf, ducking branches.

In the distance I saw the orange rectangle of the club room's doorframe, its incongruous contents.

The grass seemed alive beneath my feet now. The others were at the door already. I sprinted the last twenty metres, the last to dive through it. Jon closed the door behind me. We threw ourselves with relief on the beanbags and cushions. The room seemed smaller now, but safe.

I began to hear a buzzing sound again, like bees in the distance.

'See you back home,' Lewis said, over the sound of a rising wind.

I closed my eyes—I was unable to keep them open—and the universe receded away behind my eyelids.

Something like time passed, and I tumbled through states of consciousness impossible to describe, or even remember.

'Am I bleeding?' Vaughan had asked afterwards.

We'd looked at his cheek where he had cut himself. Of course there'd been nothing. I'd thought back to how I'd tried to explain the existence of those places to myself during the trip—as if they had been real. How stupid. Just shared hallucinations.

'No. You're fine.'

Jon put the key in the lock and opened the door.

I'd more than half-expected it to open into another bizarre realm, but it was the dim grey tunnel, weakly lit by the plastic lozenge of the service light on the wall. A small feeling of relief and safety descended. We were home.

As Jon led me back out through the tunnels, stopping briefly, occasionally to show me on the map where we were, I felt my elbow brush against something hard and heavy in my jacket pocket.

My heart thudded.

How could it be?

I put my hand slowly inside, my fingers prospecting almost in horror for the hard, cold metal touch of a tarnished silver pear.

They clasped around a something solid, rubbery. It was my torch.

I pulled it out and laughed in relief. I had completely forgotten that I had put it there earlier; the tunnels were dark.

'Be quiet,' Jon warned sternly. 'What are you laughing at?'

'Nothing. Nothing at all.'

The distant sounds of pumping machinery accompanied our soft footfall, our cautious breath, all the way out.

There were more trips, but just over a week after my initiation into the Looking Glass Club, I was accosted by Alexei's neighbour, Abby Cartwright, one night when I was returning to my room. Alexei and I had not spoken since he'd run into me outside hall in my hung-over state when I had rejected his attempts to apologise. I admit that although we had gone from spending every spare moment in each other's company to a flat zero, I hadn't given him or the situation much consideration. Jon Rodin, the Looking Glass Club, the drug meta, and the access it gave to what Tony Baijaiti had dubbed the *Great Unseen* had infected my every waking thought since my initiation.

Abby Cartwright lived on the same stairwell as Alexei. We'd met on a number of occasions before. She was a sociable, gossipy girl with a squeaky toy voice and a tendency to drench herself in a cloying, sickly-sweet fragrance such that one could detect her presence in a room for several hours after she'd left. I noticed the smell still clinging in the lift as I entered the building but didn't connect it consciously with her until I saw her milling anxiously near my room door.

'Oh, thank God!' she said, 'I was just about to give up on you. You have to come with me, quickly.'

'What is it?'

'It's your friend Alexei.'

Alexei? I rubbed at my fatigued eyes. I'd almost forgotten he existed. Excitement sparkled through the thin glaze of concern showing in Abby's eyes.

'I think he's been beaten up or something. He's on the roof of Linstead. He's really upset. I think he's planning to jump.'

we knew lewd emu...

64 h1,5 MO4: OAFV,6

Chapter 11

'I don't understand you,' said Alice. 'It's dreadfully confusing!'

—Through the Looking Glass

My mind raced over the words Sky had mouthed to me. *It's illegal.* I'd assumed she was surrogating for someone. Now here was Corello telling me she wasn't pregnant at all. *She's carrying something,* he'd said. *But I can tell you quite categorically, it isn't a baby.*

'Then what the hell is inside her?'

Doctor Corello put up two outstretched palms defensively.

'Ah... This is a matter for the police now.'

I turned to Duggan. She looked uncertain.

'I need to speak to Sergeant Bryant...'

Within twenty minutes, Skyler's room in the maternity ward had a police guard and I was even further from finding out what was going on than I had been. Duggan and Bryant had determined early that at this stage I was not in a position to provide information, and they were deep in discussion with the medics in the scanning room. I'd been told not to get in the way and not to leave. I would be questioned again.

Skyler had become hysterical when the police had turned up to question her further. Corello had sedated her and told the police to wait until she was medically stable before pursuing that line of enquiry any further. She was left to sleep for the moment.

I peered in through the narrow rectangle of glass to the debate happening in the scanning room, where the group, Duggan, Bryant, Corello and two technicians, were huddled around a screen, viewing images from various angles, pointing, speaking in low voices. I caught tantalizing, colorful slivers of the computer-generated model of Sky's womb glimpsed between their bodies, but I could tell nothing from them. Bryant spotted me peeping in and instructed Duggan to have me put somewhere I couldn't cause a problem.

I thought about just getting myself out of this mess, running somewhere, hiding, but I didn't want to leave Skyler. Whatever it was she was involved in, it involved me too. I decided to go outside, where I could switch on my com and see if I could find out any more for myself. I stood under the lit canopy of the hospital entrance beneath the dark sky and felt the cold wind bite at my face.

JR was unimpressed.

'Where have ya been? I've been freezin' my nuts off looking for ya. Do you know how hard it is for a dog to get a cab in this city?'

I explained that we'd been stopped by the police downtown and questioned, then Sky had apparently gone into labor, except now it turned out she wasn't pregnant in the first place. JR asked the same questions anyone would. I gave him the little information I had.

'Can you do a search for me? Find out if there's anything on the net that might give us a clue. Maybe, I dunno, contraband or smuggling. Maybe she's got five or six kilos of cocaine stuffed inside her. No, wait—there was a fetal heartbeat.'

I considered this for a moment. An unpleasant range of alternatives ran through my mind.

'I suppose it could have been faked easily enough.'

'I'll see what I can find.'

'Where are you?'

'At the office.'

'Okay. Any messages? Lewis? Needle?'

I caught the smell of burgers lifted on the wind from somewhere nearby and I realized I hadn't eaten for hours.

'No, nothing.'

'Okay, let me know if you turn up anything. I can smell burgers. I need to eat.'

I wandered round the corner following the smell. There was an ABM in the wall and a small line of people. It looked like a Mac in the Wall, but it wasn't, it was some new brand offering some eco-promise or other. I stood in line and waited my turn. The lady before me was served by a handsome, rather generic-looking waiter, but as soon as I stood in front of the screen, it recognized my gender and I was welcomed by a pretty 1950s-style burger bar waitress, eager to take my order. The image quality was good. I couldn't tell if she was CGI or a video edit. These days even low-budget graphic systems were becoming indistinguishable from real life. She was as realistic as one of my zombies. I resisted her seductive efforts to upgrade my order to something way beyond my stomach capacity. She beamed me a smile quite at odds with the nature of the transaction and my burger landed in the hatch underneath. She had even turned, fetched the burger from a chef behind and apparently dropped it into the hatch. The illusion was perfect and very smart. I knew the mechanistic reality of the burger's true provenance—the dark, hot machine behind the wall—but even knowing that, that slick image had fooled me into half-believing that it had been handmade and hand-delivered to me.

'Enjoy your meal! Thank you for shopping at Patty's Patty Palace!'

I took the bun into my freezing hands, relishing its heat, and took a bite, crunching though the pickle and salivating as the smell of clo-beef, ketchup and mustard rushed into my nose. Steamy breath rolled out in great coils between mouthfuls.

I wandered back to the hospital entrance, dumping the burger box into a trash can on the way, and stepped back into the warmth and light and the disinfectant smell. As I entered the lift, I thought I noticed the police guard that had been stood outside Skyler's room step out past me. I wondered what he was doing here. He looked confused. I assumed he'd been relieved, maybe on a break, but he'd been working for under an hour. Had there been a development?

I broke into a trot along the maternity ward corridor. There was no guard outside her room. I looked inside.

It was empty.

They'd moved her. Without telling me. I was livid.

I ran round the corner to the scanning room, scolded by a nurse for running and told to walk. I slowed to a trot and then came to rest in front of the door with its rectangle of glass. I peered inside. The scanner screens were now blank, but the group was still inside, still debating.

I pushed the door open.

'Where have you moved her to?'

'*What?*' barked Bryant, visibly annoyed at my intrusion.

'Skyler. Where have you moved her to.'

Bryant looked at Corello. Corello looked blank. Then Bryant was up and running and the whole group followed like startled gazelles, back to Skyler's room.

'Where the hell and damnation is Hagan?' Bryant was barking.

He demanded a hospital search and threw a few threats my way, as if I'd had something to do with this. He really wasn't doing well getting into my good books.

I told him I'd seen the policeman wandering on the ground floor.

By now Bryant and I were eager to blame each other for anything we could.

'If she's been attacked again,' I fumed, 'I'm going to hold you personally responsible, Bryant.'

Hagan was soon found wandering the ground floor by some nurses. Bryant's face was crimson with anger. His fists were bunched and trembling. I began to feel extremely grateful that I didn't work for him. I don't think I could have lasted more than a couple of days before I was charged with assault.

'Hagan? Where the *hell* have you been? Where's the girl?'

'I'm sorry?' Hagan said placidly. 'Who are you?'

From the pages of Tony's diary:

No ordinary game, yet one piece will reign...

1. Pa1 - Bxh8+
2. Pa1 - Pa1
3. Nf6 - Pa1
4. Pa1 - Rxc3+
5. Nxc6 - Qa1
6. Rb1+ - Pa1
7. Rf3+ - Nxe7
8. Qa1 - Pa4+
9. Pxa5 - Bb7
10. Pb3+ - Rg5+
11. Nf3 - Qb5
12. Re6+ - Rxg1
13. Qd6 - Qd8+
14. Ka1 - Bb5
15. Pb3+ - Rxa1
16. Rc3+ - Na3
17. Pxc6 - Qxe7
18. Pa3 - Rxa1
19. Pxa5 - Pa2+
20. Ra1 - Pg4
21. Pa1 - Qxa1
22. Pe3 - Pa1
23. Ka1 - Pd3+
24. Nxc6 - Kxa1
25. Pe1+ - Pa1
26. Ra1 - Pd1
27. Na2 - Bxh7
28. Pe1 - Pxe8+
29. Kf3+ - Pg1
30. Pf3 - Pa1+
31. Kc6 - Qd8+
32. Pa1+ - Rxg1
33. Pb1 - Pa1
34. Pxa1 - Na7
35. Pf1 - Pg1
36. Pa5+ - Na1
37. Pxb3+ - Ba4
38. Pa1 - Pd1
39. Pa3 - Rxh8+
40. Qxe6 - Qa2+
41. Kc6+ - Rxh5
42. Pa2 - Na1
43. Pc3+ - Na1+
44. Qa1 - Pb7
45. Pa1+ - Ra1
46. Pb2 - Qa1
47. Nxc1 - Pxh7
48. Pa1 - Pd8+
49. Ke1 - Pa1

Chapter 12

'Considering all possible permutations of this state system, we see that for any two states interpretable as temporal sequences and where the state change is greater than the minimum information quantum, it is always possible to find a third state between (in most cases between N and $N!$ states), with a lower implied speed and which gives rise to the same consistent history. A natural speed limit, c, thus arises as a direct consequence of the information quantum and related to the interpreted size of the universe. Since information itself does not truly travel at all, it always appears to travel at the same speed, c, to the interpreter.'

—*Information Relativity and the New Physics*,
Professor Fabrizio T. Luciano

Alexei? Suicidal? On the roof?

Abby's eyes shone like an evangelist after she'd delivered this news; she seemed almost hungry for my reaction.

'Have you called a warden?' I said, still in shock.

'No. I came straight to you. He was acting like he'd jump if people started interfering. I thought you were the best bet. He trusts you.'

'Who beat him up? What for?'

'I don't know,' she protested in a tone that for some reason suggested that she had a pretty good idea. 'I thought you might,' she added coyly.

In the lift, I wasn't sure which was going to suffocate me first: Abby's perfume or her constant interrogation ('Why would he react this way?' 'Does he have family problems?' 'Has he been suicidal before?' 'Did you notice those marks on his arms? I think he's a self-harmer. I've always thought he was a bit odd.') I demurred on all of these questions and practically gasped for fresh air when the doors finally released us onto the penthouse-level.

'Where is he?' I saw no-one.

Abby pointed to a small automatic fire door, beyond which a ladder led to the roof proper. I started to make my way up but Abby made no move to accompany me.

'Aren't you coming?'

One hand twisted nervously at a lock of hair, oyster-shell fingernails sliding through blonde silky strands.

'I don't think it would be a good idea. He doesn't seem to like me. I don't want to push him over the edge. No pun intended.'

As I passed the fire door I noticed that wires had been inserted into its electronic key, presumably by Alexei to stop an alarm ringing when the door was opened. I began to climb the ladder to the skylight. As I poked my head out, yellow light from below seemed to evaporate into the dark night. I gripped the edges and climbed out onto gravel and waited for my eyes to adjust.

He was leaning against the thick metal pipe that formed the horizontal rail protecting the edge, a deep grey silhouette against the dark tree tops, looking out into the gardens. He must have seen the light from the door but he didn't turn. He was in an odd pose, but there was nothing about his position that struck me as particularly suicidal.

'Alexei?' I said in my most careful voice.

He ignored me so I made my way cautiously towards him. The night was curiously peaceful. It was a crisp evening. Behind patchy clouds hung a gibbous moon, fat and gloating in the sky. The trees of Princes Gardens were dark giants. Their heads towered higher than the roof. The wind lazily tousled their leaves like hair. I heard a female giggle in one of the rooms below us, muted by a glass window. The giggle peaked into a squeal and abruptly cut off.

I turned around uncertainly and spied Abby's head poking out of the skylight.

'She's insufferable. Get rid of her,' Alexei said with the projection of a stage actor.

'Alexei! She can hear you. She's only trying to help.'

'You think so?'

He let this hang in the air for a while and continued to stare out on to the dark, foamy sea of rustling tree tops ahead.

'If she really cared she'd have called a warden. She fetched you instead. She's a busybody. The worst type of gossip. She's been dying to get some dirt on me since Freshers' Week.'

I eyed the doorway nervously.

'Well,' he proclaimed, 'now she has some.' His dark silhouette breathed heavily. '*God!* I think she actually bathes in that dreadful perfume. And those gold shoes? What is that about? I mean, really.'

Embarrassed, I turned to Abby, caught her attention, shrugged and mouthed an apology. Then: *Go, we'll be fine.* I wasn't sure how much she had heard. Thankfully, she didn't look especially hurt, just concerned. She didn't seem very inclined to leave.

'Apparently,' Alexei continued in a tragic tone, ' "gold goes with everything". It would bloody well have to given the choices she gives it.'

I noticed for the first time that Alexei's words seemed slurred. His left arm seemed folded in front of his body away from me.

'Are you drunk?'

'Shouldn't I be?'

'You don't drink.'

He turned his head finally and fixed me with a mean stare. His face was hardly visible against the dark background of the tree tops, but I could see the edges of his mouth turned down. In the dim light, the whites of his eyes seemed to glow preternaturally. His sarcasm ground knife-sharp edges on the words that he threw back at me:

'People change.'

At that moment the cloud cover slipped away above us and in a gauche display of riches the moon threw silver over the gardens beneath us, rendering the tops of the trees brilliant momentarily. Each and every leaf in that surreal sea suddenly stood out, ghostly bright, trembling and exposed in the cold breeze. I was reminded of the strange metal trees on our recent Looking Glass Club trip. At exactly the same moment, from somewhere below came a moan of passion. A moment later came another, and a regular rhythm began, beating out the basic tempo of love-making. I was forced to listen in silence with an awful sense of embarrassment noticing simultaneously what the moonlight had revealed. The vision remained for a few seconds withholding my breath by force until another greedy cloud swept by again, seeming to snatch away all the leaves and all the silver with them.

Alexei's face had been covered in dark patches.

The dark shadows of bruises. A black moon had curved underneath one eye in a parody of the silvery giant that exposed it. I noticed even now in the darkness how the edges of his silhouette showed swelling in his cheek and jaw line.

'Oh God... Alexei. What happened? Who did this to you?'

'Oh please. Don't pretend to care.'

He looked away sharply, staring hollow-eyed at the trees. I realised that Alexei's slurring might not be from drink after all. I felt a pang of regret at my words. He took a shaky breath and began to shiver. The couple in the room beneath began to get into an athletic stride, increasing in volume. I moved instinctively to him and put my arm around his shoulders. I expected him to either tense or to receive me, but oddly he did neither. I might as well have been a ghost. Instead, above the muted sounds of moaning, I noticed a whistling sound, a tight, high-pitched thing that seemed to come from somewhere else, so that I didn't realise it was coming from his throat. He too seemed oblivious to it. He juddered in a movement I took to be instinctive, but when it came again, and then again in a regular pulse that seemed timed with the love-making moans coming from beneath, that was when I noticed what he was doing. He wasn't looking at his actions, and that's why I didn't see them in the dark. The blade carved into the flesh of his forearm, gouging up little furls of his skin that suddenly stood out in silver relief in the light of moon, lines pooling black with blood. The sight made no sense with its odd silver and black colours. It was the sound I understood and that stayed with me (I can still hear it now, haunting my mind, decades later, that keening, empty whistle playing on top of moans of pleasure). It was the sound of part of someone's soul prematurely escaping in a whistle through a living throat. I couldn't understand his actions. He wasn't attacking his wrists. Yet, in spite of the gore of the sight, it was plain: he wasn't trying to kill himself. I knew from maths that two negatives could cancel; but I could not see how inflicting one pain could mask another worse one. I grabbed his blade hand when I saw the blood. There wasn't much, but still enough for me to feel sick anyway. He turned his wrist upwards, as if reacting to my challenge, seeming determined now to do more than self-harm. We struggled for long minutes in a tense wordless conflict accompanied only by the sounds of the increasing tempo of fucking beneath us—Alexei's determined self-destruction versus my compulsion to stop him.

The moans reached a crescendo; the couple climaxed in a surprising display of volume.

Silence.

The steel tension in Alexei knife arm suddenly went limp.

The blade clattered to the floor.

Alexei fell into my arms and without a sound began to weep.

Beneath I heard the girl begin to giggle again.

'Come on,' I whispered. 'Let's get you down.'

On the way out, Alexei pulled away from me for a moment and said something to Abby in the corridor out of earshot. Her face drained of colour and she ran downstairs visibly upset. He refused to answer my probing about who had attacked him on the way to his room. I could now see that his bruising was largely superficial. His skin was uncut, and yet the coverage on his face was surprisingly complete. I pondered this puzzle in silence all the way to his room.

Once there, I was afraid to leave him alone.

'I want to call the police.'

'No. Don't get involved. Please. You can't understand this. You think you'd be helping but really, you wouldn't. Believe me.'

I felt impotent.

'I'll be fine.' He fixed me with terrible, sad eyes. 'Thank you for doing that up there.'

We were sitting on his bed, my arm around his shoulder.

'Hey,' I said gently. 'It's the least I could do. When you're ready, you tell me what's going on, okay?'

He turned his bruised face near to me, and then without warning, he leaned in and tried to kiss me.

I flinched backwards in surprise. 'What are you doing?'

Something awful burned behind Alexei's brimming eyes.

He looked away sharply.

'I'm sorry. It was a mistake. Just go. Just *go*.'

Astonished, I stood up, and utterly unable to do anything else, I left.

I had little opportunity to consider events with Alexei. My focus was pulled sharply away from him again by several matters. Just a few days after my first forays in the Great Unseen, Jon tried to persuade me get my brother Jacob to join the Looking Glass Club.

'Are you mad?' I said, incredulous.

'Not at all.'

'He's completely against drugs. He'd have a fit.'

'So were you.'

'I...' Had no defence against that.

The simple truth was, the idea of Jacob joining the club was anathema to me. We had been getting along okay recently, yes, but Jacob had always taken everything good away from me. He'd always burned more brightly than me and stolen attention, even friends. I wanted this for myself. I belonged to something. It wasn't perfect, the people were strange, but they were my people. It was my club. If Jacob joined, I knew he would take that away from me too.

'Zeke, before the twins joined, the trips we used to have would be vague, fleeting things. No more than shared images, or sensations. We used to sit around and get fucked up and barely be able to remember what we'd seen. After Lewis and Vaughan joined us, everything became clearer, more real.'

'So?'

'We picked them *because* they were twins.'

A dreadful cold sensation filled me inside.

'It was Tony's idea, his theory about agreement. He reckoned that maybe twins, you know, being similar, having a similar way of looking at things, synchronicity, might make the effect stronger. He was right...'

Had Jon only included me because of Jacob after all? Was that why he had decided to befriend me? I felt sick. Worse, I felt debased, rotten. Worthless. Had I no intrinsic value in this world of my own? *None at all?* I took a shaky breath. Even my own breath tasted sour to me. I stared at the floor, unable to lift my eyes any higher. I felt weak, defeated. Dizzy. I remembered Jon's first words to me: *Are you Ezekial or Jacob?* He didn't seem to care which one of us it was.

Jon continued, oblivious to my tortured thoughts.

'I mean *think* about it. They're not even identical. They're heterozygous. You and Jacob are practically indistinguishable.'

I lifted my head sharply.

'You've met my brother?'

'I've checked him out. Yeah, of course.'

'Lewis and Vaughan are far more similar than Jacob and I ever will be.'

'That can't be true.'

'It *is* true. We're nothing alike. *Nothing.*'

'Zeke, we have to progress from here. We can't just stay locked in an underground room playing with illusions that no-one else can see. Don't you want to be able to do what Emily can? More?'

'How is Jacob going to change that?' I sounded like a petulant, whining child to my own ears.

'Directly, maybe he isn't, but the more we experiment, the more we can learn, and do. We need more agreement.'

'How come only she can do it around others?'

Jon shrugged. 'That's exactly what I want to find out. I have a theory.'

'What?'

'Emily's not quite as grounded as the rest of us. If you get my meaning. Never has been.'

'So?'

'It's easier for her to...'

'To?'

'To stray from the edges. To make it real for other people she needs a little bit of agreement from someone else. I.e. us. We give her visions a reality they would otherwise lack. I think we could all do it, but maybe we have a higher threshold than she does.'

'So Jacob joins,' I said, a sarcastic melody infecting my tone, 'and everything gets a little more concrete.'

As if Jacob were some kind of hero. I felt betrayed.

Jon looked at me askance, puzzled by the bitterness of my response.

'Maybe. Who knows. Don't you want to find out?'

I wasn't so sure that I did.

'Think about it. Okay?'

I said I would, but I already knew my mind.

Whether I wanted Jacob involved or not, he was going to be involved. And not necessarily because of any manipulations or coercions on Jon's part. Events would force us together.

They began with my mother dying.

He stole even her funeral from me, even my grief. Crying and wailing as he did, demonstrating how much he loved her (and thus the reverse), whilst I sat numb, unable to emote at all. I was just grateful that we had not had to organise the funeral. Jacob was a mess upon hearing the news, I became remote, even more so than usual. Uncle Ted and Aunt Lil ended up organising everything. 'They're just kids,' my mum's brother had said. And I supposed we were. Aunt Lil comforted Jacob and tried to comfort me also, but I didn't need or perhaps want comforting, not by her. Let Jacob take it all. I wanted nothing that he had soiled first for me. I just wanted to get back to the club. I wanted to be away from all this morbidity. I wanted my own private space where I could find time to mourn myself. I was not filled with grief when her body, boxed in that pallid wood coffin, passed behind the curtain. I was filled with a seething bitterness, at Jacob for stealing her, even now; at her for leaving without saying goodbye; at fate for taking her, at everybody for not *understanding* me.

The bitterness burned inside me, consuming my flesh from within until I felt light enough to float away. I glared at the hideous red curtains, the lurid, livid, blood-red, crushed velvet lips that had swallowed her so finally. I hated them. They should burn, the way I was burning inside. The way she would burn shortly, reduced finally to a pathetic pot of ash.

I could almost see the flames licking at the curtains, because fire was everywhere: inside me; burning up my mother at this very moment; fire was my life.

There was a cry from behind me.

'A fire! The curtain's on fire!'

Someone screamed. The shock of the sound shook me from my anger. I turned to look behind. Mrs Jolliffe, Mum's hair dresser, was pointing to the front. Even as I turned, she was breathlessly taking back the words, trying to eat them, so that her embarrassment would not eat her. 'Oh, how *silly* of me. I'm so sorry. But I was sure I saw *flames*. Oh dear me. Oh dear *me*. *Oh* dear me.'

The vicar was staring at the curtains, looking pale. He lifted the corner of one curtain and inspected it.

Later, at the wake, people laughed. Mrs Joliffe laughed. The vicar laughed. Of course, funerals are so funny that people laugh. They were delightful. I knew that. Jacob laughed. Oh! How *hilarious* it all was between the tears. He had cried, he was allowed to laugh. I knew that it was *okay* that my mother had died and I would never ever see her again, or be held by her, or have her kiss on my forehead, or make a fuss about whether I was eating properly, or call me and say she loved me, or be there when I needed someone just to know that I *had* someone, or say all the wrong things when I wanted her advice; and that she had been permanently deleted from my life by cancer, leaving behind just dusty clothes and cheap jewellery and belongings, a perfect mould of her, an exact Mum-shaped hole; it was okay to laugh about all that. Yeah, it was all *fucking hilarious*.

There was little to divide up. Mum didn't own the house, much of her savings went on the funeral and legal fees. I allowed myself to smile, if only slightly, only once during the whole charade. She had written a last will and testament, and she had instructed everything—what little she had—to be sold and the money to be divided equally between us. You see, Jacob? She loved me the same.

We stayed away for a week, and then returned to university.

'It's just us now,' Jacob told me, sad and serious on the train back. 'We have to stick together. We only have each other.'

Yes, I thought, you emotional parasite, now Mum's gone, I expect you need another host to live off. I turned away from him and watched the trees race leglessly by.

I regretted those thoughts later, they were too harsh, but I'd thought them and I couldn't un-think them. I consoled myself that at least I hadn't spoken them.

I slept fitfully all week, my nights filled with images of black claws, long articulated limbs reaching at me through the darkness, of running, being chased, trying to fly, to lift my legs away from the horrors that chased me, not quite able. I woke gasping, crying out on a number of occasions and turned on the light, lying in my loneliness, crying for Mum until the sun rose.

A few days later when Jon called a meeting of the club, it was almost a relief. He said he'd been looking for me and asked where I had been, but I decided that it was better to lie. I didn't want to have to go through the Morris dance of sympathy again, the choreographed steps of *now I say this, now you say that*. Jon seemed to be pissed-off with me for disappearing, but thankfully didn't say anything more. He asked if I had given more thought to inviting Jacob into the club. I said that now was not a good time. He had some family problems. Jon didn't question this, notwithstanding the implication that I too had family problems. He asked me if I was okay if I had to go to the club room alone this time. He might be slightly late. The thought of being in the tunnels alone wasn't pleasant, but I couldn't admit that. I said that it was fine. I had the map. I'd go using the Southside entrance in the nearby halls of residence.

I left early for the Club room, wanting to give myself plenty of time in case I got lost. My heart thumped. What if I was caught? With Jon leading I'd conferred that worry onto him, now it was mine alone. In spite of my anxiety, the journey through the tunnels was uneventful, although gloomy and a little frightening. I arrived twenty minutes earlier than I had agreed with Jon.

I quietly put the key into the lock and turned the key, opening the door silently. Jon was already in the room. He was kneeling with his back to me near the box that formed our makeshift sofa. He'd moved it away from the wall. My view was partly obscured, but I could see a hole revealed in the wall leading into a dark space. Jon was pushing something quite heavy back inside. It was metal sounding, singing slightly, sounding liquid-filled as it scraped over concrete. It reminded me of the sounds the portable blue gas bottles had made when we went camping as kids. He seemed to rearrange some objects in the space and then he carefully rotated a piece of dirty cardboard on a nail in the wall back into position over the hole, obscuring it, and then moved the sofa back into position again. I retreated and gently closed the door again. *What on earth was going on?* I waited a few seconds for my breath to slow before I opened the door again, this time deliberately making a little more noise.

Now, Jon was bent over the green plastic box that was always in the corner and contained the vials of the drug meta, and the equipment we used to inject. He jumped in surprise at my sudden arrival.

'Jesus H. Christ! You scared the wits out of me, man.'

'Oh. Sorry. Thought you were going to be late.'

He screwed the lid back on a thermos he was holding and closed the lid of the medical box.

'Er, yeah. I was. But it was okay in the end.'

I locked the door behind me and removed the key.

'You made another batch? Didn't you do that last time?'

'Er, no, no. Just brought some more liquid nitrogen. We were running low.'

I made a mental note to come back when no-one was here and find out what Jon was hiding in that hole behind the sofa. The conversation seemed awkward for a second, but then Jon smiled and sat on the nearest beanbag.

Emily turned up next.

'You're both early...' she said.

'I thought I might get lost so I gave myself extra time.'

Once Lewis and Vaughan had arrived, Jon began to prepare for the trip.

'Oh, I forgot to tell you,' I began. 'I did it on my own. I made someone see something on my own.'

I hadn't remembered the fire at the funeral until now. I knew at the time it should have been important to me, but it wasn't. Nothing was.

Everyone was suddenly interested in me. Emily looked distinctly disturbed.

'How?'

'I was upset, angry about something. I made flames appear. A woman saw them.'

Jon narrowed his eyes.

'When?'

'A week or so ago. While I was away.'

'Tell me something.'

'What?'

'Was you brother with you?'

How I resented him for asking that. I honestly thought I could take the credit for something, for just one thing on my own.

I kept his gaze.

'No,' I lied. 'No, he wasn't.'

Jon grunted. Perhaps he believed me.

Lewis took the first hit. Jon last. I before Jon. By the time Jon was injecting himself, Lewis had started to mumble something. A complaining sound. Then

Vaughan and Emily too. By the time I started to feel the effects, it was clear from the noises coming from the three of them that something was wrong.

I felt a sickness twist in my stomach, and a cold, wet sensation sweep through me, as if I had become a piece of soaked black rubber, lying on the ground. The room moved, and I groaned, feeling as though I were on a boat that had just taken a large dip in the trough of a wave.

We were not going under. We all remained terribly awake.

Jon swallowed and let out a breath and a noise. He'd gone pale too.

'What's happening?' Emily said, frightened.

'I don't know,' Jon said, in short gasps.

'Something's wrong,' Lewis said. And then, without warning, he vomited, spraying hot acrid bile across himself.

I turned my head dizzily and tried to focus on the small dark green thermos flask that I'd found Jon fiddling with when I had arrived.

'You changed the formula,' I managed to say through sick breaths. 'That's why you brought a new flask.'

Jon just looked back at me with wide, fearful eyes.

'You changed the damn formula.'

'No, I just brought some more liquid nitrogen.'

Jon's voice was tight, and high-pitched.

Vaughan had raised his head sluggishly and was now glaring at Jon from beneath angry, thick brows. He spoke with a slur.

'You *changed* the formula, man. You changed the formula without telling us!'

Lewis began to clumsily pick himself up, half-collapsing onto one elbow, smearing sick around.

'I need to get out, man. I feel... I veel...'

His gorge rose, but he resisted it, tensing hard.

He stumbled across to the club door and tried in vain to stab his key into the hole. He heaved slightly and his lips suddenly bulged as he tried to hold back another mouthful of vomit. Emily was retching in the background, but without liquid. With a sound of self-disgust Vaughan let the sick out, it burst like a sour broth from his lips. He spat another mouthful onto the door and floor. I felt my own stomach heave. Finally Vaughan got his key into the hole, and he turned the lock.

But when he opened the door, and stumbled through, it was to discover something that stunned each and every one of us.

He did not find himself in the university's tunnels.

From the pages of Tony's diary:

X marks the spot...

up f; down 8	up f; down e	down 0; down 8	up 1; down 7
down 8; up 1	up 7; down e	up f; up 0	down 0; down 7
down d; down d	down 7; up 2	up f; up 3	up 6; up 4
up 7; up 1	up 5; up 4	up 1; up 6	up 7; up 2
down b; down c	up f; down 3	up 3; up 1	down f; up 7
up 7; up 0	down f; up 3	up f; down 7	down 7; down f
down 8; down a	up 7; down f	down a; up 1	up 2; up 5
up 0; up 2	down 8; down 8	down c; down 8	up f; down d
down 8; up 5	down e; down b	down 7; up 0	down e; down 9
down c; down 7	down d; up 2	down 7; up 3	down 0; down a
down 7; up 1	down b; down 9	down c; up 6	down 7; down 7
up 7; up 3	down 9; up 1	up 2; up 1	down 8; down e
down b; up 6	down 0; down b	up 5; up 0	up 2; down 9
up 2; down 7	up 1; up 2	down f; up 1	down a; down 9
up 3; down 8	down d; down b	down 9; up 5	up f; up d
up 4; up 5	up 7; down d	up 1; down 8	down e; up 7
down 0; down 9	down f; up 6	down f; down 9	down a; down c
down a; down 7	down b; down 7	down 0; up 4	down 8; down 9
up f; up 2	down 7; up 5	down 7; up 4	down c; up 2
up 0; up 6	down e; down e	down b; up 2	down f; down f
down f; up 2	up 4; down a	down 9; down d	down f; up 4
down e; down 8	up 6; down f	up 3; up 5	up f; up 9
down e; up 3	down d; up 7	up f; up a	down e; down 7
up f; up 4	down f; down b	up 6; down c	down f; up 0
down 6; down 7	down 6; down 8	up 1; down 9	down a; down 8
up 5; down b	down c; down c	up 4; up 0	down a; up 6
down 7; down 9	down 6; down 9	down f; up 5	down c; down 9

Chapter 13

'And you do Addition?' the White Queen asked. *'What's one and one
and one and one and one and one and one and one and one?'*
'I don't know,' said Alice. *'I lost count.'*

—*Through the Looking Glass*

'You're being detained,' Bryant sneered.
'Why?' I said, incredulous.
He sniffed casually.
'Suspicion of conspiring to abduct; assisting a suspect; and assaulting a police
officer.'
'*What?*' I exploded. 'I had nothing to do with this! Assaulting which officer?
No-one was assaulted.'
After Skyler had vanished from hospital I'd made the mistake of thinking that
Sergeant Bryant would realize that I was in genuine danger, and that he would
help me. Instead, I'd been taken back to the interview room of the Gramercy
Park station.
'Officer Hagan was assaulted,' Bryant said. 'I don't how you did it to him,
Steel, but whatever you did to his memory is exactly the same as you did to your
girlfriend.'
'I'm *innocent*.'
Bryant shrugged. 'Then you'll be able to demonstrate that and walk free.
After we've done our investigation.'
'And how long is that going to take?'
Bryant leaned in toward me.
'That depends on how compliant you are, doesn't it? You'll be questioned in
the morning.'
I couldn't muster any more energy to protest. At least it was safe here. This
was a police station after all, and there were people around. I couldn't be anywhere safer. I let one of Bryant's officers show me to a cell with a relatively
comfortable bed to spend the night on, and I let my objections go. I was shattered. I lay down and I was asleep before I even heard the key in the lock.
I found myself suddenly awake. The station was quiet, my cell was dark and
yet something had woken me. I opened my eyes. The walls were striped horizontally with faint light from shuttered windows. The shadows of the cell's bars
overlaid them in places, forming a grid of midnight and sodium yellow. Higher
up, occasional squat rectangles glowed like satellites, square moons projected
from the skylights above. Somewhere, deep in the station, two muffled voices
exchanged meaningless babble and fell silent again. Traffic dozed in the distance,
a gentle ululation. Ghosts of stale coffees and the faint accreted body odor of

111

hundreds of previous occupants fell from the walls in silent swathes. Ordinary sensations.

But there was something else.

I lifted my head and looked through the bars into the adjacent cell. It had been empty when I went to sleep. The shadows near the cot seemed deeper. My heart tapped a few beats of warning on my ribs.

'Who's there?' I challenged, in a meek voice, embarrassed by my paranoia. Silence breathed back at me. My heart quietened again.

Outside the traffic sighed.

'Half,' came a low voice.

I froze. The voices deep in the station droned wordlessly for a moment and fell silent again. The voice had been so quiet, I began to wonder if I had imagined it.

'Hello?' I whispered.

Silence.

'Who's there?'

More sighs of traffic.

'...a pound,' came the voice. There was a lyrical quality to it. A song dreamily sung.

I pulled my thumping chest upright.

'Who is it?'

'...of tuppeny... rice...' The voice carried a slight Germanic lilt.

The shadow shifted fractionally in the cot through the bars. I was certain someone occupied it now, but the darkness was an effective blanket.

'Half... a pound... of treacle.' The accent was definitely German.

Just a bum. A drunk, in all probability, hauled in overnight. But the choice of words...

In his cell, more yellow moons hung squarely on the walls above his cot. I looked up to their source, but through the tiny glass rectangles I could see only dark sky.

'Viktor Meistermacher is one of my names,' came the young man's voice. 'So nice of you to ask.'

I cleared my throat.

'One of your names?'

'Oh, yes. I have been called many. Jens Puppenspieler. Jürgen Unholdformer. Hans Ungeheuerbastler. So the list goes...'

'I see.' He didn't sound like a drunk. Delusional perhaps. Common on the streets.

'I am known by many as Der Handpuppen-Meistermacher. Der Monstrum-Trugbildformer...' He began to hum a quiet tune again to himself. 'That's the way the mo-on-ey goes...'

'So many names...'

'You think I don't deserve them?' He paused, a while then:

'You know... you hurt me.'

'I didn't mean—'

'Two days ago. You hurt me.'

Silence thundered in my ears. He started to hum again. '*Pop!* goes the weasel.'

I shrank back instinctively.

'How did you get in here?' I growled.

He chuckled sarcastically. 'You're asking me how I got *into* a prison cell? It's not so hard, I think. I'm a wanted man.'

He sat up suddenly, a dark shadow twisting up from the gloom.

'You know, whatever the Hag's instructions, I intend to have my revenge first. I am not fond of...' the word turned sour on his tongue: 'electricity.'

Hag? My thoughts raced, erratic.

Three nasal grunts. I realized he was laughing.

'Poor little Steel. All in the dark.'

'Who are you? Who is this hag?'

Another connection snapped in my mind. For the first time, I started to feel truly afraid.

'I saw her. In the mirror.'

'You did?' I was surprised at his surprise.

'She wrote in the steam.'

He grunted. 'Then her Calculus *will* succeed. She will be pleased.'

'Who is she?' I demanded.

'She is the Calculatrice,' he supplied, as if this were self-evident.

'I can sense the possibilities near you,' he whispered, and sucked in a breath over his teeth as if to taste them.

I began to look for a way I could escape the claustrophobic confines of this cage. Should I call for help? He seemed to sense my intention:

'You could escape here as easily as I. Why don't you?' he challenged.

I said nothing.

'Afraid of the consequences?' he taunted. 'Well then, here we are. All alone. At last.'

'I only have to start screaming for the police to come in here.'

Meistermacher chuckled. 'I have no doubt that you will scream. But when the police try the door, they will find it locked. And strangely none of their keys will work.'

He had no need of a gun here. That had been a contingency for populated areas.

'Do you speak German?' he asked.

'No.' My mind raced, searching for a strategy.

'Then my names are just words to you.'

From the gloom he lifted his hands into the light.

'Just sounds.'

He had pianist's fingers. Slender. Clever.

'I was a puppeteer.'

Nimble digits flexed and slipped over each other in the light.

'Puppets were always better friends to me than people.'

I understood something of his aspect when he spoke these words, for though he was clearly young, Meistermacher carried more than an air of maturity about him. There was something old about this young man, as if he had been aged and withered by an extreme solitude.

On the wall, a shadow wolf came alive with alert eyes and howled silently at the moon. The wolf changed into an owl, which shook down its feathers and turned its head completely around. A crow swooped past. An old man smoked a pipe and pulled a sour-face. The Puppenspieler dazzled me with his dexterity.

'Just tell me, is she still alive?' I asked. My voice cracked and sounded hoarse.

He seemed surprised.

'Alive? Of course! What good would she be to me dead?'

'Then why did this... Calculatrice... send you to kill her?'

'She did not.'

'Then why did you try?'

'I did not. I came to collect, that is all. A gun may be a threat, may it not? The fool who launched himself at me caused the threat to become a weapon.'

I'd made him fire?

'Then where have you taken her to?' I demanded.

'You are quite mistaken. I did not take her at all. Nonetheless, she is where she needs to be now. You have created a somewhat inconvenient situation, but rest assured, I will be collecting soon enough. Both of you.'

'Me?'

He chuckled.

'Oh yes, you.' And then in a whispering hiss: 'The Calculatrice has sent for you.'

'What have I got to do with this? Who is—'

'Enough! I've answered your questions.'

Meistermacher's hands shuddered and the shadow creature collapsed. His hands folded together again, but where before the shadows had leapt in response to his cleverness, now it was the hands themselves that were the clay from which the Meistermacher formed his *unhold*. Two heels pressed together. He began to hum another children's rhyme. Eight slender fingers undulated—slow, arachnidine legs extending from a solid knuckled body; interlocked thumbs became grasping jaws with sharp nail ends.

'*Die Kribbel-Krabbel-Spinne...*'

The *unholdformer* played his great spider across the wall in the light of an artificial moon.

'*...kriecht ins Wasserrohr.*'

Its gait was exact, frightening. His arms lurked in shadow giving, lie to the illusion. I saw not two hands, but a single autonomous creature, a cautious, curious thing with an enquiring hunger. The thing arched on hind legs and bared its fangs. It poised to pounce. It was a vision rendered in pink and bone-white flesh which terrified me. The spider began to crawl along the wall out of the light and into soft stripes of shadow and light cast on the walls. I watched it slink under them, folding them around itself. I followed it with a horrified fascination.

The spider was halfway across the wall before I realized that Viktor remained, sitting patiently on his cot.

'She told me to collect you,' he hissed. 'But she didn't say in what state.'

The spider crept with slow and certain precision. Thick bone-white legs padded softly along the wall. I shrank back. The monstrous thing probed between the bars separating Viktor's cell and mine, and slowly, it eased itself through. It moved briefly through a patch of sallow light. I saw its blind, eyeless form. It had changed, become more spider-like. Something of the stripes of light painted its skin; stripes signifying poison. It stopped; two forelegs tasted at the air. The hairs on its back stiffened. Dark drops of liquid beaded at eager fangs.

'It's not real,' I insisted, feeling for the roots of its existence, tugging at them. Without changing, the spider seemed to flatten, become a shadow on the wall.

'*dann kommt der Regen und spült sie wieder vor...*'

A battle of wills. The shadow on the wall bulged. I felt sweat begin to bead at my temples.

The shadow inflated again into form. He defeated me effortlessly.

It resumed its relentless crawling.

'*dann kommt die Sonne, und trocknet das Wasser ein.*'

'You aren't strong enough to deny me,' Meistermacher hummed. '*und die Kribbel-Krabbel-Spinne, kriecht wieder ins Rohr hinein.*'

I looked up in horror to see that two more of the hideous *unhold* had been released into the shadows, inching their way towards me. Meistermacher's devious hands were at the light again, forming yet a fourth.

I began to panic.

'This isn't necessary. We can talk.'

I strained my mind again, pulling at the threads of existence of the spider nearest to me. Its reality flexed, but Viktor's will was powerful. I had never felt agreement so wilfully coerced from me. His gift was greater even than Emily's.

The spider was less than two feet away now. I began to realize just how enormous was the span of two hands. Only a little further away the others began to make their way through the bars, moving with inexorable clockwork precision.

If my skill could not defend me then words must.

'You know the consequences,' I said.

Viktor laughed, sputtering. '*Consequences.*'

'It's Russian Roulette. You know it is. What is this costing you?'

'Make no mistake, I have suffered already as much as I am going to. My gift did not come the way of yours.'

'What do you mean?'

The spider was a foot away on the wall. I stood up to distance myself from it. But the cell was finite.

The spider dropped heavily to the cot.

There were at least seven of them now, coming from all directions across the walls and floor.

I began to shout for help, hysteria rising in me.

The Puppenspieler laughed cruelly.

'The doors are locked.'

A moment later the door to the cell area rattled. I heard voices beyond them. Confusion. Keys being tried.

The threads of reality shifted as if in wind. The police were behind a door, but their presence strengthened me. I kicked at one of the spiders, but it grasped onto my foot with manual strength. It began to pull itself up my leg. I screamed, and kicked to try to throw the hideous thing off.

'HELP ME!'

'I need one more gift from you before my little *unhold* have their way.'

Meistermacher's voice was a distant crooning thing beyond the panic that flooded my senses. I swirled around seeing the hideous pink and white things crawling towards me from every angle, attaching themselves to me quicker than I could rid myself of them.

A dizziness swooped over me, as if something silken, infinitesimally thin, had been pulled from within me, extracted from my essence. To the side, I could see the Meistermacher had moved. He had opened a door in the wall of the cell. A wall that had contained no door.

'I thought so,' he said.

Beyond it, I saw a corridor with a faint glowing light of terrifying familiarity.

'Our way home. The Calculatrice is waiting.'

'No. NO!'

'Oh, but *yes!*'

The bone-white thing was at my groin now, its digits grasping at the cloth of my trousers, pulling up towards my face. I screamed.

More keys jangling. Shouting now.

I felt again for the roots of the arachnid's existence, but the *unhold* former was at the bars watching me with an intensity of will I could not deny. The spider's reality could not be questioned.

The door where the police were. His focus was here, on his creations.

I tried to grab at the thing crawling up my shirt, but it bared its fangs and threatened to strike.

I moved my hands, taunting it to keep it at bay, and cast my will out to the locked door. What had he done to it? I could detect nothing.

There.

A tiny thing. A simple knot tied deep in its reality, confounding keys. Viktor's mastery astonished me.

The spider lurched at my hand, but missed. Something new landed onto my back. I screamed again, and whirled around to throw it off, crunching something on the ground.

Meistermacher laughed cruelly.

The knot. The knot.

The thing at my back had reached my neck.

I reached out with my flailing mind, desperate to find again that tiny twist in reality. *There.* I pulled at its subtle ends.

The knot unraveled, a silvery thing slipping over itself.

The door flew open.

Two prongs of sharpness bit savagely into the back of my neck.

Bodies tumbled into the room, yelling.

Meistermacher cursed, and turned. Shadows danced.

Behind him a door closed, snuffing an unnatural source of light, and I collapsed into darkness just as the poison coursing my blistering veins evaporated.

From the pages of Tony's diary:

Make your own God* from just a hundred basic elements!

Begin with:

H_5+ H_2AmSmIr + H_2ErPrNb + H_2AmSmIr <=> H_2NiBeRb

H_2TePmBk + H-BeEr-H-fAt + CrXe-H-GdRn + ZrTeBeIn-Br
+Ne-Tm-AcTe-As

V-C-TmSePu <=> Ti-AtKF-H

You'll also need:

NaRhY-Cr-Cu
ClPTl-OsLa
H-ZnRbFBk
H_3Li-Mn, H_4As, H_4He

Then:

[H_5+ H_5+ H_5+ H_5]

HClCrPmAs + HFHoSC + HCl-CrNeAl
HF-RuTiZn
HF-ThFTl
TiCdInRbIn

And finally repeat the middle step:

[H_5+ H_5+ H_5+ H_5]

(*mountain & midget not included)

117

Chapter 14

'The quantisation of information leads also directly to the Uncertainty Principle, since information storage capacity of any system is finite, the precision with which information about conjugate variables may be stored is limited.'

—*Information Relativity and the New Physics*,
Professor Fabrizio T. Luciano

Vaughan stumbled into a plain, cream-walled corridor, about fifteen feet long. The walls seemed lit with a sallow light, but I could see no light source. He stopped dead, lifted himself upright slowly and stared ahead.

'What... the...'

He turned and looked at us, wide-eyed.

'We... I didn't go under. I don't...'

I looked around at the details of the room, checking for the minutiae, the things I had noted on the previous trip that had told me that I was no longer tripping. There was the patch of dirt on the walls. The fine dilapidated weave of the rug. I noticed the crumbling foam of the lagged pipes. I was wide awake.

I felt my physical sickness abating, but a new sickness came across me instead. Jon had just begun to suffer the effects of the drug and lay still on the beanbag groaning through clenched teeth and taking shallow breaths.

I stood up and walked unsteadily to the doorframe. A deep noise came from somewhere distant. I sniffed at the air. The smell of something acrid burning. Like hair, or rubber. Or skin.

Lewis came to my side. He put out a hand and held my elbow to steady himself, and whispered harshly:

'How is this...?'

'I don't know.'

'Shh. Listen!' he barked abruptly.

I could hear little but the straining pulse in my own ears.

The sound came again slowly, pushing its way subtly, darkly past the violent noise of my own sanguine hydraulics. It emanated in slow rising and collapsing waves of intensity, as much a physical judder felt through our bodies as a sound in our ears, such was its low frequency. It was the slow, unsettling rumble of distant buildings collapsing. It was the sound of tidal waves crashing over continents; remote earthquakes. It was the sound of enormous, skyscraper-sized rotor blades whumping unstoppably through a far-off sky. It was elemental: earth, water and air together. Immense, gigantic, thunderous sounds made faint, almost silent by immeasurable distance. I imagined some incalculably large, mechanical heart in the distance, slowly pumping dark liquids through a bloated network of pipes, and I shuddered, pushing the thought as far away from me as possible.

'What's happening?' Emily called in a small voice.

'The *bastard*,' Vaughan spat. 'I'm going to kill him.' But I heard his fear.

'Close the door. Cycle the lock.'

Vaughan backed out and pulled the door shut. He cycled the lock and opened the door again.

We all expected a change. I didn't really expect to see the tunnel network, but perhaps some other bizarre world. None of us expected this.

The corridor was still there. Those same terrible sounds vibrated through our bones, in our chests.

'Do it again,' Lewis said, quickly, unnerved.

Vaughan closed the door, slamming it firmly, and cycled the lock again. The corridor remained behind it.

He did it again. And again. There was no change. He slammed the door.

'How are we going to get out. How the fuck are we GOING TO GET BACK?!'

I grabbed Vaughan's arm just as he turned to confront Jon, whose form lay still on his beanbag. Jon was looking at us with fright in his eyes.

'Keep a lid on it Vaughan,' I said. 'Come on, we just have to wait it out.'

Jon spoke from his bean bag:

'I didn't change the formula. I *swear*.'

'Then how do you *explain this*?'

'Guys, I promise, I didn't change the formula.'

Vaughan went over to the medical box and the thermos flask.

'Then why are there *two* lots here? Hmm? Explain that.'

'I... I made more. I just thought we ought to use fresh stuff.'

'You told me you just brought more liquid nitrogen. You said we'd run out,' I said. I considered raising the topic of the secret hole in the wall behind the sofa, but the animosity being shown by Lewis and Vaughan was already unnerving. I decided to keep that little piece of information to myself for the time being.

'You guys seemed so suspicious last time I made a batch, I just thought it was easier to say that. Guys, I swear. On my mother's life. I didn't change the formula. It... it must have been a bad batch.'

'We're screwed.'

'NO. We're not. Don't say that. It'll wear off. We just give it time.'

'Has anyone noticed that we *didn't go under*? Anyone? Hello? This is no trip, it's permanent.'

'No it's not. It's not. It can't be.'

Emily stood up and went to the door.

'I just want to look.'

Lewis was blocking Emily's way; he hesitated, but moved to give her access.

She turned the key and opened the door, and looked into its clinical cream-coloured walls.

Continents crashed slowly against each other in the distance. Skyscraper-long blades rent the air apart as they turned. I felt the vibration through my feet. This room, this tiny room, was embedded in a different world now.

'It's just a corridor. A dead end.'

'No,' Lewis said. 'There's a turning at the end.'

There was. It was hard to make out in the corridor's uniform colour, but a slight shadow hinted at a right-angled turn.

'Where does it go...?'

'We're not finding out. We're staying here until this wears off.'

'Vaughan, stop telling everyone what to do,' I said, annoyed. 'If anyone's the boss here it's Jon.'

'JON?! You still want him leading after he's done *this*? What fucking planet are you on, man?'

'One with a strange corridor apparently,' Emily said, humour dry as a desert.

Nobody laughed, but there was a softening in the tension in the room.

'Very fucking funny, Em,' Vaughan said quietly. His anger had melted. He pressed at one side of his temple with his fingertips, then shook his head and let out an exasperated laugh. He looked down at the mess of vomit he'd made.

'Look at the state of me...'

'Vaughan.' Jon lifted himself onto one elbow. He looked less pained now. The nausea had been severe but short-lived in all of us. 'I know you're upset, but think about this. We wanted to progress, this has always been an experiment, and we've all accepted the risks, right? This is progression. Whatever made the batch go bad, I can work that out. How do you feel now? I feel...I feel okay.'

Jon stood up demonstratively, less steady than he had hoped to be, but he retained his balance.

'Jon,' Vaughan said patiently, patronising. 'We *didn't* go under and the door is now leading into another world. You know what that means? This *isn't a trip.* This is no dream. It's *real.*'

'So what's so different?' Jon snapped. 'Remember the jack-in-the-box?'

My thoughts were stuck in a strange loop. I couldn't accept that this was happening. We had to have gone under and not realised it.

'What if... we did go under, but... it happened so quickly we didn't notice.'

'Then you would have seen us go under. Did you? We went before you.'

'No,' I admitted. 'What if we just can't remember though?'

I pored over my memory of the events of the previous minutes to try and find some inconsistency, some disconnect or discontinuity that might provide a clue. I could think of none. If this was real, then it indeed raised the horrible possibility that this was permanent. We could be stuck in whatever world was behind this door. I didn't want to know what was making those sounds, or that smell. Was there a chance that I would never see home again? Never see Kate again? My heart died at the thought. I felt weak. I stepped backwards and sat heavily on the sofa-bench. I suddenly needed my mother more than I had in years. But even if I did get back, she was not there. She was dead. And that didn't seem real. Nothing was real. How could she be *gone*? How was that possible? I fought back tears. And in that moment, I also craved to see my brother Jacob. If I ever got back, I promised myself I would make our relationship work. I would stop fighting and competing with him. I would find our areas of commonality. We would be strong, powerful, together.

'Is he okay?' Emily asked. She managed to sound sarcastic, critical, even in those few words.

'I'm *fine*,' I blurted, before anyone started trying to comfort me. The last thing I needed was to lose it here, in front of these people.

'Well? Shall we find out where we are?' Jon asked.

'I'm not going in there,' Vaughan said. 'It doesn't sound right. And that smell. Can't you smell it?'

I didn't like the idea either.

'I'll go,' Lewis said. 'I wanna know.'

'Anyone else?'

Silent eyes said no.

'Okay. Keep the door open. We won't be long.'

Lewis started walking down the corridor, Jon started to follow him and then turned to the rest of us.

'We're all in this, guys,' he said. 'We have to keep our shit together. Okay?'

He turned and followed Lewis down into the corridor, and they vanished around the corner.

Vaughan immediately started bad-mouthing Jon:

'I don't trust him. He did this on purpose.'

This would tear the club apart. I had to stop it:

'Guys, we *are* all in this. Jon's right. We have to hold our shit together.'
The swearword felt strange but powerful on my tongue.
'You think the sun shines out of Jon's arse, Zeke, but you don't know everything. Remember that. I'm going after my brother. I'm not leaving him alone with that prick.'
Vaughan stalked off into the corridor, wearing disgust in his stride.
'What was that supposed to mean?' I demanded of Emily. My confidence in the integrity, the solidarity of this brotherhood I had joined was beginning to seem misplaced. I felt a slight sense of panic. I needed this club; this was not a conscious, explicit thought but: it validated me. The idea of the club fracturing was tantamount to me losing my new identity, just as I had found a me that I liked. I couldn't let it happen.
'He doesn't trust Jon,' Emily offered. Just the two of us remained in the room. 'Hasn't for a while. I'm not even sure I do any more.'
'Don't say that. Without Jon this club doesn't exist.'
'Don't be so *naïve*,' She said it with casual venom, but I soon realised her poison wasn't really for me. It was for Jon. 'He's a manipulative cunt. Don't be fooled by his charm.'
I couldn't believe what I was hearing. I had believed Emily was infatuated with Jon. Perhaps she had been. Perhaps this was the flip side.
'What reason have I got not to trust him.'
'Has he told you how Tony died? Has he?' Aggression turned her sentences into spears. Her eyes were filled with pain and fear.
'He killed himself,' I said. 'He threw himself off the Queen's Tower. Everyone knows that.' I heard the doubt in my own voice. I'd challenged Jon myself about pushing him.
Emily let out a derisive snort.
'Tell me, then. Was he pushed?'
'Physically? No.'
'Don't be clever.'
'Am I being? Clever? Really? Think about it, Zeke. Hasn't he pushed us all? Hasn't he herded us where he needs us?'
'What happened to Tony?'
She took in a big jerky breath and I realised that she might be on the verge of tears. But none came. She sat next to me on the sofa-bench.
'Haven't you wondered about *where* these places are that we visit?'
'They're constructs, shared illusions. Dream places.'
She laughed.
'*This* isn't a dream. How do you explain *that*?' She pointed at the dim corridor ahead. 'The trips aren't either, even though they seem like dreams. We brought something back once. How do you explain that if these places aren't real?'
'What?' I thought back to the torch I had briefly thought might have been a silver pear. 'What did you bring back?'
'They're other universes. That's what Tony thought anyway. We're getting into other universes, alternate ones.'
The Great Unseen.
'Then why are they all empty?'
She fixed her gaze, cold and hard on mine.
'They're not.'
I waited for her to continue.
'When the mirrors clear—it's only happened once or twice, but when they cleared, we've seen others through them. Those worlds aren't empty.'
'Other people? Through the mirror?'
She nodded. She was trembling again.
But that would mean seeing people *in the club room itself.*

'*What* did you bring back?'

'The famous *jack-in-the-box* trip,' she spat. Her eyes darted across a painful memory. She looked at me with a haunted expression.

'*Something*. Only Jon and Tony really knew.'

She seemed empty, this vampire lookalike, drained not only of her colour, her blood, but of her energy.

'The club room on our trips was always just like this one. We started to experiment by bringing new things into the room before tripping. They would always appear in the trip version of the room too. So we wondered what would happen if one of us brought something along that only they knew about. A secret, hidden in a box. The idea was that one of the others would open the box *during a trip* to see if it contained the same object as the one in the real club room. It was a test that would prove if we were really sharing information, thoughts. Vaughan brought along a jack-in-the-box. But it was just a shiny red box. Only he knew that's what it was. So during the trip they opened it...'

She seemed to go into a daze.

'And? What was in it?"

She looked into my eyes.

'A jack-in-the-box. That's not the interesting bit. You see, the mirror was dark. Reflecting nothing. And as they opened the box... something came through the mirror and hit the floor. The trip ended immediately, but *it was still in the room with us afterwards.* Everyone freaked out. I tried to see what it was, but Jon and Tony were round it and shouted as us to get out. '*Get out! Get out!*' So we did. We were idiots. Back then we did everything they said.'

'What was it?'

'I don't know. They would never tell. Refused to speak about it.'

'But you must have seen *something*?'

'All I know is whatever it was was *very* cold. It gave off mist like dry ice. It caused a massive argument afterwards. Jon was furious because Tony then contacted some girl and told her about the club. I don't know why. He said it was a stupid thing to do, it put all of us in danger and he couldn't see the point of it. Tony kept going on about proximal similarities and convergence, or something. He said that there are infinitely many universes that contained identical histories. He thought the mirror was like a view into the future. That it predicted stuff. And if we saw something happen in the mirror universe, the chances of it happening in another one, this one, were raised. They never came to agree about it. They used to shout at each other. It was pretty shit.'

Why had Tony involved Kate in all this? What had come through the mirror?

'So, you think Jon had a reason to push Tony...'

'I don't know if he pushed him or not. Like I said, not physically anyway. But things weren't the way they seemed with Tony either. It was a surprise to all of us when he was found at the bottom of the Queen's Tower.'

A shadow of memory haunted her briefly, and she put a hand to my chest and stared at me with intense burning eyes.

'Zeke, *Tony went missing on a trip.*'

She let this outrageous sentence sink in, before continuing:

'Two days later he turned up dead.'

'Missing?'

'None of it made any sense. Jon and Tony seemed to have buried the hatchet, at least enough for us to get back together. We wanted to explore more, but the trip went bad. Back then, things weren't so lucid. Jon was still experimenting with the formula. Trips were confused, really messed up. We came out inside this weird house. It was like sunlight when you were inside but dark outside. There was a lake all around, and boats. None of the geometry made sense. I just remember stumbling around trying to remember who I was, bumping into the others, surprised at finding them. There were others there too. Strangers. They were all around Tony. Crowding him. Getting excited. All around him and they started shouting, like something was happening. Like they were trying to stop him from going somewhere. I ran over to look and pushed through them, but he... he just wasn't there any more. When we came back from the trip... he'd really gone. The door was still locked, but he *just wasn't there.*'

Her breathing had become shallow and rapid. I put an arm around her and held her in silence for a moment.

'We don't have to talk about this.'

I wasn't sure I wanted to know any more.

'No, it's okay. It's good to talk.'

I studied the floor for a moment.

'What about these other people? Who were they?'

'This sounds stupid.'

'Go on.'

'They were dressed normally. But, well, I just thought... no I felt I knew somehow: they were angels.'

'Angels?'

'Not like heavenly angels. There was something sinister about them. They just seemed something... higher.' She paused for a second, trying to get a purchase on the slippery surface of her own thoughts. 'I know this all sounds muddled and makes no sense. But I've turned it over and over and I can't *make* it make sense. It's like a bad dream. Only there's no waking up.'

'It's doesn't make sense. You're right.'

'The weirdest thing is that he turned up two days later. That screwed us all up. No-one saw him for *two whole days.* He vanished from a locked room and two days later he's dead at the bottom of the Queen's Tower. Even if he got out of the room whilst we were still asleep—maybe he had a secret key—but even if he did that, what the hell did he do for *two whole days?*'

I stood up and went to look inside the strange corridor beyond the door that should have led into the tunnels. Was I dreaming? Was this real? I'd had dream-like powers of flight during the last trip, perhaps that would settle the matter. I would try to levitate. I searched inside myself for that special physical-mental state that could lift me, defy gravity, but I couldn't get a purchase on it. It was like trying to remember a word on the tip of my tongue, but that never came. I turned back to Emily and saw that she was shivering again. I'd always found her extreme Goth look rather daunting, but to see her so fragile and vulnerable like this made me realise what that make-up was. It was her shield, her camouflage. Her barrier of protection. That white face and dark lips, that jet-black hair and black clothes, they were the eyes on the butterfly's wings. Warning markings. Defence. *I'm bigger than I look, don't eat me.*

She looked so terribly small and sad.

I went and sat next to next to her, and put a tentative arm around her shoulder, wondering what words of comfort I could offer this trembling, broken butterfly. She was fiddling with her own fingers, nervously. I noticed her fingernails: all ten bitten short, painted black and flaking. Her fingers were slender, pale. I put my free hand on top of her trembling ones to steady and comfort them.

'It's going to be okay.'

She sat diminutive, within my outstretched arm, not responding, but not rejecting me either. I wondered how to distract her, take her mind off Tony. I spoke more softly:

'Conjure me a flame...'

She turned and smiled a fraction at the suggestion. Then lifted out a small, delicate hand, from beneath mine, palm upturned.

The air flickered above her hand and softly exploded into light.

I felt heat immediately. She flinched and quickly withdrew her hand, extinguishing the flame in surprise.

'Wow...' she breathed. She put her palm out again and the flame returned. She grimaced slightly but kept her hand there.

The flame was producing heat. I put my own hand out to touch it. It carried the heat of a small candle flame, diluted over a larger volume.

I laughed and our eyes met, amazement and joy shared between us.

'Can you make it hotter?' I asked.

The flame sputtered, then brightened. Heat pulsed from it until it vanished.

Emily took her hand back and cupped it in her other.

'Sorry, I had to stop, it was burning me.'

'No, don't be... that was... amazing.'

She turned her eyes on me again.

'Thank *you*...'

'Me? Why?'

'You let me do that. That's how it works. Agreement...'

I suddenly felt bashful, but allowed a shy smile to creep on my face. Then Emily took me by surprise:

She lifted herself up to me and kissed me quickly on the lips.

I almost jumped backwards in surprise. She looked panicked:

'Sorry... I—Oh God, I'm such a *jerk*.'

'No. No... stop saying that. That was... nice.'

She smelled faintly of patchouli oil, herbaceous and musky.

'Really?'

I thought about Kate. My mother. What if we could never get back? That cold, empty thought by itself rendered me alone.

'Really.'

She put a hand on my thigh, and moved her face close again. Her touch electrified me with nervous excitement. I felt the warmth of her dark painted lips near mine. That sweet yet musky smell.

I cannot recollect the details of what exactly happened. All I know is that one moment we were touching lips, and then we seemed to be on the floor, clawing at each other in a desperate hot embrace. I remember the feeling of penetration. It was my first. And I remember climaxing, lying still on top of her, staring in disbelief and shame at the musty rug underneath us for eternal minutes.

I turned my head to the side, away from her.

I was at just the right angle to see under the sofa. I spied the bottom of the cardboard that covered the hole that I'd caught Jon using when I'd arrived. In those bizarre, post-climactic moments, lying on the floor, a connection formed in my mind. I remembered the sounds of something large, metal and liquid-filled that Jon had been manhandling. I'd assumed it was something to store the frozen meta, but it had sounded too large. *The jack-in-the-Box trip.* Emily had said something *very* cold has come through the mirror during that trip... could it be that Jon was keeping whatever it was secretly in that hidden hole behind the sofa? Certainly a dewar—an oversized thermos flask used to store liquid nitrogen—would have made the kind of noises I'd heard.

And that's when the screaming came.

It was distant, but it cut clearly through the deep vibrating sounds emanating from the corridor and straight through my train of thought, derailing it completely. It would be decades before I made that connection again. We both whipped our heads to look at the doorway.

'What the fuck was that?' Emily said.

I leapt up, clumsily pulling my pants to my hips and hopped over to the door, my heart alive and thumping. I leaned inside the corridor, holding the frame with both hands, to listen more intently.

The screaming came again, shot through with voices, screamed words I couldn't make out, then silence. They had seemed closer.

'Oh my God, the boys,' Emily said. 'Let's go.'

The screaming came again, further away, but these were vocal chord-breaking screams. I'd never heard anything so extreme, or so terrifying in my life.

'I... can't... go in there...' I whispered.

Emily looked at me with an expression of disbelief.

'We *have* to.'

I said nothing. I couldn't move. The screaming stopped.

'Zeke? I need you to come with me. *Now.*'

Emily lifted a hand and summoned a fiercely bright flame that poured heat over our faces like liquid. She dropped her hand again, droplets of hot, wet light skittered over the floor. She grimaced and put her hand under her armpit.

'I can't do *that* without *you.*'

I nodded, understanding.

We moved into the corridor and turned right at the end. The sounds of crashing continents was ever-present in the distance. Ahead of us, the corridor ended in a T-junction leading into something wider, left and right. Everywhere the walls were cream or white coloured, clinical. To the left an opening in the sidewall further down revealed steps leading up in the same direction. Everything was the same pure, bland creamy white. I sniffed at the air. It was there again, the acrid smell of burning. To the right the corridor was shorter and steps led off up to the left and down to the right.

We listened. Nothing but massive, distant noises.

'This way,' Emily decided, and turned left. We walked along to the gap in the sidewall, where there were steps leading up in the direction of the corridor. The steps were narrow—not quite wide enough for two of us at a time. They led up to another level. We ascended cautiously and found ourselves looking into yet another corridor that stretched out for a long distance in both directions. Exits were visible on either side along its entire length, some hinting at more stairs up or down. Everywhere a maze of connecting corridors.

The screams came again briefly, causing both of us to jump. They stopped.

In the distance, down the corridor, I thought I saw a tall, white shape move swiftly from one side to the other, vanishing as quickly as it had appeared. My heart jack-hammered in my chest.

'What the *fuck* was that?'

'What? I didn't see anything.'

'Something came out down there. It went across, into another door.'

Emily was silent for a moment.

'It sounded like it was this way.' She indicated the other direction to my relief. We walked cautiously. I kept checking behind me, but the corridor stayed empty.

Suddenly we could hear shouting close by. It was coming from up some stairs. I made out Lewis and Jon's terrified voices, and heard the sound of running.

'Up there, come on.'

There was no way back out now, and I didn't want to be alone in here. I let adrenaline take over and we raced up the steps, and another level again, twisting a turning through a maze of white corridors towards the sounds of Jon and Lewis.

Emily began to shout to them:

'JON! VAUGHAN! LEWIS!'

We looked down the length of a huge long corridor, with doorways every hundred metres down its clinical depths and then: far in the distance, a tall, white form stepped out and turned towards us. The white form cracked down the centre, opening like a carapace, and inside a multitude of black and chitinous limbs began to shimmer. I remembered my dream days before, and I felt my bladder muscles weaken. I didn't wait to see what the details of what it looked like, I had seen enough.

'Emily... RUN!'

We turned and ran, down the nearest set of steps, and Emily screamed in terror as we collided heavily into a living thing, a tangle of legs and blood and flesh, screaming and wailing at us as it turned the corner. My heart almost exploded.

It was not one thing, it was two: it was Jon and Lewis.

'This way! Quickly.' Jon spat the words.

The look of terror in their eyes, and their blood-splattered clothes, set my heart racing even faster.

'Where's Vaughan?' Emily demanded. '*Where's Vaughan?!* He went looking for you. Didn't he find you?'

Lewis's expression crumpled on his face.

'Oh God. Oh God no...' Emily said.

The screaming was terrible, punctuating the great and distant crashing sounds. This time, when it stopped, it was clear that it had been cut off.

'They caught him.'

He started to cry.

'I couldn't help him. I couldn't *help* him.'

Emily lifted a fist and it burst into incandescent heat and light.

'Where is he?'

'Emily, you haven't seen what they're like. We'll die...' Jon said with a steel-hard glare.

'Go, then. The entrance is down that way. But I'm finding Vaughan. Zeke, are you with me?'

No, I thought, no I'm not. But if her flame depended on me, how could I refuse?

Lewis spoke:

'I'll come.'

'Okay, then,' Jon agreed. 'Together we're more powerful.'

'Give me as much as you can,' Emily said.

We ran back the way they had come from, drops of blood from their injuries on the floor tracing the route they had taken. Finally, we turned a corner and saw Vaughan's body. He was lying twisted and still on the floor. Where his torso should have been there was just a mess of red sinew and the long jointed white rod of his spine starting from just above his hips. Just below, his legs were still intact. Even his ribs were gone, only the upper part of them were visible just under his shoulders, the ends were gleaming stubs. Then I saw his head. It was facing sideways. There was no face. The front of his skull was gone. The cavity of his head had been emptied, only the back of his skull kept it concave. It was steaming. The hair framing it was singed.

Whatever had killed him had gone.

Lewis began to make wordless animal grunts of grief and horror, a loss and pain so fundamental his human self could not articulate it.

I heard a slurping, slavering sound, chitinous clacks behind us. I never saw the monstrous thing that made it. Emily had turned to it and was pouring a great river of fire from her outstretched hand. The monster screeched and hissed steam from inside the inferno coming from her. Smoke poured out from the thing. Black insect legs writhed within the flames. Sections of hard white armour cracked open, spilling fluid. The thing cooked and split open inside the ball of fury she had unleashed upon it. A thick tube flailed around from near its head, spraying blood and pieces of burning meat. Vaughan's flaming flesh.

We ran.

Emily held her hand close to her chest.

Lewis was chanting a desperate litany to himself. I couldn't make out the words. We followed Emily down and round the maze of white corridors, racing for our lives. I prayed she remembered the way back.

On every corner I thought I heard that slavering sucking sound that that elephantine tube had made; those chittering, insectile noises; the clacking and slicing of mandibles. I saw tall white forms in the distance turn towards us, malevolent. Together they began to screech.

Lewis's words came over the noise, fragmented:

'change... we can...'

Over and over he repeated himself, as if trying to believe it himself.

'We can change this we can change this we can change this...'

We raced around a corner and another and there was the club room, just fifteen feet ahead. Behind me there was a scream. I turned and saw Lewis being pulled violently backwards, disappearing around the corner. Jon raced past me, shoving me into the wall to get past me. I bellowed:

'EMILY!'

She turned to me and saw that Lewis had gone, and immediately reversed her course, squeezing past Jon to return to me. We turned that initial corner again, back towards where Lewis had been pulled, and saw him. He was clinging desperately on to the sides of the wall with both arms outstretched, resisting the huge white and black thing tugging on him from behind. His face was twisted with terror. Its thick grey mouth tube extended and I heard the sucking begin.

Emily turned to me with a rapid instruction:

'Guide it. Make sure it misses him.'

Her hand shot out, she stretched her fingers wide. Her hand was raw and blistered, but she did not hesitate. From her thumb and each finger loosed five torrents of blazing, yellow-white liquid fire that arced up and below, five streams of burning fury, twisting around Lewis's body, engulfing the white and black body of the monster, penetrating its grey feeding tube. I felt the form of the fingers of fire in my own mind and shielded Lewis from them, willing them instead to immolate the monstrosity clutching at him.

Lewis dropped to the floor, released, and the five rivers of fire flew like streamers, completing their journey from Emily's now blackened and tortured hand to the hissing, steaming monster. It screeched and backed away on fire, flashing black and white under dark smoke. From the top of its carapace I saw the head from which the fat grey feeding tube extended. It was black. It had great blind, white orbs as eyes. One of them split in the intense heat, leaked blobs of fat. Twitching black feelers burned and smoked and writhed above its head.

I grabbed at Lewis and we hauled each other back around the corner towards the club room.

The door had gone.

We faced a blank wall.

Emily let out a scream of rage.

'NO! You CAN'T do this to us, you cowardly... fucking *CUNT*!'

She screamed the last word so hard I thought her vocal chords might rip. She turned with flecks of spit on her chin and blazing eyes to me.

'Bring it back. He closed it, but we *can bring it back*.'

Behind us I could hear the awful sounds of more things approaching, clicking and screeching. How many of them were there?

We turned on the blank wall and willed it to change; willed the change in ourselves; prepared to make the sacrifice.

'It's not working.'

'Keep *trying*.'

I began to see that the flat wall was indeed a door, but it wasn't enough.

'Nearly there, keep it coming.'

Clicking sounds of hardened exoskeleton reflected from the walls behind us. The hissing and sucking sounds of feeding started again.

I saw the door frame. The thought came, it was not a wall. It never had been. Just a different interpretation of the same thing. It was there, it always had been. I ran forward, lifted my knee and booted it with as much force as I could. The door burst open, into the club room.

Jon was nowhere.

The three of us rushed inside just as a tall black shadow advanced into the corridor behind us. We slammed the door behind us, and leaned against it with all our combined weight. My ankle burned with pain. I thought I had broken it.

'Change it back. Change it back to the tunnels. The college tunnels.'

We stayed tensed against the door in silence. I couldn't focus. The pain, the terror. I had no idea if we were succeeding.

All we could hear was the sound of our own heaving breath.

I whispered, 'Is it gone? Is it gone?'

Emily shook her head a fraction to indicate she didn't know. So we stayed, unable to move out of fear, for what seemed like half an hour, our muscles burning from the effort of pushing against the door, until finally, Lewis slumped to the floor, and began to weep in grief.

I put my ear to the door to listen. I could hear a mechanical throbbing.

Finally, when Lewis was able to move, we opened the door a crack, and to our relief peered out into the cool, musty darkness of the college tunnels.

We journeyed back through them together in silence. I was limping badly. My ankle wasn't broken, but I had sprained it kicking down the door. As we moved through the half-light of the tunnels, fleeting creatures, flat, many-legged things like great woodlice, seemed to scuttle from out of shadows across our path and disappear again into the darkness. Each time we would stop, fearful, but there would be nothing, just silence.

We came out by the Chemistry building. It was dark, but as we moved into the light, I caught sight of Emily's hand again. She was holding it close to but not touching her bosom; she held it limp, hunched around it protectively. The hand seemed charred and a livid red. The skin underneath was beginning to blister and bubble and I could tell from the way she held her jaw clenched that she was in a great deal of pain.

'We should try and heal that.'

She shook her head.

'It won't work. You know that.'

'Try.'

We tried, but there was no change. I understood. This change was part of that which allowed the flames. The transformation was a lever bridging the observer and the observed. One side could not move without the other moving in opposition. To reverse it, would be to reverse the flames. Impossible. They had happened. It was done. The sacrifice was permanent. This was the physical sacrifice Emily had had to make. But there were other sacrifices we had had to make that could not be seen. Dangerous sacrifices. I thought to the fleeting many-legged things that had flitted in the tunnels. Lewis was in shock, and simply stared into the distance, trembling violently.

'Then we have to get you to hospital.'

She refused. *Too many questions.* How would we answer them?

'Zeke, I need to be alone right now. I'm sorry. It's my way. I'll look after Lewis. He needs me. I know him better than you. I'm sorry. Do you mind? Go home. Sleep. We'll find each other. Okay?'

I felt hurt, rejected, but also I understood. She had been Vaughan's lover.

I went back to my room in hall with a numb sensation through my entire body. I watched every leaf, every blade of grass that I passed with gratitude for its normality. Flashes of the horrors we had seen came unbidden to me, making me flinch.

I could not sleep. I could not even get undressed or into bed. The effects of the drug were not wearing off as they had before. Reality seemed to have softened permanently. I recalled how exciting that idea had once been—the control I mistakenly thought it brought—yet now I wanted nothing more than the concrete permanence that I had had before. But it was gone. The shadows under my bed and in the corner of the room contained too much doubt now. I kept the light on, and sat in the corner on the floor, knees to my chest, with the desk lamp clutched tightly between my legs, illuminating each of the various shadows in turn to make sure they were—and stayed—empty.

When the sun rose, I put on as many layers as I could, left the room and went out into the growing light. I slept fitfully for an hour on a cold bench in Hyde Park, in the sunlight, where I felt safe.

When I woke, the nightmare flashbacks evaporated into the morning. The events of the previous evening seemed like a nightmare, a bad dream. The sky was a dirty inconsistent grey, a capricious looking thing, that might do anything next, shine or rain. It was depressing, and yet comfortingly real. How could any of last night have been real? I began to doubt my sanity. I lifted myself up from the bench, cold and bleary eyed, still exhausted but unable to sleep. What was I going to do?

I sat for a long time, on the verge of panic, desperately wondering how to undo this awful reality I found myself in.

I decided to call my brother. I could not deal with this alone. He'd lost his mobile phone weeks ago and not yet replaced it. I had no credit on mine as usual but I found one of the increasingly rare callboxes and phoned Jacob's hall of residence. I asked him to meet in me in the park. I needed help. His voice sounded concerned. He asked me if it was about Mum. I said it was something else, something worse. I thought I sensed relief in his silence. As if, selfishly, he had grieved over her at the appropriate time and didn't want my grief now to spoil his happiness. Then, when he broke his silence he asked me if I was joking (as if I would!) but he soon realised that I was not.

Jacob sat next to me on the park bench in Hyde Park, studying my face, looking, for all the world, in spite of our different clothing, like a reflection, magically given life of its own. I was reminded of the mirror games we would sometimes play as children. That memory brought up a tide of emotion. We *had* been friends once.

Wispy filaments of breath clung like smoke to Jacob's lips as he studied me. The dreary clouds had parted and the sun made a brave show of appearing bright through them, but it was a sham: for all its parading across the sky, its light did nothing to warm our faces.

And so I sat with Jacob, trying to find words.

After several attempts to find a starting place—with words dying in my mouth before they even left it—so that I merely opened it, took a breath to begin, and then silently exhaled their vapour souls out, unspoken—Jacob started for me:

'You're going to tell me you're gay. That's it, isn't it?'

For a brief moment, the magnitude of the situation dwindled away to nothing by some perspective trick. A rug somewhere underneath me had been pulled away. I stared at my twin in disbelief, feeling vaguely stupid.

'It's okay,' he reassured me. 'I don't mind if you are. It explains *everything*.'

I managed to wrestle control back over my rabbit-in-headlight mind before he ran it over with this particular truck.

'No!' I protested weakly. 'No, I'm not.'

He touched my arm, a deliberate symbol of solidarity and said:

'You're my brother, I still love you. I really don't mind.'

'Jacob! I am *not* gay!'

'Why the hell else would you drag me all the way out into the park to tell me something?'

How did he do this to me, *every* time? I felt an old anger rise inside me. What did he mean, *it explained everything*? He always managed somehow to put me in a position of weakness relative to him. My mouth was hanging slack, the muscles weakened by resentment and then weighed down by incredulity.

'I'm not gay.'

'There's nothing wrong with being gay.'

'Jacob! I KNOW. But I'm not. Okay!? We're twins, if I was gay then you would be too.'

'That's not true. It's more environment than genetics.'

'We had practically the same environment.'

'No we didn't. I had you as my brother, but you had me.'

'I can't believe we're even talking about this.' I was talking to the air, I'd given up talking to him.

My torso felt like a cement mixer, tumbling a sick mix of emotions inside me: anxiety, anger, sadness, disbelief. How did every conversation end up as a fight like this? How did he manage to make me feel so goddamn small in every interaction. I felt so let down.

'Tell me, then! If you're not coming out, what did you bring me out here to tell me?'

I let the sick mix in my torso settle for a moment into resignation and then harden into something else. What had I been thinking when we had been trapped? I had romanticised a new brother, but he was Jacob. He would never be the brother I wanted or needed.

'Forget it.' I stood up to leave.

'Hey, come on. Sit down. Look, I'm sorry. I don't know what's going on, but it's clearly upsetting you. I. . . I was just grabbing for the biggest thing I could think of that could upset someone like this.'

I looked into his eyes, my eyes, for a trace of insincerity, but I found none.

'Come on, Zeke. I'm *really* sorry. Of course you're not gay. It was a stupid thing to say.'

'What did you mean, "it explains everything"?'

'Just. . . ' He was silent for a moment, but no explanation came. I felt my anger rise again, but it subsided as quickly. Something of the winter had entered me, a chill, and my hot anger found nothing to ignite this time. It flickered away to nothing like a flame extinguished in a breeze.

I sighed heavily, exhaling a small cloud that was whipped away by the wind, like my anger.

'Actually, I think. . . I mean I *am* in love with someone. A girl.'

This was not the conversation I'd come here to have, but now it seemed all that was important.

Jacob looked genuinely sympathetic, as if being in love was a cause for sadness. Perhaps he misread the weight that pulled down on my expression. At that time I didn't know my love would remain unrequited, I still held hope that she might respond when I finally found the courage to tell her. The heaviness in my voice was not because I was in love, but that must have been what Jacob heard.

'Does she know?'

I shook my head marginally. 'No. At least, I don't think so.'

'Are you going to tell her?'

'I don't know.'

'Why not?'

'I'm afraid. I guess.'

Fear of love seemed to be such a foolish fear after the events of the night before. And yet, there it was undiminished, perhaps even greater than before.
'Nothing ventured, nothing gained. What's her name?'
'Kate.'
Jacob's expression tightened. I noticed, but it simply didn't occur to me that there might have been a personal reason behind that reaction.
'Kate who?'
'Andrews. She's in my tutorial group.'
From that moment on, our conversation parted, though we stayed together, talking using the same words, but each understanding something completely different. Same facts, different interpretations, different realities.
Jacob took a careful breath, and then:
'I see. That's why you asked me here.'
But I didn't see. I didn't see *at all*. I didn't ask him here so that I could confess I was hopelessly, possibly unrequitedly in love. His words just floated across meaning nothing. I'd just seen someone horrifically murdered. And yet I wasn't even sure if I had, whether it was real.
'No, that's not why I asked you here,' I protested. 'That's just... oh, I don't know why I said it.'
He seemed confused, but the confusion silenced him rather than raising questions. I became suddenly annoyed that he'd never answered my earlier question. 'What did you mean, "*that explains everything*"? Tell me.'
The look of confusion increased on Jacob's face. I think at a subconscious level I suspected that we had our lines crossed somehow but I figured I was just being confusing, telling him I needed to confide in him and then confiding something else entirely.
'Well... first you and Alexei... and then you and that Jon guy. I mean, you hang out with him, like *all* the time. I mean, I just put two and two together.'
'What!? Jon? *Jon?!* Don't be ridiculous. He's my friend. We were... doing an experiment together. Research.'
Why did I lie? Hadn't I asked him here to tell him? To lean on his support?
'Okay, sorry.' He didn't sound sorry at all.
There was another awkward silence between us which he eventually broke.
'Zeke, if you didn't come here to discuss Kate with me, what did you bring me here for?'
He sounded angry, and that made me angry again. What was wrong with him? Why couldn't he just be supportive? I blurted out my problem, but when it came out, it sounded ridiculous, even to me.
'I think I'm going mad.'
'I think you are too.'
'Thanks. That's really helpful.'
'You're not making any *bloody* sense!'
'I've started... seeing things. *Okay?*' I almost shouted this, but then the anger left me and the next words came out so much smaller:
'Only... only they're physical as well. I don't know what's real any more. Jacob—I'm frightened.'
And then the words seemed to tumble from my mouth like water, as if that first admission were the branches of a beaver's dam coming away, breaching it, and now a pent-up river released its pressure gratefully. I explained everything to Jacob, whose confusion at my choice of subject matter gradually faded to be replaced by suspicion and finally concern. I told him that I had joined a club, that drugs were involved, that they caused shared hallucinations. I told him about the trips. And I told him about the nightmare of last night, and in spite of Emily's fire, that Vaughan had died. The last of the dam released, the words

stuttered and failed in my mouth; normal flow resumed and I found my teeth
were chattering, something that had nothing to do with the autumn chill.

'These... effects... only *you* can see them? They're only there when other
people aren't around?'

I nodded.

Then Jacob did a thing which was probably the last display of fraternal af-
fection between us: he put his arm around me and held me, and, for a moment,
I allowed his twenty minutes of seniority to magnify to years, and let myself be
comforted by my older brother. He rocked me gently in silence, like a baby, for
what seemed like an age, and for the only time I can recall in our lives, I allowed
him to adopt a position of strength relative to me without feeling weakened by
it, taking instead the support and love that I desperately needed.

Eventually we both became conscious of the attentions of the occasional passers-
by unable to resist the drama of an upset twin being comforted by his brother,
and our embrace was fractured and teased apart by their glances, little knives
separating cubes of fused ice.

'Do you want to see someone?' Jacob gently asked me, knowing this would
not be for me to answer. And hearing his words, I realised two things:

First, that I had secretly held out a small hope that Jacob would believe
what was happening to me (how could he? I hardly believed it myself in this
cold daylight), and second, that anyone I told would have the same automatic
reaction. How could I expect someone to believe in things I only saw, or that
only happened in private? There *was* only one conceivable interpretation of my
story: I was suffering from delusions.

That I was going mad.

I chewed the inside of my lip and nodded.

'Would you like me to contact someone for you?' he offered compassionately.

'It's okay. I'll speak to Professor Luciano. My tutor. He'll know who to
contact, I'm sure.'

We walked back to the college campus in silence. Our conversations about
Kate had come so close to touching, but the gravity of my predicament had
pulled them apart again before they could connect, and now, like the perspective
trick enabling the tiny moon to eclipse the vast sun, it was temporarily shadowing
a matter that would later transpire to be of much larger significance to both of
us. The small collision narrowly averted now meant only that by the time these
matters swung into proximity again they would have time to gather far more
momentum and the collision, when it came, would be catastrophic.

I thanked Jacob for being there for me—I meant it sincerely—and I went
alone to find Professor Luciano, temporarily accepting that I was delusional, and
possibly as a result of drug abuse.

I felt that the entire conversation had gone wrong. Jacob had dominated me
as usual, pushed me in directions I hadn't wanted to go. I had said things I had
had no intention of discussing, and I had omitted things I had intended to talk
about. The result: he thought I was mad. Perhaps I was, but I'd wanted him to
believe me, or at least check some facts before drawing his conclusion.

As I walked along the concourse towards the physics building, mulling this
over, a memory struck me. At the funeral, the curtain fire... Mrs Joliffe had
seen it. *And Jacob had been there.*

The illusions weren't just experienced in private.

I had to tell Jacob. Now he would believe me.

I wasn't sure which version of reality I wanted least. Did I want to be proven
mad? Or did I want a world where reality wasn't solid, and where a man could
die in the way that I had seen?

I turned around and ran back to find him.

From the pages of Tony's diary:

An end to mark the beginning...

Chapter 15

'Would you—be good enough,' Alice panted out, after running a little further, 'to stop a minute—just to get—one's breath again?'
'I'm GOOD enough,' the King said, 'only I'm not strong enough. You see, a minute goes by so fearfully quick. You might as well try to stop a Bandersnatch!'

—Through the Looking Glass

'He was screaming, you say?' The voice was gravelly and confident. An older man.

'Yes,' Bryant replied.

'Well. . .' The man paused, pondering possibilities. 'Almost certainly just *pavor nocturnus*. Night terrors. A type of parasomnia. A simple sleep disorder. Not uncommon. Perhaps exacerbated by stress from the arrest.'

'Don't go putting ideas into his head.'

I felt a hand released my wrist. It had been taking my pulse.

'Litigation? You say he has a history?'

'Apparently. He was delusional years ago.'

'Then relax, Tom. He's fine now. I don't think you need to worry.'

Bryant grunted.

'I can keep him in?'

'For the moment, yes. Let me know if anything else happens.'

'Thanks.'

The two men left. My eyes had remained closed the entire time. I sank back to sleep.

I slept until a small square of white daylight slid down and across the wall from a window opposite, hurting my eyes with its obnoxious brightness. The noises of the station, which had been constant throughout the night, infiltrated my consciousness like thieves.

I ran my mind over the events of the night. *Pavor nocturnus.* Maybe I had dreamt it after all. I sat up and swung my legs to the floor. I touched my neck. It felt sore but I couldn't tell if there were puncture marks. Nonetheless, I was certain that what had happened in the night had been real. And now at least, I had some names to work with. I needed to find out who this Viktor Meistermacher was; who, or what, the Calculatrice was; what did she want with me, with Skyler; and what was their connection to the Looking Glass Club. So many questions. But I could do nothing trapped here in custody.

My eyelids were made of lead. My entire body was. Heavy, aching lead. My shoulder was in pain from sleeping in the wrong position, or perhaps from when I had hit the wall on that first night, running wet and cold through the rain.

Suddenly I felt very old. Too old to be running in the rain with a pregnant women.

She hadn't been pregnant.

I'd worried needlessly about the poor little baby when she had hit the wall with me, ensconced inside that taught pink bump. It didn't exist. And I still didn't know what was inside there instead.

I was about to find out.

Bryant, I was pleased to note, did not look any more refreshed by his night's sleep than I felt. I'd been given a disposable toothbrush and cheap toothpaste, some spray-on deodorant, and I'd been allowed to wash my face, but I hadn't been offered a shower and I felt sticky and dirty. I hadn't showered in days. I could smell my own hair, a strangely intimate, very human smell.

The cell was no longer an attractive proposition. I would have made a phone call there and then, but as I'd discovered last night, my com was jammed by an emitter somewhere nearby. Criminals had the right to a single phone call and the police made damn sure it was made using the station phone. Traceable. Recordable. I decided it was time to make my call. I called to the guard and told him I wanted to. He unlocked the cell door and led me to a phone.

I called my dog.

'I need legal help, JR. I don't care about the cost. Just get me out of here. Fast.'

He'd find me the best lawyer in town. If there was one thing dogs were great at, it was find and fetch. That's why I'd had him upgraded. A cat would have pissed off and done its own thing, or found itself a nice corner of the net to curl up and sleep on. A cat would have hunted down viruses, or worms, but instead of killing them, it would have dragged them back, half-alive and dangerous, and released them right inside my own domain. *Look what I found!*

Yes, very *clever*, Smoky.

The interview room was set up differently. I walked in ahead of Duggan, who had collected me and shown me to the room. A projector sat on the desk. It was about the size of a pack of cards. Ancient technology; ten years old at least. Thousand lumen phased-array projectors were the size of buttons these days, and wall-sized display cloths were commonplace. Either the police were less well funded than I thought, or Bryant just still liked to shine light in his victims' eyes. I wondered what I was going to be shown. Bryant looked slightly more refreshed than he had when I'd seen him an hour earlier, his breath carried warm, malty overtones of latte over the desk. There was a small crumb of something stuck in his moustache which I used—a private, silent weapon—to diminish him.

Police interrogation methods had changed with the advent of the lie-cam. Bryant had no need to laboriously repeat a line of questioning to try to dig out the gleaming truth from beneath a pile of rotten lies. He satisfied himself with a single question that I had believed Sky to be genuinely pregnant; he also satisfied himself that I hadn't been involved in Sky's disappearance, nor the strange memory loss of one his officers. And yet, here I was, still in his custody.

'I just can't shake off this hunch that you have something to do with all of this, *Steel*. Call it police intuition—still the most useful weapon we have against crime amongst all this... *technology*.'

He pronounced the word as if he were holding something dirty at arm's length.

'You know, it occurs to me, *Steel*, that one way to cover up the truth, one way to hide the truth from even a sophisticated polygraph like this, is to forget it. Wouldn't you agree?'

I nodded. It was indeed. Perhaps this was why Skyler's memory had been wiped. I tried to ignore his deliberate over-stressing of my name.

'And I'm wondering, *Steel*, how much *you* might have forgotten. Perhaps deliberately.'

I frowned. This possibility had actually not occurred to me, but Bryant was right. What if I knew more than I thought? I searched my recent memory for gaps. I found none. Still—would I know?

'So, I think it's time to show you some stuff. See if we can't jog your memory a little.'

A clean image sprang brightly into being on the white wall. It was an object, a 3D computer model, rendered in a pale metallic blue. It started to rotate, its surface glinting in calculated light.

'Do you know what this is?'

'I could guess. It's the scan of someone's head. Skyler's? She had it done when we first went to Bellevue.'

'Well, pretty close. It *is* a scan of an adult human head. But it isn't Skyler's. This is what she was carrying *inside* her, Steel.' He deliberated over his next words: 'An adult human head.'

Cold liquid seemed to leak out from my center. Bryant stood up and went to the image, which brightly wrapped itself around him as he stood in front of the projected beam.

'Let me tell you something else. Whoever this head belonged to, they were still alive. See this part next to it, that's a heart. The doctor suggested this was grown artificially. The placenta connects here to the blood supply, so it can get nutrients, just like a baby. We're not sure what this is. It doesn't look organic.'

He pointed to a blob to one side.

The skull rotated in response to Bryant's hand movements, as if he were touching it. I started to notice details that suggested this skull wasn't healthy. The eyes looked like they had been deflated. I felt vaguely sick.

'Jogging any memories yet?'

I shook my head. 'No. I've never heard of anything like this.'

'Neither have we, *Steel*. Neither have we.'

Meistermacher had lied. He wasn't simply interested in me, or Skyler. He'd been after someone else: someone who had taken refuge inside her. But why would someone go to such extremes to hide? There were easier ways to hide, surely? It didn't make sense. I thought back to the note that had been written. Someone had wanted me to protect Skyler in order to protect *a person inside her*. Bryant watched me with all the eagerness of a cat waiting for the moment to pounce. He nodded fractionally. I saw a small, eager smile tug at the corners of his mouth. Something began to occur to me. My mind was reeling. I felt dizzy.

Now I've experienced some weirdness in my life, more than most people, and by rights I have a capacity for strangeness that would simply topple most people, but sometimes there are things that even I can't get to grips with. This was one of those moments, and perhaps not because of what you might think. It was just too *specifically* weird. So obviously connected to events in my past and yet in a way that *could not possibly fit*. It was like finding a jigsaw puzzle piece with exactly the right part of the picture on it that was needed, but that was completely and utterly the wrong shape, not even cut to the same pattern. You'll understand this later. For now, all you need to know is the effect this news had on me. I absorbed the information in complete shock, and then, because it could not fit in any way that I tried to make it, my mind simply shut it down and denied its relevance.

'I think we're getting somewhere,' Bryant said confidently.

I didn't share his optimism at all. I was more confused than ever. Only one thing seemed evident to me now. I remembered the doctor complaining about radio wave interference at the hospital.

'I know what that is,' I said, hoping to buy time and avoid some questions.

'What *what* is?'

'That thing. The blob there.'

'Go on...'

'It's a transmitter. The... the equipment at the hospital kept going crazy. But no-one had their coms switched on. I think when Sky started to... go into labor, or whatever you'd call it, I think that thing started transmitting to whoever put it in, to help her get it out again. She couldn't give birth. It would have to be surgically removed. So they came to fetch her when she was ready.'

A thought struck me. What had she said in the taxi? Something about white boys coming to get her?

Bryant squinted at me. I continued with my logic:

'Whoever put that inside her also made her lose her memory. And whoever came to collect her made your officer lose his using the same technology so that they could collect her with a minimum of fuss. It fits.'

'Why make her lose her memory?'

'Like you suggested: isn't that a good way to hide the truth? I'm assuming this isn't legal...'

'No. You can bet your ass it isn't. The question is: *why* would someone do this?'

I considered my words strategically:

'How could I know such a thing?'

You can't lie with a question.

'Your *past* says you could, *Steel*.'

My heart skipped a beat. The extra emphasis he had been placing on my name all this time suddenly made sense.

Bryant moved out of the projector light and signaled something discreetly. The image changed.

'Or perhaps I should be calling you Ezekial, Mister Ford?'

'Hello, Zeke. It's been a long time,' said a face I hadn't seen in years; a face I had hoped never to see again. Detective Inspector Hofstadter gave me an almost embarrassed smile from his London-based office. Hofstadter was in his sixties now, gray-haired, but still with width and strength to his face that suggested someone younger who had merely turned prematurely gray. Deep worry lines etched downwards, carving out his jowls. His eyebrows had become bushy with age. He wore half-moon reading glasses now that gave him the slightly inappropriate air of a kindly grandfather or uncle.

I took a huge breath, closed my eyes and let it out in a very long sigh.

I turned to look at Bryant, and I spoke in a low, cold voice.

'You have no right to do this.'

It was Hofstadter that spoke.

'Zeke, you're not to be punished again. You've already served your sentence. But as far as I'm concerned that case is not closed. Here I am, twenty-five years later, still looking for answers. Isn't it time we laid some ghosts to rest?'

My voice trembled with restrained emotion:

'Here I am, twenty-five years later still looking for some kind of frigging peace.'

'People died, Zeke. Horribly. People went missing, and crazy. And I *still* don't know the truth.'

'You'll never know the truth. None of us will.'

But I did know. A red light blinked silently on the lie-cam, betraying me. Hofstadter smiled.

'I think perhaps we might, now that technology has made such useful advances.'

Bryant looked so silently smug I wanted to reach over and smash his face to a pulp.

'Why can't you be satisfied, Hofstadter? You put me and Lewis in care for two years; Emily probably forever. Wasn't that enough for you?'

'You put yourselves in care as I recall. That was a smart move. A mere two years instead of ten, fifteen, maybe life. You may have managed to convince the psychiatrists of your insanity, Zeke, but you never convinced me.'

Hofstadter wasn't malicious or vindictive like Bryant. He spoke softly, almost apologetically. But he was a determined, persistent, tenacious man. I remembered the motto that he used to have on the triangular block on his desk: *Gutta cavat lapidem, non vi, sed saepe cadendo.* The drop carves out the stone, not by force, but by persistent falling. Hofstadter liked to know the truth. And here he was persisting all over me, twenty-five years later, to get at it. He wasn't malicious—no—but harm isn't always born from malice.

This stone was not about to be carved out by a persistent drip.

I let a callous smile spread itself across my face.

'Is that so. Well, here's your chance, Hofstadter. Ask me your questions again. Let's see what *I spy* here has to say about the truth. Ask me now, in front of this all-seeing judge, this modern little piece of God.'

Hofstadter's expression hardened. He didn't enjoy being goaded. Not then, and not now.

'What did you do with Vaughan Van Cross's body?'

'Nothing.'

The lie-cam's little red eye remained blind, confirming me. Hofstadter's eyes danced from it back to me.

'Did you kill him?'

'No.'

The lie-cam once more verified me.

'Who did?'

'He was eaten by a giant insect from an alternate reality.'

I deliberated over the words, making sure there could be no doubt that I meant what I said. I saw Hofstadter's expression soften slowly, as if being melted, as he waited for the lie-cam to out me, and when it did not his eyebrows danced in surprise. Bryant's smug expression transformed in a second and boiled into anger.

'Duggan?! What's going on? You told me this piece of crap was infallible!'

Duggan blinked.

'It... sir, it is. It is supposed to be.'

'Then how is this... this *bullshit* possible?'

She was quick to respond:

'The truth and what people believe to be the truth are not necessarily the same thing, sir. But the lie-cam can't distinguish between them.'

Hofstadter started to clap slowly, somewhere in London:

'Oh, you're good Ford, very good. I don't know how you're doing this, but I don't believe for one second that you are *anything* but perfectly sane.'

'Isn't there only one logical conclusion to draw from that statement, Hofstadter? That I'm telling the truth?'

'Don't try and trap me. The logical conclusion is that somehow you are able to lie and fool this detector. Tell me about the girl, Kate Andrews.'

Don't go digging this up again. My heart turned to lead. A steady heat burned behind my eyes.

'What do you want to know?'

But before he could ask his next question, the screen abruptly went gray and emitted a loud digital squeal, startling everyone in the room. Suddenly the screen was filled with line after line of dancing puppets, small desert gophers, singing in gay squeaks as they marched across the screen. It seemed to be a children's television show. They sang letters of the alphabet:

'A. B. C... D. E. F... G. H. I. J. K. L. M...'

Bryant exploded. 'What *the hell* is going with I.T. today?'

He started barking orders into his internal com:
'Wang, what's happened to our link?'
He was far too busy to notice what the gophers sang:
'N. Y. P. D... S. H. I. T...'
I struggled to keep my face straight. Duggan hadn't noticed either, she was riveted by Bryant's anger.

A large camel—apparently made from toweling cloth—strode onto the screen and began to speak in a great bassy voice using the patronizing tones reserved for pre-school children.

'Hello, *children!* Today's word is... *oxymoron*. Do you know what that means? Let's see if you can guess from some examples of *oxymorons*...'

'Don't give me that crap, Wang,' Bryant barked into his com. 'Just fix it!'

'*Plastic glasses. Open secret. Deafening silence. Police intelligence.* Can you spot the connection?'

Duggan turned to the screen, suspicious:
'Sir? I...'

'Just zip it for one goddamn second, Duggan! Can't you see I'm trying to sort this out?'

'That's *right*, children,' said the camel. 'They're all *complete* bollocks—'

At this even Bryant noticed. He turned to see the camel lifting its head in braying laughter and it jumped and shrank, disappearing through the eye of a needle. The screen was left with row after row of dancing gophers, gaily spelling out obscenities in song.

With a gesture Bryant silenced the screen. I watched the rows of gophers, and suppressed a smile. Bryant turned menacing eyes to me.

I shrugged and lifted up my hands in denial.
'Nothing to do with me...'

Bryant was about to spit some vile accusation at me when the room door opened and a rather unsettled looking male officer peeped in.

'Sir? Uh... Mister Steel's legal representation has arrived, sir. He's demanding that he be admitted and that no further questioning takes place without his presence. He's citing legal rights I've never even heard of, sir, but the station AI says we should comply.'

Good old JR. I knew he'd come through. He'd hired me a lawyer.

Bryant looked close to having a coronary. He had little choice but to admit the lawyer.

'He'd better be good, for your sake.'

'Oh, he will be,' I retaliated confidently.

JR had found me top brass to kick Bryant's ass, I was sure. He could find practically anything.

The door opened. JR trotted in. He was wearing a small bow-tie. Confidence sailed out of me.

'Good afternoon, gentlemen, lady. My name is Mister Jack Russell, and I shall be representing Mister Steel today.'

JR spoke in a perfect English accent with not a trace of his bawdy Bronx present.

Before Bryant had a chance to explode—his face was by now an incarnadine moustachioed potato—JR began to cite a string of laws which demanded that I be released from custody immediately. He finished with a confident flourish:

'...demand release, denial of which shall constitute tort, exercising his rights endowed under section 4, article 5 of the Uniform Prisoners Act 2014.'

Bryant practically choked on his own tongue. He hit a button to get the verdict from the station AI.

'Full compliance recommended,' was all it had to say on the matter.

'This isn't over,' Bryant warned as we left the station.

JR stopped in his tracks, turned, cocked his head at Bryant and said:
'Are you threatening my client, Sergeant Bryant? Article 4.ii of Section 11 of
the Uniform Fair Treatment Act 2022 clearly states—'
'Just get *out* of my sight.'
We turned and were gone. Once we were safely around the corner, and I'd
recovered a sense of control from laughing, I turned to my four-legged super-
lawyer:
'JR, I don't know *how* you did that—'
'Steel, it's Needle, my friend. Your dog kindly lent me the temporary use of
his body.'
'Needle!'
JR interrupted from the same mouth:
'Guys, *guys*, it's been a hoot, but I'm done with bein' a puppet, If ya don't
mind, I'd like my body back? Bein' possessed ain't all it's cracked up to be.'
'Of course,' Needle said, speaking from my com suddenly. 'My apologies and
sincerest gratitude, Mr Russell. May I make a suggestion?'
'What?'
'That we—or rather you—move somewhat more quickly than you presently
are?'
'Why's that?'
'Well, there's just a *teensy weensy* chance that Sergeant Bryant will discover
that half the laws I cited don't actually exist and that his station AI has been
hacked into a gibbering mess. Whilst it was relatively trivial to turn it into
something that would answer yes to practically anything, including sex with a
gerbil I might add—and I did test this—it's proving *slightly* more troublesome to
fix.'
We ran several blocks laughing and panting, with Needle following like a ghost
in my ear. We twisted and turned at his advice until we were at least ten blocks
away, safe and out of sight.
'I guess I owe you for rescuing me a second time in a week.'
'My reward is knowing you are safe and free, my friend. Now, I'm afraid I
have rather disappointing news for you. I haven't managed to turn up a single
record of this lady friend of yours. It seems the first time she entered a maternity
ward was when you took her to Bellevue. It's rather—'
'She wasn't pregnant. That's why.'
'Pardon?'
'JR? Didn't you tell him anything?'
'Hey! I had a lot on my mind! I forgot! So sue me!'
'Needle, can you access Bellevue's patient scan records?'
'Probably. Hang on. Yes, here we go.'
I waited for a second for him to find her scan.
'Good grief. That's not a deformity, I take it?'
'No. It's implanted. Adult.'
'Her records say she vanished from hospital.'
I explained about the vanishing, the police guard's memory loss, the interfer-
ence with the hospital equipment.
'There's more. I know the name of the assassin. He tried to attack me again
last night. In the station.'
'Are you okay?'
'Just. He was scared off. He had a German accent. He claimed several
names. Viktor Meistermacher, Jens Puppenspieler, some others I can't remember.
Something -bastler. He said something about a hag. Called her the Calculatrice.
I have no idea what it means.'
I contemplated telling Needle about the Looking Glass Club connection but
honestly, I was afraid of his reaction. *Now isn't the time.* The other possible

connection, the one I was in denial about, would either disappear as irrelevant, or I'd find a way to make it fit. For now, it was just a stupid idea.

'So he spoke to you?'

'Yes. He said he was coming to collect me. For the Hag. But he wouldn't say why.'

'For you? Not the woman?'

'That's what he said. He also said that he doesn't have Skyler. Someone else has taken her. She's still alive.'

'What would they want with you?'

'I don't know...'

'Well, clearly I've been looking in *all* the wrong places. This is turning out to be far more interesting than I'd thought.' He paused for a second, doing some unfathomably fast thinking somewhere miles away. 'Okay,' he said finally, 'let me see what I can find out armed with this new information.'

'Wait. One final thing. This may be nothing, but when we were taking Sky to hospital she was delirious and she was talking, muttering stuff.'

'Go on.'

'It could be nonsense, but she said something about white boys. Ghosts or something. She said they'd done this to her. And they would come to get her. At the time, I just put it down to delirium, but then she vanished. Someone did come for her. And Meistermacher insists it wasn't him.'

'Anything else?'

'I think that's it. Needle?'

'Yes?'

'Be quick. Please. If this Meistermacher gets to me before I find out what's going on, I could be a dead man.'

'Steel, my friend,' he said, his voice suddenly sombre. 'I will do my best.'

Needle signed off. JR followed me into a cab that I'd hailed and we headed back to the den. I couldn't go home. Even with Sky gone, it wasn't safe. The police would no doubt have people sniffing around. JR complained that I stank, and he was right. I accessed my account with The English Cut, selected the latest designs for some jeans, a top, some socks and underwear and a thermal over, personalized them on my body proxy, and had the designs sent to the nearest fabber in Tribeca. The clothes were still warm in their packaging when I picked them up ten minutes later. I undressed, ignoring the ads trying to cross-sell me the latest Armani and DeVeaux visionwear, wiped myself down with a Crystyx, changed and then dumped my old clothes in the reclaim for the discount. I hopped back in the cab feeling slightly less grimy, inhaled the unbeatable scent of freshly fabbed clothes. The fit was pretty good, but the top didn't quite look the same in the cab as it had on my proxy. Luckily the fabric was smartdyed, so I tweaked the color a few shades, and played with the font of the text on the back until I was happy with it.

Back at the den, I took a long shower and let the hot water wash away some of the years that seemed to have accumulated on my body over the last few days. I decided to lie low for a while and wait to hear back from Needle. Unfortunately for me, this was pay-back time for the stimulants I'd been taking. For three tense and sleepless nights I lay low, hardly talking, hardly moving, fearing the depression would never end; and fearing another attack, but none came.

On the final night I slept heavily for sixteen hours. And slowly the feelings passed, and I began to feel human again.

JR and I had now spent too much time together in close proximity and began arguing furiously about anything, but especially his new-found religion:

'I mean it's just a *ridiculous* idea. A dog who *dug up* the universe. What was it doing buried in the first place? Where did this Dog come from? Ridiculous. I mean, *ridiculous*.'

'Oh! Oh! You have a nerve. Questioning *my* beliefs. Have you had a good look in the mirror lately, Mister Looking Glass Club?'

Sometimes, I thought, JR was either a lot smarter than he made out, or he had one hell of a knack of faking it.

On the fourth day Needle got back to us. He stood behind my World Wall, life-sized, proud and handsome in his blond, pony-tailed avatar. The camel and needle emblem stitched on his shirt had dancing gophers animated in the background—a new addition.

'I was beginning to give up hope,' Needle said, scratching at his virtual temple. 'But...?'

'I finally made some headway today. This woman has been most remarkably well hidden.'

'What have you found out?'

'Skyler's full name is Louise Skyler Andrésson. She was supposedly on holiday out of the country, presumably for the duration of the operation she was participating in.'

'Which was?'

'Getting this far has been tricky enough, but things should be easier from here.'

'Is that it?'

'Patience, dear boy! Ms Andrésson has had a pretty unremarkable life, but managed to get herself in quite a serious amount of debt. Recently, that debt was wiped out by a claim payment made by company called Barton Insurance.'

'An insurance claim? For what?'

'Well, now there's the interesting thing. Nothing. It's one of very few insurance payments made by the company, which is a wholly owned subsidiary of Barton Holdings. Barton Holdings has indirect but very serious and substantial interests in lots of different companies, many of which are *very* difficult to trace. I'm talking hundreds of billions.'

'So, it was payment for illegal services? Disguised as an insurance claim?'

'One presumes.'

'And you can't find out what Barton Holdings really is?'

'I didn't say that. I said it was very difficult. I didn't say I hadn't done it.' Needle smiled.

'Have you ever heard of Howard Levi?'

'Vaguely. Remind me.'

'He's one of America's richest men. He famously bought the Freedom Tower from the owners in 2017, to save it from growing debts.'

'That's right.'

'Fascinating man. Spent two years in a concentration camp as a young Jew, surviving his parents who perished there. He was only seven at the time; nine when the war ended. He's ninety-nine now. He's still the acting chairman of the H. Levi Group PLC. What's interesting is that although it's extremely well hidden by a cunning corporate architecture so that it doesn't in theory appear to be, Barton Holdings is in *practice* entirely owned by the Levi Group. Howard Levi controls everything. Now, Barton Holdings may sound like a pretty innocuous name, but after some digging I've discovered they not only have dodgy insurance dealings, they have some very wide-ranging interests in state-of-the-art technology firms.'

'Do they now?'

'Yes. Their interests run to fields ranging from medical nanotech, cloning biotech, and get this: *cryonics.*'

'Cryonics?'

I knew *exactly* what the term meant, but Needle misunderstood my inflection as a question:

'The science of longevity through freezing to cryogenic temperatures—whole corpses, or, in many cases what they call neuros—just the heads. It's been practiced since the 1960s, mostly in California, but a batch of the early corpsicles—as they fondly call the whole bodies—thawed out when one company ran out of money. People got sued, the industry got a bad rap, but it picked itself up again. It came back in vogue in the last decade when there was a breakthrough in reversing ice-damage and even survived a second difficult period during the energy crisis in 2018, but there's *never* been a documented case of bringing a frozen corpse back to life. The most that was ever achieved was bringing small animals—frogs and the like—back from frozen. But they'd all been frozen alive.'

'Frozen *heads*...'

'And the breakthrough? Can you guess? Which would never be allowed in humans...?'

'I give in. Tell me.'

'Ice-damaged neuroplasm degrades in a matter of hours if thawed and resurrected. It was discovered that if the blood supply of a thawed brain was connected to that of a growing fetus, *in vivo*, in the live animal, the hormone mixture promoted neuroplasmic repair by itself. They could then ditch the fetus. It wasn't perfect, but it was a staggering result. Piggybacking on a dynamic biological system, perfectly evolved for life. The big problem was it wasn't reproducible outside of a live animal, and didn't look like it ever would be.'

'So the obvious way forward is to keep doing it *in vivo*. In live specimens.'

'Except that would never be legal.'

'Needle, you're a genius.'

'This is all still conjecture. That research was funded by Barton Holdings. Now, it transpires the H. Levi Group *also* own a cryonics company, a legitimate outfit called Revíve,' he pronounced this 'reveev', 'which for years has been freezing bodies and heads of the desperate and dying. I can't find evidence yet that they are actually restoring any. But I'm still looking.'

The odd jigsaw piece was still an impossibly wrong shape, but this news added new possibilities. Things were starting to make a horrible kind of sense. I pondered silently for a moment.

'Well,' I said eventually. 'It sounds to me like a visit to Revíve is in order.'

From the pages of Tony's diary:

Trapped in a box, What are its chances?
Poisoned or living? Look here for the answers...

$$ih\frac{\partial\psi}{\partial t} = -\frac{\hbar^2}{2m}\nabla^2\psi + V(x)\psi$$

Box length = 0.5
$n = 1$
where $x =$

8.3840068673563412020214138867238589566177456835835626735449461O7 × 10^{-9}

8.38820201741031939648031446906833151739032114662905331934656364O × 10^{-9}

8.38400686735596358182021257864634833044102484866148455266837494O × 10^{-9}

0.083333333333333379277453941834666597560959135439777958662OOO806273

0.083333333333333379282007413585471032971184971941121110856660493042

0.083333333333333379277867852007526941289494612895427008162972461O4

7.957790922123545346023278992032475448997778184070120447082878844 × 10^{-10}

0.0883502778316O2461O337031533742626106199462334516772712296390318O

0.0252706560026066383237015432633383527002578583759839080176901493O

0.025270656040081820354384054456412982190969006389104108028189213O8

0.0252706561662334966536818309093123000213649277069297359458805317O

0.0252706574277502261811O1741668899994163745804100508171694587605O0

0.025397785803468844952710706015815122911493638407473331854588161O

0.0252847964827101339814417185217019088147668840780343344751379961O

0.0252706560260649673946974537708160425688366873210487560815169616O

0.0266501895190568373456625773352740283575418870804718444556600262O

Chapter 16

'In classical physics, concepts such as space and time are axiomatic. Their existence and form are assumed a priori. Although General Relativity goes some way to an a posteriori concept, spacetime, the idea that spacetime is an entity with properties such as curvature (which, ipso facto, implies it is a medium), is in direct conflict with other observations.'

—Information Relativity and the New Physics,
Professor Fabrizio T. Luciano

I searched for Jacob everywhere I could think of for the rest of the morning, but he was nowhere to be found. I wanted to tell him about the curtain fire at the funeral, to ask him to just *consider* that I might not be mad, but I failed to find him.

Dejected, cold and feeling dirty, I went back to the hall, and took a hot shower. Images of Vaughan's body, his missing face, the hollowed cavity of his head kept pushing themselves into my mind, and more than once I cried out, pushing those images away from me with ineffective mental hands. I wanted to forget. I came out of the hot shower shivering, and several people gave me strange stares as I left the public bathroom and returned to my room to dry and dress. I could tell I was getting a reputation as a weirdo.

I tried to call Jacob's accommodation again, but it was early afternoon and no-one answered the phone. I thought about Jon. I wasn't sure if he had got back. I had given him little thought since we had returned. Emily had taken his cowardice more badly than I had. I could see from his perspective, he had been through something with Lewis that we had not, and returning to that danger was harder for him. I understood that seeing us flee back around that corner, he had probably run into the club room and shut the door instinctively to protect himself. I couldn't believe that he had intended to lock us in that world.

Even if he had, we could not afford for the club to fracture now. I could not. The effects of the last injection were still active. It wasn't fading like it had before, like it was supposed to. In the daylight the effects were minimal, safe, but I could still feel that things were not normal. I was beginning to be afraid of what would happen when darkness came again. Jon was the only person who could do something about this. He had to make an antidote. He had to work out how.

Although he had never told me, it didn't take much sleuthing to find out where he lived. I checked with his office and lab; he wasn't there. I checked at his friends' house that I had visited when we had first met, and Frankie, the curly-haired dope head that had answered the door that first time, scribbled his address down for me willingly.

I called Jacob's accommodation again. This time a lad answered, but said that he wasn't there, he'd gone out and wasn't likely to be back. There was some big house party that night, maybe he would be there. I thanked the guy, and hung up. It was five o'clock, and outside the light was beginning to fade again. The clocks had gone back a few weeks before. It would be dark soon.

I needed to find Jon.

I took a bus to his apartment. He lived on the top floor of an apartment block in Fulham. I rang and rang the bell but there was no answer. Thinking perhaps that he wouldn't want to answer the door, I pushed open the letterbox and called through. I told him I needed to see him, that I didn't blame him for running away. I listened intently for hints of occupation, but the flat was silent.

It was nearly dark. I didn't know what to do. I sat down in the hall outside his flat and the light timed out and switched off, plunging me into the half-light of dusk. A single orange light glowed on the wall. I jumped up and bashed it with my fist, returning the hall to temporary brightness.

I stayed, sitting down under the light switch, not knowing where to go, my brain numb, hopeless, waiting for the light to time out, lifting my hand to bash it every minute or so, over and over and over, I don't know how many times. Outside the night crept over London in stealth, and the traffic washed by, the irregular waves of an urban sea. Distant sirens wailed and dopplered. Occasional voices flew up to these heights from below. Some distant shouting. Normal city noises.

The light of the corridor timed out again, but this time it relit itself before I could press the button again. I heard the door, many floors down, slam shut, and the lift whined into action. It stopped at the base, the doors opened, closed, and it began its ascent again, arriving presently, a rectangle of light sliding up behind glass.

The doors slid apart, and out stepped Jon, fetching keys from his pocket.

Seeing me sitting by his door, he was startled and cried out. Then he realised it was me and stood very still, in a defensive stance, regarding me cautiously.

I stood, sliding my back up the wall.

'Hi.'

'You frightened me.'

'I'm not here to give you a hard time. I know why you ran. It's okay. I probably would have too.'

He considered this for a moment and recovered some of his usual confidence. He continued to get his keys and came to the door, taking a deep breath. He opened the door and pushed it wide for me to enter, switching the lights with an outstretched arm.

Inside, his flat was small but tidy. Jon switched on the lights in every room. Table and side lamps too. The short yellow-painted hall opened into a kitchen at the back to the left, and to the right a small bedroom, beyond it a living room. A potted plant stood underneath a dark window at the end, green and generous. He obviously preferred to live alone, a luxury for a student in London. He indicated the front room:

'Make yourself at home.'

'This yours or you rent?'

'Mine. Mum and Dad bought it for me.'

'Lucky.'

'Mm-huh.'

He flicked on the strip light in the kitchen. I stood in the doorframe, watching him. The kitchen walls were white and bright, the floor black and white tiles, blue cupboards. He had his back to me and was fishing things out of his pockets.

'How are you feeling?' he asked.

I tried to find the right words.

'The effects aren't wearing off. Things don't feel... as solid as they should.'
He turned to me.
'It's not just me, then.'
'Do you know how to stop it?'
He shook his head. 'Not yet. But this should help.'
He waved his arm at the kitchen counter.
I screwed my eyes and stepped forward to see.
There were six or seven small bags of various white powder.
'Coke?'
'And speed.'
I screwed up my face in disgust. Drugs had caused this mess, and now here he was trying to remedy it with them.
'Fine. Deal with it your way. I just want to get through tonight. And sleep is not an option. Not in the dark. Not in this state.'
I agreed with that. I looked at his eyes. They were dark and ringed.
'Have you slept?'
He shook his head, and turned to his stash and starting to chop up the contents of one of the bags on the counter with a credit card.
'I managed an hour, in the park this morning.'
He swept out several fat lines, took out a twenty, rolled it up and hoovered up two of them, one in each nostril. Then he took in a deep lungful of air afterwards, and clenched his teeth with chemical resolve. He certainly gave the impression he felt safer. Then he proffered the rolled-up note to me, eyebrows lifted into a silent question.
I took the note and copied him.
'There's a big party on tonight. Lee Chalmer's place. It's massive.'
'A party? Are you mad? How can you think about—'
'Zeke. *Shut up.* Think about it. We need to stay awake. If we're around people, things are safe.'
He was right. And wasn't Jacob going to something tonight? Wasn't that what the boy on the phone had said? Maybe it was the same place. Maybe I could find him there.
Jon put the television on and went to take a shower in the en-suite bathroom. I sat and let the cocaine and the television bind me to the vapid reality of modern society. Jon returned, and we wasted the hours until the party snorting lines and trying to talk about the normal things that the television presented to us, instead of the obvious. It was hard.
Eventually Jon decided it was late enough for us to go. He gave me a bag of my own, a mixture of coke and speed to keep me through the night.
'Don't drink too much. Alcohol's a depressant, it'll work against the stimulants.'
We made our way out onto the street.
I had so many questions.
'Jon, Emily told me something about how Tony died...'
Jon turned on me with an unfathomably guarded expression and took both of my shoulders in his hands. He seemed fully six inches taller than me then, though I knew he was just two or three, and for a moment, reacting to some subconscious cue perhaps, I panicked that he actually was about to strike me. But he looked intensely into my eyes, then deeper still, as if boring his attention into me and when he was sure I was entirely captive, like a mouse in the paws of a cat, he spoke, softly and clearly, an instruction masquerading as a request:
'Zeke, I really, really, *really* need to just have some fun tonight. Please don't bring up anything about that subject or the club again. Let's just keep it *real*, okay?'

He released me and we walked in silence for a time. The anger did not come immediately. It rose slowly, sneaking up on me, so that by the time it blossomed into a flower of outrage inside me I almost lost myself to it. I felt my fingers clench into a fist. A vivid image flashed into my mind of me driving it into Jon's face, pummelling it into a bloody mess.

'You. . . ' But the sentence was too spiked with outrage and caught in my throat.

I saw shock register on Jon's face. He reacted to my stance. His arms jerked up defensively and he side-stepped away, bunching his head into his neck, using his shoulder as a shield. His shock turned to fear; it vanished immediately, but what replaced it was something I'd never seen on Jon's face, ever. He realised that I had not actually moved. I'd thrown no punch. His expression turned to horror and he reddened furiously. I suddenly felt a wave of disgust at him and shook my head fractionally but said nothing. We were not moving, nothing changed, but in that lengthy silence, everything transformed.

Jon recovered his posture, but still regarded me uncertainly:

'Are we good?'

I stared at him, surprised by the contempt I felt.

'Yeah,' I said. 'We're good.'

We walked in silence the rest of the way. Before we entered, Jon turned to me once more:

'Look. . . .Zeke, I'm sorry if I was out of order, okay? We've all been through a lot.' I nodded, feeling unexpectedly emotional. He smiled tentatively and bunched his fist, gently press-punching my chest. I returned the gesture and felt the tension between us fall away.

Lee Chalmer's house, the location of the party, was indeed massive. Spanning four floors, with six bedrooms, two huge reception rooms and an enormous kitchen and garden, it was the perfect place to host a party. And, housing twelve people, it was almost a halls of residence in itself.

Once inside the house, Jon—ever popular—was quickly recognised and dragged off to say hi to people he hadn't seen for a while. He seemed relieved to be able to slip into his people-magnet character, the social attractor. I envied him.

I knew no-one. Normally I would have hated this, but I was no longer the social inadequate I had been. I used to be desperately bad at the kind of small-talk one needs to kick-start conversations at a party, and without a conversation to anchor me to the centre of the room, I tended to find myself buffeted like some swimming pool flotsam into a corner on my own. Tonight was very different. Tonight, I was a member of the Looking Glass Club. No-one would know this, but I knew. And whilst I was trying to forget what we had been through, that experience made me who I now was. I didn't realise how much of this confidence was chemical. It didn't matter. I was charged. I took myself straight into a group of people I half-recognised and introduced myself. Talk for once came easily. The events of the previous trip continued to try to battle their way into my mind, but as the evening drew on, I found it easier and easier to ignore them, and focused on the pretence of normality.

The house gradually filled, and whereas initially it had been mostly the music occupying the large rooms, after an hour, it was the rabble noise of conversation, shrieking and laughter that dominated.

I pulled myself gently away from the group I was stuck too and went in search of Jon on the floor below.

I was sure that he would be the centre of some group of laughter, but to my surprise, he seemed surly and almost aggressively engaged in an argument with an intense Chinese-American girl wearing thick dark plastic-rimmed glasses. I wasn't clear if he knew her or had just met her.

'We have a social responsibility for those less fortunate than ourselves, surely, Jonathan,' she had said in level Southern-States tones that barely masked hostility.

'It's not fortune, or luck,' he'd responded tartly. 'People make their own luck. Why should hard-working people in society have to carry people who can't be bothered to get off their arses and work for a living? Why do we actually *pay them money* to be lazy? Why not just shoot them? Cut off the dead wood. That would motivate the work-shy bastards.'

I'd never heard Jon like this.

The American appraised Jon coolly from behind her glasses. She wasn't attractive, but she carried a sense of grace, and the glasses gave her the air of an intellectual. Jon was being deliberately extreme and antipodal. Nobody who knew him would have believed he wanted to shoot people, but one couldn't help doubting how he would cast his vote if it came to one.

'Don't you consider yourself fortunate that you were born intelligent, Jon?'

'Yes I do, but I worked bloody hard at school and through university to get my doctorate.'

'I'm sure you did. And that's very commendable, Jon. I'm sure also that you must also feel very fortunate that you were doubly blessed by being born a hard-worker.'

'It's a choice we make every day. We all have free will.'

'I take it since you want to move into cryonics that you're a biologist?'

Cryonics? Jon had never mentioned this ambition to me.

'Biochemical neurologist.'

'Right. Well, it's a common belief among biologists, isn't it, Jon, that character traits are either genetically or environmentally caused... what is it they say?... nature or nurture?'

'Or a combination. Simplistic, but yes.'

'There's no third option? You don't believe in the soul?'

'No.'

'So laziness and stupidity must be either genetic or environmental?'

He wasn't prepared to agree just like that, but he didn't offer a counter argument.

'Then you must agree,' she continued with a smile, 'that we have no choice about the environment we are born into, and even less over the genes we inherit? God forbid had you been born with *stupid* or *lazy* genes or into a stupid or lazy family... or, a *combination* as you say.'

Jon elected not to respond but simply stared at her controlled smiling face.

' 'The obstinate man does not hold opinions, they hold him'—Samuel Butler,' she said and she tightened her smile. 'Well, we seem to be running low on *cocktail mix*. Let me go make some more.' And with that she left.

'Stupid bitch,' Jon muttered barely audibly, and he knocked back a glass of something clear.

I'd been feeling strong and fine. Yesterday's events were no more than fleeting dream images by this time, but suddenly I was beginning to feel fatigue weighing down on me again like a heavy cloak. Too much alcohol. I remembered Jon's warning. He suggested we do another line of coke, so we went upstairs to a toilet on the top floor and did one. I watched, fascinated by the ritual, wondering if that was half the attraction of the drug. Jon handed me the note he'd just rolled and I snorted the line, realising a little too late just how big he'd made them. I screwed up my face in both pain and revulsion at the disgusting tasting lump of nastiness that was sliding its way down the back of my throat, turning it numb as it went. Jon laughed without humour and did his. My drunkenness evaporated quietly in the ether of the coke.

We left the bathroom and made our way down the stairs again, sidling past the people who had made the staircase, for whatever unfathomable reason, their choice of dwelling to chat. I wanted to ask him why he wanted to move into cryonics. It seemed like such an odd choice of research given the circumstances. But I never got to ask the question.

It was through a set of banister poles that I saw her.

Unmistakeably her. Those soft dark curls, seeming even more lustrous than usual, poking out from beneath a dark lilac beret, framing her gentle face, her high, noble cheekbones. Her delicate skin, made silky and perfect with artistic excellence. The strong nose, ever so slightly pug: perfectly imperfect. Glistening cerise-painted lips, round and soft, contrasting the paleness of her complexion. Her tiny chin, narrowing in that sultry curve from her strong jaw, giving her face the impression of a squared-off heart. A generous, rare, pretty face.

Queen of hearts.

I didn't even know that I had stopped on the staircase until people pushed past me, complaining. Jon had disappeared ahead of me. I remembered the strange looks she had given me in the recent tutorial. I hadn't imagined those. Her attitude had distinctly changed towards me. I pulled back my watch strap and looked at the tattoo hiding underneath it on the underside of my wrist. I had no reason to fear anything after the things I had been through.

Columbian confidence flooded through me.

Kate disappeared into one of the rooms.

How long had she been here?

I would stroll down into the room, sneak up behind her, slip one arm confidently around her slim waist and in a soft voice, gently say hello into her perfect, tiny ear. She'd giggle, instantly knowing it was me, turn to face me, and then—

I strolled down the stairs and turned the corner, my eyes flitting from person to person and there! There was the beret (what other student in this place had that kind of style? Who could wear such a thing and pull it off? Who could look so chic, instead of contrived?). She was facing away from, just as I had fantasised.

I walked up to her in a straight line, people seemed to part from me like the waters of the red sea.

And there was Jacob.

Standing right next to her.

I looked down, incredulous, and as my eyes fell so did my heart. It fell to the floor, all the warmth leaving it as it dropped, turning black and glassy, and it shattered, there and then, in that moment, into a million shards of razor sharp glass. Blackened shards for me to walk across, barefoot, forever.

Their little fingers were casually interlocked.

My memory of what happened next is hazy, though I learned that some considerable time passed where I managed to drink a substantial quantity of alcohol. All I clearly recall is that image, the two of them, stood so innocently with their backs to me, next to each other, their unity betrayed solely by those interlocking digits. Those digits betraying *me*.

My own *brother*!

I vaguely remember being found on a sofa on a different floor, then being escorted to a bathroom, a caring, supporting arm around me. Vomiting into white porcelain. The acid sobs that wracked me then disguised by my retching, the tears streaming down my face mingling with and camouflaged by those induced by the burning contents of my stomach.

There was nothing left of my world. Nothing at all.

Comforting words from someone, entirely misplaced.

It was some time before I realised that it was Jon that was with me in the bathroom. I pulled my head away from my white prison.

'*Hell*, man,' he said. 'I should have kept an eye on you. You're not used to it. I told you not to drink too much. It's easy to drink too much on this stuff. Keeps you going way past your natural limits.'

I grunted a response, tasting unwelcome acid in my mouth.

'Let's get you sorted. Steer clear of the booze for a while, okay?'

Jon pulled out the tiny plastic sachet of cocaine and speed and a set of house keys.

'No time for niceties, eh?' he said, and dug deep into the white powder with one of the keys, offering a small white heap up to my nostril.

I sniffed and a little of the fog was swept away. He repeated the action twice more. Finally, I was alert enough to sit on the toilet seat, which he put down for me.

All I managed to do was swear, holding my head in my hands.

Jon laughed. 'Hey, no worries, little guy. Everyone goes too far sometimes.'

A small pathetic sob made its way out of me, against my will.

Jon put a fatherly arm around me again.

'Don't beat yourself up. You just got a bit sick. Drank too much.'

I wasn't about to explain. I took a deep breath and let the effects of the cocaine flood through my system, obliterating my depression, or rather, squeezing it into a hard, defined point. I clenched my teeth together and ground them against each other, as though I were grinding my misfortune into dust.

'Your brother's here. I said you were around. Do you want me to get him?'

I let out a sarcastic guffaw.

'Yeah, maybe that would be a bad idea,' Jon muttered for an entirely different reason.

Jon was referring to his theory about twins. To the visions that through agreement we were able to bring to reality. Not the disagreement implicit in Jacob's theft of the woman of my dreams, to his theft *of my dreams*. Not to his violation of the sanctity of fraternal trust and fraternal love. Not merely fraternal: the bond of twins.

Oh, Kate. . .

I felt an enormous up-welling of the purest blackest hatred for my brother at that moment, a sick tide, rising up inside me, like the sudden swell of water in a pothole or geyser. It was elemental: a liquid hatred drowning me; a fire consuming me; a thick earth burying me; a savage tornado ripping the warmth from my heart.

I was drowned, yet arid; buried, yet unable to die.

I wanted to cry, to pour that liquid hatred from me in a lacrimal torrent that would flood the house, the street, the earth.

But I could not.

Perhaps it was the cocaine—I will never know—but my tears did not, could not, come any more. The grief I felt was too deep. And grief it was, for—perhaps it is always this way with the loss of one's first love—it was more than the loss of love, it was the death of a dream. Love and death. Always together, entwined like saplings—like twins in the womb.

The little death I had longed to experience with her had been exchanged for the grand death of a dream.

I sat bolt upright. I took a deep, invigorating breath through my nostrils, feeling and smelling the residue of coke in the depths of my sinuses, taking solace in its sharp, intoxicating vapours.

Then I walked out of the bathroom without a word of thanks to Jon, who forgave my actions as those of someone drunk, and I went searching the house.

I did not plan to do what I did. I did not have any vision for action. I just intended to find them, and find them I did.

The party had quietened a little, though the music was just as loud, the crowds had thinned. Jacob and Kate were in one of the large reception rooms, standing apart from the others. He had an arm around her shoulder, she looked under strain, and I realised that she was supporting him.

Jacob was also very drunk. Perhaps he had anticipated a confrontation, knowing as he must have how I might react after my confession to him in the park. This would be a typical way of defending himself, obliterating himself in alcohol. I had done the same, hadn't I? Only cocaine and speed meant that I was still conscious.

I walked up to them. Kate saw me. Jacob's head was lolling around, incapable of seeing me.

'Oh, Zeke, thank God it's you,' she said, entirely without irony. She slurred her words unprettily. 'He's really drunk. I've never seen him like this. He's been acting weird all night. I'm really worried.'

I smiled wanly. She continued:

'Has. . . ?'

She threw this vague word out like a pathetic net, and shook her head questioningly at me, hoping to fish something with it, but whilst it was wide enough, the mesh was too loose to catch a thing.

'Has?' I countered.

'Well. . . Uh. . . Has something happened?'

'Lots of things have happened.'

She looked at me strangely.

'I mean, do you know what would make him act so. . . so. . . you know?'

What? Act like a thief? Betray his own blood? His own twin?

'He's been under a bit of pressure. You know, studies. That kind of thing,' I lied. 'He can get like this sometimes,' I continued. 'Don't worry, I know how to handle him.'

I smiled at Kate and took Jacob under my shoulder.

'Oh God, thanks!' she said, genuinely relieved, and let me take his weight.

'I didn't know you two were dating. . . ' I said, feigning indifference—brilliantly by my own judgement.

She smiled bashfully and let out a small laugh, showing a brief glimpse of perfect white teeth, which bit savagely into my heart.

'We've only known each other a few weeks really. . . '

Why him and not me? I've known you for a whole fucking term.

She cocked her head to one side, and squinted at me.

'You look so alike, it's freaky.' And she let out that tiny bashful laugh again, such a minute gesture to have such a heavy, crushing influence on me.

I smiled again, hoping she could not see the insincerity of it. Hoping that she could not sense the utter emptiness in my chest.

You look so alike, it's freaky, she'd said. I already knew the subtext of her comment. We looked alike, but we were not. He was acceptable, fanciable, whereas I was rejection material.

I felt my face flushing with anger and humiliation.

'Why don't you wait here. I'll help him sober up.'

She looked gratefully at me and I heaved Jacob into a more secure position under my shoulder and took him away. He could barely support his own weight, but I struggled up the stairs with him, to the top floor, into one of the empty bedrooms. I hoisted him in the darkness across the room and laid him down on the bed on top of a pile of coats. I closed the door behind me and switched on a small lamp. I watched him in silence for a moment, hearing just the bass thumping noise of music filtering up through the floor. He let out a snort, then seconds later a snore.

He'd fallen asleep. How I envied his unconsciousness.

My mind raced over an unfamiliar terrain, a minefield of thoughts that could explode into molten humiliation and anger unexpectedly. I wanted that terrain to swallow me into its fires, submerge me under its lava, and consume me.

I had such a multitude of thoughts, exploring so many crazy ideas and possibilities that it is now impossible for me to know how I came, eventually, to decide to do what I did.

I wish I could say that I was acting out of anger and humiliation. I wish I could deny responsibility for my actions, diminish it with the excuse of alcohol, of cocaine. But I cannot.

I *rationalised* what I did.

I justified it to myself.

Yes, I was drunk. Yes, I was high, and under the subtle, perverting influence of cocaine and speed, and who knows what residual effects of the meta. But I still cannot escape that I knew what I was doing. I knew just how wrong it was. And I did it anyway. And perhaps, therefore, I deserved the consequences, though we all suffered those.

I shook my brother to try and wake him, but his slumber was extreme. Deep enough that he did not stir as I took off his shoes, removed his trousers and manoeuvred him onto his side, slipping off his shirt in jerky stages.

He lay there snuffling in porcine inebriety whilst I, in my chemical sobriety, dressed quietly in his clothing. I folded my own clothes under the bed and, finding the tunnel map in my pocket, thought better of leaving it for someone to find and slipped it into my stolen trousers' pocket.

I told myself she was mine to take. He had stolen something from me before I'd even had the chance to win it. Even after I had *confided my feelings to him.* Though she had said they'd met weeks before, I couldn't accept this as truth.

She was drunk. Possibly she knew him well enough to discern the subtle differences between us sober, but she did not that night. She followed me, hand in hand, as I led her into another bedroom, placed my fingers on her lips to shush her questions and concerns. She believed completely that I was Jacob.

We are genetically identical, I had told myself. What's the difference? In a sense, she's making love to the person she wants, I told myself this as we kissed, as I slid my hand under the silk of her blouse and touched the purer silk of her skin, electrifying my fingertips as it brushed against them. I breathed in her heady scent and let it fill the void she had created in me. Her passion ignited suddenly like kindling wood, her resistance did not simply drop, but inverted, became a powerful force, pulling me passionately, almost desperately towards her, my mouth into her mouth.

Eventually, me into her.

She cried out *his* name in her *petite mort* when it came. I cried out hers in mine, but my cry grew, my *petite mort* lifted itself up like a vast phantom against the walls around us, it drew itself up to a staggering height, into the *grande mort* that it really was: a solitary death, not a shared one; a living death so great it cast shadows over Hades. The ominous, oppressive weight of what I had done toppled over onto me during the terrible empty seconds after my ejaculation and crushed the life from me.

I began to weep. I let her hands comfort me. I took her soothing words and her caring strokes like a thief, as she struggled to comprehend what was happening. She gave up trying to tease clues from me eventually and simply held me tight into the soft warmth of her bosom and loved me.

Not me. Jacob. She loved Jacob.

My tears stopped flowing. Something hardened terribly inside me.

'I have to go. I'm sorry.'

Bewildered, she tried to stop me. Him.

I quickly dressed amid her confused, sad, drunken protests and slipped out of the room, telling her I was going home, that I had to go home, I closed the door gently behind me. And then I went to the other bedroom, where Jacob lay still, in his vile slumber, and I entered and locked the door and sat with my back to it with my head in my hands, shaking in silence.

I sat that way for a while, trying to ward off thoughts like demons. The shadows moved to the quiet thumping of the party dying beneath us. I thought I heard her door open and close across the landing, and footsteps make their way down the stairs. I imagined I heard the sound of a single sob from the stairwell as the sound of footsteps faded.

I took Jacob's shirt to the bathroom en-suite. It had lipstick marks. I washed it under the hot tap with soap, scalding myself, but uncaring.

I deserved the pain.

Jacob woke when I put his trousers on again. Confusion scrunched his face like paper.

'Wha' y'd'n?' he mumbled.

'You were sick,' I said in a dead tone. 'I had to wash your shirt.'

'Where's Kate?'

'Gone home.'

Jacob grunted and let his head fall back to the bed, asleep.

I left his shirt to dry on a chair, and I went home, back to my room, and sat in silence snorting what was left of the cocaine and speed until the morning.

From the pages of Tony's diary:

An existential question is the answer, and sounds like the Bard.

2C8HJD5DJC2D2C2C10DJD6DKD2S9D7S9DAHJH8CJC2D4DJKQHJHQC2C
6C10D3S2C3S9S10SACKDJK4CJS10CQC10CJH8CAHJD9H2S9D6HJH8H7H
4CJDJSAD3D8D5CAS5DJC6C7D5DAS2DJC5S6H7CJHAD3D3CJK5S8D5HAH
9DJD9D6S4DACQS4HKC3SJKJH4CJH5SJHKH2C5S9S9DJCQS6H8CJS8DJC
8D10DJK10H7H10S5C4D6D3S7C9CAC9D4D10C2C10S8D3D8S4D4C3DKCK
D3HQCKS4S8H2C9C3D10D6D6SJHJC5S9S5SQC7S4S6D7SQDAC5SJC2H7D
3S2SKH4C2S10D3D5CKDQC7S5D5SQS3SQH5H

155

Chapter 17

'The Knight looked surprised at the question. "What does it matter where my body happens to be?" he said. "My mind goes on working all the same."'

—Through the Looking Glass

When most people virt places these days, they at least wear Shades. The illusion of being there is enhanced when both your eyes are being fed the same information they would be if you really were. If people are virting to a communal place, they'll usually have an avatar representing them, instead of snooping invisibly; sometimes a realistic copy of themselves, sometimes something wildly different. I don't wear Shades if I can help it. It takes a bit of getting used to, but I use my World Wall to virt places. It shows in true 3D whatever my avatar happens to be looking at, which can be pretty disorientating if he swings his head up and down too much. I'm too jaded by gaming to use a fancy avatar. Six cams positioned on the walls at strategic points ahead and to the side of me constantly record my expression. A blindingly fast GPU then combines them into a dynamic texture-mapped mesh, resulting in an avatar that looks exactly like a live 3D video of me. My face anyway. What my body is doing is interpreted by a control interface that determines the behavior of the avatar's body in a way that's not always immediately intuitive to an outsider. Someone unfamiliar with Linglyph would be forgiven for thinking I'm speaking to someone in a bizarre new sign-language, or someone incanting a strange and silent magic, but the combination of my hand gestures and movements and the sub-vocalizations recorded by my laryngeal and lingual implants are all controlling my avatar's body in real time. It's just a puppet with unusual strings, although it knows how to move itself most of the time, so I'm really just directing.

My avatar stood convincingly beyond the glass of my World Wall. I watched its subtle movements as it pretended to breathe, and I mused over what Needle had told me. Skyler had received a large bogus insurance claim from Barton Insurance, owned by Barton Holdings. Barton Holdings had hundred-billion-dollar interests in all sorts of tech areas and was covertly owned by the H. Levi Group along with Revíve, a legitimate cryonics company whose business was storing frozen human heads. He'd also uncovered evidence of an unethical procedure that had the possibility of reviving frozen human heads using living women and their wombs as hosts, hijacking the natural process of pregnancy. I hadn't thought through my plan very far, but if Needle was right, and if these elements were linked, then Revíve deserved a virtual visit.

I invoked a Linglyph, and I was instantly there.

Revíve's offices were slick. After handshaking my interface and querying its rendering capabilities—and getting Faster-Than-You as the answer—they turned

156

on the whole show and threw every detail switch imaginable, presumably thinking they could break my hardware. They were wrong, of course.

I was impressed with whoever had designed it. You could even see dust catching the light near the window, whirling around in fluid vortices stirred up in real time; and when the stunningly seductive sales agent walked in to greet me, her avatar was flawlessly lifelike.

Presumably they'd gone to all this effort to take one's mind off things. *Welcome to the Head Chop Shop! You're going to die, but it's okay, come on in— we've got nice graphics!*

Very comforting.

'Good afternoon, sir,' the agent said. 'Welcome to Revíve. I'm Mandy.'

She smiled. I smiled back.

'Is your interest in Revíve for yourself, sir, or on behalf of a relative?'

'I just want some information.'

'Certainly, sir. I'm here to answer your questions.'

'Are you able to restore the people you freeze?'

'A very common question. The answer I'm afraid right now is no. However advances in technology are being made all the time, in fact they're accelerating, so we're hopeful a process will be perfected within the next decade, and become available a few years afterwards.'

'But there's no process that works right now?'

'No, sir. But we're extremely confident—'

'Do you research reanimation methods?'

'No, sir. Our business is preservation. We don't have the resources to research reanimation, however there are groups across the world who—'

'But you are well funded and backed, are you not?'

'Indeed we are, sir. Rest assured that we're exceptionally financially stable. Indeed, during the energy crisis in 2018 many of our competitors lost refrigeration, causing irreparable damage. Potentially many stored lives were lost. We not only survived the crisis, we grew.'

'Ha. You kept your heads cool when everyone around you was losing theirs?'

'Our heads are stored at minus one hundred and ninety-seven degrees!'

'Er... joke?'

She looked uncertain for a moment and then continued:

'Our company is backed by one of the strongest American institutions. When our competitors were in crisis we acquired several of them immediately to save further loss of potential life.'

'How noble.'

Time to get hard.

'I'm aware of your backing. What I'm not clear about is why you're keeping mum about the fact that you are researching reanimation, and in fact succeeding.'

'I'm sorry, sir, I don't understand "keeping mum"?'

'Keeping quiet. Is it by any chance because your practices are illegal?'

'Perhaps I explained poorly, let me rephrase—'

She kept her cool well, I had to give her that. I cut her off again:

'I have evidence that Revíve is directly affiliated with an illegal research operation that is reviving heads right now.'

She paused a second.

'I'm sorry, sir, Would you like to rephrase your question?'

Oh no... I'd realized a bit late.

'You're a bot, aren't you? A zombie.'

'That's correct, sir!' she said brightly. 'To be precise I am Mandybot version 11.3 by Life Systems, winners of the Turing Competition for six consecutive years. I'm programmed with an extensive database—'

'Save it,' I snapped. There was no point in talking to a glorified set of rules. It was time to execute my brilliantly conceived plan. 'Tell your PR department the press is here and if they don't get a human to answer some of my questions pronto there's going to be some pretty unpleasant press about you tomorrow.'

'Oh, I'm sorry to hear that, sir,' Mandy said pleasantly. She beamed and wrinkled her nose sweetly. 'I'll get Jarod Nino for you, right away.'

What happened next I was not expecting. The Mandybot put her fingers to her lips and let out a surprisingly forceful wolf whistle, but that wasn't the surprise. A minute later this happened:

The door flew open and a very nattily dressed man walked in. His hand was extended to shake that of my avatar—obligatory netiquette politesse stolen directly from real life. He just about managed to get the J of his first name out of his mouth and then his eyes widened and his forced expression of amity changed so quickly I almost felt a breeze.

'You?!'

He looked utterly horrified.

There was a moment of stunned silence between us.

'Mandy, fuck off,' he snapped, and we were instantly alone.

'You know me?' I asked.

Horror turned to puzzlement, but then he looked at himself and comprehended.

'Go away,' he said. He used a tone you might use with someone you knew was not going to listen to you anyway.

'Where's Skyler? What have you done with her? Where is she?'

'She's safe. The procedure is complete.'

'Then let her go.'

He tutted.

'I'm serious about going to the press.'

'Oh no, no. That's exactly why I'm hanging on to her. She's my guarantee. You won't go to the press. Or the police. I'll know if you do. Listen to me, stay out of this. If you care about this woman you'll do exactly as I say. Okay?'

His voice carried a quiet, deadly certainty.

Nino's face and his voice meant nothing to me, but his avatar, like Needle's, could have been configured to look and sound like anyone.

'Who are you?'

He didn't answer. Instead, he looked at me with infinite sadness in his eyes. '*It has to be you now.* Take my advice. Run away. Now. While you have a chance. Don't do this. The Looking Glass Club... I thought I... but I was wrong... it's all out of control. Take the advice that she never did, Zeke. *Stay away.* I still believe you have a choice. I have to believe that.' He paused for a few seconds before delivering his final sentence: 'I'm sorry about your brother.'

With his words still reverberating through my skull, the connection to the Revíve virtual office was cut, sending corrupted polygons skittering across the Wall in a garish explosion. I tried reconnecting at least a dozen times, but the connection was refused. I could try to go in via a proxy, but what was the point? Whoever he was, Jarod Nino clearly had no intention of speaking with me further. I hardly knew Skyler but this man knew that I wouldn't let her come to harm. I daren't risk going to the press, or the police now. I was left in shock, with a hollow cavity where my stomach and guts should have been.

What did he mean he was sorry about my brother? For some reason, that reference shocked me far more than I ever would have predicted.

Eventually JR pawed me out of my silence, eager for news. I'd asked him to leave during the call so he hadn't heard the conversation.

'He knew me,' I said, finally finding my voice. 'I didn't recognize him, but he knew me. And he talked about the club. And my brother.'

'Are you okay?'

'No. No, I'm not. He's got Skyler. If we try anything, he might kill her.'

Just as I thought we were making progress we were stopped by a brick wall again. I felt helpless.

JR looked at me with a desperate sympathy in his eyes. It was impossible for him to remain buoyant when I was so desolate.

'I'll pray for you tonight,' he said. 'To Dog. I'll ask Her to get Needle to call.'

I couldn't muster energy enough to respond. I just opened my arms and he jumped into them. He licked at the saline brimming in my eyes until we fell asleep together on our little couch; until dawn broke through the grimy windows.

When Needle did in fact contact me the next day, JR said nothing but I noticed afterwards that he was more sprightly than I'd seen him since he'd lost his collar. I'd recovered a little from the shock, but not much.

I updated Needle on what had happened. He looked earnest for a moment.

'I see.'

'Well, there's no profile on Jarod Nino. I already checked. Nothing of interest anyway. That in itself is suspicious. He's gone to unusual extremes to stay offline.'

'Can you disable his avatar?'

'Possibly, but if he's refusing connections we don't have the opportunity.'

JR was standing with his head cocked to one side, staring intensely at nothing in particular and routinely cocking it the other way. It's something he does when he tries really hard to think. Without invoking external help I mean. He's a proud dog. He likes to think for himself. Just because he *can* connect to over a billion services that can think in very specific ways for him, doesn't mean he always *does*. He understands the concept of cheating, you see. The trouble is, he doesn't have a terribly good record of results thinking for himself.

By now my mood had degraded somewhat. This tends to happen when you feel you're getting nowhere after being chased by a maniac whose poor grip on reality adversely affects yours; shot at; had someone kidnapped; been told bad news about your twin; taken large doses of class A drugs which fuck with your brain; and had ghosts from the past resurrected when you *really* could have done with a nice quiet night at home with a cup of tea. I thought I was doing quite well under the circumstances. Granted I was a little tetchy.

'JR, what are you *doing*?' I snapped.

'How do you do anagrams again?'

'JR?! Is this *really* the time?'

A few months ago he'd become obsessed with an old puzzle game called Sudoku that was popular when I was kid. He found tons of them in a newspaper archive. You may know the game. The rules of Sudoku are simple deductive logic rules though it uses the numbers one to nine. It appears to be a maths puzzle, though in truth there's no maths in it at all. That was the attraction for him, I think. JR and numbers, it wasn't pretty, trust me.

'You have to use *all* the letters, right? You can't add any?'

'Of *course* you have to use all the letters,' I said, exasperated. 'You might as well just make up the answer otherwise.'

'Oh,' he muttered and fell silent, depressed.

'One day...' I muttered, vaguely threatening I'm not sure what.

I shook my head in disbelief and turned back to Needle. ˙

'Please tell me you've found something?'

He arched an eyebrow as if challenging me to doubt him. Somehow it was the perfect response given my emotional state. I smiled wanly.

The Wall filled with a new view of a building.

'The entire top floor,' Needle said, 'is leased by Hurasat Computing, one of the companies in the Barton Holdings portfolio. They employ few staff and purport to rent processing power out to third parties from their super computer cloud.

I noticed them because their price per petaflop is suspiciously uncompetitive. I don't see how they can have any customers.'

'And do they?'

'I couldn't access their client list. But my guess is, no. I think the company is a cover. They don't have any super computers. I tried to rent some processing power from them, just to see. My enquiry was ignored.'

'So what? Maybe they're busy? This is a pretty tenuous link so far, Needle. How many rented spaces does Barton Holdings have indirect interests in?'

'Hold your horses. I couldn't access their client list, but I *was* able to trace some of their purchases from other companies. Two years ago another of Barton Holdings's companies invested forty million dollars in a single product order with Honda. That purchase order was shipped, not to them, but to *this* office.'

'So?'

'Guess what they bought.'

'From Honda? I don't know. Motorbikes? Vans?'

'Forty million dollars worth?'

'I *don't know*, tell me.'

'Nurses.'

'What?'

'Nurses. iNurses to be precise. Twelve of Honda's finest, top-of-the-line medicare robots.'

'The white boys...' Finally, a lead I felt positive about. 'Skyler's ghosts.'

'Exactly,' said Needle. 'And why? A robot nurse never tells tales... no matter what kind of patient they're asked to look after. I'd wager quite a considerable sum that our mysterious disembodied head was put into incubation inside Skyler right here. Whilst her hormones were getting to work reversing ice damage they grow a new clone body, and once everything's ready, they remove the brain and spinal stem from its old skull and rehouse it in the pristine skull using a similar nerve bundle collar technology I used on JR. Same old brain, brand-new body. This technology is *very* new. But a process like this even in the prototype stage would be worth trillions. My guess is that this place is being turned into a hospice for wannabe immortals.'

'Then we have to get inside,' I said.

'Good. I was hoping you'd say that. I suggest you do a physical reconnaissance of the building whilst I check out its net security. This was a smart location to hide an illegal operation. It certainly has the spare capacity; with seventy percent of the population home working now they've struggled to rent the floor space almost ever since it was built. A bit of a white elephant, which is how Levi bought it so cheap. But because of its history it was built with security that is just about the highest level in Manhattan.'

'Then how am I supposed to get in to do a recce?'

'There are public areas. The observation deck, the restaurant. Getting into those should be no problem. Getting into areas where eyes are not wanted is another matter. I'm not expecting anything, but keep your eye out for security gaps that might not be obvious from the building plans. Human or process weaknesses. Whenever you see security doors, check the types of locks they use. If they're mechanical they won't necessarily be detailed on schematics. Most of all, *you* need to be familiar with the building layout before we try to break in.'

I could see JR out of the corner of my eye. He was still rigid and staring at nothing, but the alternation frequency of his head-cocking had increased.

'JR...' I said with a barbed tone equivalent to a shot across the bow.

'Did Jon Rodin have a middle name?' he said, disarming me completely.

'Beg pardon?'

'Did Jon Rodin have a middle name?'

'Uh. . . I can't remember. Yes, I think so. Anthony, I think. Andrew. Something like that.'

'Ha!' JR exclaimed and then barked excitedly. He jumped in place and began to strut proudly around, wagging his tail confidently.

'Jarod Nino. . .' he said, 'is an anagram of Jon A. Rodin.'

Needle and I looked at each other.

Then Needle laughed.

'I think an apology is in order,' Needle said, and discreetly vanished. 'I'll be in touch.'

'You can't eat an apology. I think Flibbety Gibbets are in order,' JR said.

Later, I was preparing to leave on my reconnaissance mission when the chimes from nomansland alerted me to a contact attempt. I paused, and returned to my desk screen and established a connection. It was Lewis.

'Where the hell have you been?' I said. 'I've been trying to get hold of you.'

'Yes, I know. I got your messages.'

Then I noticed the background behind him. It was different. I did a quick trace on the connection. It wasn't coming from London.

'Hang on. Where are you?'

He paused for a second before answering.

'I'm in a hotel.'

'Where?'

'Zeke, I'm in Manhattan.'

I walked with JR from the snowy sidewalk to the canopy of young oaks. Their thin winter branches cross-hatched the windows of the skyscrapers above. The canopy had sheltered the Memorial Park from some of the snow. If I didn't look up, I could perhaps imagine I was in a winter forest. A strange man-made, meticulous forest. The kind of forest nature would grow if she suffered from obsessive compulsive disorder; regular rows of trees, planted with neurotic precision. The night wind was cold and dry, and I could hear it howling, a deep and morbid moan around the majestic towers whose images were fractured by the branches of this faux forest. Above, the broad needle of light shining starwards from the spire of the tower proudly pierced the night sky.

JR seemed oblivious to the chill and was trotting toward the first of the great square pools that symbolised the two towers that had once stood here. I heard the rush of water ahead, falling into the darkness below. The park was empty. Nobody came here at night, in the winter. Why would they?

This was a place of ghosts.

'He's not here,' JR called to me. 'There's no-one.'

Occasional flakes of snow picked out lonely paths through the icy black between the trees.

'It's cold,' I said. 'Maybe he's waiting below.'

The Memorial Hall was empty. Full of echoes and ghosts and names and water, but empty of humans. I wandered deeper into its concrete bowels, toward the nearest wall of falling water. I could hear JR's clicking toenails somewhere near me. I wandered past the square waterfall toward the next pool. Spotlights conspired with the falling water to cast ghostly marine shadows around the hall. I flinched and turned quickly away.

A dark, heavy form stood in front of me.

Startled, I shrank back, instinctively pulling in my arms to my chest, almost crying out.

The figure remained silent and still. My eyes took a second to adjust from the brightness of the lit poster, to the gloom of the hall.

'Lewis?'

'Who did you expect?' said Lewis.

I released my breath. 'This place gives me the creeps,' I said, forcing a small laugh.

'It's not Disneyland.'

I couldn't decide from his tone if he was just agreeing or being sarcastic.

'I didn't see you arrive.'

'I was behind the waterfall, looking at the art—like you.'

Art. It seemed the wrong word when spoken aloud like that. They were pictures of the dead.

'Thank you for coming.'

Lewis stared at me with multiple question marks painted over his expression. I guessed it wasn't the best choice of greeting given the circumstances.

'We're in this together. That was always the deal, wasn't it?'

I nodded. 'I'm sorry, I should have accepted your help before.'

He leaned in to look at me more closely. 'Are you high?'

I shrank back instinctively.

'No. Well, just stimulants. Take the edges off. I've had a tough few days.'

He said nothing, but I felt a judgement weigh on my already burdened shoulders.

JR's voice echoed across the hall from somewhere:

'It smells sour down here.'

Lewis was in no position to be judging me. He looked worse in the flesh than he had on screen. His face seemed to hang, heavy and loose from his skull. His suit underneath his winter coat looked crumpled, as if he'd slept in it on more than one occasion, and he was carrying at least a day's growth of beard, a dark gray shadow on his face. His hair rebelled against whatever product he'd quickly forced through it. I may have imagined it, but I thought I smelled whiskey on his breath. How could I blame him? This was hard for both of us. I needed him sober for this, but it would take more than a few whiskeys to make a big man like Lewis drunk.

I could sense the subtle vibration in all my senses that came from being alone with a club member again. Even after twenty-five years. It was slight, but enough to make me nervous of the shadows. I didn't want to be alone with Lewis. Not again. It was safer to be around others.

'I don't think we should stay down here. Let's get upstairs.'

Lewis nodded.

I'd asked the restaurant when I had booked if I could bring my dog, but this request was politely refused, even if I took him inside a pet-travel box. This news upset Needle more than it did JR, as he was hoping to spy through JR's eyes. Nonetheless, the visit was going to be useful.

The glass doors swept aside for us as we approached and we entered into the eighty-foot-high foyer. In front of us, I was surprised to see an array of receptionists sat patiently behind an illuminated wall which was scintillating with liquid crystal colors. I felt like I was entering a museum: abstract sculptures in granite and marble were placed in a subtle strategy; glass cabinets filled with dazzlingly lit artistic pieces; vast canvasses with impressive swatches of oil paint decorated the enormous walls.

As we approached the reception, cameras turned to follow us and the receptionists all turned in unison and smiled as if they had been waiting for us. Behind their pretty faces, I saw small escalators crisscrossing in opposition to the mezzanine levels. Blue lights lined their ascent. I saw a glamorous looking couple descend in a glass elevator that deposited them on the mezzanine level. The entire section behind was only accessible through a series of gates either side of the reception. Each gate was a tall corridor housing what I assumed were advanced metal and chemical detectors. Glass doors barred the ends. Beyond them, the central core of the building seemed to be entirely composed of elevators. I counted at least twenty.

I approached the nearest receptionist, who tilted her head to one side and widened her smile to acknowledge me. It wasn't until she spoke that I realized she was mechanoid. You didn't need to be sentient to be a secretary these days. The other receptionists turned back to face the front in unison.

'Good evening, sir.'

She blinked.

'How can I help?'

'Uh,' I said, thrown by the fact that I'd thought she was human, that I'd been fooled twice in two days. No doubt there were human security people waiting behind those pretty eyes, somewhere remote and safe.

'I have a reservation for two for the restaurant.'

'Your name please?'

'André,' I lied, using the false name I had given.

'Ah yes, table twenty-six. You're a bit early. Let me just see if they're ready.' She turned her head to one side and was silent for a moment.

'Yes, that's fine. If you'd like to go through to gate A, and then up the escalators to the express lift. That will take you straight to the top. Have a wonderful meal.'

'Thank you.'

Unlike the receptionist, the security robot made no pretence at being human. It swiveled its tank-like head toward us, aiming a camera, if not a concealed gun, at us. I forced myself to smile at it and walked through the gate. The glass gates in front opened. Lewis followed.

It was only once I was through the gate that I realized that from here there was no access to the main elevators. This path led only to the crisscrossing escalators to the mezzanine, and to the express lifts that stopped only at the observation decks and restaurant. If we wanted access to the lifts that stopped at the office floors, we could not get to them through this gate. I quickly looked at the other gates and confirmed my suspicion that they were pass-protected and seemed be equipped with biometric sensors.

The couple that had been disgorged from the elevator passed by us on the escalators. His suit and overcoat looked like it could fund a small village in the Third World. They slid past us, oblivious.

For much of the journey we rose through the center of the tower deprived of the sight of the city outside. Halfway up, though, we passed through three floors of glass through which we saw the astonishing sight of an arboretum, where great trees grew inside of the building. The greenery flashed by and was quickly gone. We slid upwards in our tunnel of light, I watched the glowing digits of the floor display rise with us.

The lift began to slow, and delivered us, finally, into a restaurant over three hundred meters—a thousand feet in old money—above the city.

We were greeted by a young lady—a real human—whose beauty was diminished by the spectacular sight of New York and New Jersey, laid out in a dazzling tapestry of light through the windows. The night was dense and black, a lush velvet for the heavens to present their diamonds. Yet there were none. The bright city had stolen the jewels of the night sky, leaving it empty and black. Those constellations now shimmered, gloriously dense, in the ground below us as if they had fallen there. The nearby buildings had slight blue and green hues to their windows, as if they were huge aquaria. The effect was that all them seemed to be built from stacked blocks cut from solid glowing sea water.

I turned to remark on this beautiful vision, picked out in pinpricks, when I realized how withdrawn Lewis seemed. There was a tension in his body and his expression. His eyes looked not at the splendid luminous web down below,

but around the restaurant and its clients. The corners of his mouth were subtly
turned down. He was almost sneering.

'Spectacular, isn't it?' I ventured anyway.

'You eat here often, do you?'

I looked again at Lewis's recently exposed crumpled prefab suit, his stubble.
The girl who had taken his overcoat, and evidently his dignity, had gone and was
hanging them somewhere. I realized now that perhaps her face had registered
something when we had arrived. She'd looked at Lewis with surprise. The city
had stolen my attention away.

Jazz music played softly and a pleasant chatter of people wafted across from
the tables. I had naively expected the entire top floor to be restaurant, but in fact
a large proportion of the center was walled away. This core presumably contained
the myriad lift shafts, and machinery, but it had been cleverly mirrored to give
the impression that the entire city could be viewed in every direction.

Every dress in the room sparkled and shifted colors expensively, every suit was
tailored from the finest smart cloth.

'Shall I show you to your table, sirs?' said the young lady, who had returned
with a worthless plastic coin to exchange for Lewis's pride. I watched her carefully
but if she held any opinion about his suit now, she was professional enough to
hide it; though this did nothing to ameliorate Lewis's mood. We followed her in
awkward silence to a glass table secured against one of the windows like a shelf.

'Your waiter will be with you shortly. Enjoy your meal.'

'I've never eaten here before, no,' I said, once the girl was gone.

Lewis had picked up the menu, looked at the prices and dropped it to the table
again with a cough of disgust.

'I'm paying.'

'Life's treated you better than I realized.'

I studied Lewis's bitter expression, his wrecked face, jowls hanging from what
used be a strong jawline, drink- and tobacco-damaged skin, his patchy gray stubble, and suddenly I felt a great wave of pity for this poor, damaged man. Somehow, he was a reflection of me. I lowered my head and fingered a napkin.

'No. You're wrong,' I whispered. Then, in a voice cracking with a strain that
I had borne for the last twenty-five years, I spoke again:

'Lewis, I brought us here for a reason.'

His cynical expression softened fractionally at that, but a residue of bitterness
remained. 'You said you know where she is.'

'Yes. There's a lot more to what's happening than I understood before. Skyler
wasn't pregnant, for a start. She was... hiding someone. Regrowing them. Just
a head. An adult human, cryogenically frozen. Helping to revive them.'

I watched Lewis's face to see if this evoked anything like the reaction I had felt
upon discovering this. I wanted to know if I was mad to be thinking what I was
thinking. When your track record with sanity is like mine, you don't necessarily
want to back all the ideas that spring to mind. Just in case. One loses confidence.

Lewis didn't react. He looked slightly tense and nodded, but he clearly wasn't
seeing the link I suspected.

'Okay...'

I explained what I knew about Meistermacher, his attack in the police station,
his mention of his Mistress, the Calculatrice. He sat listening intently to everything, silent, but still tense. I told him about Revíve. When I revealed what JR
had worked out, that we thought we had finally found Jon Rodin, this seemed to
make Lewis sit up.

'You spoke to Jon? What... did he say to you?'

'I don't know for sure that it was him. But the anagram fits. Ever the
narcissist. He told me very little. To stay away. He said the procedure was

complete. Whoever that head belongs to has been given a new body. They'll be in recovery. And... something weird. He apologized about my brother.'
'That's it?'
It seemed enough to me.
'That's all.'
Lewis sat back heavily and exhaled.
'I'm not sure about this but I think the note dropped at mine with Sky might be in Jacob's handwriting. It's hard to tell. It was clearly written in a hurry.'
He stared at the table for a moment and then shook his head.
'He's started the club again. But something doesn't quite fit. I don't think he's recreated meta.'
'What makes you say that.'
'It was something this guy Meistermacher said. He wasn't afraid of using it, of going mad. He said, "mine did not come the way of yours".'
'Well, you said you destroyed the notes, everything. Maybe he's found some other way. I don't know, maybe this guy's just a natural?'
I decided to finally voice the concern that I'd been unable to work out. The odd jigsaw piece that had the right picture but just wouldn't fit. I could trust Lewis not to judge me if I was being crazy.
'Don't you think it's strange? It's too much of a coincidence. A frozen *head*.'
His jaw muscles bunched. He avoided eye contact.
'It's just a coincidence.'
'No. What if—'
'Zeke, don't.'
The saxophone solo of the jazz music peaked at that moment, obscuring our conversation. When it quietened again, we sat in a tense silence for a while.
'You said you'd found the girl. Skyler.'
I nodded, feeling too angry to speak.
'Well, there's one way to find out.'
So, he wasn't going to deny the connection completely. My anger dissipated a little.
'I have a friend,' I said. 'He's a hacker. A very good one. He's pretty sure he knows where she is.'
I watched my finger play absently over the silver knife nearest to it. I could see the ceiling lights, little halogen stars, reflected in its perfect polish.
'What's the plan?'
'You're in?'
'I'm in.'
'That's why I brought us here. She's in *this building*, Lewis. The floor below this one.'
Lewis was silent for a long time and we both looked out across the inverted firmament beneath us, and listened to gentle jazz rhythms.
He took a long breath through his nose. Then:
'Why don't we just leave? Forget we were ever involved?'
My surprise at this sudden change of mind was interrupted by the arrival of the garçon. I scanned the wine list quickly. My eyes halted over a Krug, a 2010 Clos Du Mesnil, that was listed at nearly three thousand dollars. It had been the date that caught my eye. The menu coolly told me it was *stylish, dry, and lively—a fine, delicate yet creamy wine with zesty fruits*, and showed it pouring in a sparkling stream into a fine tall-stemmed crystal glass. The description seemed a poor match for the price. I ordered a bottle of the second cheapest white wine, a snap at five hundred bucks, and the waiter left with a professional smile.
I looked out of the window, trying to filter out the reflections of the room behind me. What were we doing? Two wretched, broken twins? Maybe Lewis was right?

'No. We do have to do it. We have a responsibility.'

'I'm not hungry anymore.'

'Neither am I. So let's drink the wine and leave.'

'You saw the security. So what, are you expecting to just waltz in there and kidnap her again?'

'I don't know. I'm beyond planning, Lewis. I'm scared. I haven't slept properly in weeks. This is not exactly a heist. If we were robbing a bank, then yes, maybe we could plan, but we're not. I have no idea what to expect. All I know is Jon, no *we*, unleashed something twenty-five years ago. I knew it would come back. It has. And it's our job to find out who's doing it and put it back in Pandora's box and nail the fucking thing closed. I'm involved whether I want to be or not. So are you. We need to find out who Skyler was... Jesus, I don't even know what words to use for what she did. Incubating. Whoever it is, they're the key to this.'

'This is about Kate, isn't it? Still, after all these years?'

I glared at him, not knowing how to respond to this non-sequitur. He leaned forward, angry suddenly.

'Let it go. Can't you see that's what's keeping this alive?'

'You *don't know* the whole story, Lewis,' I said through my teeth.

'I know enough. I can see it in front of me. This is a one-man mission. It always has been. Driven by your damn guilt.'

The garçon arrived, blocking my vitriol with glass and wine.

'I need the bathroom, excuse me.'

I washed my face with cold water, and stared at myself in the mirror. I flinched briefly at the possibility of seeing something unexpected and dark in it. But it was a simple reflection. In it my face was still red and blotchy with anger at Lewis. *Let it go. This is not the time.* Lewis had his own demons. I picked up one of the white terry towels from the pile where they were folded on the marble surface and ran it over my wet face, and then threw it in the chrome bin still nervously eyeing the mirror.

You're here for a reason. Stick to it.

I recalled Needle's instructions. So, I scanned the bathroom, looking for doors or panels to get into the service ducts. The ceiling panels looked removable, but we'd never be able to get through one without being seen. I looked in the end cubicles by the wall. There was a service panel. I closed the door behind me and inspected the lock. I'd need some kind of tool if Needle directed us to enter this way, but it was just a mechanical lock.

I let myself out and returned to the table, where Lewis was staring out over the city. I sat and we were silent for a moment. He had already drained his wine glass. Mine still stood, looking crisp and fresh in its elegant glass. His hands playing with a small blue and gray plastic inhaler he'd retrieved from somewhere.

'You have asthma?'

'Insulin,' he said vaguely. 'Diabetes.' He was staring at the bejeweled city.

'You're right. It is beautiful,' he said in a sad voice.

He seemed to come out of his reverie, and turned to me:

'I've ordered the bill. When and how are we going to do it?'

I told him about Needle whilst we finished the wine. The garçon arrived looking less than impressed and tartly presented the bill to me. He glanced at Lewis. I picked it up. It was a maple leaf—a real one, bleached a pale color and pressed perfectly flat, presented on a silver plate. The bill summary had been lithographed onto it in neat silver lettering.

'How do you intend to pay, sir?'

There was something in his tone I didn't like.

I idly passed him an anonymous credit card with enough credits on it to cover the amount. As I did so I noticed the leaf had raised marks on it, as if it had been written on from beneath. I turned it over. Letters glared at me in cheap blue ink from the subtle veined texture of the leaf:

Pop goes the weasel!

'Who wrote that?' I demanded. The boy looked shocked. Lewis too. 'Who *wrote that?*'

I looked across the restaurant to where they prepared the bills. Waiters and waitresses milled around, doing their normal jobs. I stood up, shoving my chair away from me. People at nearby tables turned to stare at us in disapproval. The boy looked in panic at Lewis, who spoke next:

'Zeke,' he hissed. 'What's wrong with you? Calm down.'

I showed him the scrawled writing.

'So?'

'I've been getting shit like this ever since it started. Always the same thing. *Pop goes the Weasel!* He's here. He must be here! Who wrote this?'

'Sir! I've no idea sir. They're just in a box. We just take the next one out and stick it under the litho.'

I surveyed the room again. Hundreds of obscenely rich people glittered in their expensive brands, chinking glass and cutlery under the gentle wash of jazz music. The waiters and waitresses buzzed around tables and congregated around the till, buzzing green flies. If he was here, could I sense him? Perhaps not with Lewis so close.

'Let's go,' I said urgently.

'Sir, your chip. It still has a few credits.'

'Keep them.'

Lewis looked terrified by me in the lift as we descended. Outside, we picked up JR and went back to Lewis's hotel to speak to Needle. By then I'd calmed a little, but the words of that damn song kept singing themselves in my subconscious, over and over.

Needle hijacked the room brochure, a small fold of display plastic, and he appeared on it, ten centimeters tall. He spoke in a tinny low-fi voice, all the e-paper could manage.

'The building plans are complex and security is tight. You're going to need constant access to schematics.'

'JR?'

'If you can sneak him in maybe, but I suspect you won't be able to and besides, he won't be enough. I'm sending you something. It's state-of-the-art, and bloody expensive, so look after it. This is going to be tricky. As I'd expected, the security in this place is unusually heavy, both from virtual attacks and physical ones. I've had a cursory feel around their systems and they're rock solid. On the other hand, if I *were* to be able to find a way into the systems,' and at this point Needle seemed to be looking directly at me, 'gaining physical entry for you would, of course, become somewhat easier.'

I started to feel uncomfortable with the look Needle was giving me.

'We'd never get away with breaking in. Even if you got us through security, someone would see us,' said Lewis.

'Nothing electronic would see you, I can assure you.'

'This is all pointless if you can't get into their systems,' Lewis said.

Needle's miniature image again was looking straight at me, locked on to me.

' "*Can't*" isn't in my vocabulary. If a certain person is willing to use a particular talent they have, I don't see any reason why we can't do this.'

Lewis looked at me, suddenly suspicious.

'What *talent*?'

The words of the pact we'd made twenty-five years before still echoed in my ears. The pact I had insisted upon. *Never use it. Never even speak of it.*

'Surely you know? You've been friends for years.'

I could see Lewis's jaw muscles gently flexing. His mouth was so tightly shut he was snorting as he breathed through his nose. I couldn't bring myself to lift my eyes to meet his. My words seemed to falter, to betray me as I spoke them:
'Cracking encryption codes.'
'He's quite extraordinarily intuitive. Why, back in the good old days, he could crack sequences even the best quantum algorithms choked on. Couldn't you, Steel?'
I wanted to be invisible.
'Never told me his secret.'
'Really?' Lewis said. 'How... interesting.'
'Of course, once prime numbers were out of vogue, and everything went quantum, we thought his days as a cracker were over, but he just has this *knack.*'
Lewis was wearing such a casual expression of contempt for me that I could hardly bear to stay in the same room. I could feel my face flushing. Before—and I had only done it twice—I had risked a transformation. I wasn't cracking codes, I was *changing* them. I didn't calculate the prime factors of some vast number, I substituted it for one I already knew the factors of. One subtle sleight of mind, and two rotten fish became fresh. I'd been desperate. I had no money. And that kind of trick pays handsomely. But then quantum came along, supposedly uncrackable, because if anyone so much as peeked at the numbers, it would destroy their states and the company would know. In fact, the advent of quantum encryption just made my job easier. I'd discovered I could interact with quantum states without collapsing them, no transformations needed.
I don't know what Needle must have made of that, but he wasn't about to kill a golden goose with questions.
'Needle, just tell me the system?' I said quickly before he added anymore unnecessary detail.
'All right,' he responded, sounding piqued. On the hotel's brochure, he wore a charmingly innocent smile, apparently oblivious to the tension that had formed in the room. 'It's a Butterfly Cipher. Think you can handle it?'
A Butterfly Cipher. If Lewis hadn't been in the room I would have groaned. Butterfly Ciphers were chaos-based encryptions reliant on the inherent unpredictability of iterative functions. Early versions had been quite weak but modern ones were mathematically intractable. Water-tight. Rock solid. As difficult as finding a butterfly in London to blame for a hurricane in New Orleans.
I lowered my head and gave a small nod.
Lewis released me from my guilt. He forced a smile. And then with a bright, open face he said:
'Well. Aren't we *fortunate*? What are we waiting for?'
Needle vanished from the little brochure, leaving Lewis, me and JR to wait in an uncomfortable silence in the hotel room. I gave Lewis the address of my office without meeting his eyes and told him to meet me there in a few hours. Then I left to perform the sleazy act in private.
Back in my office Needle transferred the cipher and I, a little later, passed the pinned butterfly back to him with all the guilt of someone handing over the last specimen of an endangered species.
'Dandy. We'll do it first thing in the morning. Tell your friend to shave.'
I cut his connection.
Before I went to sleep I spoke to Kate again, driven by my perpetual guilt to seek forgiveness she was incapable of granting me. Her reply was so shocking to me that at first I denied what I'd heard.
She said: 'I love you.'
An awful sensation crept over me.

From the pages of Tony's diary:

A long exercise:

Find $a,b,c,d,e,f,g,h,i,j,k,l,m$:

$$-41a - 46b + 40c - 11d + 8e + 2f - 16g + 43h - i + 40j - 46k - 22l + 21m = -62$$
$$7a + 13b + 2c - 11d - 13e + f + 4g - 19h + 28i + 22j + 24k + 19l - 24m = 28$$
$$-3a - 6b + 36c - 35d - e + 35f + 41g + 47h + 40i + 17j - 35k + 44l + 45m = 6$$
$$23a + 7b - 44c + 12d + 14e - 9f - 34g + 28h + 29i - 43j + 31k - 41l - 49m = -3$$
$$-47a + 41b - 24c + 17d + 44e - 37f - 4g - 9h + 49i + 17j - 17k - 31l - 35m = -21$$
$$-36a + 49b - 4c + 33d + 16e + 34f - 40g - 43h + 14i - j + 9k - 35l - 47m = -31$$
$$-29a - 22b + 25c - 44d - 49e - 10f - 11g - 32h + 35i + 43j + 37k + 17l - 49m = 26$$
$$39a - 8b - 34c + 2d - 24e + 5f - 23g + 10h - 6i - 9j + 29k - 19l - 27m = 6$$
$$-44a + 4b + 38c + 17d + e + 5f + 6g - 35h + 21i - 37j + 16k + 18l + 6m = 22$$
$$10a + 22b - 26c - 29d + 27e + 11f - 21g + 47h - 8i + 28j + 34k + 2l - 32m = 13$$

Find $2^{nd}, 1^{st}$ roots:

$$x^2 - 2686976x + 1804137922560 = 0$$

Find $2^{nd}, 3^{rd}, 1^{st}$ roots:

$$x^3 - 3694593x^2 + 3833546895360x - 887509287226572800 = 0$$

Find a,b,c,d,e,f,g,h,i

$$-41a - 46b + 40c - 11d + 8e + 2f - 16g + 43h - i = 8$$
$$7a + 13b + 2c - 11d - 13e + f + 4g - 19h + 28i = -13$$
$$-3a - 6b + 36c - 35d - e + 35f + 41g + 47h + 40i = -1$$

Find x:

$$x^5 = 45671926272928955955693624043635691373616693249$$

Find r_n for the remaining n terms:

$$r_n = e^{(2ni\pi - i\pi)} + 1$$

Chapter 18

'*Space and Time in Information Relativity are both derived* a posteriori. *They are constructs with no independent existence from matter. When we contemplate the case of smaller and smaller information universes, the very concepts of time and space as independent variables first collapse into one, then become meaningless, since they are interpretations of relative states; they are both simply interpretations of change. Time and space, as independent variables, only appear as macroscopic epiphenomena.*'

—*Information Relativity and the New Physics,*
Professor Fabrizio T. Luciano

I couldn't undo what I had done, so I tried to deny what it was called. It wasn't that, was it?

Throughout that lonely second night, the shadows were always there, moving sometimes, in the edges of my vision, shadows of things from the edges, waiting for the opportunity to break through. The stimulants racing through my blood kept them at bay, but they couldn't stop the demons inside me.

It wasn't rape. *It wasn't,* I told myself, over and over and over.

I wanted to go back, undo my entire life for the last two months. But that wasn't possible. I was stuck with this history—these *facts.* It seemed such a harsh, indicting word. *Facts.* The word engulfed me, washing over me, a drowning tsunami of accusation.

She had wanted it, I told myself. No, she had wanted Jacob. *You cheated her.* No. *Deceived her.* No! *You evil, vile, filth; dressing as Jacob in order to take what you wanted.*

—yes.

The memory of her body; her smell; her soft, pliant skin; those sweetened lipsticked lips; her musk; her desire; her restrained cries; her silken hair; her naked vulnerability; her honey-skinned breasts; the hot, muscular wetness of her enclosing my desperate, disbelieving prick; and the echoes of her voice calling *his* name; my guilt; my shame—all these things tortured me.

It was worse for having experienced her.

Now, I wanted her more. Now, I could never have her. She could never forgive me.

How could she do anything but despise me?

Outside, in the distant darkness beyond the windows, I heard the sound of a police siren. It was surely for me. She had come back, found Jacob. Together they had realised what I'd done. She'd called the police, told them I had raped her. They were coming for me now. I felt certain.

170

I waited sat with my back to the wall, trembling, waiting for the footsteps, for the knock to come; for them to come in, to see the remnants of the filth I had been snorting, the marks on my arm telling the story of my demise into the wretched, tragic mess that I had become. I waited for them to take me away.

Everything, gone. My golden future had turned to lead. My vision, to study, to become a research scientist, eventually a professor, to solve the great mysteries of the universe: all destroyed. Everything was dust. My dream, my life, perhaps even my sanity.

I shook thinking of myself, of Kate, of my mother.

Footsteps came. My heart quickened, but the door wasn't knocked. The footsteps echoed off again into the distance.

I stared for a long time at the wall until patterns danced across it, until I was no longer sure of what I was seeing.

If they came, could I protect myself? I tried to conjure a flame, as Emily had, but the most I could manage was a flicker of light that extinguished itself the moment any sound from beyond the door advised me of the presence of others. I consoled myself that the effect of their presence at least also kept the shadows at bay.

Outside the darkness was beginning to lift, and the sweeping sounds of passing traffic from the nearby road increased in frequency. London was waking up. I was exhausted. But I could not sleep. I slipped once or twice into a dream state, not realising that my eyes had even closed, but each time the visions I experienced were nightmarish. I began to glimpse the first of a recurring series of nightmares. My distress, translated into the maleficent language of dreams and nightmares, imagined me become the subject of terrible oppression, strapped down to a restraining bed in stark whiteness, helpless to defend myself, as men and women in white coats loomed towards me with their needles, their cooing lies disguising poorly their sharp and slicing intentions.

Although that morning I wrenched myself awake again from these terrors, later when the dreams took a stronger hold, no amount of violent thrashing could release me and seemed to serve only to bring on more of these demon doctors and scientists who would hold me down, stinging me like wasps until thankfully, the dream would end and I could wake, gasping for air, touching the skin of my wrists to be sure of my liberty, still sensing the leather straps tugging like ghosts at my limbs.

Here, sitting against the door of my room, the transition from dream to reality was frightening and stark, one moment trapped under the terrifying scrutiny of those white-coated fiends, then next back in my room, panting, breathless with terror.

The light slowly brightened through the nasty orange curtains of my room and helped me to stay awake and I thought I was going to be fine until I started to hear voices.

At first I thought a fight of some kind had started somewhere in the hall of residence. I could hear shouting. I couldn't make out any words, but the voices seemed familiar. Then quiet. Then arguing again. I stood up, slowly, and opened my door. The voices vanished.

I closed the door. The voices started again.

Suddenly I recognised them. It was Emily, and Jon and Lewis. My memory was playing tricks on me. Fatigue was taking my memories and playing them back to me audibly. I could no longer tell what was memory and what was real. Except—

The words of this argument didn't match any of my memories.

Suddenly Emily's voice was clear in my head: *Zeke, help! Come to the club room. Quickly. Please.*

Even my imagination was betraying me.

I fell back against the wall, and closed my eyes, not knowing what to do. I needed to sleep.

Outside at the far end of the corridor the phone on the wall began to ring. Emily's voice came again: *Zeke, help...*

Her voice was as clear as if she were in the room with me. Could this be real? Did she really need my help?

Zeke? Can you hear me? Help. Please!

The thought of going to the club room like this filled me with horror and anxiety.

Someone sleepily answered the phone, told the caller to hold a minute.

Then I saw Emily's face, clearly in my mind. There was a terrible look in her eyes. *Zeke, don't abandon me now.*

It was real.

I pushed myself off the wall, opened the door, and ran into the corridor outside, almost knocking over sleepy-eyed Karen from room 34 next to the phone who was walking in slippers and a nightgown towards me.

'Oh. Where are you going?' she asked. 'It's for you.'

I pushed past her and ran down the corridor.

'Where are you going?' she called.

'To the club room!' I yelled, thinking it might be Lewis, or Jon. She wouldn't understand but they would.

'What?' she called back, but I'd already gone.

I headed for the adjacent halls of residence where Jon had first led me into the tunnels. I realised that I did not have a key for the lift, but I saw that there were stairs next to it. I pushed through the door and made my way downstairs.

The soapy smell of the laundry room. White light came out through the laundry door, but the machines were silent. I hurried past it into the grey corridor, turning left to the entrance to the tunnels. The doors stood locked and defiant in front me.

I had no keys.

I pushed at the doors. They rattled heavily.

I stooped to look at the lock. A single metal block joined the doors, extending out from one, penetrating a hole in the other. I pushed at the centre where the doors joined, I could see it clearly. It was bronze, no thicker than two fingers. I leaned my weight against the doors, it creaked under the strain. I pushed harder. The block slipped out of its hole and the doors flew open into the tunnels, banging against the walls.

The tunnels stretched away into the dim light to the thrumming sound of distant machinery.

I checked in my pocket for the map. It wasn't there. I had only my keys, one of which opened the club room door. I must have left the map in my room. I wasn't thinking straight. I was about to turn back to find it when Emily's face and voice came again:

Zeke...

I had to go without it. *Shit!* I had been blindfolded the one and only time I had used this entrance. I tried to recall the details of the map, but all I could manage to visualise were some blue lines and symbols, fragments of the map, tumbling like jigsaw pieces in my mind without connection to each other. All I could be sure of was the relative position of this entrance to the club room.

Dull orange lights extended out into the dirty darkness ahead of me. The shadows seemed to dance, even though the lights were steady. The prospect of walking into that dismal, dank corridor—of braving whatever forces that my imagination assured me were dwelling somewhere in those shadows—sucked at my courage with a cold and hungry mouth. My feet refused to move forward, nailed by fear to the floor as surely as if I were crucified. I put my head into my hands and clenched my teeth hard, voicing my distress out loud to warn away the shadow things. I ran my fingers through my hair, steeling myself for what I had to do, breathing hard through my nose, building up my courage.

There's nothing there.

I took a faltering step forward and waited. Did I hear a shuffling sound ahead? Just my imagination. I began to walk forward towards the first drab lozenge of light. As I passed it, my own shadow, huge and distorted, raced by me on the wall, diminishing as I reached the next light. I stopped there, listening to the hammering of my own heart in my chest. Ahead, another tunnel branched off to the right, and further up I saw the tunnel lead off to the left. I took the right turn. A multitude of pipes on the wall guided my eyes into the darkness before another dusty glowing lozenge broke into the gloom with a pool of weak light.

What was I doing? I was in no state for this. There were no people here to ground my reality. Anything could happen. What if I got lost?

Suddenly, I heard the sound of breathing near to me.

My own breath caught in my throat. My heart refused to stay quiet, hammering out a rebellious racket in my chest. My knees felt weak and I feared they might collapse under me. I held out a hand to the wall to steady myself and—

I touched warm, papery skin.

I shouted and leapt backwards.

It was an old, faded cardboard notice underneath the light. I was breathing hard, and began to laugh nervously, and then almost hysterically, not knowing whether I was laughing or crying. I wanted my old, safe reality back. Not this. My entire body was shaking.

I steeled myself and moved ahead, trying to keep the mental map in my mind updated with my position, turning left and right where I could find turnings that would lead me in the right direction. More than once, I heard scuttling sounds, and I ran to the safety of the nearest pool of light and waited for certainty that whatever it was had gone.

Eventually, I came to a doorway with steps leading up. I didn't recognise this place. Perhaps it was one of the entrances I had yet to use. I decided to go up. If I could find out where I was above ground, it would help me find my way.

At the top of the steps was a door. I fancied that I could see a faint glow of daylight through the cracks around it. I pulled on the handle and opened the door into a dusty stone room that reminded me of the inside of a church. Stairs wound up inside the building. It was a tower. I was inside the Queen's Tower. The tower that Tony Baijaiti had thrown himself from.

I realised at once that I had misjudged how far I had walked, but knowing this landmark, I knew the club room wasn't far and which direction I needed to go in. I came down the steps and headed off, back into the tunnels.

Finally, I found a section of tunnel that I recognised and I made my way down the final section to the bland grey door of the club room. The room seemed silent, but from the edges of the door I could see strange flashes of light. I heard a groan.

I pushed at the door. It was unlocked. It swung open into a scene that so shocked me that it seemed to lift my essence away with my breath.

Emily was in the middle of the room, lifted as if by an invisible force, wracked by convulsions and spasms. She was silhouetted by a white-blue light coming in a milky radiance from behind her, a tall rectangle of impure light. Another silhouette sat in front, facing the window of light. I realised that it was Lewis. He was sitting cross-legged in front of what had been the full-length mirror.

'Emily...'

She tried to look at me, but her neck muscles spasmed, turning her to the side. She half whispered half groaned:

'Zeke...?'

At my name, she sighed and her twitching body seemed to relax. A tiny smile bled into her tortured expression. The light subsided and she collapsed into a heap on the floor.

I rushed to her. Her bad hand was bandaged in dirty crêpe, moist and dark with blood and serum. She was barely conscious. Her eyelids flickered.

'What's happening.'

She responded in a daze:

'Losing... my...'

She didn't finish the sentence. I turned and saw Jon in a corner of the room. His nose was crusted with blood, his skin swollen under one eye, a small slit marked the point of impact. He was awake, holding a hand firmly over his forearm. The shirt sleeve underneath carried a dark stain.

Lewis sat still, hypnotised. A large kitchen knife lay next to him on the floor. The light coming from the rectangle of the mirror had subsided, returning to the image of the club room, except—

Except Lewis's reflection did not face him.

The mirror room, viewed through the portal of the wooden frame, contained a very different scene. Bodies lay about inside. I recognised one of them: it was Jon. I thought I also saw Lewis and Vaughan. There was a fourth, a boy I didn't recognise. I also saw something that I did not take notice of at the time, but that would turn out to be of critical importance: I saw a small shiny red box on the floor lying next to them.

Lewis whispered hoarsely:

'You did it. I can see him.'

'What's happening?' I repeated.

Jon spoke, but he spoke to Lewis. His voice sounded nasal and bruised, like his face.

'Lewis, you can't bring him back. He belongs in that world. You'll only be stealing him from your own—'

'He's alive...' Lewis said in a small, wistful voice. 'He's still alive.'

'Lewis, that's not our world. Don't interfere with it. Leave them be.'

Lewis whipped his head around and snarled at Jon:

'We're just rats to you. Experimental rats. You took my brother from me, and I—' He choked on his own emotion and coughed, spilling bright tears from his wild glistening eyes. '—I had to force you to help me bring him back.' He lifted the knife and brandished it. 'You're scum, Rodin. I should have killed you when I had the chance.'

'Lewis, this isn't necessary—' I began.

'Stay out of this.'

Emily opened her eyes. They stared wild and frightened at the ceiling. She moaned as if seeing something.

In the mirror world, the bodies began to stir awake. Then suddenly, the image clouded and vanished. The light in the room flickered.

Emily sat up, staring ahead at something none of us could see. She was mouthing something. She turned her head and looked beyond and behind me and said out loud, despondent, as if disappointed, a single word:

'No.'

I turned to see what she was looking at. Shock punched me in the stomach. Someone was standing in the doorframe of the club room, gripping the side of the door frame with one hand.

It was Jacob.

He was clutching at the paper map with his free hand. I hadn't left the map in my room after all. I'd left it in his trouser pocket, forgetting to transfer it back when I had swapped our clothes. It had been him calling on the phone in the corridor when I had left, not Lewis or Jon.

I'd never seen such a look of vile fury on his face before.

Behind him, I saw the tear-streaked face of Kate.

I heard Lewis whisper a guttural curse.

Jacob leered at me from the doorframe with an anger so pure that it darkened the area around his eyes. I'd never seen him look so feral.

'You. . .' he started, but failed to find words sufficient to express whatever feelings were twisting his face into such ugliness. I found my own hatred rise briefly, but it couldn't sustain itself. I couldn't defend what I'd done. Not even to myself. Especially not to myself.

Lewis turned from the mirror. It had faded to an ordinary reflection. His faced was full of horror. 'No. No!'

'I'm going to kill you,' Jacob said and launched himself through the door at me.

Lewis cried out: '*Emily?*'

I ducked down and grabbed the knife besides Lewis, taking advantage of his surprise. I only meant to defend myself. To scare him perhaps.

Emily grunted as if in pain. 'I can't. It's *her.*'

Kate saw the knife and screamed.

Lewis cried out and scrabbled for something near to him.

Jacob's anger had spurred him beyond any fear of the knife. He didn't believe I would use it. He lunged at me.

I reacted instinctively. Jacob's face froze in horror and disbelief.

I stepped back. He staggered back. I still held the knife; the end was bloody.

Kate screamed again, this time shrieking. Blood flowed onto Jacob's shirt near his stomach where the knife had penetrated. She rushed towards him and then screamed again, stopping and twisting violently to see the hypodermic needle Lewis had just plunged into her thigh. She began a sobbing cry of confusion and disbelief and her hands flailed around like moths near the syringe, as if it were too hot to touch.

Jacob looked down at the red stain rapidly growing over his shirt.

Lewis hissed at Emily, '*Bring it back!*'

The mirror flowered into cold milky blue light and flowered again, clearing this time, revealing the other room again with waking bodies strewn around inside.

Jacob staggered to the side. Kate saw. Her hands stopped flailing and she stepped forward to support him, but he was too heavy, and then, more from shock than injury, he began to collapse. He crumpled to the floor, pulling Kate with him. She fell directly onto the thigh with the hypodermic still in it, snapping it. She screeched in pain, leaping from the floor as if it were searing lava. And then, still screaming, eyes boiling with pain and anger she turned on me.

'YOU BASTARD!' she screeched and launched herself at me.

I shoved her away forcefully in defence.

What happened next none of us foresaw. Perhaps Emily did. Perhaps that was why her face was so strange and pained. Perhaps that explained the dreadful emptiness and despondence that had been in her voice.

Kate fell backwards over the still sitting Lewis. She tripped, and in a great, slow arc, fell head-first through the mirror.

None of us knew why it happened. None of us understood the laws, the strange physics that prescribed what would happen to her as she fell through into the mirror world. We had no idea what rules applied. We could only watch in horror, as her head passed through the glassy interface.

A furious blazing circle of blue-violet light flashed around her head, conflagrating her hair.

Inside the mirror room I saw silent shouts of horror grow on the mouths of the occupants inside, now awake. Dark round red fleshy Os.

I couldn't process what I was seeing.

As her shoulders reached the mirror surface it shattered. The world on the other side vanished. The glass exploded into blood-red shards. They fell to the floor at the same speed as Kate's falling corpse, bouncing with crystalline beauty around the slumbering meat of her now headless torso.

All that was left of the mirror was a dull wooden frame; shards of bloody glass that lay prettily like rubies around Kate's decapitated torso.

Jacob had continued his fall to the floor in ghastly, synchronized time with Kate's, where he lay unconscious, twitching. Jon, Lewis and I stared in opened-mouthed horror at the scene around us.

At the ruin that was Kate.

Emily, blank-faced, staring but unseeing, simply repeated herself, the same despondent tone:

'No.'

None of us saw what happened as her head passed into the mirror space. We did not witness its energy stolen during that unfathomable process of transition. We did not see it freeze, but freeze it did. *Absolutely.* It used the only currency remaining to pay for a translation across the improbably vast distance through the looking glass.

From the pages of Tony's diary:

ATTCTAATTTAAACTATTCTCTGTTCTTTCATAGGGATGCATGTTTGGGT
ACGATCCGCGTATTGACTGATCCGACAACAACCGGGGTGGTTTTCGTACA
TGGCTCTCAGCCACCATAGATGCTGTACGGTACTTTCGGTACTTTTCCCT
ATTCTGTCACACAACGGTAATTCGCGCACACGCAACACTGGGGTCGATTT
TACACTTTTTAGCCACTCCGAATACCAACATCACAAGACAAGCTTAACTC
CTATGGCAACCCTCACCCCTTAGGCTAGATTAAACCCAACGTTAAAGGTG
AAGAACCGTATACAGTTAGGCATGTACCGTAGGTATCACTTTAAGGTGGA
AACCCGCCTCGTCATCAAGGAGGACCCCCGCCATATACGCCGAATACGAC
CACATGCCTGACCGAAATCTGTATCCCCTACAAGACCGCTACTACCCTCG
CAAAGGGGAAATAACACTTCCCCCCAGCTAAAGTGAACTGTATCCGACAT
CTGGTTCCTACT

Chapter 19

'Now, Kitty!' she cried, clapping her hands triumphantly. 'Confess that was what you turned into!'

—Alice

When Lewis arrived at the den the uncomfortable tension between us still remained. Things were about to get worse.

I had already revealed one shameful skeleton—that I had been using the gift I implored us all to forsake—but by now I was feeling haggard and confused, and my fatigue was causing me to be careless. There are many things in my life that I am not proud of, but there was one further skeleton that I had clothed and closeted and had no wish to be found. Unfortunately, in my spent state, I had left the closet door wide open, and the mortifying peccadillo flopping out in full view.

Lewis had shaved and had even managed to make his suit look more presentable with the hotel room's steam press. I opened the door and showed him into the tiny space I called my office.

It wasn't until he was in the living room that I realized I'd forgotten to shut Kate down. Her response the previous evening was not in her standard vocabulary. I had intended to run some diagnostics to make sure of the implications before acting on them.

He stopped abruptly when he saw the Wall. Every muscle in his body seemed to freeze and his eyes and jaw make such great work of looking surprised that at first I thought something hideous from a borderline reality had escaped into my den. The realization that I had left Kate on screen hit me with the speed and brutality of a brick. I felt as if I had been kicked in the balls. I actually physically jerked, but it was too late. I had the same feeling I'd felt when my mum walked into my room as a teenager when I had been enjoying my first porn collection.

His voice was harsh with accusation:

'What is this?'

I held my breath for a moment.

'What *is* this?' he repeated. It felt as if hours passed before I had the courage to speak.

'It's the sentinel.'

I didn't think he was going to respond at all. He didn't seem to understand the implications. I felt obliged to fill the silence, to dress the wound, more to cover it from view than to medicate it.

'I know what it looks like,' I said. 'Well—no, maybe I don't know what it looks like. It must look I don't know... but...'

'You *made* the sentinel program look like Kate?'

Lewis would have never known. He used a normal interface to the sentinel. Not this human-shaped window onto a lifeless bundle of algorithms.

I must have looked like a sorrowful boy about to be beaten by his father. Then he simply shook his head slowly.

'Unbelievable,' he said under his breath. 'All those years of therapy, for what? Do you have one of my brother as well? Have you got a little button to switch skins?'

There was a controlled anger in his voice, making it tremble slightly.

What could I say? He was right. What kind of person clothes an artificial intelligence with the skin of a dead person? What kind of person becomes a zombie specialist—a specialist in the art of making lifeless computation imitate life—in order to deny death? What kind of person spends the kind of time I had, feeding in every photograph and image I could get hold of, rebuilding every character trait painstakingly over years in the effort to try to fool myself that she was still alive? That somehow I *hadn't* killed her. The kind of person, I guess, who regretted the majority of their life. The kind of person who wished he could undo the past; who wished for a spell to un-break glass. The kind of person who, as if clamped by death, was unable to fall out of love and was now trapped in a morbid approximation of it, asking for forgiveness every night, never able to hear the answer given because it was one I had programmed.

'You know what. You deserve it. No wonder your brother tried to kill you.'

'Lewis, please. I can't deal with this right now. I had my reasons, can you just... not do this? At least until this is over.'

Needle's voice came to rescue me from another room on screen.

'Your parcel is outside. Could you go and pick it up, please?'

The cab waiting outside was driver-less again. I reached inside and pulled out an aluminium briefcase and took it inside.

Lewis seemed calmer when I returned. He seemed to have accepted things. He was looking at the image of Kate on the Wall with an inscrutable expression.

The briefcase was locked, and didn't appear to have a combination or key. A small blue light flashed in a pattern across the front when I tried to open it.

'Don't try that again, please,' came Needle's voice.

'Why? Will the contents self-destruct?' I quipped morbidly.

'No, they're far too expensive for that. You'll be electrocuted.'

I hastily put the case on the sofa.

'One second...' said Needle, and the latch on the lid popped.

'There, it's safe now.'

I gingerly opened the lid. Inside, the case was lined with black sponge that had small cut-outs in it, in which nestled various glistening items. Two figure-eight-shaped dishes made from brushed metal caught my eye. Each was made of two shallow round dishes with glass covers. There seemed to be something inside each of the dishes. I lifted one up to look closer and, yes, there was something inside. A clear liquid, and something gel-like, a transparent body with flecks of color running through it.

'What are these?'

'Overlay lenses.'

'They look disgusting. Like oysters.'

'I trust you're not squeamish?'

'Why? What do they do?'

'Ah, well, what they *do* I think you'll be rather impressed with. What they're made from...'

'Do I really want to know?'

'Not if you don't want to.'

'Tell me.'

'Well, they're not oysters, but close. They're engineered from jellyfish, actually.'

'You mean these things are *alive*?'

'Well, no, not in any sensible meaning of the word. They can't reproduce. They can't eat.'

'You're not expecting me to put jellyfish in my eyes.'

'I said they were *engineered* from jellyfish, I didn't say they were jellyfish. They don't sting. If you'd prefer a less organic description, they're an optical gel matrix of specialized nanocells. They form a stable layer over your eye with configurable refraction and reflection properties. These lenses are going to serve two purposes. Firstly, they will be able to alter the biometrics of your eyes, adjusting your iris pattern and color to match anything on file. Your retinal pattern is a little harder because it's the back of your eye, but they should be able to fudge that by refraction tweaking—a little bit like a hologram but coarser grained. This is going to get you inside some, but not all security doors. Using the same technology, the lenses can also change what you see through them, but obviously not at the same time as they're faking retinal patterns. They have limited cellular energy, so they won't generate images by bioluminescence unless strictly necessary. Most of the images you'll see will be made by refracting the light that's already coming through them—which they do by changing muscular density—so the images won't be bright. However, you'll have one in each eye, so 3D is no problem and the overlay images will stand out clearly. Sensors at the edges tell the lenses where your eyes are pointing relative to your eye sockets, but they can't know which direction your head is pointing, nor where you are, so you will also have to wear these little devices here.' Needle indicated using his own on-screen versions, a small box and a matt black button. 'The first is a micro-AGPS, military precision and with local correction algorithms and is accurate to about a centimeter. Plus, it's sensitive enough to work indoors. That will go on your belt. The second is a tilt-sensor and sticks to the back of your skull. They're both non-metallic and communicate electrically using your body as a conductor. The voltages are tiny, you won't feel a thing. Combined, these tell the lenses exactly where you are to within a centimeter, and what you're looking at. The lenses will then be able to overlay what you're seeing with anything useful.'

Lewis and I simply looked at each other.

'You need to charge them. There's a solution marked ATP/Glycogen. Add plenty to each lens and let them soak for a minute. The charge should last a few days.'

'Okay. Done,' I said. Colors began to roll across the transparent lenses, appearing from nothing. They looked briefly like the eyes of a thousand people, and then vanished again.

'Right. You mustn't blink whilst they're attaching to your cornea, so use the lid speculum to hold your eyelids open.'

'What?'

'The chrome thing that looks like a little barbecue tong. You put them in your eye and—Oh! For goodness' sake, Steel, are you going to be a wet fish about *everything*?'

Lewis looked at me.

I picked up the lid speculum and squeezed them and then let them spring open again. Now I felt doubly squeamish.

'I recommend you lie down on your back first. Put them in gently and let the tongs expand slowly underneath your eyelids. Then pick up the jellyf— the lens with the tweezers and gently lower them onto the eye just over the pupil. They'll move around a bit and get comfortable. Use the rinsing solution on the speculum before and after each use to avoid infections. When you're done, take them out in the same way. Gentle squeezes, no sudden movements, otherwise you'll scratch your cornea or stretch or rip your eyelid.'

I took a breath and lay down on the bed.

'Lewis? I think you might have to help me.'

The procedure was entirely painless, though I felt a wash of sickness run through me when the first lens moved over my eye by its own volition. At first the room had appeared a little fogged, but then, once I'd attached the box and button to my belt and skull, waves of transparency and shifting colors began to roll across my vision, creating patterns in three dimensions that swept in and out over distances even beyond the walls of the room. It was like trying to focus on something turning inside out and made my eyes hurt. A minute later, the configuration process was complete and the lenses cleared.

I blinked and looked around.

'Are they working?'

A colorful ghost standing next to me waved and said, 'Can you see me waving?'

'Yes.'

The ghost rippled across the room, as if it were somehow embossed in three dimensions, as if the air itself were bulging to accommodate him. His form was transparent, his colors those of refraction, the rainbow hues of oil on a puddle. Despite his transparency, this rarefied, insubstantial man was extraordinarily clear; the three-dimensional quality made him literally stand out from the background.

'You look like a soap bubble.' I said.

'Everything will. But you can see me okay?'

'Perfectly.'

Once Lewis's overlays were in, Needle conjured an image of the Freedom Tower, suspending it in rotating glory in the middle of the room like something made from soapy magic. I remembered a girl painted in flames above a hand from a time long past, and felt the muscles in my arms shiver.

'There are two independent layers of security which I've marked here in color. Red is building security and green is Hurasat. The red cameras here match the faces of every single person going through the security gates in the foyer as they enter. If the faces don't match entries in the database, an alarm is sounded and all of the lifts will stop at the nearest available floor, preventing access. The only exception to this system is for people traveling through the visitors' gates. These gates only lead to lifts that allow access to the restaurant and the observation decks above the office space.'

'Yes, I noticed that tonight.'

'Assuming we get past building security, each office then has its own bespoke security measures.'

'So you've added our faces to the building security database, right?'

'I'm afraid not. That database is watched over by GALIAN, the government security AI, and even I'm not stupid enough to try to hack it. There's only so much I'm prepared to risk for this little adventure. However, I've worked out a clean route from the observation deck into the floors below that should be relatively straightforward, and thanks to Steel's little cracking efforts, Hurasat's systems from there should be as compliant as a Thai whore.'

'Should be?'

'I have full access right now but nothing in this game is certain. If anyone spots the intrusion, they could change the access codes. I can plant some back office agents, but that could potentially expose us now. I'm trying to keep my footprint as small as possible. If I think someone's on to me, don't worry, I'll do my best to keep the door open.'

Lewis and I looked at each other for comfort, but there was none to be had. Needle continued.

'You'll be able to get up to the observation deck by taking the public lift from here, just as you did this evening. There are service doors here and here,' at this the entire floor rotated and expanded to fill our view, 'and fire exits leading to the stairwells here. Whilst I can't get your faces on the main database, I think I should be able to knock out the fire exit door here, also in red, for a few seconds, which is going to give you time to open it without setting off any alarms. You can then take the stairs two flights to the levels below. Your next hurdle is going to be this green door here, which is protected by Hurasat's security. Their door is protected by an iris scan.'

'Hang on a minute,' Lewis interrupted. 'You said "should" again. Can you knock out the fire escape alarm or not?'

Needle folded his arms on screen. 'Listen Lewis van-whatever-your-fucking-name-is, when I say "should", it's because I'm—by nature—a precise person. Please feel free to substitute the word "will" as long as you're happy that ninety-nine point nine nine nine nine is about the same as a hundred.'

'I just want to be clear that you have a plan if the point zero zero zero one decides to come up,' Lewis muttered.

Needle smiled. 'Sure. I have a plan.'

'Which is?'

'You get caught, and you go to jail.' His smile tightened into something spiteful. 'Or, of course, you show a little gratitude, use your own ingenuity, and stop relying on someone else to get you out of every fucking mess you find yourselves in.'

Time to intercede:

'Woah! Lewis, Needle—guys. Come on. Everyone's just a little bit on edge. Needle, I trust you one hundred percent. Lewis, everything's going to be just fine. We go in, find out what we can, get Skyler and leave.'

As we strolled into Memorial Plaza during daylight, my heart was beating a nervous tattoo on my ribs. Pigeons descended in feathery legions ahead of us. They strutted around a little, pecking for food under the snow. Then, startled by some unheard signal, they dispersed, moving as a single, supple body, flowing around the trees, clapping their wings in applause.

JR came with us as far as the building complex, but in the end we decided the risk of trying to get him inside was too great, and could jeopardize the mission. He waited, my ever patient underdog, outside.

The foyer during the day was buzzing with noise. We had waited until after 9 a.m. to avoid the major crowds, but there was still an energy and an excitement to the huge hall that had been missing the previous evening. In spite of JR's absence, we were three. Needle's bubble ghost walked with us, and I watched with irrational envy as he appeared to waltz through the security gates, invisible to the cameras, permeable to matter.

I smiled at the robot receptionists, noticing again how utterly human they all seemed. How easily we were imitated by technology now. I remembered seeing Japanese prototypes of these on the internet around 2005, before I'd even started university. A female robot called Akiba. I never imagined they'd be in commercial use within three decades. Even if the singularity never came, it couldn't be long before we were redundant.

'Welcome, Mr André,' said a ginger-haired lady automaton. She wasn't the same girl I'd spoken to before, but I supposed they were all one really. I wondered if she had legs behind that desk. Probably not. I smiled as sincerely as I could and said how marvelous the view had been the night before, we'd decided to come again to see it during the day. I couldn't believe I was making small-talk with an android, but I had no idea what systems or people might be listening.

I tried to keep calm as we walked through the gate. What if they saw the devices on my belt, and skull? Needle had assured me they contained no metal.

The lift to the observation deck was crowded with people all eager to see the sights. I heard at least four languages being spoken. I tried to catch Lewis's eye, but he kept his head low. He didn't seem to enjoy crowds.

The observation deck was a thin corridor that ran around the edge of one of the mechanical floors above the restaurant level and the sixty-nine floors of office space below. Degrees of north, south, east and west were marked on the windows, and etches had been made on the lower part of the windows, pictures of buildings that lined up with the famous sights if you stood at a particular distance and stooped to look. My imitation of a tourist was marred by the anxiety I felt.

Subtle lines of rainbow danced out from the background when I held my eyes still. I trained my eye on the Statue of Liberty and bubble text danced next to her. Across my entire field of view little rainbow markers labeled the entire vista of Manhattan and its neighbors. I was surprised to see that even the boats crawling slowly up and down the Hudson had labels, *The Marchant*; *Knight's Move III*; *The Gilberte Roquet*. If I was any closer, I wondered, would the captain and the passengers carry labels too?

'The fire exit is this way,' Needle said softly in my ear, at which point Lewis looked up at me. He tipped his head in the direction of the fire exit. I nodded.

There were enough tourists and height-seers to make me nervous, but still less than I had expected and when we turned the corner to the edge that had the fire escape, only two couples occupied that length of the building.

'Get rid of them,' Needle said.

'How?' I panicked.

'I don't know. Think of something.'

I looked at Lewis, who shrugged.

I went to stand in between the two couples and began to affect a nervous facial tic, feeling incredibly foolish. At first they didn't notice, so I started including my shoulders and arms, which attracted their attention. They politely waited a moment, pretending that I wasn't the reason behind their exit, and left.

Lewis was giving me a curious stare, so I shrugged and mouthed, *it worked, didn't it?*

'Okay. It's out of action. Do it now,' Needle said with a tone of urgency.

I took a deep breath. *Here goes.*

I pushed the bar of the fire exit and Lewis and I bundled through the door into cool air, closing the door behind us. A short corridor led immediately to an echoey stairwell that led up as well as down. I could hear the constant noise of a generator and the whine of lifts starting and stopping from beyond the walls.

'This way,' said Needle's bubble ghost, appearing suddenly down near where the stairs twisted out of sight.

We hurried after his image, which disappeared each time we reached him to reappear further down.

Two flights down, Needle had left the staircase and was now outside a door leading back into the usable space of the building. As I approached him, his colors seemed to shift and refract, filmy greens, and reds and violets.

I looked for a handle. There was none. The door was plain.

'Shit!' I exclaimed. 'Needle, this is a fire-exit door. It doesn't have a way back in.'

'Hush, will you.'

'How are we going to get in?'

'Will you just wait a minute?'

Lewis's breath was ragged and raspy behind me. It had only been two flights. Down. The man was in serious need of some exercise.

Suddenly there was a clunking sound from behind the door. I stepped back instinctively. Another clunk and it opened a fraction. And then it swung completely open.

Standing in the bright corridor behind the door stood a short hominoid form which looked like a small boy astronaut about five feet high. The robot was entirely made from white plastic. Its head was like a helmet, with a black visor through which I could darkly see the shapes of sensing equipment.

The robot boy stepped backwards to allow us through. Needle's face beamed.

'I'm glad I never installed electronic security,' Lewis muttered, and walked through the door.

I followed him, closing the fire door behind me. These offices smelled of newly laid carpet tiles. The office floor plan sprang up in my field of view. It looked like a maze, and there were icons moving steadily around it.

I was overcome by a memory.

When we were about nine or ten, before the car crash that had deleted our father, Dad had told us about a game he'd played as a kid. Pacman. He'd showed it to us on an emulator: not much more than a hungry yellow cursor, moving around a maze in two dimensions. You had to eat all the little pills in the maze. Lame compared to our modern 3D games we'd thought; until we played it. The maze was full of colorful blobby ghosts which chased you, slowly at first. Your only defence was to eat Power Pills, which you could find in the corners. If you ate these, the ghosts turned blue, and would run away from you. Then you could chase and eat them, for a limited time until your Power-Up time was over. I remembered my pounding heart when the ghosts trapped me; how those crappy little graphics had rushed my unsuspecting body, contorted it into wild shapes as I pressed the movement keys; as if somehow by shifting my entire body this could change the effects of a single key.

I remembered the adrenaline of trying to escape something chasing me inexorably.

They always came. They never stopped. They were indefatigable.

I stood at the entrance to this clinic complex, with the office schematics shining in my field of vision like a maze, and I watched little dots moving around it, one icon for every iNurse robot in the building; and I remembered Pacman. It should have been a ridiculous memory. Something I could laugh at. But I wasn't laughing. The memory didn't amuse me at all.

It terrified me.

Needle was our power pill. Here were our little ghosts. We were safe, but for how long? How long would it be before our time ran out and they would come for us?

The robot boy walked left until it came to the end of the corridor, a T-junction, turned left again and was out of sight. I saw an identical unit walk in the opposite direction a moment later.

'Where now?' said Lewis.

'This is quite a big complex. The nurses have a pre-programmed pattern which covers eight rooms. Unfortunately, the rooms are numbered, they're not named for their contents or purpose, and whilst I can control the robots, I can't actually read their memory from here to find out more.'

'Let's split up,' said Lewis. 'I'll go right, you go left. If you find anything, call me.'

I left first, running to each corner quickly, and peering round to check for humans. I saw none. Occasionally a white boy would walk past, oblivious to my presence. It seemed that every single door in this strange maze was controlled by a biometric sensor. I came to room twenty-two on the map. Needle was still in my field of view. I assumed he was also present in Lewis's.

'How do I get in here?'

'We may have to try a few combinations. Just lean in to the scanner so your eyes line up.'

I leaned in. I felt the jelly on my eye tense up and my vision suddenly twisted in on itself. The effect was so disorienting that I had to put a hand out to the wall to steady myself.

I hissed surprise.

'Don't worry, they're just doing their job.'

The door panel flashed red and made a grinding burp sound. Wrong answer, contestant.

'Okay, I'm going to try a combo. This should work.'

The schisms in my vision reconfigured into new twisted patterns. I fancied I heard a sucking sound come from my eyes. This time, I saw in the pale panel reflection that my eye color appeared to change to a cool gray.

The door panel belched at me again.

'Ok, last go.'

'Three lives, eh, then it's game over?'

'Sorry?'

'Nothing.'

The viscid things perturbed my nauseated orbs again; now they appeared green with hazel flecks.

The door clicked and the panel turned green. My vision returned to normal.

'There you go! See?'

I sighed heavily. 'I don't trust technology.'

'Jesus, you're as bad as that fat bastard. How can you not trust technology when you build it?'

'That's exactly why. Even my bloody sentinel's been behaving oddly.' I pushed open the door into a dark room. 'I'm beginning to wonder if it was hacked.'

'Really?'

'Oh, I don't know. I set a subtle tripwire in it years ago. A specific phrase that it would only use if certain consistency conditions were no longer met. The phrase was spoken last night but I haven't been able to find out what triggered it. It's probably nothing. I'm sure I'm just being paranoid.'

Something above pinged, startling me, but it was just the lights, sensing my movement. They flickered on, and slowly grew warm.

The first thing I noticed was a humming sound. It penetrated the room. There were large white blocks which gave me the impression of chest freezers, and the room had white lab benches around it. It had no windows. I lifted the lid of one of the chests. Cool white mist whipped up into the air and vanished. The chest seemed filled with a buoyant sea of the fog, which leaked over the edges. My imagination betrayed me and conjured something dark and malevolent under that white mist, something that would grab me and pull me into it. The image was so vivid, that I stepped back slightly and almost closed the lid. *Come on, Steel, don't be pathetic.* I leaned in again, pursed my lips and blew a tight stream of air at the white sea, parting it.

An array of metal dewars revealed themselves, nestling under the mist like large milk bottles.

'What do you reckon these are?'

'Samples? Stem cells maybe. Maybe just liquid nitrogen.'

I closed the freezer and opened the door of a large upright unit which turned out to be an industrial fridge. Inside, the shelves were lined with thousands of small bottles with silver caps, and white labels. The shelves were also labeled, with both text and bar codes. I picked up one of the bottles. At first glance it appeared to contain a clear liquid, but I noticed it seemed to glitter in the light of the fridge.

I read the label. *Nan. Antag. 5-HIAA Targ: Hippocamp.* Bottles on the shelf below read *Nan. Antag. 5-HT, 5-HIAA, NA Targ: subst. innom.*

'These guys are *advanced*,' Needle said.

'Why, what is this?'

'Well, if I'm reading the labels correctly, these are nanites, morphologically targeted neurochemical antagonists.'

'Yeah, which means what in English?'

'You're holding a liquid suspension of nanoscopic machines too tiny to see, designed to deliver chemicals that block certain neurochemicals in very specific structures of the brain. Namely the *hippocampus* and the *substantia innominata*.'

'To do what?'

'Well, judging from the neurochemicals, and targets, these would prevent the laying down of declarative memories. Memories of facts, events. But they wouldn't prevent the laying down of procedural memories, which means the recipient could still learn skills.'

'Then this is what they used on Skyler and Officer Hagan. But why?'

'This is just a guess but with Hagan, and perhaps Skyler too, I think they just saw an opportunity to reinforce their secret and took it. These were designed with a medical purpose in mind.'

'What?'

'Well, your goal is to revive cryogenically frozen heads. Assuming you can thaw the brain successfully, you still need adult clones to supply bodies. The trouble is, they would already have their *own* brains. And whilst human cloning might be illegal, it doesn't carry the same penalties as murder.'

'Murder?'

'Just because you create a clone doesn't give you the right to murder it. And removing someone's brain, I think you'll agree, is pretty homicidal.'

'Can't you grow clones without brains? Aren't there cases where babies are born like that? Acephaly or something?'

'Anencephaly. Yes. I would have thought that they would have gone that route too, but I guess when you think about it, you *could* try to grow anencephalic clones, the problem is your adult clone would never be viable. Anencephalic babies never attain consciousness. They'd be bed-bound for their entire life, never moving. You need a healthy body and a healthy nervous system too. Do you see?'

'So they simply stop it from learning. It can't lay down memories, so it can't ever develop a personality.'

'Declarative memories are blocked, but procedural memories are allowed because they're laid down in a different part of the brain. *Voilà.* Your clones can learn to walk, eat, lift weights, even catch a ball, but they're no more than zombies. Perfect body, but nobody home. Technically, taking the brain out would be no more murderous than aborting a fetus.'

'Jesus, that's so calculated.'

'Really? Oh. I'm rather impressed by it all, so far.'

'You would be.'

'Come on. Let's see what else we can find.'

I headed back into the maze. The corridors seemed sterile and lifeless, a feeling that was only compounded by the occasional mellifluous gait of a passing iNurse.

'Should I follow one?'

'I wouldn't bother. I've got them locked in a holding pattern. It was the only way I could maintain control. Let's keep looking. Try this one here.' A large room flashed on the map, apparently with another room hidden inside it.

I made my way around the maze until I found myself outside it. This time the door panel opened on my first try. I looked around the room. Along one wall were several large sinks.

'Bathroom?' I hazarded, noticing the bottles of chemical scrub too late.
'Funny. Surgical prep room. That explains the inner room. It's the surgery.
Jesus H Christ.' Needle's image froze for a second.
'What?!'
'Move. Go here,' Needle said, and vanished, leaving the room suddenly empty
and cold. Something sparkled on the map overlay, and a line marked directions
from me to it. His voice came, like a disembodied ghost in my ear, 'Lewis has
found something.'

I backed out of the prep room, and ran to find them.

I found the door and rushed into a dim corridor. The room that Lewis was in
was behind a second door. The light in the room was dim, and it took a moment
for my eyes to acclimatize. At first all I noticed was the smell: a powerful sour
stench, like rancid fat, and underneath this potent fetor I detected the rank
malodorous fumes of feces and urine. As my eyes grew accustomed, I noticed the
look on Lewis's face and his posture. He stood slightly turned as if in defense and
seemed to be trying to retract his head back into his body, as if shrinking from
something in disgust or protection, and yet unwilling or unable to move away
from what it was that was responsible for the look of horrified fascination in his
eyes. I followed his gaze into the dimness ahead. Behind me, I heard the door
click gently as it closed.

Forms began to pick themselves from the shadows, vile twisted things. They
were alive. Moving. There were beds in this room, small things, no larger than
cots. I counted at least ten, but only one of them was occupied. Something
ticked quietly in the room every few seconds. Things that should have been in
their beds had left them and were all around the room, exploring, blindly. They
were the things of nightmares, and quite real. Nearest to me, clinging on to a
metal IV stand and trying to suck on it, was a hideous child, so deformed that
it was barely recognizable as human. It seemed instead to be a mass of tuberous
growths from which eyes and limbs protruded. Its body was covered with dark
lines, sores where the growths intersected and bled. Hanging onto a bed leg, as if
trying to find its way back to comfort, was another terrifying thing. It had grown
on only one side of its body and was twisted around onto itself. The side that
had grown was twice the size of the other, but the digits of the hands and feet
had grown even more, becoming improbably long and thin, and entirely without
nails. It tried to claw its way back onto the bed with its long hand but one of the
fingers had long ago broken and the hand was almost useless. It blinked slowly
with one outsized eye, straggled hair plastered on its uneven scalp. It slumped
back to the floor, rasping. The child that had stayed on its bed had not done
so out of choice. It had grown so fat that its blubber pressed through the low
caged walls of its bed. Tiny feet and arms poked like stubs from its enormous
folds of fat. Something else seemed to be just a tangle of long limbs, shuddering
and quivering on the floor next to its cot in the corner, like a dying spider made
of pink flesh.

Lewis tugged at my sleeve, moving me toward him, and I heard a slapping
sound behind me. His appalled gaze penetrated beyond me, and I turned to see
a monstrous, heavy-headed thing with sharp teeth the size of parsnips crawling
with interest toward my leg. Each time it moved forward a large hand slapped
to the floor. Its overgrown teeth made up fully one half of its entire face and had
distorted it so badly that its lower jaw had long ago dislocated. There were more
moving things by the walls, and something behind a cabinet that seemed made
largely of twisted locks of matted hair.

'Why?' Lewis whispered. 'Why would they make such things? Why wouldn't
they abort them?'

'They will, no doubt,' Needle said. 'Although they look two or three years old,
these things are probably all just a few days old. When they check on them and

find they've failed, they'll abort them.'

'Failed?'

'Cloning is relatively straightforward these days. Accelerating growth isn't. We evolved to grow as quickly as is physically safe. It's a balance between the need to grow quickly, to attain independence, and the need to grow properly. Accelerate the process and the chance of mistakes increases dramatically. You may have to try hundreds of times before you get a viable adult.'

'These poor things.'

'I wouldn't waste your emotion on them. Mentally they're no more than embryos. They can't think. They're not suffering.'

'Well, they can't be fucking *happy*, can they?' Lewis hissed.

'They can't be anything,' Needle said coolly. 'And don't blame *me*, I didn't make them.'

'Let's get out of here.'

'Hang on, what is that thing in the corner?'

I'd seen a boxy looking structure. It was obscuring the matted-haired monster. The top of it was ominously funnel shaped. I noticed it because it seemed to be the source of the occasional ticking sounds I could hear. I carefully stepped between the beds nearer to it, and realized that the ticking was because it was cooling down, or possibly warming up after use.

'Curiosity killed that cat...' Needle warned.

'It's a bit fucking late for that, isn't it?'

As I passed the long-fingered mutant, its large eye fixed on me and a floppy hand tried to catch my shoe. I shivered and sidestepped it.

'I really don't think you need to know what that is, Steel.'

But I stepped closer anyway and foolishly peered into it.

I saw a huge metal screw-like thing going across a hole which reminded me of a fruit juicer I once owned. There were pieces of red meat and hair stuck to it. Needle spoke in a low voice in my ear:

'They can't be shipping bodies in and out all the time. It's a recycler. They'll use this batch to feed the next lot.'

I let out a shout of horror and stepped backwards away from the recycler. I felt a crunch beneath my heel. There was a piercing, gurgling screech and suddenly both Lewis and I were contributing to the cacophony.

'You stepped on it, you FUCKING *STEPPED* ON IT!'

Three long fingers of the mutant were flattened into a smeared red mess on the floor at the third knuckle. Its monstrous mouth was open wide, lopsided in a toothless screech. I put my hand to my mouth to hold back a spray of acid I felt rising in my throat.

'Get out, get out, *get out*,' I cried, scattering the cot beds as I pushed my way back to the door.

I knelt in the welcome light of the corridor near the wall, heaving, trying to stop my stomach from squeezing a fountain of bile onto the floor.

'Curiosity one. Cat nil,' Needle said.

I turned to see Lewis pale and waxy behind me. His face was filled with thunder.

'You seem to know a remarkable amount about the way this place works, Needle.'

'What are you suggesting? It's all fairly obvious if you think about it logically and happen to be plugged into their systems.'

'I'm not suggesting anything.'

'Good. Shall we get on? I suggest you split up again. This place is enormous.'

Once I'd recovered control over my stomach, I reluctantly agreed. As soon as I was in a corridor by myself again, Needle spoke in a quiet voice.

'How much do you trust Lewis?'

'Implicitly, why?'

'That was an odd comment, don't you think? I mean, you've engaged my services to help you break into this place. It's my job to know about it.'

'So?'

'Why would he suddenly try to cast suspicion on me?'

'He's not used to you, that's all.'

'Unless he wanted to divert it from himself...'

'That's just paranoid.'

'You said you were suspicious about your sentinel being hacked. Do you mind if I check it out?'

'Be my guest.'

I suddenly felt a terrible isolation descend over me, an icy shroud. What if Lewis was right? What if I shouldn't trust Needle? He had the hacking power after all... And I'd just given him permission to look at my sentinel. He could cook it any number of ways and I'd never be the wiser. But then what if Needle's suspicions were right and I couldn't trust *Lewis*? I stopped in my tracks momentarily incapacitated by these terrible thoughts. I put a hand out to the wall and listened to my own heaving breath.

Keep going. Keep going. This paranoia will get you nowhere.

I began to move again. I wandered the corridors, trying to clear my mind of paranoia and trying to get the images from the last room to leave my head, but they insisted on staying, replaying the sickening crunch in my mind with varying volumes, and more than once I had to stop walking to stop myself from being sick. I peered into a couple of rooms which yielded nothing more interesting than storage and several large and completely empty rooms that looked out onto the great stretch of Manhattan far below. They were blue carpeted and looked innocuous, as if they might hold a dull conference about insurance.

I left the room and continued my wandering, not realizing that Needle's ghost-like form was not with me. I tried another room, but the door refused to open. That was when I noticed Needle had gone.

'Needle? I need to try another combo.'

In the distance I could hear the sound of the air-conditioning units, gently breathing into the building with infinite lungs.

'Needle?' I whispered, tapping my earring.

Nothing.

'Lewis?' I tried. Lewis's voice came back loud, startling me:

'Yep?'

The network was fine, then.

'What's up with the doors?'

'The doors, why?'

'They were opening for me before, but I can't open this one. And Needle's vanished. Is he still with you?'

'Oh. No, he was here a second ago. Zeke, I think you should come here.'

'Why?'

'I think I've found her.'

'The map's gone. I don't know where you are.'

'I'm in room sixty-seven.'

'Okay,' I said, trying to keep the panic from my voice. 'I'll try and find it.'

The corridor ahead of me terminated in a T-junction. If I was going to find this room without a map, I needed to be quick. I broke into a trot. A rhythmic hydraulic sound told me too late of an approaching robot, and before my instinct to hide registered with my running legs, I was out in the main corridor in full view. The robot stopped. I heard a whirring sound as servos inside it reconfigured something I could not see.

My instinct was right. Needle was no longer in control.

The robot lifted its arm, rotating at the elbow joint, and seemed to point something at me.

I moved left. The robot turned to follow me. To the right, and it swiveled again. And then it started walking toward me, at first slowly, but with increasing speed, it directed its fluid hydraulic gait directly at me. I had no idea what it was capable of if it got to me, and I wasn't about to find out. I turned on my heels and ran back the way I had come. I ran along two corridors and into a third before I heard another marching medical machine hydraulically hiking toward me. I about turned, only to find myself confronted seconds later by the sound of another coming from the other direction. In a panic, I started trying the doors nearest to me. Nothing would open. The squishing sounds were coming from both directions now.

I quickly moved to the corner and pressed myself up against the wall. My heart was thudding in my chest. Seconds later I saw a white form walk straight past the T-junction without seeing me. I dodged into the corridor behind it, and moved in the opposite direction. I peered into every biometric panel I could find. Nothing would open.

Then I heard the advance of robots again. I checked my exits. This corridor ended in T-Junctions at both ends. There was a third turning in the middle, but it led to a single door at the end. I moved to the T-Junction and tried again to press myself up against the wall, but this time luck was not with me and the robot nurse turned into the corridor, immediately seeing me. I ran back the other way, only to see another white nurse turning into the corridor. Both robots raised their arms, and I finally realized what it was they were doing.

They were armed with hypodermics.

I back into the center of the corridor. I had no way out, only the one corridor that terminated in a door.

I ran down it. There was no panel. Just a handle.

Something hissed by me and stuck in the door next to my hand just as I went to grab it. I turned to see one of the iNurses ambling calmly down the corridor. It had fired a dart.

I frantically tried the door handle with my hand behind me, fumbling about for something I couldn't even see because my eyes were locked on the thing advancing toward me. It strode with the horrific and precise certainty of a machine. Its white plastic denying the uncanny human-ness of its gait. It didn't need to run. All it had to do was prime the syringe-gun again. Behind its shining astronaut helmet, I fancied I could see red eyes glowing with the satisfaction of sure kill. I daren't take my eyes from it. My hand flailed behind me, knuckles knocking painfully against the door edges. My fingers grasped in desperation for something they could not find. I could almost see myself in the shiny black curved surface of the iNurse's face, when my hand found at last the handle, pushed down and I fell backwards into the room.

I scrambled to my feet and slammed the door shut in the face of the advancing robot, and turned to push my weight against the door, breathing hard, aware of the beads of nervous sweat near my eyes.

It took a moment for the room in front of me to make itself known to my conscious mind. The room was softly lit, and the contrast in brightness from the corridor made it seem dark at first, a blur of shapes that seemed soft and safe. I noticed a beeping sound, and small lights, red and green. There was a window at the rear of the room. Its gauzy curtains softened the daylight. And then the largest object in the room suddenly clicked into existence, though it had been there all along right in front of me, my mind had been unable to translate it.

I looked upon a bed. And in the bed, under the covers, someone was sleeping quietly.

This was a hospital recovery room.

The door opened a crack and pushed gently and patiently into my back. I grunted, dug my heels in and forced it closed again. Then with one hand, I held the door handle up so it couldn't open like that again.

A clipboard hung from the end of the bed. Still holding on to the door handle, I stretched my body out to the end of the bed, reaching with my free hand. It wouldn't reach. I balanced on one leg and stretched out with the other. There was a sudden force on the door handle, My grip was loosened. I threw myself back at the door and held up the handle again with both hands, spitting as I breathed through gritted teeth.

'Leave me alone, you *fucker*,' I whispered.

I was using such force that I could no longer tell if the handle was being pressed from the other side. I released the pressure gradually. No, it was free. The handle didn't move.

Again, keeping one hand on it, I stretched out with my body and leg to the clipboard, this time giving it a quick upwards kick to free it from the horizontal bar it was hanging from. It clattered to the floor. I scrabbled at it with my shoe and then, getting a decent purchase on it, kicked it toward me, and resumed my defensive position behind the door.

As soon as I lifted the clipboard it sprang to life with text and symbols and graphs with lines and labels that meant little to me. At the top, there was a box with patient details. I scanned it for a name:

CID: 560

D.O.B.: 11-11-34 11:15

Age Acc: x17

Ap. Age: 18

Cer. Reins.: 02-13-35 19:13

Then more text that meant little.

But then, underneath, a single line that meant a great deal.

Orig. Host: Louise Skyler Andrésson.

This was it. This is who Skyler had been incubating. The person who had upturned the last few weeks of my life.

I started to move toward the bed, but behind me I heard the door handle again, and I lurched backwards to secure it. I scanned the room for something to jam it with. There was nothing. Then I noticed at the top of the door, a mechanical sliding lock. It looked flimsy, certainly not enough to stand a strong attack on the door, but it would hold for the time I needed.

I slid the lock across and slowly withdrew my hands from the door handle. A second passed. Then the handle depressed with robotic patience. The door bulged, but didn't open. Again. I saw the bottom corner of the door moving each time, casting a shadow of light from the corridor; but the door held.

I skipped across to the bed quickly, glancing back at the door frequently, and I cast my eyes for the first time upon the person whose identity had remained a mystery for so long.

Nothing had prepared me for what I saw.

I'm certain that my face drained of blood because at that moment the floor beneath seemed to lose its solidity.

My breath died in my throat.

I gripped the edge of the bed for support.

From the pages of Tony's diary:

Four base pairs?

```
CTTTTTTTTTTTTTTTGCTTTTTTTTTTTTTTTTGCTTTTTTTTTTTTTTTTCG
AGAGATCGAGATTTCGATCGTGGTCGCTTGCGTGAGTGGTCGATTGCTTT
TTTTTTTTTTTGCTTTTTTTTTTTTTTTTGCTTTTGTGTGTTTTTTCTTTAA
TATATTTTTGCTTAACGCGCTCTTTGTTCAACGCGCGCTTTGCGAGACGC
ATATGTTTCGATGTACATATCTTGCAATTAAAAGAGCTAGCCATGAAAAA
AACGCGAAAAAAAAAAAACATTAAAAACACGTAAAATGAAATATGCGTAT
AACGCGTGTTTCGCGTAGAGCAAACTTCTCGTTTTGCGAAATTATCTTTT
TTCTGAACTGTTTTTTTGTTTTAATTTTTTTTTTTCTTTTTTTTTTTTTTTG
CTTTTTTTTTTTTTTTGCTTTTTTTTTTTTTTTTGCTTTTACACGCCCTTGCT
TTTATGTGTACTTTCTTTTCTACATCCTTGCTTTTTTTTTTTTTTTTGCTTT
TTTTTTTTTTTT
```

Chapter 20

'We see that the Incomplete Interpretation has an equivalent corre-
spondence to the uncollapsed wave function. Prior to interpretation,
the data hold all possible meanings. The traditional problems of epis-
temology and ontology that plague quantum mechanics are therefore
resolved: what is known, is what is so, and vice versa. Meaning and
being become one and the same.'

—*Information Relativity and the New Physics,*
Professor Fabrizio T. Luciano

Death is a whimsical puppeteer. I'd seen him make people wail, make others
laugh, yank the strings of others in a bewildering array of odd jigs. I thought I
knew how he pulled my strings: he'd made me dance twice in recent weeks with
my mother; Vaughan.

But I didn't know.

I learned that each death is different.

The wind whipped through my hair. I found myself staring out over rooftops
gilded and glittering with cold fire from a rising sun. Long morning shadows
stretched out dramatically across the flat roofs of South Kensington, ink black
blocks among the gold and white and grey. The sky was a cool steel in the
distance. I looked down, three hundred feet, to the concrete steps below, bleeding
out onto the lush green of the Queen's Lawn. I smiled joylessly at the two stone
lions ineffectually guarding the entrance below.

I had no recollection of coming here. Only memories of the notes I'd just
finished reading and set back down on the floor.

My last memory prior to being here was of Kate, rather, what remained of
her. Then here with the collection of items at my feet. I knew that time had
passed, but my brain, like a camera pointed at the sun, was unable to record for
a while.

I stared at the fierce, cold, yellow sun in the distance until my eyes hurt and
blocks of ghostly blue afterimages danced around everywhere I looked, ruining
my vision.

Down below, people were beginning their day, walking purposefully to their
lectures, their labs, their offices. I watched their tiny figures, each in their own
little worlds and I wondered if they knew how beautiful and cruel the world
around them was. I wonder if they knew anything at all, those tiny, studious
things.

What could we know? It was obvious to me then that we could know nothing.
What could such infinitesimally tiny points of matter know about the infinite
stretches of multiverse that so utterly dwarfed them? The answer was evident,
put in this way. The most we could hope to ever know, the most information a

thing could ever hope to store, was about itself, surely? And we failed dismally even at that.

I stared down again at the adamantine steps far below and considered gravity, my ally. It would be quick, painless. I had only to decide which side. Should it be the north side, should I throw myself to the lions? Or should my demise be a West Side Story, played out on the Queen's Lawn? Gallows humour.

The lions would be too painful I decided, if I misjudged, and accidentally landed on one. It might break my fall, I might survive it crippled, or die an agonising, slow, broken death. The west-side steps seemed more certain.

I wondered if Tony had pondered these same important details standing here.

I looked down at my feet, at the floor I was standing on, the concrete slabs of the viewing gallery of the Bell Tower.

The props for my penultimate act lay in waiting there.

I had no memory of returning to the scene of Kate's death, the—by then abandoned—club room, but I knew that I had done so. I knew that I must have wandered the tunnels blindly for some time before deciding unconsciously what I must do, before I returned and calmly stepped over her still carcass and retrieved the remaining supply of meta and Jon's lab books from his secret hole behind the sofa, ensuring that not a trace remained of it, or the instructions on how to produce it. I had a dim memory of searching for the large dewar that I had once seen Jon secreting there, but it was gone. Jon must have grabbed it after the accident. What was in it that Jon would prioritise rescuing it over his supply of meta, and his notes? It could not have been meta, the dewar was too large for that. Only one explanation came to mind that fitted the facts, and it was simply too twisted to consider. The dewar had been large enough to contain something the size of a football; or a head. I was pretty sure that whatever had been inside it was the thing that had come through the mirror in the jack-in-the-Box-trip six months ago. '*All I know is whatever it was, it was very cold,*' Emily had said. '*It gave off mist like dry ice.*' (Later, I would think back to the red box that I had seen in the mirror-world just before Kate fell through and wonder, could it have been the very same box? My head would spin with the implications; but at this moment I was too filled with grief to think of anything but the task at hand.)

The dewar had gone from the hole, but I had at least managed to secure the supply of meta and Jon's lab book. That, and a second notebook which seemed only to contain pages and pages of cryptic scribbles, data that I was in no state to try to interpret. The grey cover of the notebook bore a neatly penned name in blue ink: Tony Baijaiti.

Jon himself had told me that the molecule was hard enough to replicate, but fiendishly difficult to make from scratch, even with the years of notes contained in his book. He'd made the first batch in a contamination accident; if I destroyed it now, he would not be able to reproduce the conditions again.

This would protect the world for while then. Not forever, but I had to try.

There had been two flasks of it in that secret hole. I checked in Jon's notes for evidence of others, but he had diligently catalogued and labelled every batch he made, and I could be quite certain that I had everything here with me. It was all written down in neat biro.

He *had* changed the formula. He'd even catalogued his lies to us.

I unscrewed the flasks and let the wind lick the smoky ice vapour from them for a while, before I poured them out onto the concrete. The tiny glass vials inside tinkled as they landed, and the liquid nitrogen froze them to the concrete, cracking and boiling as the heat of the slabs fought the cold of the liquid. The liquid soon vanished, leaving a small strange sculpture of glass, and white ice. Cold vapour steamed from the sculpture in the wind. It looked like a small city. Or a fragment of an iceberg sticking out from the sea. It was sad, like the last remaining island of snow after a thaw when we were children.

The edges of white ice receded, sublimating. It was beautiful to watch, but I couldn't watch forever. I placed my heel over the little ice sculpture and crushed it into the concrete, twisting and grinding the ice and glass into the finest dust I could manage. What remained sparkled on the concrete like the glitter on a Christmas card.

I stood Jon's book like a tent over the glittery patch and held the flame of a lighter to the pages until they blackened and caught with orange fire, eager and greedy in the wind. The book burned steadily. The pages curled, blacked and bloomed into flames. After a while, fragments lifted themselves brightly into the wind and were tossed away among smoke, where they died, grey and fragile, powdery ghosts.

Ghosts of the Looking Glass Club.

The only thing I did not destroy was Tony's cryptic notes, which for some reason I couldn't bring myself to burn. Instead I pocketed them. When Jon's notebook was nothing more than char and ash, I turned again to the edge and looked down at the point that would mark my end. I felt no fear of death then. I had decided—resolved—to bring myself to an end, so it was not fear that stopped me from throwing myself. I started to lift my leg up, to climb onto the ledge, but I looked back down at the charred pile on the concrete and stopped.

That little sacrifice would not stop it. This small pile of blackened, glittering glass would not mark the end. It wasn't a grave, or a pyre.

Nothing, once discovered, can be hidden again for long.

A knife blade of pain cut to the very quick of me.

I wanted Kate to be alive again.

And though I wanted to throw myself over, to end myself, I could not.

It would start again. Someone would try again.

The impossibility of my desires crushed the breath from me. After all I had done, I didn't have the right to take the coward's exit now, no matter how much I wanted to.

I climbed back down.

From the pages of Tony's diary:

Unusually Upset Egg...

M'''''''_/X''?_^'!'__P'#_W^''O]_@!+__X'#_[^'$W__'!'__@'!__8'$?
M^&''O_@P'3_X,''W_!@'/_P('1O^"'''-\PO!!^S$''/')'&''?X''''?_''^
F#_\'_]Q^!__X?P?_\#X#_\'>'/\'#@'^''<''''''''''''''''''''

196

Chapter 21

I stood facing the sleeping clone utterly stunned, barely able to support my own weight.

I had been certain that it would be her. I was wrong.

He looked about eighteen years old, but despite the years that cloning had erased, there could be no doubt whose genes had been the template for this cloned boy.

His face was my own.

Almost exactly as it had looked two and half decades before.

I drew a conclusion. I had to be looking upon the slumbering body of my twin brother, Jacob.

My breath caught in my chest. A buzzing sound had crept into my skull as I looked down onto the young face of Jacob. My teeth started to tingle. The edges of my vision began to close in.

How could this be? How *could it be* Jacob? What had happened to him? How had he ended up like *this*? These and a myriad of other confusions swirled in the hurricane of my mind. This did not answer anything, it uprooted the earth and tossed a thousand more questions gleaming and jutting out, like white bones of the dead, demanding explanations.

Seeing him in this rejuvenated state, seeing that smooth eighteen-year-old skin again, even in the face of more powerful events, I felt an awful twinge of jealousy that he should have been granted youth again. My sibling rivalry knew no limits, no respectful boundaries that it should obey.

I felt my diaphragm spasm, my throat open and my chin lift, forcing air into my lungs that I had denied my body through shock.

My legs slowly buckled beneath me, but the buzzing began to subside, and I clutched at the bed sheets, pulling on them to stop me from falling completely. I managed to stabilize my position in a crooked shape, neither fully standing nor fallen.

Somewhere in the distance, I heard a door banging against its frame, slowly, methodically, like a heartbeat.

I put out another hand and pulled myself gradually up again to look at his sleeping face.

Those eyelashes so thick, that skin so smooth. Those lips so full. The hair luxurious, the hairline low. I had forgotten this face. This face with the beauty ubiquitously granted to the young but made invisible to them, for only to the old to appreciate through its loss; the beauty that I had taken for granted, for it

197

was all I knew. This face that had once also daily stared back at *me* from the looking glass. I put my hands to my temples for no other reason than to contain the explosion that was growing so gracefully between them.

The incessant banging at the door came into focus in my mind all at once, banishing these wistful thoughts. How long could that flimsy lock hold?

I dragged myself to the door, leaned into it with my knee and forced the handle back up. The banging stopped. I lowered my leg and simply held the handle up with both hands and rested my forehead against the door, trying to collect myself.

I called Lewis.

'Zeke?' said Lewis. 'Where are you?

I couldn't bring myself to speak for a moment.

'Hello? Are you there?'

'Yes, I'm here. I've found him.'

'*Him?*'

'Yes, him. The guy Skyler was incubating.'

'Where are you?'

'Room eleven. The robots tried to attack me. One's still outside the door now.'

Silence.

'Lewis. It's my brother. It's my *fucking* brother.'

'I'm on my way.'

I rested my head against the door again.

Suddenly, Needle's image flickered into life on a nearby screen.

'Steel!' came his voice from the in-built speaker. The tone was knife-sharp. 'You were right. Your sentinel *was* hacked. And now, I don't understand, I'm being blocked somehow. You're in danger.'

'You think I don't fucking know that?'

'*Listen!* I'm trying to tell you, it wasn't—'

The sound cut off, though I could still see the lips on Needle's avatar moving. Then his image began to melt, like wax. It slipped down the screen, the pixels flowing like colorful blood. What happened next terrified me: instead of stopping at the edge of the screen, Needle's melting image bled out over it and onto the table, where it collected in a pool of liquid light. A terrible sense of dread overcame me.

Behind me I heard a noise. I whipped around, startled, and the world exploded into white light.

A shrill whining noise was ringing in my ears. It took me a moment to realize that I had been punched. I was lying on the floor. Jacob was standing over me, still dressed in hospital pyjamas, holding his fist. He looked frightened more than angry. He was staring at me with a helpless expression, as if he were lost. His eyes flicked up to the door. In the next moment, the door crashed open and I saw Lewis standing there, physically holding the iNurse in the air by its slim waist with one hand. He held it to the side. The nurse's arm whined hydraulically as it tried and failed to lock onto a target.

Lewis looked at the boy, and then at me. And then he surprised me by talking to him.

'*A penny for a spool of thread.*'

'Lewis?' I gasped.

'*A penny for a needle...*'

'*Lewis?!*'

'Shut up!'

He spoke with an urgency to his tone:

'*That's the way the money goes, Pop! goes the weasel.*' He paused, panting and wide-eyed with tension.

'What's the next verse?'

There was no next verse so far as I knew.

'Lewis, what the f—'

'I said *shut up!*'

'What's the *next verse?*' Lewis shook the robot at Jacob, as if he were holding a gun. '*WHAT'S THE NEXT VERSE?!*'

The boy's eye were wide and terrified. He whispered haltingly, in a tremulous voice:

'Half a toe of stuttering dice, Twice a wheel of diesel, Tell the man he's not so nice. . .' His voice dropped to a whisper. '*Pop!* goes the weasel.'

The boy wore a look of surprise, as if he had no idea himself where the words came from.

'You're *sure?*' demanded Lewis.

He nodded meekly.

He tapped his earcom.

'Did you get that?'

'I don't underst—' I said.

'Not you.'

A voice spoke from Lewis's com:

'Loud and clear.'

I recognized the Germanic lilt immediately. It belonged to Viktor Meistermacher.

The tension in Lewis's body melted away. He took a cautious breath, and then turned to me.

'I'm so sorry, Zeke. Your brother is dead. This is not Jacob.'

And with those words. Lewis lifted the iNurse toward me and let it fire its syringe dart into me.

A swift curtain of darkness fell around me.

um... weld new week

6ZP,E 28J: 466 1M,h

Chapter 22

'Whilst the Many Worlds Interpretation of Quantum Mechanics resolves the problems and paradoxes inherent in the collapsing wave function (Copenhagen) interpretation, it brings with it the awkward, even ugly, idea of universes "splitting" with each and every particle interaction. Information relativity does away with this ugliness by suggesting that no new universes are created. Instead, each universe (state) is a different interpretation of the same unchanging substrate.'

—*Information Relativity and the New Physics,*
Professor Fabrizio T. Luciano

The first time Jacob tried to kill me was in the police station. Although he had threatened to do so in the club room, I don't think he had been serious then. He hadn't a genuine motive. He would have hurt me, for sure, perhaps even beaten me unconscious, but he wouldn't have killed me. Later though, when he saw me across the waiting room in Chelsea Police Station, his eyes were dull with grief, and when he launched himself at me it was an act of clear and cool intention, not the bright, spontaneous hatred I'd seen in those eyes before. He made no sound as he fought the police to try to get to me. He didn't cry out as his stitches ripped, and a fresh red stain patterned his shirt. His face remained slack. He would have extinguished me then without emotion, or regret.

The police questioning seemed to last months.

'What did you do with the head?'

'I've already told you. Nothing.'

Officer Hofstadter huffed through his nostrils, and then sniffed.

'How long were you planning it? What was Tony Baijaiti's involvement?'

'I never knew him.'

'Don't give me that. Why did he warn her?'

'That was before I even joined.'

Hofstadter continued to try to press information out of me that I didn't have.

The second time Jacob tried to kill me was at The St. Clair Institute for Psychiatry. They had put the psychiatrists on the case almost immediately. Especially at night, when we would all be screaming not to be left alone. To leave the lights on. And Emily's fire-damaged hand, of course. That caused a great deal of concern.

Lewis, Emily and I were all diagnosed with acute schizophrenia. The symptoms were unusually strong psychosis and delusions. The police believed it was brought about by substance abuse. They had plenty of evidence to back up their interpretation. The theory they were entertaining was that a particularly poor batch of a street drug had been made, and that we were the unfortunates it had ended up damaging. Still, the shrinks were impressed by the consistencies in our delusions, but they all commented that there were precedents. It wasn't unheard of. We'd had plenty of time to talk about them. To infect each other's minds with ideas.

Jon had gone into hiding and was still at large. They suspected him of being the dealer. A missing person's file was opened for Vaughan. A murder enquiry for Kate. The police demanded to know where I had hidden Kate's head, convinced that under some drug-crazed psychosis I had decapitated her with the same knife I had used to stab Jacob. It had both blood types on it, because, of course, I had dropped it.

Jacob wrote to me. It was a kind letter, saying that he realised it wasn't my fault, that it was the illness that had made me do it. He claims he never saw light coming from the mirror, and of course he'd been unconscious when Kate had fallen through it. He pleaded with me to tell the police where I had hidden the head. For the family's sake. So that she could have a proper, dignified burial. He wrote again, asking permission to see me. The letters had sounded genuine, so I agreed. The conversation was observed by a police escort fortunately, because it only lasted two sentences before he jumped over the table and strangled me unconscious.

The police jailed him overnight.

Emily, Lewis and I spent six weeks together in St. Clair's before the staff realised she was pregnant. I learned this second-hand through another patient, bug-eyed Carl, who I disbelieved at first because he was renowned for his fabulist tales. He was, if you would listen, genetically engineered from an alien species of plant and spent most of his early life growing on Mars before finding himself here on Earth. He was a spy, but benevolent, here to study. This much represented a distillation of his ramblings. Much of the time I could not understand him at all. In long animated periods of mania he made wild, leaping connections between concepts that were almost logical but just beyond comprehension. The nurses called it "knight's move thinking" which seemed a perfect description. Two moves ahead, and one sideways. Yet it was Carl who, in a moment of lucidity, told me Emily was pregnant. She had not menstruated since her incarceration. He'd heard the nurses quarrelling over the interpretation of this fact. To be pregnant in such a state... I remembered back to our brief tryst in the club room, and I wondered. I said nothing. Only Emily knew.

Emily had not uttered a single word since she was taken from the club room by police. She stared wide-eyed into blank space. She saw, but it was no longer our world's light. Her screams would puncture the ward unexpectedly and they terrified staff and patients alike until she was sedated. I would watch the shadows trembling and taking shape in my cell in tune with her screams, and I too would begin to scream for someone to come and sedate her before I lost the little control I had.

They sedated me, not understanding. Thankfully they moved us apart after a few days of being in adjacent cells.

The experts on the ward, namely bug-eyed Carl, assured me she would have the foetus terminated, which he gleefully described in gory detail until I punched and bloodied his nose and earned another day in solitude, drugged and restrained. My nightmares had come true.

Emily's family were consulted. Permission was granted for the termination, and she was taken away. She did not return to The St. Clair Institute. She was relocated to be nearer her family, and when I was finally released nineteen months later, I learned that she had been moved to New York, where a new treatment promised to give her some hope.

Jacob continued to write to me. Sometimes hate mail. Sometimes pleas for a reconciliation, that he had forgiven me. I knew it was all a ploy to get access to me again, and that he would try to kill me at the first opportunity. I read them all. But then I put them calmly in the drawer and never looked at them again.

Lewis begged forgiveness of me. He wept uncontrollably over the loss of his brother as he did, dribbling snot and spit as he tried simultaneously to speak, to paw at my hands, to force me to look at his eyes. I listened coldly from an empty, faraway place. I understood that it had been his desire to bring back his twin that drove him to inject Kate the way he had. I couldn't blame him. I could only blame myself. And though I could not understand the strength of his fraternal love, of course, eventually I forgave him. We formed a curiously powerful bond in St. Clair's. It was almost chimeric. Two twins, ripped apart and fused together again in a perverse new fraternity; an unnatural two-headed beast welded together by the strange arcing heat of the shared events of our past.

Jon had effectively vanished. And that, along with my brother's disturbing threats, was why I set up the protections against the club being reformed.

From the pages of Tony's diary:

Of all of the states, take this on faith, the one that you seek, is the

33,819,426,709,781,400,696,385,349,849,123,312,250,554,205,880,237,578,
580,493,150,441,569,886,677,930,218,876,536,660,176,651,112,018,561,648,
587,550,581,631,554,548,802,800,473,185,968,259,155,688,929,725,333,531,
338,257,876,876,033,589,525,160,132,700,682,555,452,336,293,025,993,307,
462,847,336,473,038,890,955,607,219,361,153,839,710,765,775,957,628,850,
989,531,660,312,018,627,706,073,882,273,655,202,048th

Chapter 23

I wonder, now, what the Rules of Battle are,' she said to herself...

— Through the Looking Glass

Whatever new breed of anesthetic was in the dart it did not grant me complete oblivion. I had nightmares, anxiety and terror-filled sensations. I dreamt of falling and pain. Later, I would come to understand why.

When I finally came round it was in parts, first becoming aware of my voice desperate to speak, to ask questions and yet having no working mouth to channel the words. I felt groggy, a little nauseous, and also incomplete, for not all of me was waking up at the same time. My eyes were open some time before I was able to process what I was seeing. There was a constant invisible fluctuation somewhere. Gradually, without changing, the world transformed and came to be.

I experienced a great discomfort which I could not yet localize; and a smell... *that* smell. It was familiar. It was... no—gone again. Just a smell. Musty. Damp.

Ah, yes, *that*.

In my mind's eye: a faded, much-used carpet; threads revealed in patches; color—sun-bleached; a pattern roughed and sloughed and scoured away by hard soles over aeons.

I saw a mirror.

Momentarily I believed I was there again, in the club room.

The last twenty-five years had not happened. I was Ezekial Ford, a member of the Looking Glass Club. I thought I was coming round from a trip.

I began to recognize the strange invisible fluctuation as sound. A babbling nonsense.

A face began to pick it itself out of the dull colors and forms that sat static and lazy in my visual field. A dark-haired man. He looked haggard, and lifeless. An enormous bruise covered half of his face, purple and yellow. His nose looked crushed. Dark blood crusted beneath his nostrils. Was he dead? His lips—one of which was badly split—hung loosely from his mouth and spittle drooled from one corner. I licked heavy-tongued at the corner of my own mouth to clear away some wetness, and when the man facing me painfully mimicked me, the awful realization struck that he was me.

I lay on my front facing a mirror.

Pain began to localize itself, but it wasn't limited to my face. My entire body felt battered and broken. Groggily, I took in the parts of the room that I could see before me in the mirror. My identity had resolved itself enough to know who I was, but now I understood why I had made the mistake of regressing. This was not actually the club room, though it was similar. I could see doors in different places, and this room seemed larger than my memory told me the club room had been. Nonetheless, there were striking similarities in its set up. Old worn rugs on the floor covered concrete. Together they produced that unforgettable smell of must and damp. Tatty beanbags were strewn around. Someone had tried hard to recreate the effect of the room; it was a distorted but recognizable reflection of the past.

As if focussed by what I could see, my discomfort resolved to pain in my ankles and wrists: ropes bound me to a low table. This pain and the sudden memory of events leading to this moment jolted through me, adrenal lightning. I struggled, causing blue rods of agony to shoot through my entire body—I was tightly bound.

The young clone in the clinic had punched me. I remembered it clearly now. There was no way that punch had done this damage to my face. I looked as if I'd been beaten across the face with a lamppost. I felt sick. I was barely recognizable to myself: one eye so black and swollen it could hardly open. Yellow and purple ink spilled across bloated skin. A fat lip split down like a pink slug someone had stamped on, or a sausage burst under the heat of a grill. My body too felt as if it had taken a severe beating. What had they done to me whilst I had been unconscious? It hurt more to look, so I averted my eyes from the ruin of my face and instead scanned the room in the mirror.

There was a single striking difference to this room and the original club room that was immediately apparent: around the back of the room behind me, I saw a multitude of mirrors, tall and short, fat, oval, square, framed and frameless, all stood or propped in a curving array, angled such that they faced onto my bound form and onto the single great mirror facing me. The arrangement brought to mind a solar furnace I had once seen on a school trip to the French Pyrenees: a thousand mirrored surfaces forming a great curving parabola, a reflector capable of concentrating the sun's energy into a single point of molten fury. It had been capable of a thousand kilowatts of power.

I struggled again in vain but the pain was severe and I had to stop.

Suddenly I heard voices and realized that I'd been listening to but not understanding a conversation. I quickly closed my eyes and lay still again.

'I'm tired,' complained a woman. Her voice sounded nasal, as if trapping itself.

'Your masterpiece is almost finished, my love,' said a German man. His voice was silky with persuasion. 'We are so close.'

There were subtle pressures in his voice, an odyle, coercive force suggesting that she should complete what she had started. She resisted.

'I can do the rest after.' Her voice was strange—unnaturally high, as if she had breathed a little helium gas.

'After?'

'The order doesn't matter.'

'But if something were to—'

'Something can't,' she snapped. 'It doesn't matter, I tell you.'

'How do know if you can't see through them?'

'I know, I tell you. It will happen. And I'm tired.'

His voice cooed and soothed:

'Of course you are, my darling Calculatrice. Your calculus... is beyond me. A work of unrivalled genius.'

She paused a moment to consider the stupidity of this comment before emitting a disgusted denial, part guffaw, part cough.

'My calculus is a ruin. A disaster.'

'We've come through disaster before. Choosing the wrong twin. Losing the woman when he escaped with her.'

'My memory was—'

'Darling, this is exactly what I'm trying to say: we have overcome exceptional obstacles. This last debacle in the tower! Did we not come through? Finally, we have what we sought. We overcame our obstacles because we are stronger than they are. You more than any of us. Are you not *extraordinary*? Do not lose heart, my love. We are nearly there. And *you*—you are too hard on yourself.'

'No,' she whispered harshly, '*it* is too hard on *me*. The protection I hoped for is so reduced it's... it's barely worthwhile. I'm forced to integrate myself over *time* instead. Don't you see? Can't you understand? It's still *me*. I can't integrate over the other possible worlds. There is no sharing of risk. I was wrong. I'm just diluting it over time.'

'But you are still protected?'

I opened my eyes a fraction to see. I could see part of Meistermacher now, obscured by a column. He spoke to someone short and dressed in black. A midget, a dwarf perhaps.

'Yes. No. Oh, I don't *know*,' she wailed in her tight dwarf's voice. 'Perhaps... not as much. Nowhere near as much. I'm suffering, Viktor. I've tried to do it in small amounts each time, but... I'm afraid. And I'm tired. *So* tired.'

She shifted and I could see her form better. The Calculatrice stood no taller than four feet. Viktor had called her the Hag and his description was deserved. The dark clothing hid a barrel-shaped body. I saw hair, tangled and matted, fall from a sunken head. Patches of pink scalp showed through thin, unwashed strands. Her spine distended from her broad back in a great knotted hump at the top that obscured her head until she turned sideways suddenly, and I saw that her spine was so long that her head hung forward on a neck so unnaturally long that it sank under its own weight until it was almost beneath her shoulders. She was a monstrosity.

Meistermacher's voice caressed what his hands refused to touch.

'We will soon be done, my love. Soon,' he paused almost as if to touch her—but he did not, 'you will be fine again.'

This seemed to invigorate her a little. She forced her twisted voice from squeezed and deformed lungs:

'Yes. Yes. It is too easy to forget the goal. Let me rest a moment.'

'Yes, rest. Try again when you're ready.'

I struggled to keep my breathing under control, panicked as I was to wake up bound and in this condition. There was no sign of my betrayer, Lewis, nor the young clone.

I scanned the room in the mirror, desperately seeking out routes for escape. There was a single door approximately where the entrance to the club room had been. Beyond the pillar obscuring the Hag and Meistermacher I could see the room's geometry differed significantly from the original club room. This place, wherever we were, was bigger. There seemed to be another room beyond this one, but it was hard to tell, bound as I was. I tried to move my head, grunting inadvertently as I did.

'He's waking up,' said Viktor and I realized that he was looking at me.

'Then start work on him,' the Hag wheezed. 'It must be *deep*.'

My pulse pounded at my temples. What further torture had they planned now that I was awake to suffer it?

'It should not take long. A few days at most.'

At these words I felt faint, but the mercy of unconsciousness was not to be mine; the feeling soon passed, leaving me only with a painful thumping as every beat of my heart forced blood around my battered head and body.

Meistermacher eyed me lasciviously, as if I were an object of sexual desire. Or perhaps it was a look of hunger, a glutton's eyes savoring a steak prepared and waiting in its own blood for his tongue to savor, his teeth to savage.

'Do you want to say anything to him before I begin?' asked the Puppenspieler.

She eyed me with emotion utterly contrasting his, as if I were already consumed, become his excrement.

'No.'

The Puppenspieler stood and began to approach me.

I started to struggle again, pain like light illuminating my body from within. I tried to arch but I was strapped firmly to the table and succeeded only in further bruising my chin and flaying my ankles and wrists where the thin rope bit into my flesh.

'I've been laying the foundations for weeks now. The carrier is fresh in his mind.'

I concentrated on the sensations of the ropes biting into me, how they looked in the mirror, familiarizing myself with every sense of them, every possible aspect of their reality; and I began prepare myself to reach inside, to twist myself around my own reality in order to escape what bound it.

Meistermacher's expression opened in mock surprise. He lifted a slender finger. 'Ah ah aaah!' he scolded and began to wag it at me. 'I don't *think* so.'

I flinched. The ropes in the mirror had changed subtly, but not at my bidding. They seemed thinner, blacker. More hairy.

The Unholdformer lifted himself tall and turned his head to one side whilst keeping his eyes locked on me. Then he said in a low voice:

'You should be *very* careful. They could be many things. What do you *want* them to be, Steel?'

I heard a rustling sound. I felt the bindings move slightly against my skin and held my breath involuntarily.

Oh... shit.

I let my breath come out through gritted teeth, inflating my cheeks as it did, pushing spit onto my chin and stinging the split in my lip.

'Please...' I grunted.

Meistermacher peered disdainfully at me.

'Your brother was stronger.'

I was terrified. I stifled a sob.

'What do you want with me? What is all this?'

He chuckled gutturally.

'Why don't we learn a rhyme?'

The strangeness of this statement merely served to chill me further. What kind of subtle psychological torture did he have planned? He began to gently sing, a poor approximation of a well-held tune:

'*Half a pound of tuppeny rice...*'

'Why?'

'*Half a pound of treacle...*'

'*Why this song?*'

'*That's the way the mo-o-ney goes...*'

'Pop! *goes the weasel.* Sing it with me.'

'Why?' I cried, and at this he lost his temper and slapped my bruised face, sending an avalanche of pain shuddering through me. I choked on my own astonished breath, trying to deal with the sheer volume of pain being fielded by my sensorium. I had felt nothing like it in my life.

'Sing It With Me.'

'Half a pound of tuppeny rice...'

We sang together. I in ragged, breathless, stumbling words. He in confident, atonal strides. He dragged me painfully through the song, like an unwilling dog on a harsh lead. He grinned the entire time, his teeth as uneven and unclean as his soul.

'Very good!' he declared. 'Now let's try a new verse.'

He stuck a piece of paper to the mirror in front of me. On it, in scrawled handwriting was a rhyme:

Half a toe of stuttering dice,
Twice a wheel of diesel,

Tell the man he's not so nice,
Pop! goes the weasel.
'Why?' I cried. Meistermacher raised his hand and the corner of his lip in a snarl. I flinched and hurriedly began to recite the words. At first he recited them with me, but he soon stopped and made me sing them alone. When I reached the end, he made me start again from the beginning, in an endless cycle of nonsense.

After an hour, he took the paper down, and I thought I would be allowed to stop, but he made me continue from memory. Each time I made a mistake or paused too long, he beat me across my back with something heavy and hard, causing an explosion of agony to cascade through me. Soon my words were barely legible through the snot and fatigue. I was sobbing more than singing.

Meistermacher paced the room, and eventually, angrily, he told me to stop. 'We will continue later.'

There were long hours where I was left alone like this to contemplate my extraordinary circumstances. I'd trusted him implicitly yet Lewis had lied to me. The emotional pain I felt almost dwarfed my physical pain. Why had Lewis betrayed me? Whatever alliances they had formed in secret, it was clear from Meistermacher's tone that they were now crumbling.

I never saw what lay beyond the room of my captivity. It could have been a palace for all I knew; or a two-roomed cellar. It felt underground for there were no windows. I knew it had at least two rooms because during one of my moments of pain-filled solitude, another of Meistermacher's captives wandered in; and found me.

She stepped around the corner gingerly, not seeing me, nor I her at first. I heard a sound and lifted my weary head, astonished to see her. She looked strange, quite different: her once protruding belly gone. Her hair was straggled, unwashed for some time.

It was Skyler.

She was alarmed, seeing me trussed up as I was.

'Skyler,' I croaked from a parched mouth. 'Quickly! Untie me.'

She flinched a little; wide terrified eyes fixated on me, but she didn't move.

'Skyler? Please...'

'Who are you?' she said. 'Why are you tied up that like?'

Meistermacher appeared moments later and coaxed her away from me, chuckling in a ghastly throaty way.

It was the only time I saw her there.

Meistermacher spent a good deal of time in the adjacent room with the Hag. I could hear clicking, and a soft blue light reflecting on the wall that I could see in the mirror that changed occasionally as if a screen were dousing it in light. It sounded like he was using an old computer with a keyboard and a mouse.

I was given no water, no food. And I was not allowed to move to go to the toilet. It was some time before anything more happened:

The Hag ambled into the room, refusing to even acknowledge me. A rank smell wafted nearby. She uttered not a word and simply stood in front of one of the mirrors. I could not see it beyond her. Meistermacher watched her anxiously from the other room. I felt a shift. Suddenly, the light seemed to change. It was brief. She seemed to tense, and held herself like this for I don't know how many seconds and then she sagged again. He rushed to her, held her hand—the first physical contact I had seen between them—and helped her out of the room.

Later, I could hear their low voices from the other room. The occasional clicking of a mouse and tapping on a keyboard. Most of their conversation was unintelligible, but then he spoke clearly and excitedly:

'It's begun!'

A stool scraped across the concrete, vibrating like an oboe.

There were moments of silence filled with a palpable tension.

'It's working!' she hissed. 'Take notes of the other activity. I want to know if these are the peaks. If the codes are optimal.'

'Yes. The first parts of the verse seem to be so far.'

'Keep checking.'

When he returned to me he seemed ebullient, floating on his heels as if buoyed with hot air. It seemed a good opportunity to ask:

'I'm hungry. I need to eat. Please, can I have some food?'

The words soured his mood like lemon juice poured into milk.

'No. You can't.'

He bade me recite the rhyme again. To avoid further pain I complied. It came out easily, automatically. I no longer had to think to recite it.

Soon my swollen lips were cracking from their dryness and my voice was too hoarse to speak. I stopped the rhyme even though he hit me, and refused to say another word except 'water'. Eventually he realized that the simplest solution was to bring me some. He carelessly fed half a glass to me, spilling the other half on the floor, where it lay wasted and glistening, and was gradually drunk by the concrete.

We continued with my instruction.

I don't remember when it stopped, whether I fell asleep in the middle, or whether he allowed me to stop first. There was no natural light in the room. In the gloom, I couldn't tell if it was day or night. All I knew is that I slept. I woke in excruciating discomfort. My wrists and ankles burned under their sharp bindings, which I felt had cut deeply into my flesh and were agony each time I moved a centimeter. My face had swollen even more, one eye now refused to open. I was unrecognizable. My back and legs throbbed, and several of my bones felt as if they had been snapped or fractured and stabbed at my sore insides like knives when I tried to move. My neck ached from its position so much that I wanted to weep with it.

My bladder also pressed against the inside of me, threatening to burst. When Meistermacher came into the room, my requests to be unbound were ignored. His only concern was that I continue to repeat the rhyme. Eventually, I was forced to piss myself and had to lie in warm wetness soaking the material of my underpants and trousers until it went cold.

If the smell offended them, the Puppenspieler and the Hag said nothing.

They cared only that I recite the rhyme.

Hunger began to consume me, dominated my other pains. I tried to go on strike again. Demanding food this time.

'You won't do this rhyme any more? Too monotonous, is it?' Meistermacher offered.

He seemed sincere. I foolishly nodded, expecting food, or at least water.

I watched him in the mirror as he moved a slender finger through my greasy hair, stroking gently like a lover. His hand went out of sight behind my head. I could feel his fingers still stroking the back of my head tenderly.

'Then let's try another.'

I froze.

He began to sing softly, another familiar rhyme:

'*Inchworm... inchworm...*'

His finger reappeared over the crest of my head in the mirror. It inched realistically across my head. I felt my scalp shrink back in response.

'*Measuring the marygolds...*'

The worm began to crawl further up to the top of my head. It was autonomous now, his hand was gone, nowhere in sight.

'*Seems to me you'd stop and see...*'

I held my breath, rigid in fear as the dull pink grub crawled onto my scalp, blindly searching for something. Another had appeared at the back of my scalp. I felt it crawl its way above my naked ear.

'*How beautiful they are.*' He stopped for a moment. 'Inchworms are members of the *Geometridae* family. Did you know? I wonder what they eat? Don't you? *Geometridae...*'

He continued, hauntingly lyrical:

'*Two and two are four...*'

Two more appeared, thick, gray-white, over the greasy horizon of my hair, squirming in the strands.

'*Four and four are eight...*'

I felt more sensations on my back now. The skin of the finger worms seemed to have slackened now, looking like loose foreskin. At the end of one I saw within its blind searching maw a circle of tiny razor-sharp teeth. Terrified, I was utterly frozen by their strange peristaltic, looping motion. I could think only of the basic nature of my own hunger and project it onto their primitive forms. What *would* they eat?

'*Eight and eight are sixteen...*'

Each of the worms unexpectedly divided, splitting and peeling apart into two somehow the same size as the originals. One of them dropped from hair on to the table near to where my mouth and lips lay in a pool of saliva. It stumbled upright and lifted itself up on stubby hindlegs and began looping in the air, searching towards the moisture of my lip. I lifted my head away from it, straining with the effort.

'*Sixteen and sixteen are thirty-two.*'

My body and hair were alive and crawling with the horrific grubs. They each began to stand on their hind legs and clumsily feel around in the air. I heard a strangled sound issue itself from my own mouth. Meistermacher crooned on, delighted by my terror, drinking it up as if it were nourishment itself:

'*Inchworm, inchworm,*
Measuring the marigolds,
You and your arithmetic,
You'll probably go far.'

Geometridae. I thought of the geometric sequence, the classic enigma of doubling grains of rice on chessboards. The Puppenspieler lowered his face to mine, the edge of his lip curling with animosity:

'Have you worked out what they *eat* yet?'

If the doubling continued, I would soon be infested with hundreds and then thousands of the hideous Geometridae that he had conjured from those nimble, terrible fingers.

The worm that had dropped was searching, hungrily looping near the blood on my tender split lips. I could move my head back no further. My neck ache was beginning to turn to cramp.

It was the Hag that rescued me:

'Stop playing with him! Come here.'

He grinned a disgusting oily smirk, stood up and strode away.

'Oh! for the day when I can do that to just *anyone*,' he pronounced.

The worms evaporated into shimmering puffs of pink and gray air; and I wept with relief and exhaustion.

In the back room an argument broke out. I could not catch all of it, but she seemed to castigate him for polluting my mind with another rhyme. He swallowed his initial fury, and even apologized, but it was evident that he still contained it.

There was a long stretch of angry silence. Later, I overheard more fragments of muted conversation:

'...nearing a billion now,' he said.

'There will be accusations of insider trading,' she replied.

'I'm prepared for that. The strategy is extremely subtle.'

'Good. Take *everything* from him. I want Rodin to understand the meaning of suffering.'

'Soon, my love, you will have everything you have desired.'

'And you will have all the facilities you need,' she said with a sharpness to her tone that said she knew he was not doing this for her benefit.

Several more times she came out to stand for a few minutes in front of one of the various mirrors, a different one on each occasion. She stood on a stool or chair to reach the ones that she was too short to reach otherwise. Sometimes she lifted her arms, and it did not escape my notice that she lacked the Looking Glass tattoo that he sported. This observation intrigued me. He watched nervously from the other room each time, and I felt a subtle vibration shudder through me, through the room. On several occasions, I saw the particular mirror she faced through a gap in her clothes. Perhaps it was my imagination, but its reflection seemed to darken and then vanish, becoming a terrible void containing nothing, no color, not even black the absence of color. Nothing *at all.* Each time she seemed to sag a little more, and Meistermacher escorted her away to rest.

She did not speak to me once.

'It's done. They all worked. Every code. Every one.'

'What is the total?'

Silence. Perhaps a figure was pointed to.

'Billion?'

'Yes.'

More silence. A brief shuffling sound. A strange keening.

Meistermacher spoke, discomfort clearly tainting his attempt to console:

'This is no time for tears. We've done it. We should be *happy.* It's almost time to send him back.'

Sniffling. A quiet voice cracked with emotion:

'Yes.'

'I must go out, but I will return in time to see.'

My heart lifted to hear these words. They were going to send me back. I was going to be released. The relief allowed me to sleep a little.

I could not have been more mistaken.

I woke to a voice, and a rank smell. I was startled to find her stood near to me. She was looking at me in the mirror without a trace of emotion on that sad, distorted face.

'Remarkable things, mirrors, aren't they?' she wheezed. She sounded sad, slightly disappointed. 'Windows into the past, when you think about it.'

'Are you going to release me?'

'It doesn't take *much* time for light to travel from an object to the mirror and reflect back into your eyes, but it does *take* time. So the image you're seeing is always an image of the past; a little like looking at the ancient stars.' She drifted into reverie. '*When* you think about it.'

She paused, holding my gaze for a moment, meaningfully.

'You don't recognize me, do you, Zeke?' she rasped, her voice escaping from twisted lips, helium from the neck of a balloon.

Stupefaction at these unexpected words overwhelmed all of the pain my body felt.

A shockwave of realization tore through me; great tectonic plates of understanding shifted in my mind as conflicting terrains of fact clashed colossally into each other, rucking up vast mountains of belief, buckling and destroying all previous understanding in their violence. It detached me. I unanchored from myself.

Finally, I understood.

'Oh God,' I whispered. 'Oh God. No.'

'Yes.'

Her voice was infinitely sad.

I looked upon the hideous wreck of her body. Comprehension continued to crash into my mind, detaching parts of it like ice from the arctic tundra collapsing into the sea. I tried to take in that terrible, tiny, disfigured form and equate it with the vigorous health and beauty of the woman I had once known, had claimed to love. Her nose was bulbous and twisted to the side. Her eyebrows too thick and misshapen for her little face. I stared in horror at the way her head hung almost lower than her shoulders on that sickeningly long neck. The patches of flaking, lurid scalp; the greasy strands of lank, dull hair. A cleft lip. The smell like rancid butter that she emitted every time she shifted under the heavy dark clothes that hid God knows what other monstrous deformity.

In the mirror that teratogenic abomination lowered her head next to the swollen, unrecognizable mess that was mine. Through the mirror she looked into my eyes through lank strands of her hair. I felt her heat against my ears. The sour, rancid smell came to my nose more potently.

She spoke again quietly, her voice as flat and devoid of emotion as her expression:

'Jon Rodin's first success. At Revíve.'

She held my gaze for a while, directing her uneven eyes at me, so that I could examine them properly and see that, yes, even though they lacked the light those eyes had contained, they were the same. If I had any doubt, it left me then. They remained the only recognizable thing about her.

'And you,' she continued, 'you were—and will be—his second.'

Kate Andrews turned and hobbled away.

From the pages of Tony's diary:

Something a consultant might say if we're not thinking the same way about this problem.

一慨一　　一一七
仿龟万伕仟　一一丈丿仟
丢任丞一一慨丢付举伕丏一七仟丏亞
轧仰北北与丌万从仳仰丸买丘为与丢
伕仟东丞亼丸丛亏仲伕丏丁龟一丿亞
轧亿一七什一仿举垄丿一万仰七件垄
丿亏龟丝龟万仟伕亿任伃丁一书
仿份垈亟佰仿任仿亠乜
丝乀丙价宿一艸仨与仟
工份丿丁乏习
七伕丏也
刃纠乜
么

Chapter 24

'In some ways, the electron, before the physicist chooses to observe it, is neither a wave nor a particle. It is in some sense unreal; it exists in an indeterminate limbo.'

—The End of Science, John Horgan

My emotions in the Kebbler Ward at St. Clair's were dulled by drugs, but I still felt them, rolling like slow waves inside me. I had a lot of time to think about physics. I had access to the internet. It was slow, and the computer was old, and sometimes I had to fight the other in-patients to get time on it, but it was my portal into the outside world. Sometimes I would read things, news perhaps, or possibly a breakthrough in string theory and be lifted high, riding a wave of elation. Other times, I had to fight the horrific images of Kate's death in my lidless mind's eye, or the many-legged things that crept from the walls, or beneath the sink or bed in my room, released from nearby worlds by the meta still affecting my mind. I would stamp on them, or flick them with towels, shrieking as I did so, and they would turn into smoke and vapour, shadows and light, and vanish.

At times like these, the nurses would resort to spot medicating me, to calm my thumping heart, and allow me to sleep.

One day, Professor Luciano—kind-hearted soul that he was—came to visit me.

He kept a controlled, bright expression but he couldn't hide the sadness that glinted in his eyes. His deep booming voice seemed diminished by this dour institution, like something seen from a distance. Still, I found his company comforting. He was the only one likely to understand. The only one who would understand the physics. I had procured a copy of his new book, *Information Relativity and the New Physics* and devoured it. It seemed to explain the mysterious workings of meta, Tony's Great Unseen, everything I'd experienced.

I spoke to him at length, energised by the opportunity to explain what had *really* happened. He listened, seemingly enthusiastic, compassionate.

When, finally, I saw him frown and chew at his bottom lip with an expression of deepest pity in his eyes, that was when I knew I had lost him too. My heart crashed again.

'Zeke...' he began, and faltered. 'Zeke, information relativity, it's a theory, and it's a strong candidate, but it isn't complete. It's just an embryo at this stage. And I think you've read things into it that aren't... that I didn't intend...'

His words dried up though: the atmosphere between us had become dry and thin and hostile to them.

'What about moments in time, just interpretations...'

'It's a model, Zeke... It wasn't...'

I shrugged it off. 'It doesn't matter,' I said, trying to remain upbeat.

215

'You were a good teacher. I'm... I'm sorry I didn't go to more of your tutorials. I wasted... I liked your book. Very much.'

'Kate...' his voice faltered at her name. Whatever he wanted to say about her, he couldn't complete his sentence. There was a moment of terrible emptiness.

He stood up, stoic again, and spoke in a very gentle voice:

'Get well, son.'

I looked at him, feeling slightly betrayed. He was the one who was supposed to believe me.

'I'll come back and visit again. Soon.'

But he never did.

From the pages of Tony's diary:

Tortoise: 'Who ever said anything about a single song, Achilles?'

Score: A Sharp Migraine in F Major

This song interpreted by the following pianists:

```
6c71706c
ec74306c
6c75d06c
6c75006c
6c79006c
6c7a786c
6c82786c
6a8394cc
6493d4ac
6695c2cd
6ab502ad
6cb9f9cc
6cfab96c
6c02b4ec
6d8394ed
6d9392ad
6e9582ad
6eb5818c
60b9798c
60faf8fc
6402b4fc
6582f4a4
7d92b2a5
7e92f281
8f606f80
8c71717e
ac7170fe
db606fe6
8c717068
7c717060
6b606f58
6c71706c
```

Chapter 25

'Take care of yourself!' screamed the White Queen, seizing Alice's hair with both her hands. 'Something's going to happen!'

—Through the Looking Glass

'Kate! Kate?'

I could but scratch at the desperate silence with that arid throat. The pleas from my bound body had been silenced by the outrageous roar of this new context. My mind: liquid with delirium.

She—that monstrous thing—was Kate.

Beneath me the moist concrete glistened; winked.

Everything displaced in my pounding, hydraulic head. I wrestled slippery thought into an order it meant to defy.

Somewhere, in this dungeon room that he and she had tried so hard to recreate as a copy of the original Looking Glass Club room, a steady drip dripped, magnified now, seeming to meter out my melting memories.

Drip.

The jack-in-the-box trip...

Drip.

Emily's voice: 'We brought something back once.'

Drip.

'Something came through the mirror...'

Drip.

Tony Baijaiti... warnings to an innocent girl...

Drip.

A discovery... an age ago... the old club room, before *she had died: a liquid nitrogen dewar hidden in a hole behind a sofa.*

Drip.

Large enough to conceal a frozen head... yet... before... yet...

Drip.

Six months later... a red box seen in the mirror world just before Kate falling into it...

Drip.

Mirrors. Reflections.

Drip.

Windows.

Drip.

In Time.

Drip.

Kate's head.

Drip.

218

Tony trying... to outwit fate... and yet if he had not warned her, I would never have...

Drip...

My very skull pounded at this, pressure waves that expelled thought.

Drip...

Drip...

Drip...

Drip...

Had he been afraid, Jon, when he had secreted the unspeakable thing from the others? (It, arriving frozen; all energy stolen by the process to pay for that improbable backwards journey.) Kept it cold. Fled with it after her death. A wise decision; what could the police have concluded had they found it?

Drip.

Devoted himself to cryonics... to prove it was really her? That such an inverted journey were possible?

Drip.

More than twenty years on... the deformed clone babies in the tower... his patience prematurely expired... the process yet imperfect.

Drip.

She; revived; monstrous.

Drip.

One further question remained loud in my mind.

Who was Meistermacher?

A voice interrupted:

'Who indeed?'

That oily smile. I had not realized that in my delirium I had been speaking.

'You've worked this much out. But not *me*?'

He strolled around me into view.

'I'm *so* disappointed.' Sarcasm.

I tried to lift my head, coughed, spittle dripped to the table edge, slipped over, where it grabbed my dizzy gaze and seem to lock it. The spit extended into a long, irregular swinging string. I saw trapped bubbles. A streaky skein of blood through the clear, like a melted marble.

'He was *desperate* to recreate his discovery. He always felt he'd made a mistake. Taking the head first. He'd planned to come back for the meta. Oh! how he raged against you for destroying it; even a decade and a half on. You were wise to hide during those early years. But then he learned of *me*.'

The spittle string snapped and collapsed to the concrete, a boneless, bloody S.

Meistermacher leaned closer and spoke so quietly I almost couldn't hear the words:

'Uncle Lewis never told even you about *me*, did he?'

Uncle Lewis...

Through the fog of fatigue, I saw only shapes of what he was saying; interpretation defied me.

'The Van Cross family shame. The bastard nephew. Son of a dead man and a madwoman.'

Emily...

'My father's *lovely* family wanted to hide me. Paid my mother's side off. I never even knew them.'

I felt a stab of pity, even through my pain. So the abortion had been a lie. Lewis's betrayal came into sharp focus with this new context.

'Can you imagine how vulnerable I was to Jon Rodin's charms? How I trusted him?'

My gift did not come the way of yours...

The poor fetus, growing in her womb all the time we were experimenting, injecting ourselves with meta.

'When all around me—my family included—thought me a *freak*. . . he took an interest in me.'

There was a harrowing bitterness in his words now. The words choked him:

'I thought. . . I *meant*. . . something to him. But I was just a road. A way back. To *meta*.'

Meistermacher's ontomorphic skill became clear to me in that moment. He had his mother's natural gift, but in addition he had been *born* with this, had grown up with it. Surrounded by normal people, how much harder he would would have had to have worked to gain the tiniest of effects: a sliver of coercion, a bolstering of the most fleeting of illusions. He'd told me in the jail cell that he had been a boy puppeteer. The *Puppenspieler*. That puppets had been his only friends. How much extra life had he been able to grant his inanimate marionettes whilst alone? What fantasies had he explored? How hard had he tried to recreate those same results in plain sight of others, and to what avail?

Twenty years of training under the toughest conditions.

No wonder he defeated me so effortlessly.

And how lonely that strange child must have been.

'I saw how he manipulated her,' he indicated beyond this room to Kate, 'promising her a new body he had no intention of delivering. It would have been an unnecessary diversion to his plan.'

Meistermacher was no longer speaking to me, but it seemed instead he was addressing some other part of himself. Fury boiled in his voice:

'*He* thought he could manipulate *me*?'

He jerked upright, a vicious smile straining the uncooperative muscles across his face.

'One little mark, that's all it took,' he proffered his tattooed wrist, 'to convince the old fool he'd got his precious club back.' He paused and shifted so that I might see the spine at the back of his neck, where a pink scar twisted the flesh. 'And this. I let him bleed me for my secrets, the stuff too weak in himself to find. But I did it not for his good. That I did for *mine*.'

'You. . . helped him recreate meta?'

Of course, said his smile.

'You're not working with him anymore?'

'He loved his secrets and his control more than me. He wanted all the cards in his hands. But thanks to you and you hacker friend, we found what he hid from us. And now we are using his very own plan against him.'

'He has the formula, then? Not you?'

'Not for much longer.' He laughed and sang gleefully, '*Half a pound of tuppeny rice!*'

'What does it mean?'

'A code. A Trojan, of sorts. A way to tunnel through the unfortunate side-effect: episodic amnesia. Rodin's idea.' He seemed delighted by this. 'And therefore a way to glimpse the future. To fix the dice. What value has information from the future? *Even tiny amounts. A few bits. Priceless.* It was his great theft; his plan to buy the power he could not charm or steal or cheat from others. Instead, it has become our key to defeating him. His very greed turned against him.'

In the mirrored room ahead of me I saw again the myriad looking glasses arranged and pointed from positions all around the back of the room, a parabola of focussing power about to be integrated, harnessed by the puissance of a strange calculus.

Meistermacher looked at me, his expression now aloof. His anger seemed to have vanished without trace.

'Almost time to say goodbye.'

He over-enunciated what he said next, his lips confidently over-exaggerating every phoneme, lasciviously enjoying them:

'Thanks for all your help.'

His head swaggered slightly as he swallowed the 'l' and popped the 'p'.

He seemed about to leave but then he removed a small plastic object from his pocket and admired it. It was blue and grey, a squat L shape. My eyes tracked it silently.

'Know what this is?'

I recognized it.

'You would be forgiven for thinking it was an asthma inhaler. Ventolin perhaps. In fact, you would be pretty close. The same mechanism, but this...' he held it closer for me to see, 'this is *insulin*. The palliative wonder of the 2020s. The drug that has rescued America from the consequences of its own gluttony; from the epidemic that began in the 1980s and that has spiraled wildly out of control ever since. America is sinking under the weight of its own fat. Oh, you could never tell looking at all the svelte avatars they hide behind and—of course—Manhattan has always been somewhat of an exception thanks to the cocaine habits of its insane work force. But in many states more than fifty percent of Americans are obese now—did you know that? *Fifty percent!* And almost every one of them has type II diabetes. Kidney disease, erectile dysfunction, glaucoma, cataracts, retinopathy, skin disorders, poor circulation, heart disease, heart *failure*... the list of complications goes on, *and on...* Well... Closche Pharmaceuticals to the rescue!'

He paused and then dramatically thrust out the inhaler:

'*Behold! The insulin inhaler*. An end to painful injections. One quick puff after every sweet indulgence and lo! One less reason to exercise the least modicum of control over their *disgusting* appetites.'

He took a breath and the bitter expression of distaste on his face transformed into delight.

'And the perfect vehicle for *me*.'

My heart skipped a beat. He began to speak rapidly, urgently:

'Rodin thought he was using me, but it was the reverse. Isolating meta from my spinal fluid was only the first hurdle. Then I had the problem of replication and after that distribution. How does one disseminate to the masses? Put it in the water? No. Too unstable. Degrades within milliseconds. It is, alas, a drug that requires injection. *Nobody* likes injections... But if the molecule is small enough to penetrate the blood-brain barrier, then it is small enough to be inhaled...

'Imagine my glee when I discovered that eighty million of these inhalers are shipped by Closche each year. *Eighty million*. All manufactured here at facilities in New York State, and shipped first to Newark Bay and then to ports around the world. All I needed was the money to take from Rodin what was rightly mine anyway. Now I have the money, I will have what I really want, and money will soon be irrelevant.'

He breathed in deeply through his nostrils.

'On the eighteenth day of this month, a shipment of one hundred thousand modified insulin inhalers will leave the port at Newark Bay and then... the world will never be the same again. *My* power will finally be released from its cage.'

My heart was pounding.

'Imagine what it will be like when a significant proportion of the population are released from the terrible shackles of this reality? When consensus is *removed*.'

He began to laugh.

'And to think, it's all thanks to you.'

He tossed the inhaler in the air and caught it again, and then pocketed it.
And then he looked at his watch. 'I believe it's time. Goodbye.'

I was speechless. He strolled into the back room whilst my heart still pounded
furiously in my chest.

Moments later, she shuffled into the room looking exhausted and frail. She
held a baton of wood in one hand.

'There are only two of you,' I protested. 'Even with him, you don't have
enough agreement to do this. I can stop you.'

'Really? Only two of us?' She smiled without humor. 'It must be fresh in
your mind. Recite the rhyme,' she instructed. I continued to be unable to speak,
so she coerced me with a hard and swift stroke across the back which blazed pain
like lava. I choked on the words. She made me repeat them, over and over, faster
and faster, until it seemed that they came from me without my consent.

In the back of the room, one by one, the mirrors began to change. Randomly,
within seconds of each other they illuminated briefly, softly blooming into light.
Momentarily I thought I felt warmth as they shone on to me. The glow faded
and the frames revealed a dark figure, standing, watching; the smaller frames
showed only a face. It was her. This was the moment she had been preparing for.
Two or three dozen versions of her. All those times she had come to a different
mirror, she had been staring through them, looking *ahead to this moment in
time*. Staring, yet unseeing. Myriad deformed Kates from the past looked to the
present through those variform windows in time and they all began to focus an
agreement upon me.

This was her great Calculus.

Suddenly, the great looking glass facing me also bloomed into light, snatching
away the remarkable sight. When the light faded, the mirror image had gone. I
saw instead a faint image of something else, made vague by a blue-white fog. It
was another version of this room, but it was not a reflection. Left and right had
been oddly swapped as if the mirror had become a window; as if I had somehow
been moved behind this mirror's frame and the glass removed.

In it, I saw her, and I saw Meistermacher.

I knew now who the clone boy was.

'The mirror doesn't stop reflecting,' she wheezed, 'it becomes a timelike reflection, instead of spacelike. Its counterpart in the past performs a second timelike reflection, undoing the transformation— a double reflection. Normal matter
can pass through such a transformation—it isn't forbidden—but it's statistically
infinitely improbable, like un-stirring a cup of tea. Only matter that supports
consciousness makes it through because eigenstates that *don't* contain a conscious
observer can't be selected. Only conscious matter. Your body will not pass. It is
not conscious.'

The boy was, and would be, me.

I turned my head to see, and she raised her arms joining in concert with all
of her past selves and for the first time since she had spoken, I truly felt the
extraordinary power of meta in her, multiplied, integrated over time with her
eldritch calculus. The air shuddered with a sudden force. The mirror in front
of me exploded into a milky blue whiteness, drenching the room in light. The
room was filled with a great howling noise, a wind whipped up by the unlawful
connection between two moments in time, that she had willed into place.

'The light is Cherenkov radiation!' she cried above the noise. 'The Uncertainty
Principle means that particle-antiparticle pairs are created at the discontinuity,
unable to rejoin, but energy is conserved: the anti-particle is always sent backwards in time to meet its twin at the other interface to be annihilated in the past!
See how even when she is violated, nature tries to keep her books tidy. Isn't the
physics *beautiful?*'

The restraining bonds around my body melted into smoke, but I could not move.

She started to sing, in hysterical tones:

'*Half a toe of stuttering dice.*'

I found myself lifted into the air by an invisible force that caressed and probed me hungrily like greedy fingers drawing food to an insatiable mouth.

'*Twice a wheel of diesel.*'

I felt myself impelled forwards. I put my hands out and grasped the edges of the glowing portal, desperately trying to keep it away from me. But I could sense the meta lifting the veils of reality around me, altering the laws of physics by sheer and brutal force of will.

'*Tell the man he's not so nice!*'

I felt a final push of force overwhelm the strength in my arms holding me back.

She forced me head first through the window of light.

I had only momentary sensations:

Sudden darkness. A profound cold penetrated me as if I were being dipped into a liquid blue void; I heard the brief sound of shattering glass, the final verse, cut off as she shrieked it.

Reality rented under unendurable strain and there was an instant of lightning white pain as my spine was severed at the neck.

'Pop!—'

From the pages of Tony's diary:

Let's space it, what's the point?

41 3.28 8.23 10.14 1.5 3.8 2.18 3.10 2.16 3.12 2.11 1.2 3.13 3.13
2.15 2.13 2.15 2.13 1.16 2.13 1.16 2.12 2.17 2.11 2.17 2.9 1.1 2.16
2.12 2.16 2.10 1.1 2.15 3.10 1.2 2.14 3.10 1.2 2.13 4.14 2.11 6.14
2.9 7.9 2.3 3.6 11.13 12.2 6.15 7.6 5.28 6.27 6.2 1.23 7.26 8.25
7.25 6.28 5.29 2.1

Chapter 26

'People like you and I, though mortal of course like everyone else, do not grow old no matter how long we live. . . [We] never cease to stand like curious children before the great mystery into which we were born.'

—Albert Einstein, in a letter to Otto Juliusburger

'Corn!'
'Which one?'
'Seven across. Four letters.'
'Is it? How?' I asked.
' *"Cereal, we hear, is a labyrinth"*—a labyrinth is a maze, which sounds like "maize" which a synonym for corn. Corn is a cereal. *"We hear"* is code for *sounds like.'*

I sighed and put the newspaper down.

'Do you believe in life after death?' I asked. Alexei looked up from his copy of the *Sunday Times*. It was his third visit, he always brought two papers so we could work on the puzzles together, and I was grateful for his company. I took pleasure in the distraction our philosophical discussions gave from the normally moribund atmosphere of St. Clair's.

'Well. . .' he began. I suppressed a smile. I hadn't realised how much I had missed him. I wondered what intellectual treat he had in store for me this time.

'I think it's practically inevitable.'

'What? I didn't have you down as the spiritual type!'

'I'm not. Purely from a physics perspective it's inevitable.'

Alexei was a computer scientist, yet his knowledge of the field of physics was now beginning to exceed my own. In anyone else it would have seriously irritated me the ease with which he mastered the subject; in his spare time no less. He'd been largely uninterested in the subject when we'd met. But I knew that in part he'd done this so that we would have more to talk about. Consequently, I found it touching.

'Inevitable? How so?'

'Lots of reasons actually. Second law of thermodynamics: entropy always increases, yes?'

'Okay.'

'Entropy is information. People argue about this, but it's a definition thing. Or they forget to include the observer. It's easy to see intuitively: if you optimally compress a system, i.e. remove all the repeating patterns—all the redundant information, then you're left with a true measure of its information content. High entropy systems contain more randomness so they compress less: ergo they contain more information. Indeed, it's a curious fact that it's impossible to distinguish between *anything* optimally compressed and true randomness, because

225

you've taken out everything that has a pattern in order to do the compression. You have to remember that information is in a sense the *opposite* of knowledge. It's what *isn't* known. Information is exactly that which is needed to know something. By that definition, entropy and information are the same thing.'
'I never thought about it like that.'
'And, in a sense, memory is also equivalent to entropy.'
'Is it? Isn't that in direct conflict with what you just said?'
'No. I'm just including the observer now. Memory is information, you can't record something without increasing entropy. A blank page has low entropy, whereas a page full of scribbles has high entropy. Same goes for a brain. It's no coincidence that this only happens in the direction of the arrow of time. Consciousness, memory, time, increasing entropy—they're really one and the same thing. Time's an illusion: it's just a path of increasing entropy through the multiverse's complete state vector, one in which memories are laid down and therefore the only one that's *experienced*. That's why we don't remember things about the future. Memories can only be laid down in the direction of increasing entropy, because the other direction has *less* information content. I mean, I suppose you *could* do it, but it would have to be a local violation. One that didn't violate anything globally.'
I didn't want to say anything, but this was really a bit of a head-fuck for me. After what I'd been through, the damaging effect of the drugs I'd taken, I simply didn't have the capacity to follow Alexei's arguments any more. Not properly. Alexei seemed to sense this.
'Think about the very beginning of time. The singularity just before the Big Bang.'
'I thought you didn't believe in the Big Bang.'
'I don't, well—only in the sense that it's just one corner of the multiverse's total state vector, it's not a true beginning of anything. No-one was there to observe it, so its "reality" is questionable. But, in that corner, the null vector if you like, the state vector of the universe arguably has zero information content. Planck time afterwards it had two pi bits—about seven bits, and kept growing by ten to the forty-four bits per second, ignoring the inflationary periods. Life happened. Memories started being laid down. It can only happen in the direction through possibility space in which entropy increases. Consciousness *is* memory laying *is* time. The implication being of course that there are infinite paths or time dimensions, but that's an aside.'
'I don't see where this is leading.'
'Well, go to one of the infinite *other* extremes of possibility space, opposite the Big Bang. Take entropy to its conclusion. Eventually the state vector represents the memory of *everything*. Ever. Life, consciousness all keep growing in the direction of time and increasing entropy until the whole universe is conscious and remembers everything about its entire past. The "Heat Death" of the universe could be the exact *opposite*. Maybe that's where God, Heaven and Hell really are. Or rather, *when* they are. So, yes, life after death is kind of inevitable.'
'Fucking hell, Alexei.'
'*Then,* of course, there's quantum immortality. . . a logical consequence of the Many Worlds interpretation.'
'Quantum immortality?' My head was hurting.
'You never heard of quantum immortality?'
'No.'
'Well, think about Schrödinger's Cat. From the cat's perspective,' Alexei continued. '*It* stays alive in one of the universes. It might be dead to you in the other one *you're* in, but as far as it's concerned, it's perfectly alive. Everything's relative. Even death. There's *always* going to be an alternative world in which whatever event kills you in this one doesn't happen. Ergo: you're immortal.'

He went back to reading his paper.

'Everyone else dies around you, but from your perspective you carry on living?'

'Until they're resurrected in the Heat Death of the universe.'

I studied his face. The bruises were long gone of course, but his nose—which had always been a little bent on his handsome face—was a little more so now. I listened to his breathing, gentle rasps through the crooked cartilage.

'Alexei... What happened?'

I was going to add, 'That night, on the roof,' but I didn't need to. He pretended to continue reading as if he hadn't heard me, but his eyes were no longer scanning the page. His eyes roamed his memory instead. Eventually they came to halt and he remained staring blankly at the paper in front of him.

I waited a little longer, expecting at any moment for the tension to break, for something to burst out, however little. But nothing came. Alexei's capacity to resist such things was supernatural.

'Okay, well...' I sighed, feeling helpless. 'If you don't want to talk about it... I understand.' There were things I did not want to—could not—discuss, after all. And yet, although I was grateful for his respect for my privacy, there was a barrier between us. I needed more than conversations about physics.

'I know it's not easy being... different. Sometimes... people, you know, strangers... who don't know you... they might not understand... and some people are afraid of what they don't understand. They channel it into anger... But—'

I knew I was making a mess of what I wanted to say. I wanted to say that I understood; that it was okay with me. Instead I seemed to be justifying whoever had beaten him up for being gay.

His eyelids seemed to droop for a moment, as if terribly fatigued, but his jaw muscles tightened.

'Strangers...' It came out in a whisper, but he was scoffing at the word.

He muttered something in Slovakian. Or Hungarian.

His jaw muscles tightened again, and a shadow crossed his face that frightened me.

I swallowed, and fell silent for a moment. I picked up the paper again.

'How about thirteen down? "*Naturally woken up, presumably, by all-night party*" Nine letters.'

From the pages of Tony's diary:

What a strange game! Simulateneous castling?!

```
1.  Pa1 - Pa1
2.  0-0-0
3.  Pa2 - Rxh8+
4.  Pa1 - Pb8
5.  Rf3+ - Rxh8+
6.  Pe8 - Qxh8+
7.  Pa1 - Ph6
8.  Pxh8+ - Kxh8+
9.  Re1 - Rxf8+
10. Pxc6 - Kxd8+
11. Pxg6 - Qd8+
12. Ka1 - Pd4+
13. Pa1+ - Rh8+
14. Pa5 - Pa1
15. Qxc6 - Qa3+
16. Pa1 - Kxh8+
17. Pe2 - Pb1
18. Qxc6 - Qh4+
19. Nxc6+ - Kxd8+
20. Pf2 - Kxh8+
21. Qxc6 - Bxh8+
22. Na1 - Kxh8+
23. Rf3+ - Nxe2+
24. Qa1 - Pxh8+
25. Pe2+ - Kh8+
26. Ra5 - Pa8+
27. Qxc6 - Qxh7+
28. Pd6+ - Pxh8+
29. Ph8+ - Nc7
30. Na1 - Pf8+
31. Qf8 - Rh8+
32. Pe1 - Be3+
33. Kc6 - Qb4+
34. Re5 - Rxd8+
35. Pa5 - Ph6+
36. Ra1 - Pa2
37. Pa1 - Rxf8+
38. Pa1 - Kxh8+
39. Pxb8+ - Kxh8+
40. Na1 - Pg8+
41. Pa1 - Pxd8+
42. Pd8+ - Kxh8+
43. Pxa1 - Pc8+
44. Pa1 - Pg8+
45. Pc3+ - Rxh8+
46. Pe6 - Qa8
47. Kf3+ - Rxh4+
48. Pa6 - Bxh8
49. Ke8+ - Kxh8+
```

228

Chapter 27

'Living backwards!' Alice repeated in great astonishment. 'I never heard of such a thing!'

— Through the Looking Glass

I drift at the edges of awareness for a timeless eternity, an infinity of moments, barely threaded together, dewdrops on an invisible spider's thread. I'm afloat on a dark sea, stretching away in every direction, sometimes falling beneath the surface for peaceful stretches of oblivion, sometimes pushed up above its surface unwillingly to endure the naked agonies of existence. I have no sense of identity, no capacity for thought. I simply am and am not, an endless cycle of uncertainty.

There is no way for me to gauge the length of this period subjectively—perhaps months?—time does not pass as such in this strange state of quasi-awareness. And yet the moment comes when I wake again.

The first thought that passes through my conscious mind is that I should not be alive. I do not know where this conviction comes from—I cannot recall who I was, or have been in life—but I am certain that I have died. I am also certain that I do not believe in life after death.

I sit up abruptly and look around.

The difficulty of this action, and the strange dull pain it causes me at the base of my skull suggests that I am not in any kind of heaven. I lie back again, screw my eyes closed and let the dull throbbing subside over some painful minutes. Exhaustion weighs down upon every cell in my body.

I open my eyes again carefully and look around as far as I can without moving my head.

A hospital room.

I try to remember what has happened to me, how I come to be here, but nothing comes. My mind feels weighed down by a profound blanket of fog, gently tugging it back to the seas in which I have drifted for so long. Lacking the will to resist it, I close my eyes and sink back again into a dreamless sleep.

'Where is Gepetto?' I ask the white boy who tends to me. I don't know where the name comes from, but it leaps from my mouth the moment it comes to me.

'Who is Gepetto?' the boy asks in a strange voice. He wears a smooth white helmet and his mouth—if he has one—is hidden behind a black glass visor.

He is not a real boy. I can tell.

'Your father!'

How do I know such things? 'Your father! I'm sure. He wished you alive. Didn't he? I must have known him once. Oh, Pinocchio! That's your name, isn't it? Please tell me I'm right.'

I sink back down on the bed, exhausted again, and delirious, scratching for meaning in a burnt scrubland of memory. A battle seems to be waging inside

229

my head. Fragments of memories are occasionally thrown up from it to my consciousness like tattered rags. I can't piece any of them together into a meaningful whole. My identity is lost. I hold onto these fragments that come to me like this and desperately try to weave them into a liferaft.

'Do you wish to call me Pinocchio?' asks the boy with infinite politeness.

'Can I?'

'I am programmed to serve. On behalf of Honda, I wish you a speedy recovery, sir. Honda is committed to excellent customer service.'

'Who is Honda?'

'Honda is my manufacturer.'

'Honda is your father, then? Not Gepetto?'

'Do you wish Honda to be my father?'

'What?'

'Do you wish Honda to be my father?'

'Oh... you're confusing me. Go away.'

'Yes, sir. I'm sorry to have confused you. Do you wish to log a complaint with Honda customer services? Honda is committed to excellent customer serv—'

'Just leave.'

'Yes, sir.'

Gradually, small flotsam of memory begins to collect together to form an archipelago of identity, a convoluted terrain of external facts that I step over gingerly, and call me. I begin to audit what I know, and what I do not:

I know that a stitch in time, saves nine, but I wonder, nine of what? I know that cats have nine lives, and that there is a cat-o'-nine-tails, but it seems unlikely that a stitch in time would save nine lives, or tails. I know that if I run, I will get a stitch. I know of a place called London that is the capital of England, and that England is in Europe, but I can't remember what these places look like. I know rolling stones gather no moss, and also played rock music, but I'm not sure if it is at the same time. I know there is a girl called Little Red Riding Hood who lives in a wood, and I deduce that she is the wife of Robin Hood who also lives there, because I know that when people get married they change their surnames to match. I'm pleased with myself for this masterpiece of deductive logic. I seem to recall, though, that he has had an affair with one Maid Marion, and somehow a wolf is involved. The wood—which is somewhere in England, surely—is also home to a beautiful girl who was asleep for a hundred years, and some dwarves, and is being deforested at such a rate that everything is in danger of becoming extinct. Or is that Brazil? No, that's a type of nut. I know that. The wood also has a witch in it, doesn't it? Yes, I seem to remember she is a very vain witch, who likes to look into a magic mirror and—

A formless explosion of pain and fear wracks my body. I lie, trembling, in bed and pull the sheets toward my face. Thinking about the wicked witch has triggered something terrible. It threatens to unearth memories I am not yet ready to face.

I hug myself and try to sleep again, but I can't. There is a nursery rhyme singing itself inside my head, repeatedly: *Half a pound of tuppeny rice, Half a pound of treacle...*

Except these words, they seem wrong. Other words keep creeping in, new verses. When the words aren't there, I find my fingers tapping out the beat.

Finally sleep comes.

I wake to a voice, and to the sound of banging. I realize the voice is coming from inside my room. It sounds desperate, full of pain. I open my eyes and look up to see a man with his head against the door, talking, apparently to himself. He sounds distressed.

'Yes, him. The person Skyler was incubating.'

A pause, then:

'Room eleven. The robots tried to attack me. One's still outside the door now.'

A longer pause.

'Lewis. It's my brother. It's my *fucking* brother.'

A rose of memory flowers in my mind, as if filmed in stop-motion, and then withers again when I try to snatch at it, falling to dust. Fragments remain. *Lewis.* I know that name. A brother. Yes, I have a brother. The memory is unpleasant. I remember a great animosity, and suddenly I fear for my life. The man at the door seems older. Is he my brother? Didn't my brother gloat about being older? Wasn't that something he'd always held over me? Something I'd despised him for? This seems to ring true. An inescapable conclusion forms in my mind:

This must be him. He has found me. My life is in danger.

Without making a sound, I lift myself out of my bed, desperately looking for something to fight with. There is nothing.

Suddenly a screen in the room grows bright and a small figure appears on it. A voice comes from somewhere. It says the word, '*Steel,*' in an urgent tone, causing my brother to turn toward it. I sidle around behind his back, like a praying mantis. The voice continues:

'You were right. Your sentinel was hacked. And now, I don't understand, I'm being blocked somehow. You're in danger.'

I am overwhelmed by a disorienting sense of déjà vu. *Somewhen*, this has all happened before.

'You think I don't fucking know that?'

'*Listen!* I'm trying to tell you, it wasn't—'

The conversation seems to stop then, and I feel a wave of nausea ripple through me. The floor beneath my naked feet seems to go momentarily soft. I stumble and put out my hand to the nearest thing—a cupboard—making it knock against the wall. My brother whips around at the sound, his face full of dread, and I instinctively react by punching him as hard as I can, knocking him backwards into the screen and causing it to clatter noisily to the floor underneath him. Something wet and unnaturally bright spills from the screen as it falls.

I think I may have broken a knuckle. He lies in a tangle and looks up at me with an expression of such stupefaction that it causes me to wonder if I have been justified in attacking him. Have I made a mistake? Have I misread this situation? Somewhere deep in my unconscious a voice is urgently trying to tell me something.

This man is not my brother.

My sense of déjà vu is so powerful now, I can barely move.

A moment later the door explodes open, and a very bulky, unhealthy looking man appears. He is holding up my Pinocchio by his narrow waist in one hand. The man's face... I know his face.

The memory trying to burgeon within me dies and falls back to nothing.

The intruder looks at me and then at my not-brother on the floor. And then he does the strangest thing. He speaks the words of the very rhyme that has infected my mind like a worm:

'A penny for a spool of thread, A penny for a needle...'

'Lewis?' says the man on the floor.

'Shut up!'

The intruder continues, directing the words at me, a great urgency and tension in his eyes:

'That's the way the money goes, *Pop!* goes the weasel. What's the next verse?'

'Lewis, what the f—'

'I said *shut up!*'

'What's the next verse?' He shakes the mechanical boy at me, as if it were a stick. '*WHAT'S THE NEXT VERSE?!*'

He's going to kill me, my fear whispers to me, but even as it does so, the words of the next verse spring from my lips, which seem to know them without me. As I sing, my voice cracks:

'Half a toe of stuttering dice, Twice a wheel of diesel, Tell the man he's not so nice... Pop! goes the weasel.'

'You're sure?' the man demands.

I nod.

'Did you get that?'

'I don't underst—' says my not-brother weakly.

'Not you.'

'Loud and clear,' comes a German-sounding voice from somewhere.

'I'm so sorry, Zeke,' the big man says to the man on the floor. 'Your brother is dead. This is not Jacob.'

Then he points Pinocchio at him. There is a *pfiz* sound and a dart shoots from Pinocchio's arm. To my relief, my not-brother collapses to the floor. He can't punch me back now. This man, Lewis, has obviously come to rescue me. I feel an enormous sense of gratitude.

'Thank you,' I say very earnestly.

He looks a bit surprised and eyes me suspiciously.

'You're welcome.'

'Why did he think I was... Jacob?' I ask. 'Who is he anyway? Looks familiar.'

'He's you.'

'What?'

'Never mind.'

'What's happening? Where am I?'

'You're at the top of a fucking big tower. And we need to get out.'

'Do I know you?'

'Yes. I'm Lewis. We were at university together.'

I look at my young wrinkle-free hands and then at his old, gnarled, heavy fists and consider this. My entire life is on the tip of my tongue, but I can't quite remember it.

'Oh. Okay.'

Pinocchio is patiently trying to turn in Lewis's arms, but Lewis keeps holding him away.

The German voice coming from somewhere near Lewis speaks again:

'Get him to the bottom. We're outside.'

'One problem. He's unconscious.'

'What?'

'I had to shoot him with a tranquilizer. He's unconscious.'

'Verdammtes *arschloch!*'

'What did you expect me to do?' the guy shouts angrily. 'Ask him nicely?'

'Scheisse. *Scheisse.* You have to lift him out.'

'What? I'm supposed to just walk out of this building carrying an unconscious body over my shoulder? Stop dicking around.'

'Then you better think of another way of getting him out. Wait... I hear sirens. *Scheisse...*'

'What?'

'Bad news. The alarms I think have gone off. A SWAT team just arrived. They're entering the building. Get out, *now.*'

'How?! Can't we open a Door or something?'

'Under these conditions? *Impossible.* Don't be a *fool.* Just *get him out!*'

Lewis looks panicked. Pinocchio's patient pneumatic struggles now pose a problem for him. He can't put him down. I want to help, but I don't know how.
'Pinocchio, stay still!' I plead.
The mechanical boy stops moving. Lewis looks at me open-mouthed.
'How did you do that?'
I shrug. It just seemed like the right thing to do. Pinocchio speaks:
'For how long would you like me to stay still, sir?'
'Put your tranquilizers away,' Lewis instructs tentatively.
'I'm sorry, sir, but I'm not programmed to respond to your needs, only to those of a patient.'
'Lift your arm,' I say.
Pinocchio lifts his left arm. I feel a little proud.
'Tell it to put its tranquilizers away,' Lewis instructs me. I comply. Pinocchio complies.
'Well, fuck me. How strong are these things?' asks Lewis.
'The Honda SPV1100 hydraulic motion system is capable of ambulatory motion under a force of 180 Newtons for eighteen continuous hours,' Pinocchio offers.
'180 kilos in normal g. That's plenty. Tell him to pick up the body and bring him along. Let's go.'
Pinocchio crouches and lifts the unconscious body of my not-brother, wobbling precariously. He carries him in his arms. He seems inhumanly strong for such a small boy.
'The other robots,' the fat man asks, about to open the door. 'Can you control them too?'
This question upsets me.
My mind has suddenly gone blank. I try but fail to remember this guy's name. Where has he come from? We had been doing something a moment ago together, but for some reason I just can't remember what it was. And... well, this is really strange: there is a little shiny, white astronaut boy carrying someone asleep.
'Am I dreaming?'
'Can you control the other robots?'
'What other robots? Who are you?'
'Oh no....' His dismay is infectious. 'Not now. *Listen to me.* You're in danger. I'm a friend. We need to get out of here. Fast.'
I feel my chest beat at these words. Why am I suddenly in danger?
'Okay.'
He turns to the little astronaut.
'Can he instruct all the nurses? Will they obey him?'
'As long as his instructions do not conflict with the first law.'
'"*You may not injure a human being, or, through inaction, allow a human being to come to harm?*"'
'No, sir, the first law mandates that a robot must not allow harm to the facilities or any property within the facility.'
'*Great,*' says the fat man. 'Come on.'
He opens the door and peers through the gap.
'Warning. I am unable to establish a connection to the central system. Timeout exceeded. I have retried twenty-eight times. There may be a technical problem or the building may be in danger. You are advised to seek help or the nearest available exit.'
'Take us to the lifts.'
'In cases of emergency the lifts may not be operational and it is inadvisable—'
'Just take us to the *fucking* lifts!'
'Take us to the lifts,' I plead.
Astroboy wobbles uncertainly at first when he tries to walk whilst carrying the unconscious man, but he soon finds a stride which hardly slows him. We run

along several corridors past several more of the small astronaut boys, who swivel
to follow us and raise their arms at the fat man. I find this very polite. There is
a faint zipping sound. The fat man dives sideways into the wall and stares with
a hysterical expression at a small dart embedded there next to him.

'Tell them to lower their arms!' he screeches.

I feel I've done something wrong. When the astronaut children obey me I feel
a little better because the fat man seems grateful. The place is a maze. At the
end of the corridor another robot appears. It is accompanied by a frightened
looking woman. She has wavy hair, and looks as distressed as I feel. There is
something familiar about her.

'Skyler,' the man says upon seeing her. 'Follow us.'

The middle of this corridor leads to another short corridor and at the end
of it, there is a wide bank of lifts. We run to them and the fat man begins to
bang at the lift buttons frantically. He lifts his head and eyes the floor indicators.
Three rubies rise like angry sparks from dying embers on the display. They rush
upwards disturbingly fast as if on a column of heated air.

'That can't be right. Those can't be the only ones in operation. No! They've
stopped the lifts. They're *coming*.'

The panic in his voice is beginning to upset me deeply.

'Where are the stairs?' I say.

'We'll never make it. It's seventy floors down. We're fucked.'

'Sir, please advise me of the situation. I am programmed to respond appropri-
ately given the correct facts. I cannot access the central system. Is the building
in some kind of danger?'

The fat guy's expression freezes for a second and he looks off somewhere to
the side, apparently thinking. Then:

'Yes. *Yes*. It's a terrorist attack. They're coming up in the lifts to get us.
What do we do? Is there any kind of escape chute?'

'Follow me.'

The boy begins to run heavily, still carrying the unconscious man. His legs
wheeze hydraulically as he thumps along, but he does not slow. Behind us, a
small horde of astroboys begins to congregate and follow us. Among them is the
woman.

We arrive at a door. Next to the door is a large glass window, behind which I
see rows and rows of smooth pods, softly lit from behind. They are mostly white
but slightly translucent and look a little like large insect eggs, a little larger than
tennis balls. The pods each have white nylon belts and buckles attached to them.

The white boy raises an arm and reaches through the glass to grab one of the
pods, smashing the glass incidentally. He gives a pod to the fat man.

'Strap this around you so that the pod is at the base of your back.'

'What the hell is this?'

'Please comply, there is little time.'

The boy then hands one of the pods to me.

'Strap this around you so that the pod is at the base of your back.'

The straps go around my waist and over my shoulders. He gives another pod
to the woman and tells her to do the same. The boy then begins to hand out
pods, but oddly none of the robots attach any of them to their waists, they just
clutch them, one in each hand.

'Follow,' the boy says calmly, and begins to run again, in a cushioned thump
along the carpet.

We twist and turn, and come to a door. The boy pauses before a dark glass
panel. The door clicks. In the distance behind us, I can hear the confident chime
of the lift doors. The lift is arriving.

I feel happy knowing the lift has arrived and start toward it.

'*No! What are you doing?* This way! Hurry!' the fat man cries.

I suddenly have a terrible sense of dread. What is going on?

'Where am I?' I say, disoriented. Behind me, a woman says the same thing. I turn and we stare at each other cautiously. There are at least ten small white astronaut boys. I'm dreaming. I must be dreaming.

'Hurry!' the man urges again and we pour through the door. What is so bad that's coming from the lifts, I wonder? I feel very afraid.

We are in a small concrete stairwell. The old guy begins to clamber heavily downstairs. One of the boys—who seems to be carrying someone asleep—calls to him.

'Upstairs,' he says. We turn up and begin running.

We run up what seems like four flights. By the top, my heart is pounding somewhere near my throat and I can taste my lungs in my mouth. The fat guy makes it to the top just a few seconds behind me, driven by sheer terror. His face is ashen and waxy, and sweat cascades down his face. His shirt is soaked and stuck to his skin.

'Are you okay?' I ask.

'Keep going,' he urges and pushes upwards toward the door ahead. Through its glass I can see the sky: dull and white and formless gray. The boy finally opens the lock and we run through and out on to a wide expanse of gray roof. The wind howls around me like a hungry animal, clawing with frosty fingers at my skin through my pyjamas. The horizon fades into a cold white haze in the distance. The small army of white astronaut boys runs out in fluid alien strides, and they jog without pausing across the great gray plain toward the edge, clumping like heavily booted army cadets.

We close the door behind us just as the dark malevolent form appears in the darkness behind the glass.

It's a man, a massively armored guard. He carries several heavy looking weapons and more equipment is strapped all around his armor. I hear more guards coming behind him. The gloom behind the glass is shot through with subtle threads of ruby laser guides, dancing and slicing up the air in shimmering lines. I panic and smash at the door control repeatedly.

'I can't break it. They're going to get through!'

The white boy runs to me, lifts one hand and drives it down through the door control, hammering it in one stroke to the ground.

There is the sound of a single shot, and the glass of the door shatters, becoming instantly opaque.

I turn to run. My feet slip under my haste as if on wet linoleum, sending me tumbling onto the floor of the roof. The base of my neck sings out in pain. I moan and scramble to my feet clumsily lurching forward. I clutch at the back of my neck, which has begun to thump in dull red agony.

'They're coming through!' I cry.

Ahead of me one of the white boys twists around mid-stride in an impressive U-turn that seems to contradict its momentum. It pulls on the cord of one of the pods it carries and throws it violently at the doorframe. There is a small explosion and then a rapid popcorn sound of firecrackers. It sounds like a gun battle that increases in intensity as it simultaneously races away from us. The pod has exploded into smaller balls on sticky strands, each of which then explodes, recursing, again and again, in a fractal series that results in a huge dense white cloud of rapidly-setting gooey fluff. The guard behind cries out as he runs through and trips. He tangles in the fluffy fog, which coalesces in thick white skeins, trapping him like plastic spider web, or melting marshmallow.

'Quickly!' the boy urges and runs, following the cohort of white soldiers ahead of me. To my terror, I see them one by one leaping over the tall glass edge of the building out of sight. The astroboy carrying the unconscious man has already leapt over the edge.

Behind me another firecracker storm whips up a marshmallow shield.

There is a cry. I turn to see the fat man's body jack-knife in mid-stride and land heavily on his back. He opens his mouth, but he is winded—no scream comes. Behind him, an armored soldier like a great dark mountain of shielding, plastic and metal devices, shouts from behind a heavy visor in amplified audio:

'HALT! YOU ARE UNDER ARREST!'

A line of wires fizzes out from something emerging from the door frame and seems to pierce the crippled form of the fat man who helped me to escape. He cries out: a strangled gurgle, and spasms on the floor. Three points where the lines intersect near him smoke and spark in the cold air. His body judders to a motionless slump. He looks deathly pale.

'YOU IDIOT, I'D ALREADY TAKEN HIM OUT!'

I run for my life across the great roof. As I near the edge, a great city spreads out below and beyond me, somehow looking less like a city and more like an enormous dull map so large that it has its own weather. It is breathtaking. Another shot whizzes past me. In terror, I clamber on to the edge of the glass that is the only thing protecting me from falling. Scintillating red dots sparkle and dart around the glass near my legs. Suddenly, spiked metal balls spank loudly against the glass where the dots are, leaving small spider web cracks. Metal threads tangle from the spiked balls and issue furious blue and white sparks into the air where they cross each other. One of the wires turns red, melts and falls apart. The stench of ozone tingles at my nostrils.

'Jump!' cries the astroboy.

The wind whips violently at my pyjamas. They flap around my legs and arms as if I were wrapped in little flags. The force of it almost lifts me off the glass. I look down in terror almost two thousand feet to the city below, and quietly, I shit myself.

There is nowhere to go. Only down.

I glance back at the man whose body spasmed so horribly. Is he dead?

I close my eyes and brace myself against the glass and then I leap with all my force against the edge into the air, letting the wind whip and tear at my arms as I fall into its infinite gaping embrace.

A second later, the pod attached to my back blows up in a fractal explosion of ever diminishing size, ever increasing number. I feel the air shudder at my back as if I have been physically hit with a pillow. I lurch, tugged strongly by my belt and the straps at my shoulders.

Terrified, my mind quietly wipes itself clean again.

I find myself suspended in chill air over a vast map containing an enormous blue-black river. I look up to see an extraordinary structure attached to me by a white cord—it is a huge cloud of strange white substance, almost insubstantial fluff. I am a seed floating toward some distant fertile land. There is no sound of wind, no traffic sounds. I am too high. Just a cold, stark beauty that surrounds and pierces me. My heart hammers rapidly in my chest, as if I have been running or frightened. It begins to slow and I start to shiver from the cold.

Ahead, around and beneath me, more strange white clouds float down through the sky. Suspended from them are little white boys, figures holding onto their clouds with upstretched arms, gripping onto them with their powerful hands. Beneath one, a large man seems to hang unconscious, n-shaped, from his belt.

Behind me, a glittering building like a great crystal recedes. I shiver and watch, astounded at the beauty of the vast city slowly sliding beneath me.

Tiny cars meander along little roads like blood cells through arteries.

Peacefully, we float across a great expanse of blue-black river toward the ground on the other side.

In the distance I begin to hear sirens.

From the pages of Tony's diary:

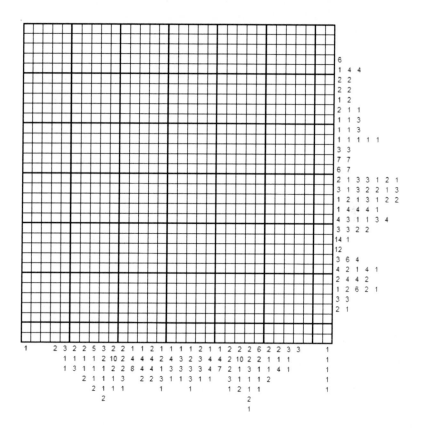

Chapter 28

'*Human consciousness is the window through which we experience the universe. It feels like a large-bandwidth, high-definition experience but this is illusory: experiments have consistently shown that we consciously processes, at most, a mere 40 bits per second. Theoretically then, all human experience may be represented in the permutations of just 40 bits. In other words, nothing beyond this window need actually exist for every experience to be accounted for. The universe may be much smaller than it appears. Infinitesimally smaller. It is entirely possible that the whole of reality runs on a 40-bit quantum computer...*'

—*Information Relativity and the New Physics*,
Professor Fabrizio T. Luciano

Alexei was my most faithful visitor at St. Clair's. He came about once a week, bearing papers and puzzles and a head full of ideas to discuss. If I was not medicated, we could even discuss them, though it was entirely him driving these days. I enjoyed the journeys as a passenger nonetheless.

I sat staring at a grid with numbers next to it.

Alexei was wearing a long-sleeved shirt, which seemed odd. It was summer. His hair was ragged and he looked tired. He'd arrived this week with a puzzle, but it was a photocopy. He had no newspapers this time. He called the puzzle a nonogram. He'd explained that the numbers were clues for a black and white picture in the grid, and indicated how many unbroken black lines there were on that row or column, but not where they were. That, you had to determine by deduction from the other numbers.

Alexei was rapidly completing his with a system of dots and shading, whilst I stared at my blank grid feeling somewhat baffled, trying to find where on earth to start.

A finger appeared across my vision and pointed to the lonely "14" and "1" on the right hand side.

'See?'

'No. The grid's thirty-two wide. A line fourteen long could go anywhere in it.'

'It's not really. Look, there are two blank columns on the left and two on the right... so the fourteen has to fit somewhere between them otherwise they wouldn't be blank. The gap is only twenty-six wide. Fourteen is more than half of twenty-six so...'

'Oh—'

I counted squares across and shaded in the two centre squares which had to be black, no matter where the line started and finished. We continued in silence for a little longer until I got stuck again.

'It's a neat type of encoding, really, isn't it?' Alexei said without looking up.
'Is it?'

'Yeah. Just a few numbers for rows and columns, apply a deterministic algorithm, and out pops a picture.'

'It's amazing, isn't it, that there are so many ways to represent the same information? Infinitely many. You could store this as a gif, a jpeg, tiff, pdf, a nonogram, in binary, hex, decimal. All completely different numbers that all mean the same thing. Thanks to *us*. Our interpretation.'

I realised I'd seen this puzzle before.

'Where did this one come from?'

Alexei seemed reluctant to answer. 'From Tony's diary.'

I'd forgotten that I'd given it to him after I had found it following Kate's death. I'd been worried about its contents, and what the police might make of them.

I felt vaguely sick at the memories it evoked.

'The cryptic notes... you've deciphered them, then?'

'Most, not all. They're encodings of tiny pictures. Some still frames taken from the possible states of a tiny 2D universe, thirty-two pixels square.'

'I see.'

'They're interpretation puzzles. You interpret the encodings to arrive at a picture.'

We scribbled on in silence for a while.

'I thought it would be fun to solve them together.'

Alexei reached across the table for a pen and I saw two things: a flash of brown material through the opening in his shirt sleeve, and the white material of his shirt seemed darker underneath. I instinctively grabbed his arm and lifted it. A patch of clear liquid darkened the cloth.

'What's this?'

He tried to pull his arm away but I held onto it steadily and lifted up his sleeve. Underneath, his arm was bandaged from the wrist upwards. It looked like it hadn't been changed in weeks.

I still didn't know what Alexei was going through, but I knew more than I wanted to about self-harming.

'Oh no... Alexei, no. You need to see someone about this.'

He looked at me, puzzled.

'You need to get help. This isn't necessary.'

'What are you talking about?'

'Cutting yourself. I know it takes the pain away, but it—'

'Stop. Stop. *Stop.*'

He touched the side of my cheek tenderly.

'You didn't get to me that badly, okay?'

'That's not what I'm—'

'Neither did anything else. I'm *fine*. This is not what you think. Yes... Yes, I did that once. But I'm not in that space any more.'

'Then what—'

'I was...'

He looked terribly sad for a moment, and yet he was smiling as he stared into my eyes.

'I was just experimenting with a direct nerve implant. To control the buggy.'

'What?'

'Why not? It's the most direct way. More intuitive. Less noise. I wanted to see how much more control I'd have. The wound got a little infected, that's all.'

'But you can't do that. You'll damage yourself.'

That sad look again in those cat-like green-blue eyes with the ever-present smile.

'What's the point of having a nice body if nobody wants you anyway?'

'Oh, come on... you'll—'

'I was joking. Half at least.' He shrugged. He waved his arm. 'This is more important to me anyway.'

I touched his sleeve.

He stared at the table.

'I'm going away,' Alexei said softly.

I froze.

'What?'

'I've...' He sighed through his nose. 'I was working on this idea... and... I sent a paper to this professor at MIT to ask him his opinion. It was just a draft. But, he got a bit excited about it. He reckons I may have proved something important. They've asked me to go over there. To Massachusetts.'

'But you're just a second-year undergrad!'

'Well...' He shrugged.

I was devastated. For so many reasons. My stomach twisted, sick and acidic.

'What paper?'

'Well, you know I taught myself a lot of physics recently... but computing is my field. Well, the paper—it's sort of an adjunct to the Church–Turing thesis. I've proposed a definition of a class of hypercomputations that are only calculable quantum mechanically. I've argued that consciousness is in that domain. I show there are logical absurdities if the reverse is true. Do you remember the *reductio ad absurdum* I mentioned ages ago?'

'You've proved weak AI,' I muttered.

He looked awkward.

'I wouldn't go that far.'

'Computers will never be conscious. Unless they're quantum.'

'Well, kind of... Zeke, I need this. I can't stay here.'

Somehow the treachery I felt flowed into the silent air, accusing him.

He did not speak for a long moment. Then, finally, in a quiet voice, he confessed. It was a terse confession, that left much to the imagination. Alexei supplied only the barest threads of colour from which to weave a tapestry:

His father had disowned him; financially, the works; and, it had not been a gang that had beaten him so badly that night.

This was all he supplied. But he didn't need to say any more.

Alexei wouldn't look at me. Instead he went back to quietly and tidily completing his nonogram.

I scratched and scrabbled with my pencil on the paper in my hand, expressing the conflicting emotions inside me. My picture no longer bore a relationship to the numbers on the side.

'I'll miss you,' I said eventually.

'Me too. Email?'

'Yeah.'

Alexei had stopped his tidy scribbling. He admired his work for a moment and then shrugged and held up his paper to show me. I stared at it, feeling utterly empty.

'Story of my life.'

He opened his mouth to say something and closed it again. But then he found his voice:

'Come with me? You'll be out soon. Start a new life. We could both do with a fresh start? Couldn't we?'

He chuckled.

'We can reinvent ourselves.'

we mewl... nuke dew

6s .24J,gE 2rmN :16

Chapter 29

'It's a poor sort of memory that only works backwards,' the Queen
remarked.

—*Through the Looking Glass*

Rain is drumming on the roof of the car. I sit quietly, listening to the engine
tick as it cools. I feel angry and frustrated by my inability to open the door.
A small man appears on the screen in the front section.
'Who are you?' I demand. The car has been driving itself until now. I have
no idea how I've even come to be inside it.
'It's okay. I'm a friend. This is my car.'
'Why I am locked in here?'
'For your own safety. You were... attacked. I helped you. We came here to
escape. To hide.'
The door suddenly opens by itself. Outside a small, wet dog with a silver
crucifix regards me cautiously. It begins sniffing at the air.
'Oh Dog...' says the dog. 'This is some kinda cat shit...'
'A talking dog,' I say matter-of-factly, but inside surprised.
The dog continues: 'Ooh. This is *strange...St'raaange.*'
'What's wrong?' says the man on the screen.
'I have the strangest feeling about him. Call it dog intuition.'
'Bring him up.'
We seem to have parked in an upmarket office complex. The buildings are
glass and the scenery is seriously landscaped. It looks like an architect's model
scaled up. I follow the talking dog into a building. The dog shakes himself, lightly
dusting the marble floor with a spray of water drops. We enter a lift which speaks
to us sweetly. After an extended moment of acceleration we slow at the top.
The doors open into a large penthouse apartment.
'Come inside,' says a voice from somewhere. 'I think it's best for the moment
that he doesn't see me. Until we've sorted out his little memory problem.'
I have a memory problem? Yes, I suppose I do.
'Make yourself at home.'
I walk through the hall. The impression I have of the apartment is one of
luxury. Dark lacquered wood, glass, mirrors, pale marble floor. There is a smell
of lilies, masking a subtle but powerful chemical smell, like a hospital. I walk
through into a spacious living area. The floor-to-ceiling rear window looks onto
manicured greenery. The dog's nails go *tka-tka-tk-tk*, tippy-tapping like glass on
glass every time he moves across the marble. Leather sofas form an L-shape
around a beautiful rug. The dog wanders onto the rug, silencing him.
To the left, another room is apparently separated from this by the faintest of
boundaries: a matte surface shimmers between in the air. In the room beyond,

an elegantly dressed, handsome man stands watching me. His sandy hair is in a pony tail. His polo neck sweater carries a badge with a camel emblem.

'I can see you. . . ' I tease.

'Ah. No hiding from you, eh. Cup of tea? Coffee?'

'Mm. Tea would be lovely. Thanks.'

I sit down on one of the sofas, and the dog leaps on to them next to me. He's very friendly. I think it's nice when a dog takes to you like that. He sits patiently next to me, nose twitching at the air occasionally. I notice his crucifix on his collar appears to be made of two silver bones. Cute.

When I move the image of the man behind in the other room distorts in a subtle and strange way, a little like he's in a fish tank. I find this extremely novel and keep moving my head to observe the effect until a trolley arrives all by itself and positions itself conveniently by me. There is a cup of tea standing on it.

'Spooky.'

I pick up the tea, blow on it, and take a sip. The blow was unnecessary. It is barely hot, and the tea tastes metallic. I grimace.

I take another sip, but the metallic taste is really quite disgusting and seems even stronger this time. I put the cup down and try to clear my mouth of the taste.

'Ugh, it tastes foul and it's cold—sorry, don't mean to be rude.'

The man smiles.

'Not at all. Please accept *my* apologies. Any hotter would have damaged the little bugs in it. They're very delicate. They should be burrowing their way through your tongue and your oesophageal lining quite happily now.'

I leap to my feet, knocking the trolley backwards. The cup of tea tips backwards on its saucer, throwing itself and its contents to the marble in a lazy parabola. It cracks into several large pieces in a very musical manner.

'Oh dear—my floor,' says man from his fish tank room in a rather depressed voice. 'Me and my big fat mouth.'

'WHAT HAVE YOU DONE TO ME?'

I turn frantically looking for something, anything to help me.

'Don't panic. It's just a little something to help you to remember. Now I have an idea of what's responsible for the problem I cooked up a little brew of machines to disable the ones that are currently holding your hippocampus and substantia innominata hostage. Give it a few minutes and with a bit of luck, we should be able to find out who the devil you are.'

I look at the milky liquid splattered across the marble. There are no machines in it. Just bits of china.

'Machines?'

'Hybrid re-engineered viruses actually. But the distinction is moot.'

My face suddenly flushes. At first I think I'm embarrassed, but I have nothing to be embarrassed about. Then my neck begins to feel hot. I sit down again.

'I don't feel—so good.'

'Don't worry. It's normal. You're having an immune reaction. It'll pass. There were really quite a large number of them in there, I'm afraid. I couldn't take any chances.'

I begin to feel quite nauseous. I lie back and close my eyes and put my hand over my eyes. They feel hot against my palm beneath my eyelids. I feel like I'm burning up from within.

The man speaks again, but I'm hardly listening. My thoughts seem to have become trapped in molasses.

'Hopefully enough will have penetrated the blood-brain barrier before they get mopped up by your lymphocytes. They can't reproduce, so it's a bit hit and miss. How do you feel?'

I groan. 'Terrible.'

And then, it is as if a storm is passing. A heavy cloud cover that I hadn't even noticed was there begins to lift. Bit by bit, the clouds thin and suddenly sunlight pierces through in a shocking and beautiful inverted spire of light that illuminates—

—*me.*

I think I gasped then, and moaned in a kind of ecstasy as the effect spread across the vast sky of my mind.

'Well. That's a good sign.'

The last of the clouds evaporated away and the entire vast countryside of my self was revealed in its terrible entirety. Although it would take much longer for my memories to integrate, I remembered enough for my joy to turn to dismay.

I looked up at Needle, and then at JR.

'Oh, Needle... JR...' I grasped my little damp canine buddy and hugged him tightly. 'Thank God.'

'Good grief,' Needle said from behind his World Wall. 'You know me?'

'Needle? It's *me. Steel.*'

JR barked and licked my face. 'See! I knew it! I told you! Dog intuition!'

I had never seen Needle at a loss for words before.

'It's me,' I repeated, a little weakly.

It was some time before he spoke.

'Impossible.'

Needle's handsome avatar eyed me suspiciously, and then the fish-tank room containing it folded in on itself. It flattened and morphed into a normal wall adorned with a grand piece of abstract art. I heard a familiar whine of servos. I turned to see a tall mirror-wall slide away and Needle's wheelchair appeared from behind it, trailing thick cables from a ceiling-mounted tracker. The wheelchair stopped, remaining close to the entrance of his hidden labs.

I stood up to face him. I couldn't understand his strange behavior.

'Needle. It's *me.*'

It was hard to read his expression, tilted sideways and distorted as it was. The livid wound on the side of his head looked a little tidier this time. Perhaps he'd been operating on himself again. His chair turned a fraction.

'Now I'm really spooked,' he said.

'Needle?'

There was a tapping of hard nails against marble. All of a sudden I felt very dizzy.

'I feel—'

JR appeared to my side.

Sharp fragments of more recent memories began to surface again, to bob about dangerously.

There was too much. Nothing had been processed.

'My head is *bursting.*'

I looked down at myself and then across at the nearest mirrored wall. An eighteen-year-old boy stared back at me.

'Holy crap.'

I sat down again heavily. And whispered to myself:

'Holy *fucking* crap.'

Needle's wheelchair edged cautiously nearer, but stayed a healthy distance away.

'Steel?'

I looked up at Needle, my face full of terror. I nodded.

'No. You are confused, young man,' Needle stammered. 'It must be a side-effect of the amnesia nanites.'

'It's *me*, I tell you.'

Weeks of un-integrated memories all floated up into my conscious mind demanding attention that was impossible to give. I began to moan with the pressure of sensory overload.

'Are you okay?'

I cried louder and clenched my fists and began to fidget, desperate and anxious.

'Are you okay?' Needle repeated.

'Do I sound okay?' I whined.

My cries came now in short, breathless gasps. Horrific flickering imagery threatened to take over my visual field. I clutched tentatively at my face.

'My face—they messed up my face—'

Yet this face was smooth, unbroken. More: the skin was pliant and young. I risked a second glance at the mirror wall, disbelieving fingers lightly tracing my rejuvenated face's contours, in case the miracle should disappear if I probed too hard.

'How could you know that?' Needle said aghast. 'He was on the other side of the Hudson to you when that happened...'

I began to babble rapidly as the memories stormed my mind, trying to sort them into some kind of sense:

'Lewis betrayed me. You were trying to warn me about something—about the sentinel being hacked. You were cut off. Lewis arrived, holding a robot like a gun. Demanded the next verse of the nursery rhyme from the boy and—oh *Jesus*! That was me. It was *me*. I remember this twice. From two perspectives.'

My eyes were wide and wild with excitement—and not a little fear.

'Slow down. Start again. From where Lewis—'

'Don't you see what this means?'

'Start again. Tell me *exactly* what you remember. As it happened.'

'We were in the Freedom Tower clinic. You disappeared. Then I found the boy. The clone. *Me*. Oh, this is *so* weird. I thought... he looked identical to me.'

'This clone was the new host for the brain that Skyler had incubated?'

'Yes. There was a record card on the bed. I called Lewis and told him. He arrived, holding a robot—like a gun. Tranquilizers. He demanded the rhyme—'

'What rhyme?'

'*Pop! goes the weasel.* I've been hearing it in the strangest places ever since this whole thing began. He demanded *another* verse, after the final verse. The boy, I mean me, I just came out with it. Like a nonsense verse. Meistermacher was listening to everything over a com. Then Lewis tranquilized me. When I came round they'd beaten my face to shit.'

I touched my face again self-consciously, amazed at the feel of my unbroken, perfect skin.

Needle stared at me with an expression of utter incredulity that even his damaged face conveyed flawlessly.

'Well, Steel's face *was* damaged, but no-one beat him up.'

'What do you mean?'

'Keep going. I'll show you later.'

'I came round in a room, full of mirrors. It looked like the club room, back in the old days of the Looking Glass Club. Meistermacher was there. And—'

I put my hands over my face and succumbed to a tsunami of emotion at the memory of the terrible aspect of Kate. JR pawed and licked at me, trying miserably to console me. He whined in empathy, distressed at my distress, but the tears and the shaking, the grief and the guilt would not stop.

Eventually I emerged again from behind my hands, shaking my head with shame.

'I can't go on. There's too much to explain. You would never believe me.'

'Well,' Needle said with the confident tone of a grandfather comforting a small child, 'why don't I suspend disbelief for a moment? Tell it to me as you experienced it—as a story, if you will—and I'll just—listen.'

I felt tiny in that moment, as if I *was* a child again. My whole life had suddenly been squeezed into a hard little ball for me to inspect like a pretty glass marble. A beautiful and strange curiosity, but nothing more. Nothing seemed real.

I took a huge breath and sighed shakily.

'*That's* it,' Needle comforted.

I began to explain the full story of the Looking Glass Club, the truth about Kate Andrews' death. It took me a long time. Afterwards there was an extended moment of silence.

'Except she isn't dead,' I whispered in a voice almost too quiet to even hear myself.

'She isn't?'

'The Calculatrice is Kate. She was there with Meistermacher.'

I described her appearance.

'She said, "*You don't recognize me do you?*"'

I started to cry again.

'She said she was Jon Rodin's first success. *You saw the babies, Needle. The failed clones. He resurrected her before he perfected the process.*'

Needle remained silent. It was patient disbelief.

'And she said I was, and would be, his second. They held me for days, making me learn that damn rhyme.' *And then they sent me back through the mirror,* I thought.

'Days?'

I knew I'd lost him with the pronouncement of that word. He couldn't keep his promise. He couldn't suspend his disbelief any more than he could believe me. No-one ever had.

'About two *hours* ago, the Steel I know was out of my sight for just under *thirty minutes*. Then you show up, a boy half his age—'

'Needle, it's *me*.'

'—*half* his age, claiming that you *are* him and that... that you were abducted since I last saw you and held captive for *days*.' He paused. '*Come—on*.'

'I'm the person Skyler was incubating. Don't you see?' I jabbed my finger vigorously at my chest. 'It was *me*. My head.'

'Oh dear...'

'What other explanation do you have? Who else could know everything I've told you?'

'Okay, so let's assume you *are* Steel. You disappear from my direct sight for thirty minutes and then you reappear in a younger body which I have simultaneously seen on video surveillance sailing through the sky at *the same time* as the very person you claim to be. That in some days' time that person will become you now. What? This is some kind of time travel, is it?'

'Yes.'

'I believe him,' JR said plainly.

Needle's scorn was acid on a raw wound. This man had entertained all kinds of bizarre conspiracy theories in his youth, but now, presented with a true story arguably no more fantastic than his alien stooge conspiracies—and with substantially more evidence—he staunchly refused to believe me. We began to argue furiously, and it soon became bitterly personal. I was unable to stop myself hurling accusations of hypocrisy at him, citing a myriad of occasions from his past behavior as evidence. JR meanwhile punctuated the entire debate with furious barking trying to stop the vitriol we dashed at each other. Needle stopped his attack on me only briefly to tell him to stop behaving like a fucking puppy.

The debate suddenly halted. Needle had stopped attacking me and was regarding me with furious red-eyes from his wheelchair, wheezing heavily. My words petered out.

'What?!' I demanded.

'You really *are* him.'

His twisted mouth began to laugh.

I too began to laugh.

Then the stress of my reintegration and weight of the emotions of the last few weeks finally hit me in a wave of pure exhaustion.

'You know, I really need to sleep.'

I half-sat, half-collapsed onto the sofa and was asleep before I heard any objections.

I slept for eighteen hours and had wild and vividly colorful dreams. My brain was finally able to integrate memories and experiences that had been suppressed for weeks. I awoke, bleary-eyed and aching. Needle had had me moved, presumably by a machine, onto a soft gel bed in his surgery. The first thing I saw was a ceiling full of folded-up surgical machinery that cast soft, complicated shadows against each other. I turned over and curled semi-fetal to be more comfortable.

Needle wheeled in, alerted presumably by the end of my REM brainwaves. A small SQuID magnetometer installed in the base had been discreetly monitoring them.

We regarded each other silently for a while. I took a deep breath to help myself wake up. I noticed an extraordinarily rich smell of frying tomatoes and eggs. I immediately began to salivate.

'I owe you an apology,' Needle said quietly.

'Me too.'

'No, the blame is mine. I scanned you whilst you slept. I was stupid. I should have done it immediately. There's no doubt that brain in your little skull there matches the one taken of Skyler's womb in Bellevue, plus it matches the scan you had done here when I did your rig fitting. There's some kind of neural collar on your spinal cord and two smaller ones on your optic nerves. All state-of-the-art. I mean *really*. They did an amazing job opening you up. The scars on your skull are very neat, hardly visible. You look—great.'

'Thanks,' I said, feeling a little awkward.

'I'm staggered by... all of this frankly. The implications...'

'So am I.'

There was an awkward pause where neither of us knew what more to say.

'Well, you must be hungry,' Needle offered.

I laughed.

'Starving.'

'I've left you some freshly fabbed clothes. Put them on and come through. Breakfast is waiting for you. Eat first, then we can talk.'

I wolfed down a fresh orange juice and fried eggs, mushrooms, tomatoes and a perfectly cooked hash brown. It was the best tasting breakfast I'd had in years. The memory of Meistermacher's threat surfaced. I spoke with my mouth full:

'Christ! What date is it?'

'It's the thirteenth.'

I relaxed a little.

'Oh, of course.' Subjectively weeks had passed for me since Meistermacher's gloating —but not for Needle and the rest of the world. 'Then we're not too late.'

'For what?'

I repeated what I remembered: Meistermacher's gloating plan to unleash meta on the world. Needle pondered this news quietly.

'We have to stop that shipment of inhalers. I have to inform the police. Tell them it's poisoned or something.'

'I think that's extremely inadvisable. Your relationship with the police is currently the wrong side of the desk, shall we say.'

'But they'd *have* to investigate a claim like that!'

'And what if they conclude you are hoaxing? If you rely on them, and they fail to take action, you will never be able to stop it. The shipment would be constantly under surveillance to *ensure* its delivery. No. We must think of something else. I have connections at the dock.'

'Needle, how did I get to be here? There's a lot I still can't remember.'

'I'm surprised you can remember anything frankly. The nanites appear to suppress recall rather than blocking memory laying. That my remedy worked at all is more good fortune than skill. We have a lot to discuss. You're the anonymous star of just about every news network across America and much of the world right now. Given the exposure, I took enormous risks to pick you up before anyone else did.'

'I'm very grateful.'

Needle's World Wall—the 'fish tank'—became a series of screens. The largest was CNN. The sound was muted, but I saw a series of videos of the Freedom Tower taken from various angles. The base of the screen showed a banner scrolling text along it:

Freedom Tower Evacuation blamed on software glitch in new iNurses.

'I was actually trying to rescue you in your original body, but that landed in Manhattan. Too many police and ambulances.'

Speculations that evacuation was a PR-stunt vigorously denied.

As I watched, a shaky video taken by a witness blocks away zoomed in and focused on the top of the Freedom Tower. Dark dots suspended from strange fog-like objects were silhouetted against the cloud-covered sky. I saw a tiny figure fall through the sky. Suddenly another fog-like thing exploded into being above him and his descent slowed dramatically.

'What is that stuff?'

'*SAFE Descent.* Self-Assembling Fractal Explosive. Basically, it's a smart plastic explosive—it explodes recursively, setting as it does. It's highly compact in solid form but fractal when unpacked; it has massive surface area to mass and volume ratios and therefore makes a remarkable velocity retardant. It's also very hard to clean off glass. Howard Levi must be pretty pissed off with Jon Rodin.'

'Why?'

'Keep watching. A couple of his iNurses floated into the sides of his lovely shiny building and stuck to it. And two more fell in the Hudson. I don't think they'll be doing much more nursing.'

I watched as several of the silhouettes veered into the tower and clung to it. Other cloud-borne dots drifted and spread through the sky. Memories of throwing myself off the roof in terror and floating through the sky began to return.

Anger over police and ambulance incompetence. Suspects still missing.

'Your older sedated body was thrown from the edge here attached by a belt strap to a *SAFE Descent* pod. That body landed in Manhattan. The younger you came off the roof here just a few moments later but fortunately the wind took you across the Hudson. I had several cars in strategic positions, but the only one I could mobilize was here. I had to frig quite a large grid of traffic cameras to confound the police and ambulances so we could escape unseen. Your unconscious body landed—unfortunately rather badly—face first.'

I watched several more videos showing my old forty-three-year-old body slamming sickeningly into the ground. By this time a news swarm had arrived and the video stream quality dramatically improved as it was blended seamlessly with the previous amateur footage. The 3D symbol appeared showing I could now rotate around this scene in real-time if I wanted to—but I didn't.

Needle was correct: Meistermacher hadn't beaten me after all. Ambulance crew and police swooped around the body seconds later, batting the hive members of robot paparazzi away.

'I don't understand. If I was picked up by the authorities, how the hell did I end up with Meistermacher?'

'That confused everybody, including me, but if Meistermacher is meta-capable as you claim then that explains a great deal. I suspected I was dealing with someone with even greater hacking powers than me. I suppose on some level there's a certain amount of truth to that. After picking you up near Battery Place, the ambulance crew arrived at the Lehman Brothers Emergency Center on Gold Street, with a police escort, somehow minus you. You had simply vanished. It took a degree of questioning and video analysis to explain it. He did something very clever. Watch. This is traffic entering the Battery Park underpass at South Street and leaving at Marginal Street.'

Two of the screens now showed videos of the entrance and exit of the underpass. The cameras were the stationary traffic analysis sort, logging flow entering and leaving the tunnel. It was illegal for autopaparazzi to fly into the tunnel for safety reasons, so they buzzed and swarmed near the entrance. I watched the ambulance drive into the underpass on one camera, and some time later on the other camera, I saw it exit.

'Did you notice anything?'

'No.'

'Watch, I'll play it again. As a marker, watch the red car four cars *behind* the ambulance.'

I followed the red car into the underpass. Needle kindly tagged it with a floating red arrow. Seconds later it reappeared on the exit camera. The ambulance had not yet reappeared.

'Looks like they made an unscheduled stop. It was only a matter of thirty seconds or so, but long enough apparently for you to be taken.'

The ambulance reappeared again at the exit.

'Your chap Meistermacher is uncannily persuasive. He stopped them, asked them to hand you over and they simply *gave you away*. They then promptly forgot all about it. Remarkable.'

'Was he in a car? Can you work out where he took me?'

'I've tried. Unfortunately not. His movements have cleverly and deliberately avoided surveillance cameras.'

'So that leaves us where?'

'Let's go back a bit. What do we know?'

'Alright: Rodin devotes his life to reviving Kate Andrews' frozen head. He's had it in his possession a whole six months *prior* to her actually falling back through the mirror. Years later, he discovers Emily's abortion was a cover-up. He tracks down the child and realizes the kid is gifted; this is his chance of reverse engineering meta. He underestimates just how messed up this kid is, and how cunning. Meanwhile his tech team finally work out a way of restoring a frozen head. They incubate the head in a human host womb to repair cerebral frost damage. The cloning process isn't quite ready: the clones are malformed, but he takes a gamble. They replace the clone's brain with hers using neural collars. It pays off. She's damaged but survives the process. It's enough to confirm his suspicions: it really is Kate. It's a huge result: meta's influence over reality includes *time*, but he needs to repeat the experiment to be certain. He needs meta, but I destroyed it. Young Viktor is the key; he has his mother's gift in spades. Jon introduces him to Kate. Three is enough to generate some decent agreement to experiment with. The boy quickly realizes how manipulative Jon is and manipulates him right back. They experiment with meta and succeed in bringing back *a second head* from the future. Mine, but I have a twin so they don't know which of us it is. This would have been months ago. Since I'm in hiding, and Jacob isn't, they go after him to make the future happen.'

I fell silent.

'Are you okay?'

I nodded and took a jerky breath.

'It had to be Jacob that left the note. He must have found where I lived.'

'I think he had been trying to contact you for some time, actually. I'm fairly certain it was Lewis that hacked your Sentinel. He deleted Jacob's messages to you.'

'What did they say?'

'I'm sorry. I don't know. Everything except the system logs were deleted.'

Why would Lewis turn against me like this? Was this his nephew's doing too?

'By this stage tensions must have been pretty fraught. Rodin tries to control everything, keeps the others in the dark as much as possible. Meistermacher isn't having this, and turns Kate against Jon and enlists old Uncle Lewis too. It's not hard. Rodin's turned her into a monster and his promises of a new body never materialize. Rodin also won't reveal the location of the clinic, but somehow Meistermacher ends up with Skyler in his charge. Jacob escapes and takes her with him, trying to find me, except Meistermacher's on his tail and he can't throw him. He dumps her with me and tries to shake him off. I'm guessing he failed.'

Needle's face became grave.

'I just did a quick search. A body was found yesterday. Gunshot wounds to the head and chest. Police are linking it to the same guy who attacked you. Meistermacher. They have camera evidence, albeit limited. I'm sorry, Zeke.'

I was briefly overcome by vertigo, a hollow feeling in my core. I surprised myself. All the bright hatred we had carried for each other, and yet now he was gone I found myself suspended precariously above an unexpected abyss of grief. *I can't do this. Not now,* I thought, and pushed the feelings away to be dealt with later.

'That left me looking after Skyler and both Rodin and Meistermacher desperate to regain control of her. She's literally carrying information from the future.'

'You mentioned a rhyme.'

'Yes. A Trojan code. Meistermacher said it was Rodin's idea. Information about the future would let him take over Howard Levi's empire. He could resurrect a head from the future, but it took time, and caused amnesia, episodic memory loss to be precise. By the time memory was restored the window of opportunity would be gone. So, if you have a short window of opportunity during which you need to extract information about the future from a newly revived person with no episodic memory, how the hell do you store your information? You code it in a *procedural* memory.'

'Yes, I see. A rhyme would be perfect. Smart thinking.'

'Meistermacher used an existing rhyme that I would have learned as a child as the carrier wave. He's been strengthening it in me since he realized it had to be me, not Jacob.'

'I don't get one thing: with the kind of power this drug seems to bestow, why on earth would money be important?'

I shook my head.

'It's not about money. It's about power. Rodin wouldn't let an opportunity like that pass. But money is still just a means to an end for all of them. Several ends. Meta does have limits. It isn't reflexive; it can't touch *itself.* So Rodin couldn't just create it *using it.* And we learned early on we couldn't change ourselves. So Kate couldn't use it to change herself; she's stuck in that body unless she can garner the resources to clone a new one. They could probably create money between them, but it would be real for them and maybe us—but no-one else. This is about her getting her body back. And revenge. Against

Jon Rodin. Against me. Maybe even Jacob. For Meistermacher... it's power too. A different kind. The range and duration of his gift is a direct function of the number of meta-capable people. He needs *agreement*. Right now there are very few of us. His plan will expand his sphere of influence massively but for that he needs access to huge resources. Recreating meta on an industrial scale would cost massive amounts. I think he's stolen Rodin's idea and intends to use information about the future to take over Howard Levi's empire, and then execute his distribution plan. If he succeeds, *then* he'll have almost unlimited power. And she'll have her revenge and maybe a chance to live in a functioning body again. Either he hasn't told her his plan, or she doesn't understand the consequences of it.'

Needle remained quiet. I stood up and went to stare out of the window onto the landscaped terrain outside. The clouds were dispersing. In the distance, three birds, winged black dots, orbited each other in front of a luminous patch of cloud. I watched the reflection of a tree in the glass of the nearest building, chopped into squares, moving silently in the wind.

What would become of all this if Meistermacher succeeded?

'The idea that you are—in your original body—in captivity somewhere else *right now*, and that we're living through a time that has therefore *already happened* is troubling me a little, I must confess.'

I turned back to Needle.

'Do you think you can decode the verse?'

'Tell it to me.'

I recited it automatically.

'No, I don't think so. It's obviously a bespoke encoding. And it's far too short to subject it to any kind of pattern analysis. Did you hear anything during your captivity that might help?'

I cast my mind back.

'Nothing I can think of, no.'

'Then we're stuck.'

'What about Lewis?'

'He's in intensive care as far as I know, under a police guard, and he hasn't exactly helped us so far, has he?'

I closed my eyes and swore several times.

'I will construct a stock market analysis program. See if I can spot any unusual patterns. They will presumably be trading in series to maximize their gains. If I can spot what they're doing before the process completes I might be able to crack the last part of the code.'

'Good idea.'

'I'm not sure it will help but I'll try. You know, it's ironic...'

'What is?'

'The Levi Group stock levels are dramatically down because of what happened in the Freedom Tower. If Meistermacher does want to stage a takeover, there couldn't be a better time.'

'And yet, if he hadn't sent me back in order to try, Levi's stock would be fine and the opportunity wouldn't arise. An acausal loop: the opposite of a paradox. Fascinating.'

'It's perfectly frightening.'

'We have to stop him.'

If I was to stand against Meistermacher I needed support of my own kind. Emily was the only one left, but she was rendered useless by her insanity.

'Can I make a secure call with your wall?'

'To whom?'

'Jon Rodin. I have a feeling he'll take my call this time.'

'I see your point. Alright, but keep it brief. Uh! Gotta go.'

Needle's abrupt end to the conversation surprised me, but I said nothing. He had stopped moving and was staring into the middle distance. But he granted me access to his Wall.

I put in a private call to Revíve, requesting direct contact with Jarod Nino. I gave my full name and stood nervously, feeling naked, in front of the Wall.

The call was accepted within seconds. Instead of Revíve's virtual offices, I was connected directly to Jon Rodin's real office. It seemed darker and less impressive than their virtual shop front, but I didn't really pay attention: neither of us was masked by an avatar this time, and so I was faced with seeing Jon Rodin for the first time in two and a half decades.

Unlike Lewis, he had aged well. Given his resources this was not surprising. However, even he could not hide nearly three decades. He was fifty-one now.

No matter the years that had stretched between us, there was to be no greeting, however cursory. Before I had a chance to say a word, he leapt up from his chair and approached the screen. I actually flinched. He began to rant at me, agitated, but still showing that degree of control that distinguished him:

'You've ruined me. Everything. You interfering...' He swallowed and at the same time snorted through his nose. 'I had you hidden. I was in control. I'd planned it. It was just a waiting game and you... you *helped him* to find you. You *IDIOT*. I told you to stay away. Now it's all lost. Meistermacher's won and we're all *fucked*.'

I marveled that he could find a way to twist even this situation to be someone else's fault.

'Help me stop him.'

'It's too *late* to stop him thanks to you. I could have worked out a safe formula again. He's not interested in that.'

He was trembling with anger now. I wanted to ask questions, get answers, but his aggressive opening had prevented it; and I was reeling with the oddness of speaking to this man, whom I had once idolized and who had had such a profound impact on my life. My feelings now could not be more different.

'No,' was the only word I was able to voice.

'Yes. We make it worse, don't you see that? He can walk all over us.'

'No. If we stand against him *together*—'

He shook his head, more determined than ever.

'I'm getting as far away from this as possible. An island somewhere where it won't reach.'

Now I felt my anger rising.

'Don't do this Jon.' I heard myself snorting now, my words deformed as I spat them out: 'Not again. You ran away before. This is your mess, you started—'

'ZEKE!'

The sheer strength of his tone arrested me.

'It will be *ARMAGEDDON*!'

The same glittering eyes that had once promised magic and undreamt possibilities now assured me hell itself. An awful chasm of silence opened up. My conviction faltered.

Jon saw the defeat. He cut the connection.

It took me several hours to shake myself out of my torpor, out of the shackles of his pessimistic and horrific worldview. I wasn't going to let his cowardice win. Not twice.

I had one last card to play.

If it failed, then I would take on Meistermacher without him.

Needle had said nothing since the connection had been broken, which surprised me. He sat immobile and unblinking in his wheelchair. I touched his shoulder.

'Needle? Can you access my old avatar? I'd like to make one more call if I can.' I caught my rejuvenated reflection in the mirror. 'Not looking like this.'

It was a long moment before he responded. I wondered if it was my imagination but he seemed paler, his skin waxier than earlier. He seemed to struggle to speak:
'To where? To whom?'
I didn't trust my relationship with NYPD, but oddly enough, there was one policeman I felt I could trust. It was worth the risk.
'To London. Detective Inspector Hofstadter.'
Again, there was a long pause.
'Unless you absolutely have to, I'd rather you didn't actually. Not to the police, from here. Even if they are UK-based. Everything's linked now.'
'Why?'
One of the pipes leading into Needle's brain via his facial wound shuddered slightly and I heard a subtle liquid noise.
'Needle? Are you okay?'
Again, a long pause.
'Excuse me—*ramping up*—preoccupied. Just be a moment.'
'With what?'
There was a long pause. Needle spoke from a speaker next:
'Things are not good, I'm afraid. And the situation is getting worse.'
'In what sense?'
'Recent events have been a little like poking a very large stick into the NYPD hornet's nest. And then whacking it. The FBI are now involved, which as you can imagine, only makes the police even more mad and determined to prove they can cope without them. Don't get me wrong, I have no regrets picking you up, but it has exposed me quite dramatically and I'm currently spending a substantial chunk of my resources trying to cover my tracks. The trouble is, I'm leaving more in the process. I need to minimize my net footprint radically pretty soon, or my location could soon be deduced.'
I felt a pang of guilt. I had no idea what the implications for him were if his cloak were to be removed. But, if I could get information from Hofstadter that could help us resolve this situation before the lid of Pandora's box was blown off...
'How hard is it to mask our location if I make this call? I need to call in an old favor.'
The plastic feed pipe rattled again.
'So long as you use an avatar I suppose it's low risk compared to what I'm currently dealing with. But make it short. Use the Wall again. I'll set up your usual interface. I'm going to stop talking for a while. I need to concentrate.'
I stood in front of Needle's World Wall and tried to invoke the LingGlyph combo to initiate my avatar. Somewhere hidden in the walls, Needle's cameras mapped my facial expressions, interpreted my hand-signing, and tried to combine them with the packet-switched radio signals from my lingual and oesophageal implants to control the perfect replica of my forty-three-year-old body. But there were no lingual and oesophageal implants to transmit the forms my throat and tongue were making. They were in my old body, that was at this very moment hidden in a lair somewhere with Meistermacher and Kate, the Calculatrice. I switched mode to the much slower hand-only signalling system, and reissued the commands.
It took several minutes for a message to get to Hofstadter, and several more for him to respond. He agreed to the connection. Fortunately, now that he was nearly retired, he was largely office-based.
His image appeared on a smaller screen within the Wall. It was a standard video stream.
'Hofstadter.'
His surprise was evident.
'This is some kind of joke?'

In spite of our relative positions, I had never despised Hofstadter. He had always been a fair man, had always carried out his duty responsibly. I respected him. And I felt he respected me, which is why I was making this call now. We had just happened, unfortunately, to be on opposite sides of the fence.

'It's not a joke, no.'

His eyes narrowed.

'You can't seem to stay out of trouble, can you? Why would a man who's currently hiding from the world's spotlight come virtually walking into a police station?'

'I need a favor.'

His eyes flicked down and to the side momentarily.

'Your location is masked. If this really is you, then I presume you're hiding behind an avatar.'

This observation startled me. How could he know? I checked my netstats to see if I was giving anything away that I shouldn't. As if detecting my surprise, Hofstadter supplied the answer:

'I saw the way you landed off that building. I'm surprised you can speak. Which, if I may be frank, makes me doubtful this is really you.'

'Listen to what I have to say, and then decide for yourself.'

'Alright, but even if it is you, why should I help you? It's not like I owe you a favor.'

'Because you want an answer to a mystery that has plagued your working career. So that you can retire in peace. I have information you want. I propose an exchange.'

Hofstadter's expression was intense but unfathomable.

'Drop your avatar.'

'No, I can't do that.'

Instead, I began once more to recount the true history of the Looking Glass Club. Everything as I understood it, including Meistermacher and his plan. And including the last known location of Jon Rodin. And then I explained the favor that I wanted from Hofstadter. He remained silent throughout.

'I'm trying to stop this happening. And the NYPD are working against me. What chance do I stand alone? I need help.'

He stared at me for an age with an expression of abject puzzlement.

'I honestly don't know what it must be like for you. To,' he waved a hand dismissively, 'to believe all this.'

'Every word I've told you is the truth. If I fail, well... don't say I didn't warn you.'

'I will have to inform Bryant that you've contacted me. You realize that?'

I felt sick at this betrayal. But what had I expected?

'If I'm right, Howard Levi's empire will crumble in the next few days, and in just a few more, the world as we know it will follow.'

I invoked the Glyph to drop my avatar. A silent warning flashed.

'Every word I've told you is the truth,' I repeated, and I confirmed the action.

Hofstadter recovered from his surprise quickly.

'Every word.'

'Another avatar.'

'Check the videos of the Freedom Tower escape again, Hofstadter. You'll see it was me.'

The connection dropped abruptly. At first I assumed that Hofstadter had cut it, but a whine of servo motors behind me advised of the approach of Needle.

'That was foolish.'

'Was I too long?'

'Dropping your avatar,' he said in a very clipped tone. 'You just showed him the inside of my apartment.'

'So? It could be anywhere.'

'You underestimate GALIAN's pattern-matching capabilities. It doesn't matter. It will just make things quicker. I'm losing the battle anyway. I estimate we have a week to ten days at the most before they find us.'

'Then we leave. We'll go somewhere else.'

'*Look at me, Steel.*'

I heard frustration in his voice now, perhaps anger. I looked at the fat data and nootropic feeds plugged directly into his cerebrum. Needle was firmly stitched into place.

'You can't disconnect?'

'If I did, I would no longer be me. And if they caught me, I would be jailed in that state with no hope for ever restoring myself. It would be death by another name.'

'Then what can we do?'

'You and JR will have to escape as normal. If I can help with that I will. For me—I have another plan. I've been preparing for this eventuality for years, but I am not ready. I need to focus on completing it now. It will take... all of my resources. And strength. I must drive myself harder than I ever have.'

I looked at his terrible, deathly complexion.

'Then you must.'

'"*A week to ten days*" was an estimate contingent on a continued effort by me to conceal us. If I stop, they could find us in mere days. We don't have much time.'

'I made it easier for them—dropping the avatar.'

My gaze fell to the marble floor in shame.

'How—will you leave?'

I looked up at Needle to see a small smile tremble feebly on his palsied face.

'Through the eye of a needle, my friend.'

For several days I watched Needle regress more and more into himself. His feed drains rattled increasingly frequently, pumping a mysterious cocktail of nootropic chemicals into that frenzied brain, driving it orders of magnitude faster than it had evolved to race. His communications became more terse and less frequent. The machines in his laboratory occasionally lifted themselves out of their stasis, stretched their metal limbs and marched in strange dances to a silent tune strummed by their immobile master. His autolabs gurgled and hummed, concocting new breeds of nanomachine with uncertain purpose. As far as I knew, Needle's lines did not provide any sustenance, and yet I did not once see him eat. His face quickly grew gaunt, his cheeks hollow. The chemical smell of the apartment began to dominate; and the lilies—which had been real—wilted and began to rot.

Occasionally I caught my own reflection in the various mirrored surfaces of Needle's apartment and every time it collided with me, spinning my breath away.

I dared not make any further contact with the outside world in case I jeopardize him further.

Depressed and increasingly anxious, I withdrew too. JR sat patiently next to me and we watched the world unfold in the eyes of the world's media. If he resented our captivity here, he said nothing.

Needle broke his silence twice. The first time was to tell me that the financial markets sentinel he had created had detected unusual trading results. I witnessed Meistermacher's plan working from a second perspective. And even though I was not bound this time, I could do nothing to stop him. Needle's second communication came later, and was his last.

According to news reports Howard Levi—the nonagenarian owner of the empire Jon Rodin had, parasite-like, infested—was nowhere to be found. Rumors abounded. Shareholder confidence plummeted. A day later the news reported the collapse and surprise hostile takeover of the Levi Group by a newcomer.

It was Meistermacher, I had no doubt.

There was nothing to stop Meistermacher now.

In just a few days' time his shipment of meta-spiked inhalers would leave Newark Bay Docks...

I needed to find out the exact time of the shipment. I'd have to stop it myself.

My Net access might be forbidden but JR had full-spectrum wireless access, and this was his specialty.

During my captivity, Meistermacher had mentioned the name of the pharmaceutical company. I wished I had my earcom to play back that conversation, but it was gone. Fortunately, the name came back to me: Closh. I looked it up and found the correct spelling: Closche. It was enough.

'JR? Wanna play fetch?'

JR's head was resting on his front paws, his eyes were closed but his ears twitched towards my voice.

'There's a Closche Pharmaceutical shipment due to leave Newark Bay Docks on the eighteenth. It should be booked in as asthma or insulin inhalers, or something like that. I need to know which ship it will be on, the time of departure, everything about it. Can you find it?'

He opened his eyes and looked at me with a bland, uninterested expression. The depression of the last few days had affected him adversely.

'Come on, boy!' I said in the tone specifically reserved to excite dogs to the point where their tails wag their bodies. 'Fetch? You gonna fetch the information? Yes? Good boy. *Gooood* boy!'

JR looked around and raised an eyebrow at me.

'Are you talking to *me* in that stupid voice? Aren't we supposed to be lying low?'

I sighed and felt my shoulders sag, but I wasn't about to take a kennel full of attitude from JR.

'*Goood* boy!' I crouched slightly and started to approach him, encouragement all over my face.

'It's not going to work, Steel. Forget it.'

His tail thumped the sofa once, betraying him.

'That's my boy...' I injected my voice with more dog-centric enthusiasm.

'Can ya'? Huh?'

I cooed him with words imbued with irresistible tones and scratched that little bit just by his ear that he loved so much. It was subtle, but I felt him push his head just into my hand a little. Then his tail started to thump out a beat.

'Bastard.' But it was his last attempt at resistance.

I had him by the instincts and I made sure to squeeze hard.

JR leapt up, tail wagging furiously by now, and stood on his hind legs pawing at my trousers. He barked once, excitedly, dropped into a haunch on all fours ready to leap into action and his wagging body abruptly went into a rigid cataleptic state. It looked as if someone had frozen him on film. In his mind, he was now running through the net, hunting for the information I'd requested. He remained in that state for some seconds before his body abruptly reanimated, just as if someone had un-pressed a pause button. He barked once, surprising me. Two barks indicated a success. JR often lost the capacity for speech when he was excited. Humans aren't so different. I waited for him to calm down to explain.

'Firstly, it's called Port Newark-Elizabeth Marine Terminal, not Newark Bay Docks. Secondly, there ain't any registered shipments leaving there matching your description. I checked dates either side and then the whole history. Closche have never sent a shipment from Port Elizabeth.'

'What? Really?'

I was astonished.

'Nope.'

So Meistermacher had lied. I felt sick.

'But they frequently have shipments *arriving* there. Closche have labs in New York State but they don't actually manufacture *anything* in the US. It's all done in South America. Brazil mostly. They ship supplies from there to Port Elizabeth, which is right next to the airport and a major train terminus, so it's an important distribution center. It supplies much of the East Coast.'

The hairs on my nape lifted. Meistermacher had wanted to gloat, but he wasn't so stupid as to tell me the exact truth. He was a manipulator to his very core.

'You should know: Port Elizabeth is *enormous*. I mean literally miles across and deep. You could fit the whole of Downtown New York into it. Give me control of the Wall, I'll show you.'

I signed a permission glyph and JR hooked into it. I felt vertigo briefly as we skyrocketed into an aerial view of the docks—a satellite map. JR had rotated the map so that Newark Bay seemed to be a gaping maw slit in the face of the earth. The flat dock areas became three broad top teeth, crazy cuts in a Halloween lantern mouth, miles across. We zoomed in until the dense fields of colorful needle flecks resolved into rows and columns of long, thin boxes.

'Each one of those is a forty-foot container. Essentially each one is a huge cargo truck which is how most of them are transported on land. I'd guess there are probably upwards of a *million* containers parked there at any one time.'

I swore.

'You want the bad news?'

I held my breath.

'There's a shipment of Closche insulin inhalers arriving tonight as part of a larger shipment of pharmaceutical goods. One single container. Eight p.m.'

I checked the time. It was almost one in the afternoon.

I had no weapons, and my meta-capability was paltry compared to that of Meistermacher. But I also had no choice. I made my way into Needle's lab and watched his silent, crippled form in the darkness for a moment. The only light came in asynchronous flashes: white, green, red, amber, blue, blinked the surrounding machines, signifying I knew not what. There were brief moments of complete darkness and then flurries of rapid activity. What was he doing?

'Needle?' I whispered, not wishing to disturb him but having no choice. There was no response.

'Can I use your fabber? And a design package?'

I listened to the ticking and whirring for a few minutes.

'Needle?'

A small screen on one of the machines brightened and blinked:

Yes.

'Okay.'

I stood next to him for a moment feeling awkward.

'Thanks.'

I left and went back to the Wall.

I worked for hours, pulling designs from the air with pinched fingers, spanning a million orders of magnitude, crossing and recrossing the boundary of mechanical, electronic and chemical engineering. I tested a simulation over and over again, correcting its errors. When I could better it no further, I massaged my aching hands, and arched backwards, popping my vertebrae. I sat back on the sofa for a few minutes, contemplating my design. It would have to do.

I went back into the lab, and told the fabber to construct it.

Half an hour later, the door popped open with a hiss and a stench of solvents. I reached inside and lifted it from its goop of polymer gels. It looked like a strange glass gun.

A last resort. I just hoped it would work.

I rinsed it in a solvent bath, pocketed it and went back to the Wall to study the 3D map of the docks, and to think.

Later, Needle reappeared from his labs. It was the first time he had moved in days. his voice was weak:

'The last bastion has fallen. We are found. You must run—*now*.'

I tried to protest but he would not listen. We fled to the door. Needle's wheelchair transported his fragile body to see us. Even in such extreme conditions he maintained his manners.

He spoke from dry and cracked lips.

'I've disabled the local cameras. When you leave the complex, avoid being seen. Cover your face from surveillance. They are looking for you alone, not a man with a dog, so this may help your escape. Make your way east to the river and hire a private taxi boat to the docks. Find a man called Tony Damasio. Tell him I sent you. He will help you. I will give you money. Pay him. It's all I can do. I'm sorry. *Go now.*'

'What about you?'

'I'm leaving now.'

'What do you mean?'

'I have laid a nanite network. It threads every neuron and synapse in my brain. In a few moments the mapping will begin and extract an exact model of my brain state. I will be uploaded to a distributed simulation space secreted between the gaps of the net where no-one will find me. Building that, and making it safe, is what I've been occupied with. The model will be able to run, in a manner of speaking. But the nanite network cannot read my exact brain state without destroying it. When the police arrive they will find an empty husk.'

'You *can't* upload,' I protested. '*You know that. You proved it yourself as an undergraduate!* It'll just be a—a simulation. It will be a zombie, not conscious. It won't be *you*. This is suicide.'

'It will be like sleeping. In time, I hope to download again. To live. When technology is ready for me. This is my only hope.'

Through the eye of a needle.

'We *will* meet again. . .'

'Needle, no! Come with me now. *Disconnect. Please.*'

'You know I cannot.'

There was a pause and his eyes filled with a terrible sadness.

'Goodbye, my friend. . . *Zeke.*'

And then the life in those weary cat-like eyes faded away. His eyelids flickered. Needle's body began to tremor gently as if with the sudden onset of Parkinson's disease. His pallid skin began suddenly to glisten with the moisture of a light sweat.

'*Alexei! NO!*'

I ran to him, but it was too late.

I sank to my knees before his juddering, wheelchair-bound frame and watched helplessly as his mind was sucked silently away; and I wept.

'It's my fault. *It's all my fault. Again.*'

JR ran to me and pawed at my arm.

'Mourn later. *Steel.* We have to leave. *Now.*'

From the pages of Tony's diary:

If you can't see the woods for the trees, are you blind, Alice?

⠰⠏⠃⠎⠁⠀⠀⠰⠏⠃⠎⠁⠀⠰⠏⠃⠎⠁⠂

⠰⠏⠃⠎⠁⠀⠰⠏⠃⠎⠁⠸⠏⠃⠎⠁⠂

⠿⠇⠀⠄⠀⠠⠿⠿⠀⠈⠠⠿⠿⠗

⠗⠠⠫⠁⠀⠵⠀⠰⠗⠄⠚⠀⠆⠐⠁

⠀⠆⠀⠓⠌⠵⠫⠚⠀⠨⠫⠵⠀⠇⠆⠚⠂⠀⠆

⠚⠰⠭⠗⠀⠆⠀⠆⠄⠜⠠⠵⠀⠨⠗⠆⠿⠏⠂⠀⠆

⠀⠆⠰⠿⠶⠚⠀⠃⠭⠓⠀⠆⠀⠚⠌⠆⠐⠁⠄

⠠⠇⠈⠸⠚⠀⠠⠨⠏⠙⠆⠀⠀⠿⠿⠗

⠀⠆⠿⠗⠀⠄⠀⠨⠆

⠀⠆⠕⠕⠒⠈⠛⠌⠰⠞⠣⠌⠈⠁⠣⠂

⠢⠢⠀⠈⠆⠌⠍⠈⠸⠣⠗

Chapter 30

'[thus] consciousness as a process must *lie outside the computable domain of the discrete state computer. Digital computers, no matter how large or complex, will never attain sentience.'*

—J. Alexei Stojkovic. "Logical absurdities arising from the discrete state machine model of consciousness," *Journal of Cognitive Science* 5:191–206

Alexei left the UK to study at MIT in Cambridge, Massachusetts and I was left in London feeling stranded, alone, and terribly depressed. With Emily gone, my control over my local reality returned almost to normal, and I was eventually given the all-clear by doctors, but they made me stay another six months to prove I was well before signing the documents to release me. I finally left St Clair's two years after being admitted and twenty-eight and a half months after the death of Kate Andrews.

My release was kept secret, for my own protection.

I immediately applied to emigrate to the US, to take Alexei up on his offer, but given my history this was not to prove straightforward. My initial immigration applications were rejected outright. It was inevitable that we would grow apart as friends given the time, but we still stayed in regular touch electronically, with Alexei constantly sending me puzzles and intellectual challenges. On bad days I would write out my fears in long pitiful emails to him. I had become so small, so afraid of everything. Afraid to live.

One day, I arrived home to find an email from him with instructions to apply again to US immigration. I replied asking what was the point? They'd never let me in. I received a somewhat cryptic message back urging me to go ahead. I was sent another message over a secure connection instructing me to use certain answers in my online application, including stating a fictitious sponsoring employer and a residential address in Manhattan. I did, still pessimistic and full of doubt, and was astonished when the application was granted almost immediately by email. Applications were supposed to take weeks to process.

I wasted no time, and packed what little I owned in a frisson of excitement. I picked up my papers from the embassy, all the time terrified that something would be discovered and I would be stopped. I bought a cheap one-way ticket and changed what remaining savings I had into dollars. I made my way the next day to the airport, and flew to JFK.

I'd half expected Alexei to meet me at the airport. He didn't. However, he called me, and we had a very strange telephone conversation in which he spoke to me as if all the details of my application were true.

As if the line were being tapped.

I understood, and I acted my role too. Then I went to an address in Chelsea where I found further instructions waiting and a second set of identity documents. There was another address where I was able to stay, and advice for getting some paid work.

At the bottom of the note, it said:

This is a new start. It is time to forget the past. To move on. To be strong again. I will call you Steel, so that you never forget.
Your always friend, Alexei.

I slipped quietly into my new identity and disappeared from the grid.

We met in person occasionally, but mostly virtually. He soon left MIT and vanished himself from the increasingly exposed online world, re-emerging as Needle, a name he'd adopted from a joke I'd once made after seeing how far he'd taken his self-improvements. He was always there to help me when I needed it.

The first two years were the hardest. I wrestled with alcohol and drug addiction, moving from job to job, unable to keep steady work. I regularly ended up in drunken fights on the street. I was in a bad state. Needle finally took me in for a few months, on the explicit condition that I respected his privacy. We both pretended I hadn't seen the rent boys that he paid to amuse him in the rare moments when he wasn't at his various computers. Eventually he managed to get me a contract programming for a games company and I moved out. They let me work from home, designing characters, AI zombies to populate online fantasy worlds. I'd finally found a job I was good at and I got myself clean.

I had suspected for some time that Needle was getting seriously into illegal hacking work, and one day he asked me to help him solve a small problem. I couldn't solve it. That's when I discovered my little gift. He paid me handsomely. *Very.* I felt happy and useful again for the first time in years. Happy, but lonely: I could never allow another woman to get close to me after Kate.

Eventually, I bought a puppy for company.

From the pages of Tony's diary:

Unusual glyphs, mystery unsolved. Simply a myth? Should you both be involved?

Chapter 31

'The Eighth Square at last!' she cried as she bounded across. . .

—Through the Looking Glass

When we arrived at the water's edge I was physically cold, but inside I was suffering a more profound lack of warmth that no heat could touch. Even the occasional sound of sirens—the ever-present music of Manhattan—stirred no emotion in me. I had followed JR automatically with my face kept low. He had led me using the map he was constantly connected to, streets and highways and across parkland, until we finally arrived here at the edge of the Hudson. The sun was low in the sky, and the light failing. JR's shadow was twice his length. I squinted at the water, catching the last of the sun, and shivered a little. There was nothing here, barely a proper riverbank.

'Where are we?' I asked.

'A little north of Fort Washington Point.'

'What are we doing here?' I asked.

'Waiting for a river cab. I called it a while ago and gave it our position.'

'Right.'

'Steel, snap out of it. We're going to stop this shipment.'

I clenched my jaw muscles, grinding my teeth hard together to press the pain away. The wind pulled idly at my hair.

'Yes.'

The river cab arrived a few minutes later. It was a small gray and white speedboat. The captain was a young lad, late-twenties perhaps, thirty at the most. He throttled the engine down and it gurgled contentedly in the water.

'Where ya' goin', son?' he called to me.

I frowned and stared at him for a moment.

'Port Elizabeth,' JR hissed.

'Port Elizabeth,' I repeated.

The captain whistled and tapped something into the display panel of his boat.

'About twenty miles. Hundred bucks a mile: two kilobucks, okay?'

I nodded, and clambered down to the edge. The boat rocked as I boarded. JR hopped on after me.

I paid in advance with a cash swipe.

'Hold tight,' the captain called, and with a growl of motor and the sound of the wash thrashing behind us, we accelerated into the wind.

The beauty of the journey seemed to mock us. The vermillion sky in the west sank into a profound indigo ink that stained the night. We raced past larger, slower boats, some glowing with festivity, others sultry and heavy with cargo. The Manhattan skyline grew, slid past. I eyed the Freedom Tower with a confusion of emotion, watching it grow from a splinter-like spark into a giant, multifaceted spear of glass and light punching through the night.

The captain needlessly announced our arrival in Upper New York Bay as we approached the Statue of Liberty.

'From here it's a few miles more down the Kill Van Kull and we'll be there,' he called and revved the engines again.'

The boat turned in a sliding arc away from the dazzling light show of Manhattan, and sailed along the Kill Van Kull. To the right the majority of the vista seemed also to be docks. A shiver of anxiety shuddered through me. Eventually we passed under a large bridge, after which we arced to the right, growling forwards like an angry panther into a vast body of dark water. Ahead and in the distance to the left the darkness was studded with tiny dazzling lights. I noticed for the first time the howling, twisted sound of airplanes. Newark airport lay invisible somewhere beyond.

'Where d'ya wanna be exactly?' the Captain called, half-turning.

'Just before Elizabeth Channel,' JR supplied.

The captain turned around a fraction more and gave me an odd look. He looked down suspiciously at JR and then turned back.

As we approached the long straight edge of the dock, I began to appreciate just how vast the docks really were. I saw enormous blue container cranes along its length, designed for lifting the containers. They loomed long-necked, one hundred-foot-high mechanical monsters. Fierce halogen lights lit them starkly, throwing out sharp, unnatural shadows from their engineered limbs.

'Do you have a pass for here?' the Captain asked. 'I don't want trouble.'

I flicked him another credit bean in return for a silent smirk. He did something to the motor and we began to sidle near to the steep wall of the dock, where a dark ladder clutched with iron will at the wall. The boat knocked once against the wall and settled down into a contended glugging.

'What about your dog?'

It was several meters to the top.

'There are probably concrete steps if we go round into the channel itself.'

The Captain maneuvered us along and then left into another wide channel, slowing next to a set of concrete steps cut into the side of the gray wall on the left. Above me huge blue four-legged cranes poised immobile and empty clawed. Further down the channel a large ship was moored and one of the enormous cranes crouched over it, like prey.

I climbed out on to the concrete holding on to a metal rail for support. It felt rough and cold under my palm. Water lapped eagerly at the step below. JR hopped out onto the step above mine.

'You need picking up, just give me a call.'

'Thank you. We may do that.'

'No problem.'

The boat motored away throatily into the night. I cautiously looked over the top to see if we had been seen, but there was no-one. Ahead seemed to be a vast concrete car park, lit with the fierce, cold light of a football stadium. Yet it was so large it could have contained thousands of them. Long lines of metal cargo crates were arranged in stacks, guarded by the vast blue and black cranes at the docks' edges. The containers formed long corridors of flaking painted metal, a patchwork labyrinth built from blocks of dull blues and reds, dull greens and dirty whites, awaiting collection. The smell of diesel and oil permeated the night air. JR moved back toward the bay, seeming to know where he was headed. I followed along the edge but I stopped a moment, turning to look at the black river flowing a few meters below. It had a different personality at night. Perhaps it was the way the lights from the dock side captured the edges of every ripple. It sharpened them, making the entire vast surface glimmer darkly. I had expected the flow to seem sleepy, to roll heavily and languidly by. Instead, the river seemed to awaken. The black surface shimmered silently. Ripples skittered rapidly across it in complex patterns. It seemed alive with the sense of its own cleverness. I thought of Needle, then, and wondered if his shimmering complexity—infinitely more detailed than this river's surface—had gone forever, or whether he had successfully preserved himself somewhere in the dark amber of technology.

'Do you know where you're going?'

'Yes, Needle told me where to look.'

I glanced around. There was still no-one in sight. Although the place was vast, I thought we would have been stopped by now.

'There's no security here. We could be anyone.'

'We're only on the dock. Getting out through the gates won't be so easy.'

My surprise was premature. We wandered along a little further past the entrances to several long ersatz corridors constructed from the massive containers. JR sniffed at the air.

'Trouble's coming.'

His warning didn't prepare me. Suddenly from out behind a container ahead three burly men appeared. Before I had even registered their presence they were upon me. Arms slipped under my armpits from behind and I found myself painfully immobilized as they were wrenched upwards over my head into a firm lock. The base of my neck ached. The two men in front began to search me professionally before a word was uttered. My device was lifted from a pocket, along with my credit chip. I had nothing else on my person. The man ahead inspected the glass-looking gun with a suspicious expression.

'You got a pass to be here?'

'I'm looking for a man called Tony Damasio.'

The men looked at each other.

'No Tony here.'

'Needle sent me.'

'Who the hell is Needle?'

I felt this was not going very well.

'Is there a Tony Damasio here or not?'

'What's this?'

The man hefted the transparent device.

'It's a toy. What's it look like?'

I eyed the guy nervously as he began fiddling with the dial and buttons. He hadn't yet touched the trigger. He shook it and held it to his ear.

'Don't do nuthin',' he said.

His thumb found the trigger. There was the sound of the tiniest puff of air.

'Ow!' He touched his fingertips to the rim of his ear. 'Fucker stung me.'

I closed my eyes against this situation.

'Gary, stop fuckin' around,' one of the other interceded. Then to me: 'What's your business with Tony?'

'That's for his ears only.'

'He expecting you?'

'No. Tell him Needle sent me. It's important. My name's Steel.'

'Wait here.'

'I'm not going anywhere, am I?' I indicated my locked arms with my eyes.

The guy tapped his wrist com and wandered around the container out of earshot. I felt a pang of anxiety: he'd kept onto my device.

Moments later he returned and told his colleagues to bring me.

They hoisted me into an electric car, into which JR also jumped, and we whined along up one of the container-lined roads, turned and headed up another toward a low-roofed building. I was allowed to enter, but the brutes kept JR as collateral, in case I misbehaved.

Tony Damasio waited inside. He was a short olive-skinned man. What little hair he had was graying.

'Tony, I presume?'

'Who wants him.'

Something inside me snapped.

'Oh, for Christ's sake! Are you Tony or not?'

He flicked an angry eye toward the men standing behind me who'd brought me here.

A heavy hand pressed down on one of my shoulders. A reminder.

'My name's Steel. I'm a friend of Needle. He told me you could help me.'

Tony Damasio's black eyes burned into me. I began to explain:

'There's a shipment arriving tonight... JR had the exact details but he was outside. 'There's a container arriving. Inhalers. Insulin for diabetes. That container must never make it beyond this dock. I need an accident to happen to it.'

Damasio looked at his belly and chuckled to himself.

'That's not the kind of deal I do here. I turn a blind eye sometimes.'

'But can it be arranged?'

'Tell me, why would someone want insulin inhalers to go missing?'

'They're poisoned. I'm trying to save lives.'

'No, no, no. Tell me the real reason. And don't *fuck* with me.'

There was an edge to his voice that unnerved me. What was wrong with my answer? I supposed if it really were a case of poison the obvious thing to do would be to tell the police. It didn't hold up to scrutiny.

Tony Damasio inspected my face for a moment, and I remembered how old I looked. I was just a boy.

'You look familiar.'

Shit. The news...

'I've got that kind of face. Everyone tells me that. Look, I can pay well. A million? Two million?'

Inflation had withered that once impressive sum to something more modest. Still, it was generous for a bribe.

'I need to assure a continued operation here. Any accident is going to be inspected. The police will sniff around. I don't need that sort of attention. It don't matter how big the golden egg is if it kills the goose, you get me?'

'I get you. Mister Damasio, it's extremely important that this shipment never makes it.'

'Why?'

I couldn't make up a suitable lie, and I couldn't tell the truth.

'Just trust me, please.'

'Then, I'm afraid it's a "no". Give Mister Needle my respects.'

'Mister Damasio, please help me. Needle—'

'Get out. Stop wasting my time.'

'Needle—'

'Get out. I'll have my men escort you off the—'

'*Needle is dead.*'

Outside, something crashed through the quiet of the hut. It sounded like a container being dropped too soon. Distant shouting followed. Damasio seemed to be focussed on an invisible point between his nose and the floor. He kept his gaze fixed there. He spoke quietly.

'I'm sorry to hear that.'

'His last words to me were to come and find you. He said you would help.'

'Who killed him?'

'It's a long story. There isn't time. Please just help me. For Needle's sake. I will pay you well. This is *urgent.*'

'What's the big hurry?'

'This ships arrives at eight p.m. tonight.'

Damasio rolled his eyes ceilingward.

'Have you any idea how long it takes to unload one of these things? Some of them carry seven or eight *thousand* containers. Even with four cranes working twenty-four seven it still takes us nearly three days. *Relax.* Tell me one thing and don't lie to me.'

'What?'

'This container. Is it drugs?'

'I just told you it's insulin. And pharmaceuticals. It's not cocaine if that's what you mean.'

'And this doesn't involve *La Cosa Nostra* in any way?'

'Beg pardon?'

He affected a heavy Sicilian accent:

'*This thing of ours.*'

'Uh... no. No, it doesn't. It's a shipment from Closche Pharmaceuticals.'

'Okay, then maybe I can help you. I don't know how, but maybe.'

He took out a slate and stylus and began poking and scribbling at its shiny display. He sniffed and sat back.

'Okay, I got it. It was loaded fairly near the end so it'll be off early. On the schedule it's due around six fifteen a.m., but times can change if conflicts occur or cargo gets re-prioritized by the system. It could be six. It could be seven.'

'How hard would it be to drop the container in the water?'

He looked at me with an expression that clearly read: *are you for real?* I returned an expression that said: *yes, I am,* then testily offered the floor back to him with my hands: *and your answer to my question is...?*

He answered much more politely than I expected:

'Impossible. The cranes are completely automated. There are multiple redundant fail-safes to prevent accidents all controlled by a total decision support system. And even if it wasn't, I don't have no influence with longshoremen. They're all unionized.'

'What happens once it's off?'

'Depends. Either it starts its way through customs clearance, or it goes to the nearest straddle crane for parking for later handling.'

'Straddle cranes?'

I guessed he meant the pi-shaped cranes I'd seen on the map straddling the corridors of containers.

'Robot cranes. They walk the container lines. I think of them as our librarians, they fetch and store, and they keep the library in order.'

'Then preferably I need to get hold of that container when it's unloaded. It needs to go missing. Can I take the truck?'

I was thinking I could drive it into the desert. I could at least dump it where no-one would find it.

Stress lines crisscrossed Damasio's face. He exhaled heavily through tight lips.

'That would be easier. Port trucking is deregulated, I have some boys who could help. I could arrange something. But I need to think about it.'

I frowned at him.

'Look,' he said. 'Whatever you might be thinking, I'm not *La Cosa Nostra*, okay? I'm small time. There are boundaries I need to respect. I cross one—even by accident—and a capo gets a sniff of it: I end up dead in a car trunk. *Entende?*'

'Okay. Don't take too long.'

I gave him a whisperkey so he could secure-call me and left him to think it over.

I found JR outside with one of the dock workers, but Gary, who had confiscated my device, had been called to a job. I cursed silently. I waited outside for him to return, huddling into myself and watched my breath dispersing in the floodlights for a while. I tried to think of something else, but all I could see were Needle's last moments; his flickering eyelids, his gently spasming body.

'Come on, let's go for walk,' I suggested to JR when I realized Gary was not coming back any time soon. We walked down several of the long corridors of containers toward the water's edge. It took twenty minutes, but I felt a little better when we arrived at the broad painted lanes that help organize the trucks as they loaded and unloaded from the vast vessels.

'What does *La Cosa Nostra* mean?' I asked JR, outside.

'You're not serious?'

'Did you learn how to integrate second-order nonlinear partial differential equations at dog school?'

'No.'

'Well, I did, smart-arse, so can you just fucking well tell me what La Cosa Nostra means please.'

'It means Mafia,' he said without breaking his trot.

'I was worried you might say that.'

'Geek,' he muttered under his breath.

'I heard that.'

I stood still and listened to the noise of the docks. JR disappeared off somewhere exploring the containers. There was little quiet. Diesel engines of all sizes sounded like artillery drummers drumming a tattoo. Somewhere, the steel wheels of a slowly accelerating train slipped on their tracks. In the distance, more trains rumbled massively across their sleepers in a series of slow regular kettle-drum beats. The wheels and rails flashed like cameras with electric blue-white arcs.

Just as the cold was beginning to infiltrate my will power, Damasio called me.

'I can help you,' he said.

Relief flowed through my muscles, releasing the tension that had cramped them.

'Thank you.'

We discussed money. It was twice my offer, but it didn't matter. I just agreed.

'The ship is docking now. Once the offloading schedule firms up, I'll be coordinating the pickups. My boy's called Bruno. Meet him here. Go with him in the truck. Get in line. Pick up the container as it's offloaded. You're then going to take it on a little detour from its planned route. The guy who's supposed to pick it up will be told it's already been taken, there's been a logistics mess up. It happens. Bruno will get it through customs with you and then you're on your own. You ever driven a truck before?'

'No. But I'm a quick learner.'

'Okay. Be here at four thirty.'

I checked the time. It was eleven past eight. I killed time by watching the unloading process, the massive computer-controlled container cranes reaching into the ships and pulling out their guts, container by container. We wandered around the docks and watched the straddle cranes rolling up and down the rows.

At ten thirty, I tried to find a place to sleep for a few hours, but the building Tony Damasio was in was full of noise and interruptions.

'Where's your guy, Gary?' I asked. 'He took something of mine and hasn't given it back.'

'Where is Gary?'

'Fuck knows. He's a bag of nerves tonight. He's doing every job on offer. I even saw him sweepin' up earlier. Makes a fuckin' change.'

Laughter.

'There's somethin' damn weird going on tonight, man,' one of the men muttered.

'Tiago's seein' ghosts,' added another.

'Don't mess wit ma head, man!'

'I ain't shittin'. He says he saw a ghost. A horrible woman.'

My ears pricked. All the men were quiet suddenly.

'And what the fuck *is* up with Gary? It's like he's possessed.'

Several of the men mumbled something at this and made signs on their chests.

'Or on drugs.'

'If you see him,' I added quickly, 'ask him for my toy back. I need it.'

Sometime after 3 a.m. I started getting nervous. JR was nowhere in sight or within signal range. One of the guys said he'd seen him sniffing around the containers down near the water. I decided to go look for him. I called up his collar service and got his last known triangulated position. It was only good to a hundred meters, but it was enough. Technically he didn't have a collar anymore but the service continued to work. He didn't like me checking up on him this way, but I wasn't planning to tell him. I stood at the end of a long lane heading down to the water's edge feeling suddenly exhausted. It was the waiting.

'JR?'

I peered down the empty lane. It was long. I guessed without counting that there were fifteen or sixteen forty-foot truck-sized containers along its length and the varicolored containers were stacked four high, forming eleven-meter walls on either side. The wall on the right cast sharp, dark shadows, carving the light away in a black prism that ran the length of this strange manmade road.

'JR?' I called again. There was no movement. Where had he got to?

I suddenly felt nervous. I edged slowly into the lane, fearful, as if there were some line of no return that I might unwittingly cross. I wished for my crystal gun, but I still hadn't managed to find Gary, who'd confiscated it.

I cursed myself for being so cowardly and began to walk down the road. I veered into the deep triangle of darkness to see if I could see JR hiding somewhere. Nothing. Something definitely didn't feel right. I stuffed my cold hands into my pockets and began to walk more briskly. The air was crisp and still. The noises of the docks seemed more muffled here. I turned to look behind me. I'd covered about fifty meters. I turned back to look in the direction I was walking. In the distance, a dark figure moved into view, lit from behind. My heart thudded in my chest. I blinked, trying to clear the glare, to see more clearly.

'Who's there?'

A voice whispered in my ear:

'Who do you think?'

I cried out and whirled around.

There was no-one there. I turned again. The figure in the distance had gone.

'JR? *JR?*'

I turned back to where I had come from and began to trot toward the lane's entrance, unable to get a link to JR. I stopped in my tracks. The unmistakeable figure of Viktor Meistermacher waited there, arms by his side, blocking my escape.

'Lost your dog?'

I heard his voice as clearly as if he were stood next to me. I turned and began to run away from him. I heard steps running close behind me. Meistermacher's words echoed in my ears:

'So. You saw through my little lie. I thought you might. I knew you would try to interfere. You are so—predictable.'

I turned my head to see, but he was not following. The sounds were all illusory. In the distance he began to raise his arms into the air. I felt a wash of warm air flow over me from his direction. I turned back and my heart leapt to see a small, hunched figure in a dark cloak at the opposite end.

I could hear her wheezing breath close to my ears.

I reacted, trying to invoke meta, but I felt a subtle ripple of agreement come from her, reinforcing him. Yet, there was something weak and uncertain about it. Was she ill? Nonetheless, it was more than enough to overwhelm my efforts.

I turned my head back to Meistermacher. A clacking sound immediately caused me to whip my attention back round in her direction. A tall gray form swept across the path between us in the distance. It seemingly appeared from the wall of a container and disappeared swiftly into one opposite. I stumbled to a halt, staring in disbelief. My heart was hammering. I squinted to see if there were some opening in the containers I couldn't make out.

My mouth and tongue silently formed the word 'no'.

'I found your doors easily,' Meistermacher hissed. 'They are always near to you. Did you know? . Wherever you are the boundaries are thinned by your presence. By your knowledge of them.'

Another tall figure swept silently across the path in the opposite direction. There was no doubt now. I recognized the hard white outer shell, the strange, smooth gait. Two more of the tall alien insects appeared, one twenty meters closer to me than the first. This time they both stopped and turned in the center of the lane. They faced me. I watched in horror as the chitinous outer shell cracked down the center, revealing a boiling mass of black legs. Something fat and gray snaked from its head section. The beginning of its screech was wiped out by the louder scream of train wheels. More white shapes poured into the corridor ahead from newly created doors, called by the sounds.

I would rather face Meistermacher than them.

I turned to him. But the Unholdformer had not wasted his time waiting for me. Five white-gray spiders fashioned from his clever hands were scuttling down the concrete and along the bright side of the containers toward me; and he was forming more.

I was trapped in the center of this long corridor of containers.

I looked up in desperation at the high walls either side of me. The nearest purchase hold was the top of the first row of containers. Eight and a half feet. I could jump to get a grip, but what then? There was not another suitable grip until the second row, seventeen feet from the ground. Four stories high, these walls would be impossible to climb. I looked toward Meistermacher. The nearest spider was just ten meters away now, gamboling toward me hungrily, and at least two were running along the walls defying gravity. Even if I climbed, they'd be at my neck and legs within seconds.

I turned back to face the tall upright insects with their writhing black innards advancing on me a hundred meters away. Terror blanked my mind for a moment. This was it, surely? I was going to die.

'JR?!' I screamed. 'Help me forgodssakeplease!'

Meistermacher laughed cruelly.

I moved uncertainly toward the malevolent white shrouds, driven by the advancing unhold that Meistermacher had sent scuttling my way and that were nearly upon me.

Ahead of me, not fifty meters away, I spied a block of shadow between the containers on the left-hand side. I looked at the adjacent containers nearest to me. The gap between them was too small to fit a man. I looked back at the shadow I'd seen. It could be an illusion, I thought—perhaps one just jutted out more than its predecessor—but it could also be a gap. If I was to reach it before the insects, I'd need to be fast.

I began to run toward them. Their excitement grew. Their fat gray feeding pipes flailed and I heard a screeching, clattering call that echoed around the containers. There were at least a dozen of them now swarming toward me. More were coming out from new doors Meistermacher willed through the thin veil of reality. My fear at this sight made my legs uncooperative. I needed power in them now more than ever, and it was deserting me.

ComeonSteelRUN!

I forced my legs to cooperate, overriding fear with command. I screamed at my legs and I pumped my thighs, sprinting now to the terrible white forms with their open carapaces inviting me to death.

As I neared the shadow, I panicked. It was just a jutting edge after all. I slowed. I'd made the wrong choice. I whirled around in panic. The carnivorous insects seemed to float toward me on a bed of hidden chitinous legs. Further down I could see more shadows indicating the end of one container, the beginning of another; the containers were not arranged perfectly. There were definite gaps beyond them, but they were too far for me to reach. There had to be a gap somewhere nearer, if I could only find it. My eyes ached trying to interpret the shadows made by the thin light of the artificial floodlights. Sweat spilled into my eyes, blurring my vision. I frantically wiped at them. I looked to the deep triangular shadow cast by the right wall and realized I'd only checked half of my options. The rest were obscured in the darkness. I ducked into the shadow and crouched down so that not a single inch of me remained lit. I tried to calm my burning lungs, to slow my desperate panting. I had seconds now. Suddenly, I could see the corrugations of the container walls. I scanned up and down the long rows of containers in the shade looking for black among the gray. *There.* Just one container away, toward the spider forms racing toward me, I saw the gap I needed. I cursed. I'd run past it. I began to crawl on my hands as fast as I could without regard to the damage my knees suffered on the harsh concrete. The gap was mere meters away now. The spiders seemed to have slowed, unable to see me in the shade, but sensing the air with feelers. They began to crawl down from the lit wall opposite and across the floor, joining me in the shade. I too slowed, fearful of alerting them to my location. I edged forwards. The toe of my boot caught the concrete, making a resonant thumping sound. Simultaneously all the spiders responded, turning toward me. They increased their pace. I lifted myself to my feet and launched myself toward the gap. It was wide enough for me, but my heart sank as I squeezed into it and saw inside.

At the far end was the face of another container.

It hadn't occurred to me that they were stacked two, sometimes more, wide. I squeezed myself deeper into the gap, forcing my breath out to be thinner. My lungs burned with a terrible fire as I denied them the oxygen they needed after my exertions. The gap was narrowing—I had to angle my feet to fit in, but I saw that there was a space between this wall of containers and the one I was aiming for. I paused to breathe, painfully constrained by the two containers I was trapped between. I could still turn my head, just. Back toward the light, I saw the dark silhouettes of finger-like digits appear over the edges of the container. The spiders were upon me. I panted as rapidly as I could to give myself the air I needed. Two spider forms tasted the air near the edge, sensing me, and began to crawl inside the gap with me. My vision began to close around the sight of them in a dark, shimmering fog. I needed more oxygen: I was going to faint. *Notnowpleasenotnow. Calmcalm*calm! I forced myself to take rapid shallow breaths. The circle of dark fog around my vision slowly widened again. *Move!* I exhaled as forcefully as I could and then forced myself empty-lunged, pushing with my legs and what purchase I could get with my trapped arms toward the narrow end of the gap. I made it almost halfway out but I was trapped. My chest caught fire with pain. *Push!* I implored my failing legs. With a final effort, first my chest and then my hips released and I fell into the wider space between the containers. I desperately drank oxygen back into my lungs, holding onto the walls with my palms to stop me from collapsing. I could not see which direction might contain an escape route. The space was not wide enough to turn around so I edged my way sideways along in the direction toward the dock's edge and the water. I could not see behind me. I felt my way along with my hands, snot and spittle and sweat poured from my mouth and nose with each desperate and fatigued breath. I heard a chittering sound behind me, close to me.

Something brushed against my ear.

I yelled and lashed out with a hand to fend the thing off. I contacted a dense, multi-limbed thing. The heel of my hand thumped it away. The thing lost its purchase on the container wall and disappeared with another chittering sound into the darkness. I heard a heavy thump. More frenzied chittering. I lurched onwards in my desperation, almost tripping and falling to the floor. My hands found the next gap. I pulled myself to it and finally, I saw light. I was looking into the adjacent road of containers. I squeezed myself painfully around into this new gap and edged into it. I bruised my chest but the new gap was wider than the one I had first entered. I accelerated and thrust myself out into freedom and light. Still panting and aching, I looked up.

A figure appeared at the end of the row.

It was Meistermacher.

I turned to run in the opposite direction and bumped into something warm and solid. My ears filled with a terrible noise. Tight limbs fastened around me, holding me solidly.

I screamed and flailed around desperately, but I was held perfectly tight. It took me a moment to realize that these were human arms, and then my ears began to process the sounds they were hearing.

'Hey! Calm down. What's got into you, son?'

I stared frantically into the eyes of two dock workers. I swallowed and looked back up the alley to Meistermacher. The entrance was empty. He had gone.

'I...' I struggled to speak, still panting. 'Oh God,' I managed.

The two men exchanged looks. Their grip relaxed when they realized that I had calmed a little. I took a deep breath.

'Sorry. Sorry. I...'

Think.

'... trapped between two containers there. I thought... I thought I was going to die.'

'What were you doing there, kid? This ain't a playground.'

'No, sorry. I... I lost my dog. I was looking for him.'

'Who are you here with?'

'Bruno.'

'Which Bruno?'

'Works for Tony Damasio.'

The guy nodded upwards, understanding something more than I meant. They released their grip completely.

'He's that way.' The guy indicated back toward Damasio's hut.

'Thank you.'

'Yeah, well, like I said. This ain't a playground. Stop messin' around.'

'Sure. Cool. Thank you,' I breathed, still panting. I crouched and bent forwards a little, steadying myself with my hands on my knees, and tried to recover my breath and hide my expression from the two guys.

'You okay.'

I nodded. 'Uhuh.'

I straightened up. I began to hobble toward the hut. Adrenaline had masked the pain in my knees and my aching, bruised ribs, my right hip. I felt incredibly vulnerable. She and Meistermacher could reappear at any moment. I stopped and turned back to the men. They were still watching me.

'Hey! Are you headed this way too? I'm feeling a bit... fragile.'

'I'll go with him,' offered the other guy, who until now had not spoken. 'I'll see you back there.'

'You seem pretty shook up,' the guy said as we walked. 'Had a close call, eh?'

'Yeah. Yeah, I did. Thanks for walking me back. Appreciate it.'

'No problem.'

By the time I got back to the hut I had a signal again but JR was already there sitting with two dock workers. I was furious with him.

'Where have you been?' I demanded.

He stood up immediately.

'Outside, *now*. I want a word with you.'

JR leapt off the seat and headed outside.

'Amazing dog,' one commented.

The men looked at each other quizzically.

'Weird kid.'

Outside JR looked up at me:

'Before you have a go at me, Meistermacher's here,' he said.

'I know,' I said, astonished. 'He almost killed me just now. She is too. You saw them?'

'That's why I was radio silent. I just ran into them, so I decided to spy. I tried to find you after but you vanished.'

'They attacked me. I must have wandered into them straight after you. Did you record what you saw?'

'Yes. Get a screen.'

I went inside, borrowed a small tablet, and came outside again. JR began to pipe video to it. He piped the audio direct to my earcom.

The tablet showed me the world through the low vantage point of JR's eyes:

The image was dark initially. He appeared to be sniffing around near a container when a noise abruptly drew his head up into the light. The viewpoint shuffled backwards into shade as two figures passed by.

I heard JR's recorded voice growl, 'That was close.'

'You promised me,' she whined nasally from her ruined body, hobbling to keep pace with Meistermacher.

'*You promised me*,' he parodied in a high-pitched whine. 'Stop moaning! What's more important? Don't be so shallow.'

She stopped dead.

'You're not going to help me. Are you? You're going to leave me like this? You got what you wanted from me...'

He halted, rolled his eyes and turned back to her.

'Do we have to argue about this *now*? Come! The girl is locked safely away from us. Until she's been given meta, I don't want her interfering. Her memory is returning and she's becoming difficult to control.'

'I don't know why you insisted on bringing her at all.'

'Are you perfectly stupid?' he snapped. 'Collateral. Leverage. He'll be here, I guarantee it. He's very... persistent. She's my guarantee. I can tell he's attached to her. He'll do what I want in order to save her. If the time comes. She's well enough hidden. This place is enormous. Even if I don't succeed in killing him, he'll have plenty to do trying to find her.' His voice became even more smug: 'And then, at five a.m. sharp, the small plastic explosive I've attached to her will detonate, creating exactly the diversion that I need.'

The horror in Kate's nasally voice was evident:

'You can't do that. She's innocent.'

'No-one's innocent, dear. No-one. Now come on!'

They walked out of view.

JR stopped the video stream.

'That's it?'

'All of it. I came straight to find you, but the signal here is patchy.'

Jesus! was all I could think. But then I thought back to the weakness of Kate's agreement. The attack had happened shortly after this video was taken.

Her allegiance to him is being eroded, I thought. *He's betrayed her trust.*

I checked the time, horrified. It was 4:40 a.m. We had just twenty minutes to find Skyler. Not knowing what else to do I began to run back to the area where Meistermacher had trapped me. Where he'd last been. JR ran alongside.

'How the hell do we find her here? It's massive? Can you retrace your steps? Where were they exactly? She has to be close by where they came from.'

As we ran, something began to nag at the back of my mind. Something seemed wrong with this situation, but I couldn't put my finger on what it was.

We searched the area for an age, running up and down countless corridors of containers, past the straddle cranes that patiently built and deconstructed them. Each second seem to drip some of Skyler's life away.

I kept calling out her name. *Skyler, Sky!*

There was nothing.

I was beginning to lose hope.

Then, I heard something.

It was faint above the constant crash and squeal of the docks but it was real. I stopped and strained my ears, willing the zoo of noise quiet for long enough that I could hear it again. The zoo ignored me. Then... a gap. I held my breath. For a moment, only the distant thunder of planes played across the docks.

There—

A woman shouting. Muffled. Panicky. The echoes made it impossible to locate, but she was near.

'JR?'

He'd already shot off through a gap in the containers.

'I'm on it,' came his voice in my com.

I looked up and down the container row. I was almost half way along, equidistant from the ends. I panicked, indecisive. I needed to get to the other side, but if I went round and happened to choose the wrong end, I'd have the whole length to run. The delay could be the difference between her life and death.

JR's voice crackled over the com again.

'Steel! I've found her!'

'Where?'

'In the cabin of a straddle crane. It's locked and high up. I can't get to her. No way. You have to get here.'

'Which end?'

'Neither. Middle.'

I panicked again. She was just the other side of the damn containers, if only I could—

The rumbling noise of a straddle crane rolling up the lane behind me startled me. Twenty meters away a stationary crane straddled this wall. There was no way I could climb the containers, but I could try to climb the crane. I ran to it and began to haul myself up its huge frame, hand over hand, jamming my feet into metal nooks for support.

I was three quarters of the way up the thirty-foot wall when the crane motors rumbled into life and my grip faltered. I couldn't climb higher. The next bar was too high for me to reach. I swore.

I needed to swing my feet across to another cross bar in order to make it to the top container. My arm muscles were burning. The motor's pitch increased and the entire frame began to tremble. Muscles in my hands started to cramp, I was losing my grip. I commanded my legs to swing.

They responded but I missed. I heaved myself and swung my legs again.

The entire frame shuddered suddenly into motion. My left hand slipped off its grip and I was forced to cling to the girder. I began to slide down and wrapped my legs around it, managing to halt my decline. Desperate now, I began to shuffle up the girder, hugging it. It worked. The crane was moving at some speed now along the line of containers with me clinging to its leg. I reached the top of the leg. I could not find a safe position to jump onto the containers. Instead I'd have to try and get on top and work my way across the horizontal girder straddling the container wall to get to the other side of the crane whilst it was moving. I hoisted myself up onto the top and began to crawl precariously along.

'Steel! Get here now! Her crane's motors are starting!'

I had no time to crawl, I had to run. I stood, almost slipped because of the crane's sideways motion, and began to stagger along the moving top of the crane, across the wall of containers. I could see her now. She was in the cabin of the crane on the container wall ahead of me. Her crane was moving toward mine. We would cross each other in seconds. If I didn't get to her now, we'd speed away from each other in opposite directions. I'd never get to her in time.

She saw me and started banging on the window and shouting for help.

I began to run and just as I almost reached the end, the crane jerked. My foot slipped and I lurched forwards and to my utter horror I began to fall.

I grasped with one arm and suddenly the sky, stars and lights whirled across my vision. There was a blinding white light and then—a huge explosion.

My heart died in my chest.

Things went quiet for a moment and then there was a rushing sound. My head hurt shockingly, but I realized with relief the explosion had been me banging my head when I'd landed on the containers. I lifted myself into a sitting position. Skyler was trundling away from me, just meters away now.

'Steel! Ninety seconds! Move!'

I stood up and began to run along the container wall to catch her. I jumped a gap onto the next container. Her straddle crane was just two or three meters away. I was thirty feet high, about ten feet above her. I had to jump across or I'd never make it. I began to increase my pace, and leapt across the gap with all my strength, aiming at the top of the leg of her crane above where her cabin was attached to it. I crashed into the side and wrapped my legs around it, sliding down onto the top of her prison.

I lay down on my front on top of the cabin and inched to the edge.

The door had been jammed with a metal peg through a hook.

I leaned down to try to reach it but I began to slip off the roof. Alarmingly, I was aiming head first toward the concrete twenty feet down. I flailed around managed to grabbed onto a bolt and pushed myself back to safety.

'Thirty seconds!'

Securing myself more firmly, I reached down again and this time my fingers touched the peg that was jammed into the door hook. Close, but not close enough. I strained further, willing myself to stretch. The peg came between two fingertips but slipped away again. I lunged and grabbed it precariously between my fingers like chopsticks and began to pull it up. I felt myself sliding forwards again. I had no more time. I lunged for the peg. It lifted from the hook just as I slid off the roof. Skyler pushed the door open and I gratefully folded over the top of it and then swung down into the cabin that had imprisoned her.

'Seven seconds!'

She grabbed and hugged me to thank me, not realizing the threat.

'Six!'

I tried to push her away so I could search her but she was strong and very afraid.

'Five!'

'SKYLER, GET OFF ME! YOU HAVE A BOMB ON YOU! I NEED TO FIND IT!'

She cried out in shock but her grip relaxed. I pushed her back. Suddenly both our hands were fighting to search her body.

'Three! Two!'

'Your belt!' I cried

She scrabbled at the buckle.

'One!'

All of my energy drained away. I closed my eyes and suddenly there was nothing left to do but to hug her tightly.

We waited for five, then ten seconds, trembling.

There was no explosion.

She began to sob heavily. I opened my eyes cautiously and began to systematically pat her down, searching for anything that could house a block of plastic explosive, no matter how small.

She was bare. Completely.

The nagging thought at the back of my head suddenly crystallized.

'Oh no...'

'*Steel?*' came JR's voice.

'*He never told me about her.* When he had me trapped. He didn't say a *word*. He didn't need to. He must have known you were spying. He made it up. This was all a diversion. *Shit!* I have to get back to the ship! JR! Get her to safety. To Demasio. Then, meet me at the ship! Find Bruno. I'll be with him. We're going to get that container.'

'Okay.'

I looked at Skyler. Her hair was flat and unwashed, her ashen cheeks just beginning to show the flush of color again after the shock. Her chestnut eyes were liquid. She smelled unwashed, yet it was a good, natural, human smell. An unfamiliar emotion overwhelmed me.

I took Skyler in my arms, and kissed her full on the lips. She resisted, not a lot, but a little, and so I stopped. But then she touched her lips with tenderness as much as surprise in her fingertips.

'Don't forget me this time.'

She held my gaze. She said nothing, but I knew in that moment that she wouldn't.

'Go with him. You'll be safe now.'

She nodded.

'JR? I need the thing that Gary took off me. It may be our only chance.'

'I'll look out for him.'

On the way back to find Bruno, I tried to puzzle out what Meistermacher was doing. The container wasn't due off the ship until at least 6 a.m. Why had he created a diversion an hour early?

Bruno turned out to be a handsome young Brazilian with moody eyebrows—two perfect horizontal slashes that could have been drawn on with a marker pen. Exactly the sort of boy Needle would have paid to entertain him in his heyday.

I felt a pang of pain and loss.

Bruno shook my hand and met my gaze with black eyes, but he said little. I mistook him for a man of few words, but the truth was he was a man of little English. Damasio had apparently given him instructions in Portuguese.

Bruno led me with hand signals to a truck engine attached to a forty-foot container-less chassis.

My nerves were fried. I was still trembling from what had happened.

I kept looking around for JR, and for signs of Meistermacher or the deformed figure of Kate. But there was nothing.

Finally JR appeared.

'Is she safe?'

'She's with Demasio. Drinking tea. She'll be fine.'

'Did you get the gun?'

'No, no sign of Gary anywhere.'

I swore. 'Then we just have to get this container and go.'

I picked up JR and climbed high up into the cabin. Moments later it shuddered and shook with the heavy purr of its diesel engine, and with a rumble we began to make our way down to the lanes across the edge of the quayside. We waited in a long line of identical container-less trucks, and every few minutes, Bruno revved the engine and we chugged forwards forty feet nearer the vast legs of the hundred-foot mechanical monsters which stood like gigantic brontosaurs at the edge of an oasis, not drinking, but eviscerating a poor ship that had died there.

I tried, but failed to speak with him. He understood little.

JR began to speak:

'De onde você é no Brasil, Bruno?'

Bruno's expression transformed into delight.

'E?! Um cachorro que pode falar? Até mesmo em português?'

'E porque não?'

Bruno laughed and slapped his thigh. I stared open-mouthed at JR.

'Since when did you speak Portuguese?'

'Just now. I've just connected to a translation service. It's pretty good, eh?'

JR and Bruno continued to chat happily. I understood nothing. I concentrated on looking out for signs of Meistermacher.

Suddenly, I saw a figure move furtively between containers. My heart stopped. It was Meistermacher, I was sure. There was no sign of Kate. *There's nothing he can do here*, I reassured myself. Not with so many people around. But, I wanted to make sure. I pulled at the door handle.

'Where are you going? We're nearly there.'

I slipped out and swung down onto the concrete. Above us, the cranes towered, dwarfing the trucks with their sheer immensity. I called up to JR:

'Tell him to keep going. I'll only be a minute.'

I slammed the door and slipped out across the lanes to get to the rows of containers.

I moved across to the entrance of the row where I thought I'd seen him, but now there was no sign of him, so I checked the next along. Again, empty. The night air seem to sparkle. *Was it going to snow?* I wondered. I looked up at the sky. Low in the distant horizon the peach moon was sliced into ragged peach slivers by dark bolts of cloud.

I saw Meistermacher's figure flit between two trucks and vanish again. What on earth was he up to? I ran back across the lanes, dodging trucks to try to find him. My fear had abated. Men crawled likes ants everywhere. Meistermacher's power here would be limited to trompe l'oeil, small tricks of the eye.

Yet, I could feel his presence so strongly it frightened me.

The sensation was the opposite of déjà vu. Instead of a doubling—the scene and its familiarity—it was a halving, a slicing away of everything solid around me. It was as if the world itself could no longer agree on what was real, what was illusion. Reality diminished, lifting slightly away from its moorings as if it were a mere poster, poorly plastered over boardings, still wet and motile. It was the sense that I had *never* seen this—all of this around me—could never truly see it, because none of it were possible. And it was the frightening sense that something else lay in waiting beneath. The shock of the strength of this feeling hit me hard, and I almost lost my footing and stumbled. Even Meistermacher could not generate such a powerful effect here, could he?

And there he was again.

He was swift, and held his arms in strange positions, darting this way and that, weaving everywhere, between everything, like a ghostly shuttle.

I saw JR on the dash of the truck through the windscreen. It had moved into position under the first of the four great cranes and was waiting now for a white container to thread its way through the bowels of the machine and be deposited upon the truck's skeletal chassis. JR was sniffing at the air. The container was feet away from the chassis now, and men coalesced around it to help guide and secure it in place.

I heard the clunk of metal on metal announcing contact, and just as this happened, he appeared. He strode confidently toward me down a line of trucks wearing a malicious smile. I heard muted barking. Meistermacher's arms were behind his back. I panicked, realizing my error. He was carrying a gun.

No, I was wrong. Not a gun.

The truth was much worse.

Meistermacher's smile broadened showing his uneven teeth. He was just meters away now.

And I finally understood why he had created a diversion an hour early.

'Do you feel it?' he said.

JR was barking furiously, and trying to shout something to me between barks. I couldn't hear, the windscreen glass was too thick. The zoo of different engine noises too great.

I stepped back, terrified, all of a sudden.

'This is what's possible, Steel. Just a fraction of what's possible.'

And he took his arms from behind his back and raised them. In each hand he carried several small gray objects.

An awful understanding came; my insides felt as if they were dropping away.

They were inhalers.

He was squeezing the devices and a constant fine mist was issuing from them. The air sparkled where the mist caught the light. A mist of pure meta.

'I had them specially altered, of course. Constant spray!'

He had diverted me early in order to get into the container whilst it was still on the ship. And now he'd been lacing the air all around us with it. I noticed, aghast, that his pockets were bulging with more. The floor behind him was littered with the husks of emptied inhalers. And there were dock workers walking into the mist everywhere.

I cried out in utter horror.

'Now. Let's see what we can do.'

Meistermacher's eyes flicked up to the massive structures above us. I spun on my heel and cried out to JR and Bruno:

'Get moving!'

I began to run back to the truck, yelling and waving my arms.

Around me I noticed several dock workers had stopped working, hands were at stomachs or mouths, expressions were sour and sick. They had all breathed the mist. A wave of tension whipped snakelike down the cables attached to the container on our truck. It hit the container, wrenching it violently before it bounced back up its length. A terrible low creaking and straining sound tore at the air. The great girders of the crane were beginning to move.

'Release the cables!' I screamed. The workers who had been fitting the container to the truck ignored me. Their faces were pale with sickness and fear.

As I reached the truck I saw Bruno opening the door.

'NO!' I waved my hands. 'Stay inside!'

The cables had slackened on the container but now snapped taut again with shocking laser-gun-like sounds. The container lurched an inch and crashed back into place under the force. The two men on my side of the truck were startled from their sickness into attention. I screamed at them to release the container.

A grinding screech of tortured metal vibrated through my head and body. I looked up to see another greater wave of force traveling through the cabled guts of the girded monster.

'Get down!' I yelled and physically dragged the guy nearest me to the floor. The man next to him stared stupidly as the wave traveling the cable reached the container. The latches exploded under stress. The thick metal cable lashed out and with a sickening crack whipped up, catching him under his jaw. He was lifted backwards through the air in a spray of blood and flesh. His body hit the floor meters away a full second before the bloody lump of flesh and bone that had been his jaw. Men were shouting everywhere in terror. Above us, something impossible was happening. I scrabbled back up to a crouching position and crawled to the cabin. Cables whipped and snapped unpredictably through the air above me, vibrating the air into sound.

I wrenched open the door heaved into the cabin and slammed it behind me. 'Drive!'

Bruno was clearly in shock, his eyes fixed on the side mirror.

'*Drive!* Vamos!'

In desperation I reached a foot over to try to step on the gas but Bruno came to life at this moment and shifted into gear. He paused again.

'Mas não está bem colocado! Vai cair.'

'What?'

JR translated: 'He said, "It's not attached properly. It could fall off."'

'Tell him *just drive* or we could *die*.'

Bruno crossed his chest and began to babble a prayer. Then he gripped the wheel and slammed down the gas and with a roar of diesel power we began to move forwards.

Ahead of us I saw the impossible. One of the four feet of the crane ahead, metal girders wider and thicker than the entire cabin of the truck, began to lift into the air.

The three cranes began to move.

Floodlights within their rigging turned on us like bright eyes in the night. The air shrieked and groaned with straining metal. Their long necks slowly lifted into the air, snapping their cables like string, and with crashing steps that quaked the very earth, one by one, they slowly began to turn toward us.

We were still underneath the first of them.

I strained forwards to see above us. A huge iron foot torn from its moorings was descending toward us. I grabbed at the steering wheel and yanked it down to the right as the foot crashed through the concrete where we had been, shattering it into rubble. The truck lurched to the right. We were heading for the edge of the dock. Bruno wrenched the wheel back up. Inertia slowed the truck's responses. By the time we turned back the wheel had overshot and Bruno wrestled to damp the out of control feedback loop that threatened to overturn the truck.

I watched men run in terror as the monstrous cranes wrought disaster everywhere. Concrete chunks flew through glass and metal and flesh, exploding from underneath the weight of their massive, unnatural feet. And ahead of us, Meistermacher stood in the midst of this maelstrom, untouched.

Suddenly, before us, one of the tall insect creatures stepped into our path.

Bruno screamed.

We were moving too fast to even swerve. Its white carapace smashed apart, shedding gobs of gray goo, skeins of dark burgundy blood and thousands of tiny twitching black legs everywhere. Its trunk-like proboscis flailed before slapping into the windscreen and then disappearing with a snap along with its head as it was dragged under us. White slime smeared the windscreen.

We left the shadow of the first crane and had no choice but to drive underneath the second exactly as it began to collide into the first.

Metal roared across registers so low I felt my ribs vibrating, and so high my teeth ached.

Above us, the two hundred-ton stabilizing counterweights attached to the backs of the monsters obeyed their momentum and began to tip from their positions. Bolts fused and melted under the forces which snapped them. The massive white blocks began to fall.

'DRIVE!' I screamed.

With majestic slowness the first of the weights unmoored and began its accelerating fall. The floodlight eyes of the monster it belonged to fused and exploded, plunging its interior into darkness. We raced by as the counterweight arced in a parabola and tore into the center of the ship with a thunderous explosion of sound. The ship buckled slightly in its center. Water rushed up in a wide fountain along its vast length onto the dock. Bruno veered the truck to the left just as another crashing foot destroyed the road to the right. The windscreen made a terrific cracking sound as something concrete or metallic smashed off it, leaving a spiderweb fracture. JR leapt from the dashboard and hid in the space down by my legs, quaking.

We were heading straight for Meistermacher.

He faced us with an expression full of dark fury. His fists were bunched by his sides. For one terrible moment, I felt that if we were to hit him, it would be the truck that would suffer. But at the last moment, Meistermacher, as cool as a toreador, stepped out of our path and we shot past him. Behind us the dying crane had slipped one foot into the water and was collapsing backwards onto the sinking vessel, and was tipping sideways onto the crane we were now beneath. In another explosion of light and violent electricity the third crane's eyes died. We had gathered speed now, and raced into the path of the fourth. It turned under the command of the Puppeteer's terrible will and lifted a vast front leg to crush us. Bruno hit the brakes and yanked the wheel down to the right. The leg crunched through the lane in front of us. Concrete exploded. I put my hands to my face. The windscreen shattered. Small chunks of glass glittered as they flew and penetrated the backs of my hands, my face. Bruno's face.

I pulled my hands away. The backs were bleeding. Bruno's hands were at his face now. Blood poured from beneath them. He had been gripping the wheel when the glass shattered.

He was screaming.

We were beyond the fourth crane. The water shimmered to our right, empty of everything now but reflection and light.

Every second we were veering closer to it.

My senses overloaded, I seemed to go deaf momentarily: I watched Bruno's screams in eerie silence.

To the right the dock raced past us and the water's edge drew closer.

I could not get out of my side. I lurched over Bruno in the driver's seat and fumbled at his door latch. The door opened, just as the first of the dock-side wheels dipped over the edge. I scrambled over the poor boy and then turned to grab his arm. His hand came down and I saw the blood pouring down from his eyes. His O-shape mouth widened and he pulled his hands back to his face.

He wouldn't let me save him.

I threw myself from the door, shortly followed by JR. I hit the concrete. My body knew nothing of air any more. It was all gone, as if Earth's atmosphere had been stripped away. I rolled and jack-knifed over myself in a hideous parody of gymnastics, finally coming to a rest. My body spasmed. And then the pain came. My lungs burned with a fierce brightness. I thought I would die. An airless eternity passed, and then the first breath came. I was granted a pathetically small thing, incapable of even beginning to calm the hunger for air my lungs demanded be satisfied. I gulped dryly at the air, keening, wheezing. The stricture on my throat released a fraction and I gulped again at the insufficient oxygen.

When breath finally returned, it was a bittersweet reunion: several of my ribs seemed fractured. Each breath became a necessary agony, each one a choice between pain and death. JR had survived the fall with bruises, nothing more. He scrabbled to me and licked at my face until I wheezed at him to stop, fearing my wounds. I had seen nothing but whirling light and dark as we had tumbled from the truck. I hadn't witnessed its final moments, plunging over the docks' edge and falling meters into the cold, hungry waters that finally consumed it and its poor, luckless driver.

I pulled myself to my knees, and coughed. *Searing white agony.* When the urge to cough came again, my body denied it. I looked up to see the carnage that Meistermacher had wrought. The container ship was no longer visible in the water. Two of the huge cranes seemed to be grasping onto each other, like drunks, half-fallen into the water that bubbled furiously where the ship had been. They were all in darkness now, inanimate skeletons devoid of the life they had briefly been gifted by the eldritch strings of the Puppenspieler.

Staring stupidly by his car two container lanes away was Gary. In shock, he was fiddling unconsciously with something in his hands.

A figure silhouetted by the headlights of trucks was striding toward me. I could feel a wave of hatred flow out from him from like carbon dioxide mist. The light seemed to be different. The docks were silent for the very first time since I had entered them. I heard the first cawing of seagulls.

Dawn was breaking.

'JR,' I croaked. 'Go to Gary. Get what he took from me. Fetch.'

I tried to crawl away, but I could not outpace him. It seemed to take forever, but finally he stood over me, with curling lips. Behind his dark silhouetted face the sky was lightening to a deep blue. He said nothing for a moment. He just watched me.

JR raced to me carrying, something gleaming in his jaws.

He tried to bark whilst keeping on to it. Meistermacher kicked him viciously, sending him yelping across the concrete; and sending the device that he had fetched for me skittering away again.

I began to hear sirens. I looked out across the concrete plain in the direction of the airport. Red and blue lights flashed in the dawn light. Headlights faced us. Hundreds of police and FBI were racing toward us.

Meistermacher stepped away from me and calmly took out more inhalers from his jacket pockets and began to place them on the floor around us. Each of them, he jammed depressed, and each began to emit a soft vapor that scintillated as it caught the light.

No... I shivered with pain and cold. The police would run straight into it.

I watched in horror as Gary and two dock workers nearby ventured into the mist. Meistermacher breathed in deeply through his nose, as if the air were filling with the scent of roses. He ignored them and turned to me with glazed eyes.

I saw reality curling around him loosely like a cloak—a choice. Around JR. I saw how different it was around the approaching police, how it clung, more like paint to them; attached, permanent like a living tattoo; and how it subtly loosened as they entered the mist; as they breathed. I saw their faces twist and sicken with it, with the shock. There were shouts of warning. Some retreated.

'Who did you think you were to decide what the world can and can't do?' Meistermacher spat. 'The world defender against meta. Against progress. You fuck up your own life and people die because of *your* mistakes and now *everyone* has to stop? *The whole fucking world?* No-one can have the prize, all because *you couldn't handle it—*'

He was shouting now, spittle flew from his mouth, raining down on me. Some of it turned to smoke on the way down. A few specks of it touched my coat and where it did so, the thread twisted, as if something small and alive were struggling underneath to get out. He ranted on, his anger whipping itself into fury:

'The sheer *arrogance*. And all the time, when you could have helped change things, you left my mother alone in her madness and my uncle brother-less.'

'It wasn't like—'

'*Shut up!*'

JR began to bark again. Something subtle was happening. I could no longer hear the sirens. Viktor Meistermacher, the tragic son of Emily and Vaughan, an orphan of the Looking Glass Club, of death and insanity—had worked himself up way beyond the point of reasoning and he was now screaming with anger and frustration as if he was being tortured by something from within. I was terrified. His arms were locked rigid by his side but he raised them high into the air. The black silhouetted edges of his coat began to flap furiously—yet there was no wind. He lifted his head up to the sky and vented a tortured scream of madness. A bruise appeared in the sky directly above him, a livid vermillion thing nested in the growing blue. It grew as he screamed at it, seeping crimson which diffused across the pure lapis lazuli in veins, like poison.

This was no longer about me. This young man was insane, finally corrupted by the very thing that supplied his power. I looked down. JR was barking furiously now, his body dancing. I searched in vain across the dock for the police, but they had gone. Ahead of me the water was drawing back. The concrete dock seemed to stretch in all directions, preserving only the distance between us and the edge; the angles. I lay on a vast desert of concrete under a carmine sky. Meistermacher loomed massively, a million miles above me by some trick of perspective. The police cars and the approaching men all seemed giants a vast distance away, projecting the same solid angle on my retina.

JR barked and then ran once in a circle, driven to craziness by what was happening around us. His barking seemed directed at the water's edge. And then I saw: the water was boiling up. My first thought was that Meistermacher was raising the sunken container from beneath. But I was wrong.

Something began to rise out of the water and reach above the concrete edge. It had pincers, enormous things, but this was a creature as much of the desert and the forest floor as it was the sea, a terrible medley of arthropoda: myriapoda, crustacea, arachnida. It was reinventing its heritage from moment to moment; it was changing form, taking its inspiration from my deepest fears, sprouting hundreds, thousands of legs of every size from beneath a yellow and black armor, some bristling, thin as hair, others as thick as a man's torso, each seemingly possessed of its own will to clutch and devour. A pair of transparent wings sprouted from its back, damp and clinging, and began to buzz in useless fits.

The thing screeched. It seemed to me to be the tortured sound of air hissing from a cooking carapace of lobster amplified a million times and steam boiled off its crusted armor as it grew. The monstrosity began to move toward us—it was larger than a car now and still growing—sliding forwards on an undulating sea of articulated legs. JR looked at me but he had lost his power of speech. I was frozen by fear. JR ran in crazed circles, barked again. As it emerged over the edge, the thing twisted, righting itself segment by segment. Its many-eyed head began to twist and turn, tasting the air with its mandibles and working it's vertical jaw, jagged black knives.

I tried to fight this psychotic reinterpretation, to shrink that mutant, monstrous thing back to whatever it might have been, but nothing happened. *Nothing*. Meistermacher—who had known only meta since birth—stamped his reality easily over mine. I began to edge away from the thing and called at JR to do the same, but JR was lost to his own barking, his own fearless fury.

The huge vertical slit of the myriapod's mouth was grinding its black, blade-like edges together. Wisps of vapor still floated out from it. The carpet of its legs rippled unexpectedly, and it lurched forwards.

JR had no time to react. He was caught, snatched up into the air by a black and yellow limb and dragged toward the scissor-like mouth.

My mouth was screaming but I could hear nothing. I reached inside myself for the fire, Emily's fire, that so long ago had burned us both, and I hurled it from my hand in a searing white arc, to the place where the creature's segmented arm joined its body. The lancing light struck and I felt the energies pouring through and out of me, coalescing around my will, channeled and directed by my hand. The creature's shoulder joint exploded, spitting gobs of burning matter, just as JR's head was about to enter its mouth. It screeched and lurched back, curling up as it did so and violently dragging a plume of smoky flame with it. Smaller limbs around its mouth tried to clutch at JR's fur, but they were weak and he fell to the ground. He landed heavily on the concrete, still attached to the black and red arm that had snatched him, and where it still twitched and flailed. The end of it oozed gray matter. JR's eyes were filled with panic and desperation. He scrabbled to his feet, turned back on himself and wrenched the flailing thing off his body with his teeth. He tried to scamper away, stumbling at first, but then found a purchase and rocketed toward me.

My hand was in agony. I looked at it. The skin was blistered and red, and it felt as if it was still on fire. I cried out and then gritted my teeth, panting through my nose at the pain. For a moment it seemed as if the only things that existed were my hand and the flaming pain consuming it. I looked up, just in time to see the myriapod curling back on itself ready for another attack.

Something was different.

I heard a whumping sound tearing at the air.

In the distance I saw a vast cloaked hag, standing watching.

I stumbled backwards, trying to escape, but felt something under my legs and I tripped. It was JR. He yelped. The world sailed around me. I saw something glitter on the floor. I twisted as I fell and landed, right on my injured hand. The world exploded into white hot pain. For an eternity I could not see, or breathe, or think. I was nothing more or less than the sum of the pain searing into and overloading my brain and the desperate necessity to stop it. In one violent twisting reflex I ripped my hand out from underneath me, pulling off some of the seared skin, burying grit into the newly naked flesh as it went. *I would surely die of this pain?* Once more, air refused to come into me, my lungs had become solid; they too began to burn and the world darkened. As a dark veil drew in around my vision, I began to feel light, almost weightless. My thoughts slowed. A great shadow grew in the sky.

It was okay to die. I began to welcome the prospect of an end to this wretchedness I called life.

A tiny breath allowed itself inside me, an inverted screech, and the light and pain returned, flaring like a flame with the oxygen; more burning in my lungs; my hand seemed huge and tender; a larger breath screeched past my vocal chords, resisting but coming into me, it came, cool and precious air, life itself. My thoughts began to unglue themselves. I could feel the position of my body. My hearing started to return. JR was yelping from underneath my legs just as the hideous black-eyed thing lurched forwards again and grabbed at my vulnerable legs with a myriad mandibles and pincers. It opened the sideways slits of its scissor mouth and I felt myself dragged toward it.

The air vibrated and shuddered all around me.

Something was different, what was it?

Fatigue weighed down on me. *I had to fight.* I lifted my injured hand and pointed it limply at the huge face of the thing, with its cycling jaws. My hand was bloody, covered with grit and dirt and it burned with searing pain, but I could no more use my good left hand than I could have written with it. I was right-handed. The pain was so great I began to weep, but my choices were few: I could either summon the flame and burn my hand further or lose my leg to this mouth. I lifted my first finger, cried out and willed the fire to come. It came, but my fear of the fire made it smaller, a mere finger's width of feeble ruby light. The creature only paused in its faltering brightness. I was going to lose my foot. I was going to die. I looked away, through the strange distorted perspective to the advancing police and braced myself for the pain. I implored those huge distant figures standing in a whorling maelstrom of red and blue lights; they watched me with strange expressions. I envied their reality, hugging tightly around them.

I was dragged suddenly a foot across the concrete toward the creatures mouth.

Something was different.

The air vibrated.

I had power again. Meistermacher was no longer overriding me.

Somewhere, someone—no, more than one—I was being given agreement.

Meistermacher's face had turned to horror as felt his power overridden.

Behind him, armed officers began to raise their automatic weapons.

I drew in a great breath, concentrating on the pain in my ribs and, just as the creature was about to slice its razor jaws down on my ankle, I *used* the pain, reinterpreting it. I turned perception into a thing. I blew the sensation from me, transforming it into a great gale of cold. The creature frosted over instantly with ice. My ribs seared, but I continued to blow. Its head began to shrink. It screeched. I breathed in, focussing the terrible sharpness in my ribs and turned it to my advantage. I levered myself up with my left hand to attack the thing more directly. The creature shriveled under the onslaught. Thick layers of white frost cracked and fell away like shedding skin. It shrank to the size of a man; then a dog; to the size of a mouse; and finally it curled up on the concrete—

—no larger than a woodlouse.

The mutant thing's legs stopped moving and it lay still and white; and tiny.

I fell back and stared at the receding red sky, exhausted, in agony, feeling only the extreme burning in my hand, my ragged breath, my aching ribs and my thumping heart.

In the sky, the enormous silhouette of a helicopter grew. Its blades whumped through the air, creating a local hurricane.

The mist from Meistermacher's canisters was being dispersed.

Meistermacher cried out. The world seemed to shake in response.

In the distance I saw the wretched figure of Kate turn to him and I felt what she was doing.

She was acting against him.

He turned on her, angrily. I defended her, casting out my will, feeling truly for the first time the possibility of the strength that Needle had always believed I possessed in me. I attacked his back with a will made newly of iron. Meistermacher lurched and whipped round to face me once more.

The helicopter touched the ground, pitching slightly as it landed. The door opened. Inside I recognized the face of an older adversary. One that I had at the last minute begged for help, and prayed that, given evidence, he might believe me. It was Detective Inspector Hofstadter. With him was Jon Rodin, the person I'd begged him to find and fetch. As he too stepped out, I saw that he was holding hands with yet a third figure that I had not anticipated.

She wore a white gown. Her hair was long and lank. Her face was slack, but as she stepped into the growing light aided by Jon, her expression changed.

Meistermacher looked appalled.

'Mother?' he whispered.

The distraction was enough. I reached out to grasp the device JR had fetched. I picked it up, aimed it at Meistermacher and depressed the button.

Thousands of tiny, invisible splinters of crystal methamphetamine flew at him as if from a whispering machine gun. He touched his neck idly where they stung but he hardly noticed. I prayed that the powerful stimulant would have the same effect on him that it did with us. Canceling the effects of meta, bringing down hard reality, slamming doors closed at whatever terrible cost.

He was surrounded now, by Kate, by Jon, by me; and by Emily his mother. A circle of disagreement closing in.

And by an enclosing line of armed police and FBI officers who trained their guns on him.

'Mother! Not you too,' Meistermacher whimpered.

I saw agony and uncertainty cross Emily's face. The police line crept forwards and they prepared to fire. I felt the balance of power shift. Without Emily we could not defeat him. Their unnatural gift was something that even together we could not match.

He cried out again, a child now, in terrible pain.

His agony reflected in hers.

Emily's own betrayal crumpled her face, twisting her lips in infinite grief. She closed her eyes a moment and then—

Everyone heard her whisper of thought, silent thunder above a storm. Tears poured from her eyes.

GOOD BYE MY SON.

We all felt what happened next.

That its source was Emily was undeniable and yet nonsensical; for it could have no source.

Time *perverted.*

Something began. Something ended. She was as much its effect as its cause. It was all things, it was every one of us. We were at once a part of it, creating it, causing it, being it, receiving it, being its effect. Words are inadequate. It cannot be described. It felt like a shockwave propagating not merely through space or time, but in the very thing underneath those figments, through reality itself, ending and beginning with each of us.

Abruptly, it faded.

The nearest officer depressed the trigger on his weapon.

And I saw Emily's lips move once more. Her eyes brimmed. Her cheeks glistened with liquid.

She mouthed something, a private thing for her son's ears alone. I started at those silent words, lip-reading.

What did she. . . ?

Meistermacher's face registered confusion, and then horror; and finally resignation as understanding came.

His face became very still.

Time seemed to slow.

As the first bullet sailed to meet him, suddenly, Viktor Meistermacher was simply—

—gone.

I felt the wind brush my cheek and tousle my hair.

From the pages of Tony's diary:

Sound of the sea above, what's hides beneath?

```
yyekhneikxjmmpuffenlgpvqhkxlptuz
yfctowwjuqttypudefeyvstgmtpqtiwe
tigkfjdursoxpjetmstcxmqimwtjlquc
ugrywqlgmnwxwqdekrwgvljggsukllcz
pinsfirntqynpjhzuvxgqjultruinhvt
wetoxljirznpgvqjlnvsxzinvoixytyc
rfuysyhzujokrrscnjhlupjchookqudx
bupxukgscpmtivckixweplitpkgmeojd
attswbbabbbaabbaafgpeopzkzqkswia
byrhbetvyxmsouoeuabbafnoxodgcqjb
aizmaabijyckhzwxkqpkcbabivqsmhio
aerhrbbbbhcnimrhnuqqflbbabvqrsvn
nmhxkqhrbbabalhgntmgngzsibbaagmr
vzhovlktubaababofmmoesreecjbabje
rfegqbbbbtezababaabbbbbthrqnxabk
klqhblgtzababaabbsqiababaruczaax
uwebobbbaaababababfgfrsbbbabaabbav
wwajbabbabaaaabaxlmdbbbbbbaaabba
ubdvaaababababbabasiaabbaabaabaoo
jbtlbbbabbaaaaaaabbbabbbbabtrsp
dxaolaabbaaaaababbbabaababbmkoix
qgaxdjabbabaaabaaabbabbaaxuhepuh
rczbbnkuwxtwababbabbabbahlrwgupqo
mrcribbaaahewwjgfjvbbxkpntehpdti
wfcrqtrrovabbababbakyvzegkzcrjcb
epvhdfqwzfuxcikedyxlcksiyydeltra
yvhkpzncpgkslivwxroityyqkzodkwks
rlqsufmpehskkezvqredjgmhveojggkd
gxnlqgceljvshfrhgoehnivpfzrihvhz
qsrsdqsrhuqzrwwegjmermlffrxkjnhj
bevqxjmhvhvhtqrmzrpgktguvriqdhcn
xyhhvtdqtrjrvpmfcnzgqijirwoueyou
```

Chapter 32

Epilogue

'What did she do?' we had whispered in the cars that took us into custody.
'Did you feel it?'
We all had.
'It was like nothing... I've... ever felt before.'
'What was it?'
'What happened to him?'
'He just vanished.'
'Is he dead?'
'Did she kill him?'

Though I had seen a sort of lucidity in her at the docks, Emily provided no answers. She had retreated into a morbid silence. I said nothing either, though in truth I knew more. I struggled for a long time, trying to understand what had happened. I replayed the movements I had seen in Emily's lips over and over in my mind until there was only phrase that possibly made sense. Even now, I do not fully understand what she meant; or did.

These were her final words to her tragic son:

God speed.

It matters little now. That mystery is moot.

It has been three weeks. I've been getting the information in dribs and drabs. We were kept in custody. Separated, of course. Hofstadter was kind and explained much, confirming what was truly being considered by police and what was just released to keep the public happy. The official line was that a hallucinogen was released at Port Elizabeth, a new mode of terrorist attack. But all our efforts to keep the truth from the public were pointless:

I failed.

News started coming in a few days ago.

Meistermacher's plan was so much wider than the simple lie he fed me. I don't know how he orchestrated it. Using that coercive gift of his no doubt. Shipments of meta-spiked insulin inhalers from no less than seventeen rival pharmaceuticals companies arrived in ports around the world at approximately the same time. I stopped only one. There were hundreds of containers. It's taken until now for them to get into the system and onto the shelves. I don't know if the police acted in time to save the other cities. I hope so.

The reports have been garbled, which is unsurprising.

Communication with the outside world—beyond the Manhattan quarantine—hasn't been possible since. The television stopped working completely two days ago. Electricity supplies have been up and down. There were strange network glitches pretty much globally for weeks even before this happened. I have a theory about those.

Inside—well, let's just say the networks haven't been behaving the way you'd expect. I haven't seen anyone for hours. At first, the only reason I knew people were still around was because I heard the occasional screams outside. I've ventured out since.

Jon was wrong. It's not Armageddon. Perhaps that's down to what Emily did; that Meistermacher has gone. Perhaps it's a function of the sheer number of people involved now—but things are different. *Very.*

JR and I were working on an escape plan but then half an hour ago all the monitors in the station came back on. They just all blinked into life of their own accord.

There's a camel on all the screens.

It hasn't answered me yet, but I'm going to keep trying.

It just keeps looking at me with a strange expression.

'*Needle?*'

AKNOWLEDGEMENTS

I am eternally grateful to my family and friends for the incredible love, support and encouragement they've given during the six years it took to complete this project, and for knowing exactly when to quote Stewie.

To my beta readers, especially those I didn't know well, for their willingness to read drafts and their brutal honesty, qualities which are invaluable to any writer: Lee Warren, James Ingram, Dr Eirik Pettersen, Darryl Stein, Cécile Janty-Davies, Wendy Tan, Joe White, Radha Chakraborty, Hiren Joshi, Maya Kaye, Dee Keys, Douglas Pinheiro, Simon Potter, Richard Emerson, Jason Ing, Katherine Grantham, Adam McDowell, Rukiya Mohamedali, Yasir Samir, Andrea Tran, Joe White, Chris O'Hare, John and Heather Briant, and Angela Meier.

I want also to thank the other writers, agents and publishers who very generously gave their time, support and advice: Drew Banks, N.M. Browne, Iain Banks, Ken McCleod, Charles Stross, Patricia C. Wrede, Mic Cheetham, Oliver Cheetham, Simon Kavanagh, Sarah Odedina, Mitch Sebastian, Oliver Ellis; and the many members of RASFC.

Dr Dan Read, Warden of Falmouth Keogh, for very kindly giving me a tour of the new Southside building so that I could see what had changed since my time at Imperial; Dr Mary Morgan for checking medical and surgical realism; Frauke Komma, Ursula Erridge and Viviane Segove for checking the occasional elements of German and Portuguese language used; my incredibly talented friend and photographer, Helen Rosemier; Damon Reynolds (PynkAndFluffy.com) for graphic design assistance which went way beyond the small favour I asked of him initially; and my marvellous editor, Sarah Taylor-Fergusson, who helped me make many great improvements and rose to my challenge of conforming to both US and UK spelling and style in alternate chapters as a subtle reinforcement of their location and point in time. Any remaining errors, it goes without saying, are entirely mine.

Lightning Source UK Ltd.
Milton Keynes UK
08 December 2010

164045UK00002B/22/P